I0687231

Uninvited

Etudes in C#, No. 3

Jamie Wyman

Pajamazon Wordworks
Phoenix, AZ USA
www.jamiewyman.com

First Edition October 2016

Edited by Danielle Poiesz and Double Vision Editorial
Cover design by Nathalia Suellen

ISBN 10: 0990392570

ISBN 9780990392576
ISBN 978-0-9903925-6-9 (e-book)
ISBN 978-0-9903925-8-3 (Audio)

Printed in the United States of America

Works by Jamie Wyman

The Etudes in C# Series

Wild Card
Unveiled
Uninvited

Crash Haus Stories (Abaddon Books)
"A Scandal In Hobohemia" (included in the anthology *Two Hundred Twenty-One Baker Streets*)
"The Case of the Tattooed Bride" (included in the collection *alt. sherlock. holmes*)

This book is lovingly dedicated to the muse for Mrs. McIntyre,
my grandmother Joan Yoder.
November 3, 1920 – April 12, 2016

Love you, Pumpkin.

ONE

"FRIEND IS A FOUR LETTER WORD"

Wispy gray hair billowed in a cloud around a pink sweatband as Mrs. McIntyre jogged up to her front door. She waved to me when Flynn's car pulled into my parking space. Ever since her hip had miraculously healed last winter—thanks to some technomagic from my friend Karma—the old lady had been training for one of those glow-in-the dark 5K races.

"Happy birthday, Cathy!" my landlady sang from her front door.

I tried to suppress my cringe. Really, I did, but I despise the nickname. The eye roll is a reflex at this point. I tried very hard to hide it from her, though, as I genuinely love Mrs. McIntyre.

"Cathy," Flynn said with a laugh from the driver's seat beside me.

"She can call me that. You can't. That's not a privilege you've earned."

Flynn cut the engine and unbuckled his seat belt. "How does one earn that particular merit badge?"

"By being an adorable Fraggle who's older than jazz, and by nearly getting killed because of me."

"I'm older than jazz," muttered my friend, the god.

"Doesn't count. She's mortal."

Taking a deep breath and fixing a smile on my face, I shoved out of the car. As Flynn and I collected the grocery bags from the trunk, I gave a quick wave to my Fraggle.

"Hey, Mrs. M. Thanks for the card you left on my door. It was a very good start to a happy birthday."

Mrs. McIntyre smiled toothlessly. "And many more."

"Race you to the door, Cat!" Flynn dashed passed her and toward my apartment, a rustle of paper and plastic.

"Big fun planned for tonight, dear?" she asked, ignoring him.

"Not really. Most of my friends had plans tonight, so it's just me and that doofus." I nodded toward Flynn. "Quiet night in with movies and munchies."

He turned around mid-jog and called, "We'll keep it to a dull roar, Mrs. M."

"All right, you kids have fun." She gave a wave of her hand, sending us off like we were her favorite grandchildren.

She padded into her place and turned on her television. *Murder, She Wrote* blared out the open window into the balmy Las Vegas evening. Not only is Mrs. McIntyre arthritic but she's going deaf.

"Don't know why you're in a hurry," I shouted to Flynn. "I've got the key."

"Like that's ever stopped me before."

I conceded the point. As technomancers, we could pop locks with a thought. Flynn had taught me damn near everything I knew about being a technomage, but certainly not everything *he* knew. Of course, being a deity masquerading as a bartender, Flynn knew everything, so it would be difficult to pass on the sum total of existence over a beer and tacos. In the grand scheme of things, a chintzy little lock from Home Depot would be as much of a barrier to him as a piece of wet toilet paper would be to a runaway truck.

As I watched him bound ahead of me, I noticed a dark mass on my doorstep, a Rorschach blot in the evening. It could've been anything from a lumpy trash bag to an elephant dressed as a ninja.

"Goatfucker!" Flynn yelled.

Or it could be a— Wait, what? The gears in my mind turned. *It can't be...*

But there's only one person worthy of such a pet name. Yet, there was no reason in hell he should have been anywhere near me or my home.

"Marius?" I asked, my voice weak.

I hitched up my grocery bags and broke into a sprint toward my apartment. The closer I got, the clearer it became that the turncoat satyr sat on my stoop. It was also obvious that if I didn't intervene quickly, Flynn was going to skin him alive. When I caught up to Flynn, he was already holding Marius by the collar of his T-shirt.

"...hoped I'd have the chance, but I never dreamed you'd be stupid enough to come back," the god growled through his teeth.

"Put him down, Flynn," I said.

He shot me a murderous look over his shoulder. His eyes blazed with fury as red and spiky as his hair. Orange light coursed through the linear tattoos on both his arms as he built power.

"Put. Him. Down," I repeated sharply. My eyes drifted away from my teacher and to the visitor. His head lolled and Marius was soon facing me.

I gasped.

Marius hung limply from Flynn's grip. His long black hair was a tangled mass of snarls. The locks were matted where blood clotted at his temples, one eye was swollen shut, and a crimson crust drew a line down his beard from his fat lip. Over his cheeks, purple bruises spread out like shadowy blossoms. The satyr's clothes were torn and stained. Making no attempt to struggle, he dangled limply from Flynn's fists. His hands dangled uselessly at his sides, and his legs remained folded on the ground beneath him.

He looked like he'd lost a fight with a particularly rusty meat grinder.

"It's a glamour," Flynn said. "Trick of the eyes to get us to feel sorry for him."

"You don't know that," I said, my voice shrill.

"Does it matter? Do you need me to remind you about the last time we saw him? How he fucked us over?"

I closed my eyes. I couldn't look at Marius's broken face or Flynn's rage. What I saw in the dark of my mind wasn't much prettier, though. A fiery altar dedicated to an ancient flesh-eating god. Cultists charging forward with flashes of bloodlust and religious zeal. Mages flinging spells around the room. Me and my friends. outnumbered and unprepared to meet one of Hell's own generals.

And there was Marius.

Running away.

And with those images came other feelings. My strange kinship with the satyr, and yes, a level of affection I wasn't proud of, nor did I particularly care to acknowledge.

I swallowed a knot of conflicting emotions and opened my eyes. "Please, Flynn."

"Cat, he left us to die!"

"Business," Marius croaked.

"I know all about your *business*," Flynn seethed. His knuckles tightened around Marius's T-shirt, drawing the satyr an inch or two higher off the ground.

Marius licked his lips and shook his head. "With Catherine," he rasped. Wheezy breaths obscured his British accent, forced him to speak in bursts of only a couple of words at a time. "Miss Sharp, please. I need...asylum."

Flynn let out a puff of derisive laughter. "As if you have any right to ask."

"Beg of you."

As far as I knew, Marius had never begged for anything in his long, debauchery-filled life. And if he was asking *me* for help?

I numbed myself against the pain of seeing him in such a state, against Flynn's inevitable reaction as I answered. "Fine."

The single word echoed as if I'd struck a giant drum. It carried with it a strange finality but also a measure of ominous foreboding. I'd committed. But to what?

Flynn whipped around to face me. "You can't be serious."

"Marius," I said with all the stony resolve I could muster, "you are allowed in my home until morning."

Flynn thrust him to the ground and Marius melted with a groan of relief, renewed pain, or some combination of the two. Kicking at the gravel and muttering curses to himself, Flynn dragged his hands through his hair in frustration.

I kept my voice cold and passionless. "You can stay tonight. I'll hear what you have to say. Anything after that is negotiable."

"I can't believe this," Flynn said.

"However," I said sternly, "if you are lying, Marius...if this is some sort of trick on your part or Eris's...if you try to steal from me, swindle me, or otherwise fuck with my head, I promise you will regret you ever asked for my help."

His head bobbed in a weak nod. "Understood."

Without another word, I took Marius's arm and looped it around my neck and shoulders. I did my best to hoist him up off the ground. When I stumbled, Flynn begrudgingly took the satyr's other arm and got him to his feet. I opened the door and the three of us did a strange dance to maneuver him in.

The lights flashed on, wickedly bright, and a chorus of voices shouted, "Happy birthday!"

People filled my small living room. Dave and Mel from work. Slash and Aeo—a couple of scene kids from the club. I even saw my sister Christine's face blinking at me from Karma's tablet. Hooray Skype?

Smiles drooped and expressions melted to confusion or horror as they took in the sight of our odd trio.

I looked over Marius's back to Flynn.

Acerbic and apologetic, he said, "Surprise."

"No kidding," I muttered.

What do you say when you walk into a party with a bloody mess of a man?

"Um, hi, guys," I said with a little too much cheer. "Just give us... um... Yeah, I'll be right back."

What? I couldn't think of anything clever, and neither could you.

I nodded toward my bedroom and nudged Flynn forward. Marius shuffled along between our bodies. A path cleared in front of us, the apartment buzzing with a million unasked questions.

"What the hell?" Karma voiced one of them. Behind me, I heard her say, "Christine, we'll call you back." A second or two later she was in front of me, opening the door to my bedroom. Flynn let go of Marius, and the satyr's whole weight dragged at my shoulders, which made me launch into a strange spin of sorts as my legs buckled. I tried to heave Marius toward the bed. His arms spread out to break his fall, but he bounced off the side of the mattress, sliding to his knees on the floor. His face twisted with pain as he let out a choked noise.

"Never thought I'd see a satyr miss a bed," Flynn mused. He bared his teeth in a sickening perversion of his usual smile. He was enjoying Marius's pain too much.

Karma swatted at her ex's shoulder, but her attention was focused on Marius. Her heart-shaped face was set with concern as she stared at the satyr. "What's he doing here?"

Flynn put a protective arm around her shoulders and tried to guide her out of the room. "He's not staying long."

She shrugged away from him and pulled up beside me, taking my hand in hers. She was trembling. I looked into her chocolate eyes and saw that Karma, too, was warring with conflicting feelings about my unexpected guest. She knew some of his more recent sins, and she'd been on the altar that night when he ran away. He'd left her behind, too. But Karma—a technomage with healing skills, and a nurse by trade—couldn't just sit idly by and watch someone who was clearly in need of help.

"Do you want me to grab my 'first aid kit'?" she asked, subtle emphasis on the last three words.

I squeezed her hand and sighed with a small measure of relief.

"Don't waste it on him," Flynn said darkly. "He's faking it anyway. Let's go. I'll lock him in."

I glared at Flynn. "Leave us for a second."

"What?"

"Go. Please," I said a little too sharply. To Karma, I added, "I'll be out in a minute."

Her grip tightened for a second before she released my hand and spun for the door. She trailed a dark finger against Flynn's pale arm on her way. His jaw worked and his Adam's apple bobbed as he swallowed whatever he'd been about to say.

"I'll go get the food," he muttered quietly.

"I'll help you," Karma said.

They left the room, Flynn making damn sure to slam the door.

Marius winced as he pulled himself up onto the bed. Winded, he lay there on his back, gasping to catch his breath.

I sat on the edge of the mattress and just watched him while the tug-of-war raged in my head. Marius had been a friend. He'd helped me out of a jam on more than one occasion and even saved my life a time or two. He'd also bugged out on me during a fight when things had looked dire. Though he used magic to conceal his horns and goat's legs, it was another example of how Marius could never buck his nature. By birth, he was a satyr—a hedonistic, selfish creature—and by trade, or necessity, he was a liar and a thief. I'd known him for a very long time. Long enough to understand that what I saw could be an illusion. The other edge of that particular sword, however, was that watching him writhe in pain yanked at my heart.

Flynn didn't know the real Marius, the one beneath the glamour. I'd seen that person once. The pitiable bastard had lived for centuries under a curse that rendered him impotent, unable to feel the slightest of pleasures. In time, what should have been a jovial soul atrophied and grew sour. I'd seen Marius's truth—naked and pathetic—and no amount of anger could exorcise my sympathy for him. I'd been a prisoner once, too. I still wanted him to be free.

And now he was in my bed, a broken and bloody mess.

When his rattling breaths calmed, he rolled onto his side. His shirt stretched, the tears widening over four evenly spaced gashes. The wounds spread from his back and around his ribs. Similar marks could be seen on one of his calves.

I thought of the many versions of Marius I'd known over the years, the layers of masks he hid behind. When we'd met, he had been a lecherous playboy type, his suits always pressed and shoes shined. He'd also been an ally. A warrior with a gleaming saber, eyes aglow with magic. A con artist with sticky fingers. I'd seen through all of it once. I'd seen him naked, metaphorically—a tortured, withered, malnourished soul. Well, okay, I'd seen him physically naked, too, but I hadn't exactly wanted to at the time.

But he resembled his truest self as he lay there on my bed. Holding his stomach, eyes clenched tight with pain, he once again tried to moisten his lips.

"Didn't know. Where to go," he said, his voice dry as sandpaper.

I sighed and said nothing. In the small bathroom attached to my bedroom, I filled a glass with water and soaked a washcloth. I had no intention of playing Florence Nightingale to the bastard, but he was visibly dehydrated. And he was getting blood on my sheets.

When I returned, he was still, breathing in a reedy but steady rhythm. My tuxedo tomcat, Linux, had come out from his den beneath the bed to curl up against Marius's feet and administer purr therapy. The cat looked up at me with his golden stare, as if to say, *I've got this.*

I left the glass and washcloth on the bedside table where Marius would see them.

Music began to blare from the next room, an electronic bass beat that called to my blood. Outside of that door were people who gave a damn about me, people who didn't think about how they could use me. Some of them, like Flynn and Karma, knew about the *other* world I navigated—a place of magic, mythical creatures and all-too-real gods. The rest of them remained blissfully ignorant.

I closed my eyes and made a promise to myself: for the next few hours, that other world would cease to exist, even if I had to drown it in a flood of whiskey and red velvet cake. For one night, I'd be normal.

TWO

"OPEN BOOK"

With the final minutes of my birthday long since ticked away and the last of the guests safely home, Flynn, Karma, and I cleaned up. Honestly, it could have waited until a reasonable hour—like two in the afternoon—but three a.m. is always a good time for procrastination.

During the party, Flynn and I had played nice, and with Karma's help we managed to shrug off questions about our injured visitor. But now that we were alone, a chilly silence filled the ether. We didn't speak as Flynn and I circled the proverbial elephant in the room. He roamed with a trash bag, picking up plates and bottles and casting the occasional glance toward my bedroom. Karma did dishes in the kitchen behind me while I busied myself by putting away leftover food and nipping a few bites of frosting.

The light *click* of an opening door caught my attention. Before I could turn toward the sound, Linux bounded out of my bedroom and rammed his bulk against my ankles. With a pitiful mew and an insistent bat at my knee, His Highness made his demands clear.

I plucked a piece of turkey from the party tray and tossed it to him. "A gift of peace in all good faith."

Linux accepted his tithe and noshed, his purrs sounding more like a pig's snorts.

Flynn's trash bag rustled a bit more forcefully and plates landed in it a bit more loudly. Now looking toward my room, I watched Marius make his entrance.

He leaned against the doorframe, holding his side. He'd wiped the blood off his face and pulled his hair back into an unruly ponytail. The bruises looked a shade lighter than before, and although the swelling had gone down, one of his eyes still refused to open.

"Thank you for the water," he said hoarsely. His voice was uncharacteristically quiet, but he was sounding more like himself.

"No problem," I muttered. I turned my attention back to the countertops.

"The music stopped, so I thought I'd pop out."

"You're just in time to see the cleaning crew."

"Can I help?" he asked.

Flynn grunted. "You can jump in this bag so I can take you down to the Dumpster with the rest of the trash."

I expected Marius to take the bait and join my friend in a colorful display of expletives and insults. Instead, Marius shuffled to the couch and sat down. Linux jumped up to join him and quickly offered up his belly for devotions.

"I remember you," Marius said, placating His Highness.

Marius had only met Linux once, and it had been just minutes later that shark monsters had battered down my door. The satyr hadn't exactly had time to get to know my furry overlord.

"Careful," I warned. "You start that now and he'll expect you to pay fealty into perpetuity."

"Is he such a difficult master to serve?"

"You won't be around long enough to find out," Flynn spat. "Besides, don't you already have a master?"

Marius's voice cracked. "Not as such."

That hooked my attention. "What?"

"Eris released me."

Dishes clattered in the sink. Karma moved just a little too slowly to cover her surprise but went back to cleaning plates. Meanwhile, questions bubbled through the whiskey haze of my mind. The goddess had once held the deed to my soul, too; I knew all too well what it was like to be under her thumb. But I also knew that Discord did not just cast her toys aside.

"When?" I asked.

"This morning."

Flynn sat on the arm of one of my chairs, his limbs seemingly relaxed but his hands balled into fists. Even after Marius's confession, Flynn's tone remained sharp and snarky. "So was that before or after someone ran you through a wood chipper?"

Marius responded with a lame attempt at his signature smirk. "Think I'm pretty, Flynn?"

"Gorgeous," he answered, eyes steely and jaw set. "Wish I'd been there for your makeover."

Marius let his head fall back onto the sofa and pawed at his face with exhaustion. "Had I thought ahead, I could've recorded it and put it on YouTube for all the world to enjoy."

"I'd watch it daily," Flynn growled around his teeth. "In slow motion."

I shot Flynn a warning look. "Stop it."

"What?" The technomancer spread his arms, affronted.

My gaze held his. "I think it's time for you to head home."

His eyes blazed, furious. "You want me to leave you alone with this backstabbing son of a bitch? Karma almost died because of him, Cat."

Behind me, the water stopped running. "Uh-uh, baby," Karma said in a tone that implied she would take no shit. She left the sink and joined me at the small countertop, crossed her arms and leveled her focus on Flynn.

That night when Marius had run, when everything had changed, Karma and Flynn had been lovers that night. But that relationship ended soon after as Karma couldn't process dating a deity. I knew both of them still hurt from the breakup.

She eyed him with ferocity, and his expression—guarded and alert—said she had his full attention.

"That wouldn't have happened, Flynn," she said bitterly, "and you know it."

With a level stare I added, *"As-kunnigr"* at the same moment Marius coughed.

I had no doubt Flynn had heard me over the noise, though. The Norse phrase—"god's kin"—hit my friend like a spear of ice. He deflated, gaze trailing to the carpet.

It's true: Marius had bugged out on a fight. But Flynn had been pulling his punches in that fight. Flynn had pretended to be mortal for so long that he'd started to believe it. Unlike most other deities, Flynn did not have a pantheon. Alone in the world, hidden from his peers for eons, this god of thought could sometimes forget his own strength.

Not many people even knew Flynn's nature. Marius included.

Sobered by the reminder that I was not just a friend and student but a believer, Flynn picked up the trash bags and headed for the exit. As the door shut behind him, I had the feeling he wouldn't be back tonight. I was okay with that. If he returned and kept talking shit, I would unleash a world of anger on him—some of it deserved.

Karma put an arm around me and squeezed. "I'm going to go check on him. Get him home safe. You good?"

"Yeah." I leaned into her, my copper hair mixing with the fluff of her tomato-red curls. "Thank you."

"I've got your back, girl," she whispered. "Happy birthday."

Karma grabbed her jacket from the hook by the door and slipped her feet into her wedge sandals, pausing only long enough to give Marius a last, wary glance. Then she was gone, and Marius and I were alone.

"Charming, as always," Marius said, some of his old snark returning to that threadbare voice.

"I would apologize for Flynn, but he's got a point." I sighed and went back to work putting away food. "You hungry?"

"Starving."

"Come get something." I waved him into the kitchen. "I'm not a waitress."

He gingerly crossed the room and sat on one of the barstools by my kitchen counter–slash–dining room. Marius slid the remnants of the party tray in front of him and voraciously began to wolf down anything that would fit in his mouth. He winced, the movements of eating obviously disagreeing with his wounded face.

I poured him another glass of water. I chose what little was left in a bottle of Jameson for myself. The whiskey burned in my chest and made my eyes water. My buzz was long gone, but the drink dulled the edge of my more volatile emotions.

"Looks like I missed quite the party," Marius said. "What's the occasion?"

"My birthday."

"Bugger," he hissed. He hung his head and fidgeted for a long moment. "I didn't know."

"You never bothered to ask," I snapped.

He flinched and closed his eyes as if I'd smacked him. "Catherine, I didn't know where else to go."

The sincerity in his words pierced me, and I bled bitter venom. "Because you don't know any other suckers who'd give you a chance?"

"Because I don't have anyone else I can trust."

"Oh, lucky me."

"Christ, woman," he rasped, "you're the only being I know who doesn't have her own agenda."

"How would you know? Maybe I've changed since I left Eris and joined Loki's workforce."

He shook his head, strands of black hair coming loose at his temples. "You might wear the mark of an Asgardian, but you're too stubborn to ever truly bend to anyone, Catherine. I know you."

Closing my eyes, I counted to ten and drew slow, even breaths. I swallowed hard, listening to him grunt as he got to his feet. With just a few steps, he was beside me, close enough that I caught the scents of blood, sweat, and cologne. The unique blend triggered memories of old times with Marius, sending them playing across my mind. For most of a decade we'd both worked for Eris, the Greek Goddess of Discord. Though our indentured servitude had come about in different ways, we had both hoped to work off our debts by doing odd jobs for her—few of them legal—and more than once we'd been forced to team up. I played those times over and over, a strange highlight reel that consisted of us running from the Fae, sharing a dance floor with deities, a few missed chances and a slew of mistakes. After all we'd been through, after all we knew about each other, the bastard had gotten under my skin and I couldn't help but care about him.

And there he was, in my kitchen, turning my stomach into knots just by standing near me.

"Thank you," he said, his voice warm on my ear. "For letting me in. I know it's more than I deserve."

"You're damn right it is," I grumbled.

I opened my eyes and stared at his beaten face. Contrition looked so wrong on him, but there it was.

Just what the hell am I supposed to do with that? And what could possibly have happened to Marius?

I was too tired to ask right now, too exhausted to deal with whatever trouble he'd inevitably brought with him. "I'm going to bed," I announced. "I'll deal with you at a reasonable hour."

I stomped into the living room and joined Linux on the couch. Pulling the fleece throw around me, I curled into a tight ball.

Marius's footsteps shuffled over the carpet. "You're going to stay out here?"

I popped open one eye to glare at him. "I'm not sleeping with you."

"That's not why I asked. It's your bed. I'll sleep on the sofa."

I snorted. "And get your satyr-blood cooties all over me? No thanks. You're washing my sheets, by the way."

He nodded slowly. "Fair enough. Good night, then."

With a small effort of will, I turned off the living room lights. Marius, silhouetted in the soft glow of amber pouring from my bedroom, turned and said, "I'm sorry, Catherine."

I rolled over, my back to him, and clenched my jaw around all the horrible things I refused to say. Behind me, the door closed. My brain wouldn't shut off, though. It just kept playing those words over and over, trying to divine if he really meant it.

I'm sorry, Catherine.

I sighed. *Aren't we all?*

THREE

"COMMISSIONING A SYMPHONY IN C"

Sometime after "hangover o'clock" the next day, Marius padded out of my room. Bare to the waist as he was, I could clearly see the many cuts, scrapes, and contusions along his torso. Those wicked slashes I'd glimpsed the night before puckered beneath a black-red crust. His eyes, though, were both wide open, the flesh painted with the yellowish shadows of bruises. He even walked with less difficulty, standing at his full height.

I put down the book I'd been reading and regarded him skeptically, "Either you're getting the glamour wrong or my room has healing powers."

One corner of his moustache hitched up in a warm leer. "While I'm sure a night in your bed would do any man a world of wonders, it is not a fountain of youth. And it's no glamour," he added. "I just heal more rapidly than your lot."

The memory of another morning spent with him came unbidden. He had been shirtless, and I'd lost my pants. The night before he'd taken a ginormous bird's beak to the bicep, and mere hours later it looked less like a gaping tear and more like an angry scratch. I'd seen the proof that the supernatural heritage in his veins allowed his body to stitch itself back together with amazing speed.

Marius's recovery reached beneath his skin, too. Mischief sparkled in his green eyes, and when he spoke, I heard his usual velvety baritone once again. "You could do with a larger bed, though," he said as he crossed the room to one of my armchairs. "I know you're a small woman, but there's not much room for sport. Not anything adventurous, anyway."

"It suits me just fine," I countered.

I glanced a path down his chest, lower past the gouges at his ribs, before resting on the bare patch of skin on the underside of his left wrist.

"It's gone," I said. "Your brand."

"I told you Eris released me." He nodded at my wrist. "I see you still have Loki's mark."

I self-consciously ran a few fingers over the ice-blue rune that announced to any who cared that I was beholden to the Norse God of Mayhem. Before the rune, I'd worn Eris's golden apple, the same one I'd never seen Marius without. For centuries now he'd been working off his debt to the goddess in hopes that she would remove the curse Zeus had laid upon him centuries before.

"You balance your books with her?" I asked.

"Nothing so polite as that."

"Dishonorable discharge?"

"Of a sort."

"What happened?"

He sighed and wiggled in the chair. He might have been settling in or squirming, I couldn't tell. "Is there anything for breakfast?"

"No," I said, folding my arms. "I told you last night that you could stay until morning. You've already been here longer than that. If you're going to park it here a minute more, it's time to feed the meter. Tell me what happened and why you've darkened my doorstep."

"Pan's balls," he said, exasperated. "And I thought you were stubborn before. Working for Loki has made you a chilly bitch on top of that."

"Not doing yourself any favors," I warned.

It was a testament to just how desperate for help he was when he sighed and said, "Eris discovered some of my other...enterprises. She wasn't too thrilled about it and showed me the door."

"She found out you had deals going with Loki?"

He raised an eyebrow in subdued surprise. "And just how did you know that I sometimes moonlight for your boss?"

"Put it together after the poker game. Too many things went right for Loki for him to not have had help. I saw him palm you some cash the next morning and filled in the holes."

"Clever girl. Yes, she put that together as well, though not as quickly as you did. After I turned up without Polyhymnia's veil, she ferreted out a number of my other business partnerships, too."

"And she kicked your ass, I see."

Marius snorted. "You should know the Lady better than that. Discord would never do her own dirty work. Where's the fun in that?" I narrowed my eyes, and he answered the unspoken question. "No, all she had to do was whisper a word of my misdeeds into the proper ears, and some emissaries came to chat." He spread his hands and displayed his battered body. "What you see is what you get."

"Since you and Eris didn't part on the best of terms, I'm guessing she didn't fulfill her end of your bargain. You're still..." I searched for the right word. *Impotent? Neutered?* "Cursed?"

"You assume correctly." He simmered there a moment. "I know I'm not in a position to ask favors, but I don't suppose you'd be willing to have another go at curing me of this particular ailment?"

"No chance. Especially since you can do it yourself." I bit my lower lip, relishing the opportunity to make the satyr squirm. "Trouble falling in love?"

He shuddered. "Disgusting. I still refuse to believe that's the only way."

"Hey, don't shoot the messenger. Not my fault the gods think it's a great joke to make a satyr have to give a damn about someone else to get his groove back."

He turned his green stare to me, his face stony and serious. "Leave it," he chided.

As much fun as it was to poke and prod at his soft underbelly, seeing his mangled torso was enough to convince me that it was time to hold my tongue. Marius gazed off into nothing for a few awkward moments, fingers combing his goatee.

"What are you doing here, Marius? Really?"

"I'm not sure to be honest," he said, then laughed uneasily. "The list of people I can go to for help has shrunk considerably. Freedom isn't all it's cracked up to be."

"At least no one is there to tell you what to do," I said.

"That also means there's no one to tell others to leave me alone."

"No one to hide behind, either?" I asked bitterly.

He eyed me, one hand idly stroking the arm of his chair. Finally, he answered. "Something like that."

"Is that what you're doing now? Hiding behind me?" The old wound opened, and black ire started pouring into my voice. "Hoping that if some big nasty breaks down my door again it will come after me and give you time to run away?"

Emotion rippled over his face like waves on the surface of a still pond. Anger sparked in his eyes while sad helplessness dragged at his cheeks. "That's not why I'm here," he protested through his clenched teeth.

"Isn't it? You're like a little remora, looking for the biggest fish to swim with so you don't get swallowed up. You don't give a shit who gets hurt in the process as long as your skin is intact."

"Which it clearly isn't," he said, motioning to the slashes along his ribs.

"So someone else should take those lashes for you?" Furious, I shot up off the couch. "I'm not your fucking meatshield, Marius! Maybe Flynn is right. You got yourself into this; maybe you should get yourself out."

"They're going to kill me, Catherine."

It wasn't so much the words that stopped my heart, but the power behind them. His voice shook, a wave of anguish breaking over my name. He fixed me with a stare as serious as cancer and twice as dark. I saw something new deep in those familiar green eyes. Something raw and vulnerable. So fragile. Marius, who was usually so cocksure and aloof, was *afraid*.

Despite my efforts to immunize myself with my rage, his fear was contagious. "Who are *they*?" I asked.

"Everyone I've ever swindled, duped, double-crossed, and otherwise fucked over," he said flatly. "And I assure you that list is quite long."

"All of them want you dead?"

Marius nodded. "Give or take."

"But I thought you were immortal," I said.

He blew out a breath, making his lips flap. "Immortal, sure. Invulnerable—as you can see—is something else entirely. I'll live as long as I'm able, but if someone takes my head, that's the end of me. That's what they want. And they won't take it quickly." Marius's gaze fell to the floor, and I pretended not to see the sheen of tears that filled his eyes. When he spoke again, his voice was as small as a child's. "I don't want to die. Not like this."

I needed to think, but my brain was fuzzy, muddied with stupid emotions like compassion, sympathy, and another that I wouldn't dare name. I needed clarity. Quiet. Caffeine.

I stalked to the kitchen, and I wrenched open the cabinets with a growl, pulling down the necessary tools to perform javamancy. I didn't look at him, and we didn't speak. For a while, the only sounds were the slamming of drawers and the cauldron-bubble of percolating coffee.

In my head, I argued with a voice that sounded uncannily like Flynn's. *Hand him over*, it said. *Don't trust him, and don't feel anything but anger for him. He doesn't deserve you.*

I busied myself with getting the creamer and sugar bowl, two spoons from the drawer, and a couple of mugs. I filled the cups with French roast and set one of them out on the counter in the satyr's general direction.

Slowly, Marius rose and crossed to the kitchen, slouching on the barstool as he had the night before. His hands folded around the cup.

As I stirred sugar into my own drink, I steeled myself for what I was about to say. "So what do we do?"

"We?" he asked after a stunned pause.

"Yes. We." The coffee was bitter on my tongue. Was it just the brew, or was it the taste of what I'd just offered to jump into? "What do we do?"

Marius straightened on the stool, wiping his palms against his torn, grimy jeans. He blew out a breath. "I wish I knew."

I closed my eyes and swiped at the air, trying to erase everything and start with a clean take on the situation. "Okay, let's back up. Who exactly are we dealing with?"

"Well, a friend of Hades stopped in to say hello. Offered to take me down to Tartarus for a weekend or eternity. Yama and his puppies came by and made it quite clear that half the Hindu pantheon would like to see me fed to Kali."

"Yama?" I asked, confused. "Not familiar with that one."

"Lucky you," he sneered.

I took a draught of coffee, wincing at the flavor. I dropped another heaping spoonful of sugar into the mug, stirring as Marius explained.

"Yama was the first mortal to die. Shiva uses him as judge, jury, and—in my case—a willing executioner. He's got a couple of hounds." Marius stretched and displayed the slashes across his flank. "One of them got in a few good swipes."

If the spaces between claw marks provided any scale, the paws of Yama's dogs were as big as dinner plates. Icy dread prickled over my body, and the fine hairs on my neck stood at attention just imagining such an immense beast. My palms were damp, and I swallowed down a lump of fear. "Anyone else?"

"Let's see, there's our old friend Na'ar al Afrit."

"Afrit?" My eyes widened. "Fuck. The djinn from that job in Belize five or six years ago? The one whose lamp Eris asked us to steal?"

"The very same," he sang. "He sends his regards, by the way."

"Great," I groaned sarcastically.

That was when it hit me: I had a vested interest in helping Marius, and not just one born of kindness and wayward affection. If Eris had put out the word of the satyr's transgressions, it would have implicated me, too. I'd been with Marius on more than one of those jobs. Like the Christmas trip to Belize in search of the djinn's magic lamp.

Shit. Helping Marius was officially in my best interest now.

Massaging the growing ache in my temples, I closed my eyes. "This just gets better and better," I muttered. "Please tell me that's all."

"Aren't you adorable?" His voice was sad and sweet, as if speaking to a naive child. "Not even close. If you'd like, I'll stop listing the supernatural element and start in with the mortals that would like to discuss old financial sins...or that time I ran away with a certain Kennedy's wife."

I let out a wordless bark of frustration. "God, Marius, why do you have to be such a bastard?"

"Until recently, it has served me rather well."

"Yeah, and now they all want you dead."

"Some of them just want to eat my soul, which is—in the end—all the same thing, isn't it?"

"You have one?" I spat.

He glared at me darkly. I gave a quick half shrug, half nod of apology and moved on. "So how can you get out of this?"

"I'm sure a few of them would settle for a century or four of slavery and torture as compensation. I'd prefer it didn't come to that, however. The only way I'm likely to get out of this entirely is to, as you say, find a bigger fish."

An obvious answer jumped into my head. "What about Loki? Or are you on his shit list, too?"

"Not as far as I know. But he is not so easy for me to contact these days."

I looked to the ceiling and cringed. I should've known this was his real reason for coming to me. "How lucky that I have an in with that particular faction."

"It does help," he admitted. "But I meant what I told you before: I came to you because you're the one person who won't sell me out. You're a good woman."

I winced again, not wanting his words to worm into my good graces. I took a quick sip of coffee. Still too bitter, I scooped more sugar into the mug. "Anyone else? In terms of new bosses, I mean."

His spring-green eyes swam out of focus and his mouth dropped a fraction of an inch as he thought. I imagined him flipping through a massive Rolodex in his mind, skimming over names and contacts, and determining how they fit in his web.

"None that I could get in touch with personally. But there's someone I know who might be able to help. Assuming he hasn't been swayed by Eris, that is."

"Fine. Give this guy a call."

"There's a slight problem with that. For that matter, all my contacts may as well be burned. I lost my phone somewhere in my brawl with Yama's dogs."

"Don't you have a backup?" I asked, slipping into Tech Support Maven mode. "Hard copy of numbers or something?"

He dipped his chin and stared down his nose. "I'm sorry, Catherine, but I didn't have time to pack between Eris's volcanic eruption and fighting for my life."

I stared at him blankly. For as long as I'd known him, Marius had contingencies layered six deep for every stage of his various games. The idea that he had only the shredded clothes on his back left me astounded. "You've really got nothing here, do you?"

"I've got you." A cheeky grin flashed his dimples. When it was clear that I was not amused in the slightest, he said, "I have a few good contacts if I can get in touch with them, and I've got a storage shed full of my things. It's off the radar and no one knows about it but me. Some of the rarer items I have might be useful."

I nodded. "Fine," I said. "I'll help you find a new boss."

"Thank you."

"Don't thank me yet," I warned. "Besides, there's still the matter of payment to discuss."

Marius folded his bare arms over the tile counter. "Ah, yes. That."

"If I help you, you owe me big-time. And I owe you nothing."

"I don't think so," he said stonily.

I blinked in surprise. "What?"

"You still owe me, Catherine Sharp, for helping you with that whole poker fiasco a few years back. I made good on that bargain. You have not."

"Do you really think I owe you shit after what happened the last time you slithered through town?"

"Oh please," he scoffed. "You may be a mortal, but you are not stupid. You know damn well that's not how contracts work in our world. You already failed to remove this damnable curse of mine, and now you want me to forget our other agreement? No."

I simmered, arms crossed over my chest and nails digging into my skin. Marius's eyes glittered with a playful glee. I recognized the look as one he wore well in our past disputes. Under it all, though, he was immovable as a mountain.

Being me, I had to shove anyway. "Are you really in any position to argue with me on this? You don't get to dictate terms here if you're the one who needs help so desperately."

Marius sighed. "Look," he started, "by granting me shelter here, you've already aided me immensely. If you help me stay alive long enough to find a new employer, I will be further in your debt and more than happy to owe you 'big-time,' as you put it. But our previous dealings stand. Terrible as you may be at the whole thing, I earned a date."

I hated when he was right. I flinched and tried to cover it with another sip of coffee. "Dammit," I breathed. "Fine. You'll get your date. Beyond that, though, I owe you nothing. Ever."

"Agreed," he said, his voice carrying a low thrum of power.

He stood and rounded the counter into the kitchen. At first I thought he meant to shake on it or do something to seal the deal. Instead, he opened my fridge. After much rustling about, he turned around, brandishing a finger covered with a thick dollop of icing from my birthday cake. With a gloppy *plunk*, coffee spurted out of my mug as the icing dropped in. He stirred it until the coffee went from black to a light, eggshell brown, then tapped the spoon twice on the rim.

"There," he said, the utensil clattering onto the counter. "If that's not good enough, nothing will ever please you."

He padded away then and fell casually onto my sofa before gasping as Linux pounced on him. My boy's not too careful with the claws, so he probably upset some of the more tender spots on Marius's stomach. Soon, though, the pair fell into a steady rhythm of worship and acceptance—Marius worshipped with belly rubs while Linux purrfully accepted the offerings.

My next sip of coffee was splendid. Scratch that. It was *divine*. It melted over my tongue in a burst of sweetness, warmth, and caffeinated goodness. I stared at the liquid voodoo in my mug, then drained it.

I restrained myself from groaning in frustration. Of course, Marius was right. *Again.* He was one of those nonhumans hell-bent on making my life difficult. For years I'd denied the fact that I even found him attractive. Then shit happened. A lot of it. Regardless, yesterday I thought I'd had a clear picture of my feelings about Marius. Now, with him here on my sofa, snuggling my cat, I had to wonder if once again I had been deluding myself.

Without another word, I breezed into my bedroom, past the rumpled, bloody sheets and straight into the hottest shower I could coax from the pipes.

What the hell had I just agreed to?

FOUR

"TOUGHER THAN IT IS"

"First things first," I said, careful to put as much authority into the words as I could. "You're not staying here. Mrs. M might be deaf, but even she would notice if these hellhounds show up. I refuse to put her in harm's way again, not for anyone, let alone you."

"All right," Marius said. His voice rose in the slightest of questions.

"I've got another place you can stay," I explained. "It's off the map and under all sorts of protections. You're not likely to run into much trouble there."

I gathered my bag and my phone, then made sure Linux had enough food in his bowl.

Procrastinating, that's all you're doing.

Kicking this particular hornet's nest was going to sting. Flynn was going to be pissed...

I swiped my keys off the counter. "Come on. We're leaving."

His eyebrows rose. "Now?"

"Yes. Now."

He stood and gingerly slipped into his worn leather jacket. He'd thrown away the T-shirt. It wasn't good for anything but rags at this point anyway. He reached out to open the door, but I caught his elbow.

"We're not going that way," I said.

"Secret passage through the bookcase that leads to your underground lair? Once there, we'll speed away in the Catmobile? Is that it?"

I ran my thumb over the slick black plastic of one of Flynn's inventions. It looked like any other keyless entry fob, but it didn't unlock my car. The fob sported a single button marked with an orange power symbol. The glyph began to glow as I willed my energy into it. When my panic button was ready, the light throbbed with the rhythm of my uneasy pulse.

"The Catmobile isn't here," I murmured.

His eyebrows knit together now. "Where is it?"

I gripped his arm in the tight claw of my left hand. I squeezed the fob, pressing the button, and the orange light flared out to create a tunnel. For an instant, the rabbit hole yawned into eternity, its walls swirling with fiery grace and jewel-bright threads of synapse. My stomach fluttered and rolled with the sudden weightlessness. Beneath my hand, Marius's arm was a radiant beam of green and silver. Whispers surrounded me, endlessly spilling over one another in unintelligible cacophony.

My knees jerked as my feet touched solid earth once more, and the infinite tunnel melted away to reveal my dorm-sized bolt-hole beneath YmFy, Flynn's bar. An amber aura clung to the shapes of the room, then dissipated like smoke as my eyes adjusted.

Beside me, Marius doubled over, gasping for breath between racking coughs. Teleportation can do that even to the best of us. I stepped into the room and opened the small refrigerator to grab two bottles of water. I passed one to Marius and took my own to the corner of the bed.

When the satyr had finally calmed his gag reflex, he joined me. He sat on the edge of the bed with his head between his knees. "What the bloody hell did you just do?"

"Teleporter," I said, dangling the fob. "It's supposed to be a panic button, a way for me to get out of a jam quickly, but sometimes I just leave my car at YmFy and would rather not splurge on a cab."

Taking a pull from his water bottle, Marius tracked his eyes over the room. "We're at Flynn's bar? That warehouse?"

"Beneath it," I said, ignoring the fact that any minute Flynn could burst in here and unleash a world of thunderous rage on us. And I'd deserve it. But I went on babbling about the room anyway. "There's a series of tunnels under the bar. This isn't much more than a dorm room with a better decorator," I explained, "but it's a good place to crash if I'm too tired or too drunk to drive home. Or in case of emergencies."

I pointed to the sleek black walls casting back our soft reflections. "Sliding panels for storage. I've got a bugout bag in that closet, but it's full of clothes that fit me, not you. That door leads to the bathroom. I've got it stocked with the necessities. And the bed is comfy enough," I added, pushing down on the futon mattress. "The fridge is stocked with water, caffeine, and a few chocolate bars. Basically, everything a girl needs in the event of the apocalypse or a renegade bottle of Jameson."

Ignoring my fifty-cent tour, Marius shook his head. "That's not like any teleportation I've ever experienced," he said, voice thick with nausea. "It's not natural. Your friend come up with that one?"

I nodded. "It's one of Flynn's more exclusive toys, yes."

As if he'd been summoned, my fellow ginger materialized in the doorway. Before his body even solidified, a distorted version of his voice called out, "Cat, are you all right?" Flynn's gaze settled on me, then on the satyr. "What is *he* doing here?"

Here it comes...

"He's going to be using my room for a few days," I said, keeping my voice firm.

Flynn scowled. "You offered something that's not yours to give, Catherine."

I gulped. As long as I've known him, Flynn has never called me by my full name. His voice, so chilly and menacing, seemed foreign.

"It's my room," I said.

"Yes, but this is *my place*." Flynn's hazel eyes locked onto mine, angry and hurt.

Though my knees shook, I didn't waver. I met his stare and passed the strength of it right back.

Marius cleared his throat and rose to his feet, a warm presence to my left. "I need to pop to your loo a moment."

A blur moved in my peripheral vision, and the door behind Flynn shut. A moment later, I could hear Marius retching.

"This is my place," Flynn repeated, at a whisper now. "The closest I have to Olympus or Eden. This is my sanctum. Why would you bring him here?"

"I can't have him at my apartment. It's not safe for him, my neighbors, or me. This place is protected, though. He can stay here and go unnoticed. It's only for a few days, tops. I won't be using the room."

"And you just assumed I'd grant asylum?" he growled through his teeth.

"Oh, come on!" I yelled. I quieted my words so that Marius wouldn't hear over his puking "You know he's telling the truth. What kind of god would you be if you couldn't divine that much?"

He blanched, and the color drained from his eyes, leaving his irises the liquid silver of mercury. Flynn clenched his jaw, but his silence roared. His hair seemed fiery all of a sudden, his tattoos more pronounced. It was as if my snarking off at him had reminded him that he was not human, but something else. In front of me, he looked alien.

I softened my voice and tried to appeal to what humanity still lived in the clockwork of my friend. "Flynn, he needs help. Put your differences aside for just a few days while things get sorted out. He won't be any trouble."

At this, Flynn let out a thin, reedy laugh. Some of the color returned to his features. He clawed a hand through his spiky hair. "He doesn't know how to be anything else."

"Please," I said. "Just for a few days."

"To you it's just a few days, but it's not as simple as crashing on my couch. Offering him sanctuary means something very different to the immortal crowd. You *know* that. If word gets out that he's here, I'm all but announcing that I've chosen a side. I don't have the luxury of anonymity anymore, Cat. I have to think about this political bullshit now. And so should you."

Marius continued to heave away in the bathroom. After a particularly glorious and loud volley, Flynn winced. "Jesus, did you cook?"

I flinched but otherwise ignored the jab at my culinary skills. "First time teleporting your way."

Flynn snorted and looked at the door with a satisfied smile. "Amateurs."

"Please," I tried again. "A few days."

The god sighed heavily, staring at his feet. "Fine." He looked up then and pinned me with a stare. "But I'm not doing this for him. I'd only do this for you."

"Thank you, Flynn."

"Rules," he barked. "Limited access. He's not allowed here without you. He only goes upstairs after hours. I don't want him seen in my bar. Got it?"

I nodded.

"Give me your key," he continued. "I'll make sure it's charged before you need to get out of here."

I slipped my panic button free from its ring and tossed it across the room to Flynn. He caught it as he turned away from me.

"Thank you," I repeated. "This means a lot to me."

As he turned the knob, Flynn scuffed his chin over his bony shoulder and looked at me sadly. "I hope he's worth it."

He padded off, leaving me alone with the rapid patter of my pulse and a satyr puking in the next room.

FIVE

"Cool Blue Reason"

While Marius indulged in a shower, I made a phone call to my employer, the steward of my soul. My stomach rolled with nausea, not in sympathy for Marius but out of sheer terror. I admit that I act rough and tough when around gods—it's the only way to make sure they know you won't be cowed by that whole immortal and omnipotent thing they've got going on. In reality, though, I'm fucking petrified by all of them. I've had my soul ripped from my being, my mind twisted in knots, my body put through the wringer, and my dignity hung on the line by all sorts of deities. That being the case, I think a little butterfly in the tummy is doing pretty well.

Loki answered on the third ring, his cool voice merry as Christmas. "What's new, pussycat?"

I rolled my eyes but counted my blessings that he was in a good mood. "Hey, Boss. You got a minute...or five?"

"For you? Always. I hope you had a pleasant birthday."

"I've had worse," I dodged.

"Did you get my present?"

"Unless you dropped a half-dead body on my doorstep, then no. If you did, we really need to talk about your choice of gifts."

The god's laughter carried a note of approval. "I have better taste than that, Cat. If I sent you a body it would be completely dead or none at all. Besides, I know you're not overly fond of satyrs."

I winced. News of Marius had gotten to Loki on the godly grapevine. "So you know why I'm calling."

"I'm only surprised it's taken you this long."

"Will you meet us?" I crossed my fingers and said a small prayer to any god that would listen.

Please, just take him off my hands and let this end smoothly, quickly, and without monsters attacking me.

"An hour," he said firmly. "Sapphire. It's a club on Industrial. Couple blocks south of Sahara. You can't miss it."

"Thank you," I said.

"Don't thank me yet, Miss Sharp."

—◊◊—

Marius exited the bathroom cleaned up and looking more like himself, wearing the borrowed clothes Flynn had dropped off. While there was a height difference between the two of them, it was nothing compared to the chasm between their individual styles. Marius, who was comfortable in designer suits or torn jeans that cost more than a plasma television, now sported one of Flynn's metal band shirts and a pair of bondage pants. Chains jingled from the satyr's hips, and I'd be a liar with flaming trousers if I said he didn't make an attractive goth.

"Go on, say it," he said catching my smile. "I'm ridiculous."

I shook my head, my hair falling in my face like a curtain. "No, the chains look good on you." The words left me before I'd approved them. Heat rose to my cheeks.

"Well," he mused. His face scrunched in a wry grin. "Perhaps a date with you will be more interesting than I expect."

"You'll have to wait to find out," I said. "We're leaving."

"For where?"

"Your first—and hopefully last—job interview."

Marius followed me upstairs to a silent YmFy. The empty bar—normally a neon beacon in the dark warehouse—was dim and lifeless. Alone but for the bottles, Flynn stood behind the bar taking inventory and prepping the place for the night crowd. My friend stopped his work and stared at us with a mixture of worry and menace. I said nothing but gave Flynn a wave laced with gratitude.

31

Outside, the summer air was thick and hot as a blast furnace. Crunching across the gravel to my car, I mentioned, "Flynn set up access for you, too. Anything in the building that requires a code, just enter your password."

"And just what is my password?"

"Goatfucker," I said with a smirk.

"Charming."

"You don't get your own panic button. You're only allowed at YmFy with me. So if we need to bug out fast, grab onto me and I'll panic button us back," I added, dangling my key fob in front of his face.

He convulsed. "Don't worry. I don't plan on teleporting his way unless I'm bleeding from every orifice. And on fire."

Turning to face Marius, I pinched his cheek and put on a baby-talk voice. "What's a-matter? Somebody's tummy feeling yucky?"

"Do shut up, won't you?"

"No." I filled him in on Flynn's rules. "Anyway, you can use my room for now, but the sooner we get you another backer the better. Hopefully this meeting will pan out, and it won't be an issue."

"Where are we going?" he asked again, his voice tinged with the slightest hint of fear.

"We're going to see—"

My vision blurred, went crimson, and a wave of bliss fell over my skin in a flush of heat. The YmFy parking lot was gone, replaced by snapshots of a dark room...

A bed with silk sheets black as night. The cloying scent of sex and whiskey lingers in the air. I lie there, glistening with sweat and writhing beneath the temptations of...who? Before I can think, another wave of ecstasy crashes against me. I rock with it, arching my naked body into the eager kisses of a lover. Breath falls over my thighs, followed by prickly stubble and soft lips. Hands slide over my knees. I can only hear the sounds of my own needy whimpering, low moans of pleasure. A flick of a tongue and I cry out, my own hands twisting in those silk sheets, toes curling against a taut, muscular back.

"Catherine!" Marius said.

"Yes," I panted. Body atingle, mind numbed with the imagined orgasm, I staggered forward and fell against my car.

His hand was tight on my arm, his face drawn with concern. "Are you all right?"

Giddy and lightheaded, I let out a sigh that turned into a satiated giggle. "I'm fine..."

"What happened?"

As the pleasure ebbed away, reality slid back into place. Shame soon followed, accompanied by confusion.

Then memory. One of Marius's satyr abilities was to inject sordid thoughts into another's mind. "Did you just...?"

"Just what?" he asked.

He wouldn't be playing his mind games now, of all times, would he? No, the expression on his face was one of pure concern. He had no idea what I'd just seen. I dragged a hand through my hair. "I just...I kinda...I guess I zoned out there," I explained weakly.

Marius's eyes swept over the lot. "You're really all right?"

"Fine," I assured him. "I'm fine. Get in the car. Less chance of you being seen."

When we were in the car and on our way, I asked, "So that trick of yours that you used on me a time or two...the one that lets you put thoughts into my head... Anyone like that looking for you?"

He shrugged. "Several creatures have that ability. What sort of thing did you see?"

I flushed red and chewed my lip. "Sex," I answered simply.

He chuffed with a sad laugh. After a strained silence, he said, "That doesn't narrow things down."

"Any other satyrs? Guys with grudges?"

He shook his head. "Not really. We don't exactly keep in touch. For the most part, satyrs just look out for themselves."

The car fell silent. I didn't want to comment on that, and Marius seemed to lose himself in his thoughts for a time. I counted all the nasty beasts that could've gotten into my head. Fae? Puck had done something similar before. I cringed, as thinking of the Fae immediately brought up the sorest spot on my heart: Dahlia, my ex. The woman who had lost my soul to Eris, bound my powers, and never had the decency to tell me that I was more than human.

"Was it good?" Marius asked, his quiet tone jarring me from memories of the traitorous faerie.

"Was what good?"

He smirked. "The sex. In the vision. Was it at least good?"

"Yeah," I admitted.

—⁊⁊—

Loki was waiting for us at Industrial and Sahara, so I got behind the wheel and pointed my car southeast. Senses still flying from...whatever that flash had been about, the Las Vegas twilight swam past my car in swaths of bright colors. The filaments of energy that run through the city like veins pulsed with power. If I listened, I could hear the high-tension hum of the world blending with the low purr of my car's motor. Each spark plug that sent out another *snap-pop* of current joined the chorus. Normally, such sounds are calming and lull me into a relaxed, meditative state. Not so on that night. No, after the sexually charged vision, the city's life coursed through me, igniting me like a lover's teasing strokes. I felt alive, wicked, and ready to meet my boss with mischief to equal his.

"We're being followed," Marius calmly informed me as I turned south onto Industrial Road

I checked the rearview, but it wouldn't have mattered. I'd been so off in my own little world for most of the drive that I'd have to take his word for it.

"You're sure?" I asked. The vehicles following us didn't look like spy cars. No ominous black SUVs or nondescript white vans. Just the usual traffic—a party bus, a couple of beaten-up sedans on their last legs, a luxury car or two.

"Fairly certain," Marius muttered, shifting in his seat. "The yellow bike a few cars back."

I looked up again just in time to see a garish yellow motorcycle weave between lanes and pull up on my tail. The single light hovered in the mirror. The driver didn't speed up, didn't draw a weapon or try to flag me over to the shoulder. He just drove a standard, safe distance behind us.

"Suggestions?" I asked.

"Keep going. The meeting is in a public place, yes?"

I nodded. "Sapphire."

Marius let out a rueful laugh. "Of course it is. Loki's choice, I suppose?"

"What are you talking about?"

"You've never been, have you?"

I shook my head. "It's a club, right?"

Marius's smile held little mirth as he kept his eyes trained on the rearview. "The bike is falling back, but I'm certain we'll see it in the lot at Sapphire. Won't we?"

I shrugged. "Maybe it's just a bike?"

The satyr fidgeted in his seat, tugging at his borrowed T-shirt and shifting the chains on his pants. He drew a long breath through his teeth. "Is there anything you want to tell me?"

"You mean like that time I cheated on my third-grade history test?"

"Who are we *really* meeting, Catherine?"

"Loki. Who else?"

Marius stared at me for a long, unnervingly silent moment. Between glances at him and the road, I couldn't read the blank look on his face. A familiar discomfort began to twist and ache beneath my breastbone. A sick sort of hope choked with guilt gripped my heart and shoved it up into my throat. I liked it when he looked at me, and I wanted...what? Desire? Approval?

"What?" I croaked. "We talked about this. Loki's the only person I know who can help you. It's the best I can do."

Now I saw something there in those leaf-green eyes—wonder, humility. "It never even occurred to you to double-cross me, did it?"

"Double— No. Why would it?"

"There's probably a bounty on my head so large it would make Solomon blush. A couple of calls to the right people and you could arrange a meeting, have us followed, and when we get out of the car I'm pinned in on both sides by the guy on the bike and the god inside. Quite the elegant trap."

I gaped at him. I hadn't even thought of that. My stomach roiled at the idea. "Is this why you've been all broody and quiet since we left Flynn's? Because you think I'm about to deliver you to your enemy?"

"Or maybe Flynn made the call," he said.

"Stop."

"It wouldn't be too hard for him. He loathes me as it is."

"Stop," I snapped. "Seriously, you're driving me crazy with this shit. I'm taking you to see Loki. Done. I'm not some Judas or fucking Fredo. And neither is Flynn."

"Did you just make a *Godfather* reference?"

"Yes. Deal with it."

Marius fussed with his ponytail and went back to surreptitiously watching the traffic behind us. After a few minutes, I asked, "Is this what it's like for you? Constantly wondering who's about to stab you in the back?"

"More or less," he answered.

"Jesus. No wonder you're so lonely."

—⚒—

I parked the car beneath the blue lights of Sapphire just as dusk fell. Even at this relatively early hour, the lot was full and a steady stream of patrons drifted into the club.

"There's our friend." Marius tipped his chin, and I followed the gesture just in time to see the Caustic Lemon crotch rocket slow down. The rider wore a helmet in a similarly horrific shade of yellow with a black face mask. I couldn't see his eyes, but he turned his head and I'd have sworn he'd looked right at me.

It was as if I'd lost cabin pressure. My ears popped and thrummed with my rapid pulse, and my stomach flopped. I turned my back to the rider and...

Hot whispers tickle on the back of my neck. Fingers tighten in my hair as a tongue slides along my ear. Teeth nibble my earlobe, and I let my head fall back, inviting those lips to devour me one precious kiss at a time. I reach up to run my hand through thick, silken hair.

As I grabbed a fistful of those tresses, the flash of desire vanished. I took stock of the world around me—so different from how it had seemed a fraction of a second ago. My car was there, bathed in electric-blue light. The only heat against my skin came from the summer night. And the satyr at my back. Marius stood behind me, a steadying hand light on my hip. Quickly, I disentangled my fingers from his mane and whirled around.

"What the hell was that?" I asked.

I expected to find his signature smirk blazing from his face, but instead of smile lines, Marius's brow was furrowed. "It happened again, didn't it?"

I nodded, looking to see if we'd had an audience. "Yeah. Yeah, it did."

His gaze darted over my head as he searched the parking lot, as if looking for someone.

I pulled away from him and shuffled toward the club. "Let's just go. I need a drink and to clear my head."

I didn't mention that I might need a cold shower, too.

Besides, we'd get into the bar and find Loki, and then thoughts of lurid sex would be the furthest thing from my mind.

When I opened the door, however, I understood that I was deluding myself.

Turns out that Sapphire is a strip joint.

SIX

"INDIGO EYES"

The lobby resembled a hotel more than a nudie bar. Simple yet elegant chandeliers hung from the ceiling, their amber reflections gleaming off the marble floor. Along the walls were tubes like something out of a sci-fi movie: gray cylinders with glass fronts, illuminated with azure light. Each of these tubes held the sculpture of a female torso. Near the door, patrons queued up behind a velvet rope awaiting entrance into the main floor of the club. From the other side of the nearest wall, a deep, insistent rhythm beat out, occasionally punctuated by the cheering of a crowd.

Jogging toward me was a gorgeous man. He had chocolate skin and biceps threatening to tear the sleeves of his black polo emblazoned with the club's logo. He moved past the line of would-be customers and greeted me with a smile.

"Miss Sharp," he beamed. "You and your guest are expected. If you'll follow me, I'll escort you to your private lounge."

Marius eyed me cautiously. "Thought you said you'd never been here before."

"I haven't," I replied. I turned to the escort and gestured forward. "Lead the way."

After a short trip to the upstairs of the club, we were shown into one of Sapphire's "skyboxes." The suite boasted two lengths of black Italian leather molded into couches—one on either side of the room. Mounted onto a wall was a flat-screen television. A window offered a bird's eye view of the action on the main floor. I squinted, blinded by walls painted a shade of green somewhere between Electric Lime and Acid-Trip Leprechaun.

When my eyes adjusted, I saw the Holy Grail: a bottle of vodka chilling in a bucket of ice next to a selection of mixers sweating in their bottles. I dove forward—past the exotic dancer sprawled on the nearest of the sofas—and began double fisting cans of Red Bull.

The door shut behind us and Marius grumbled, "Well, where is he?"

"How the hell should I know?" I said between gulps.

The stripper slithered to her feet. "We could have fun while you wait for your friend," she purred. She slid a finger down her throat, over her breasts. Looking up from beneath a forest of false lashes, she pinned Marius with a glance both hopeful and promising. "I'm Candy."

I rolled my eyes. *Aren't they always Candy?* I looked her over. While she wasn't my usual type of woman, Candy was indeed tasty. With her heavy, dark makeup and multiple piercings, she'd chosen a punky-Lolita stripper persona. Her blond hair—shaved on the sides and pulled up high on the crown of her head—resembled a palomino mane rather than a ponytail. Underneath her black mesh top, she wore a glittery gold bra that almost covered her enhanced money makers. The gleaming latex skirt revealed just a hint of bare ass cheek as she leaned against Marius. Her lips grazed his chin.

Without so much as blinking in her direction, Marius pushed past Candy and over to the table where he began pouring himself a vodka and cranberry.

"He'd better get here soon," the satyr rumbled.

I stared at my can of Red Bull, wondering if I'd accidentally quaffed the booze. Had I slipped myself a roofie? Perhaps suffered a head injury at some point? Because at that exact moment I would've sworn that Marius had just ignored a stripper.

"Are you okay?" I asked.

"Why do you ask?"

"I don't know if you've noticed, Marius, but we're in the Slytherin common room of the Playboy mansion."

"And?"

"And," I said, tilting my head toward Candy, "there's a stripper, like, five feet away from you. A hot one."

He took a quick gander at our hostess, then returned his eyes to me, nonplussed. "We don't have time for this. Look, the sooner your boss gets here, the sooner we can be done with this whole hellstorm." He took his drink across the room and slumped into the empty couch. The satyr's green eyes searched our surroundings before coming to rest on the door as he waited for Loki to arrive.

"Marius?" Candy repeated. "That's an unusual name. I don't hear that one a lot."

Here it comes. The perfect opening for him to use some clever line about how she'll get to say his name all night long.

But the quip never came. Marius pressed his lips together in a scowl and watched the ice melt in his cocktail.

"Somebody's tense," Candy said, passing me a knowing glance. "I think I know just what he needs."

She glided in front of Marius—cleverly blocking his view of the door—and began to gyrate with the rhythm of the music pounding up from the club floor. Her hips made tight circles as her hands slid down the taut muscles of her body. She pulled at her shirt teasingly, batting those thick lashes at the brooding satyr. When he refused to look up, she closed the distance between them and struck a solid, wide stance. Bending at the waist, she took his chin between her fingers and angled it up so that her gaze burned into his.

"Mmmmarius," she crooned. "Come on and give us a smile."

He bared his teeth in a cynical grimace.

"You're a hard nut to crack, aren't you?" she said. "Well, let's see if we can loosen you up."

Candy peeled off her mesh top, exposing those huge breasts and that poor gold bra. With a throaty laugh, she tossed her blond mane and straddled Marius. Locking her knees on either side of him, she rocked her hips. His cheek twitched as he ground his teeth together. He turned his eyes up to the ceiling and squirmed in his seat. As Candy gave a particularly deep thrust of her hips, Marius hissed as if in pain. She rolled her head and passed me a wicked, conspiratorial stare.

Her eyes never leaving mine, she pursed her lips and looped her shirt around Marius's shoulders. Heat crawled up my cheeks, and my stomach twisted as Candy pulled the satyr into her breasts.

"Uh-oh," she sang, "looks like someone might be getting jealous."

There was no warning. Marius grabbed both her arms with brutish force and thrust her off him with a leonine growl. The dancer fell to the floor, her...*ahem*...charms bouncing out of her inadequate bra.

"Enough," Marius roared. Rage overtook his features as he loomed over her. "Get out!"

Candy made no move to leave. She just lay there on the floor chuckling. Soon, those chuckles turned into hearty laughs that changed her whole face. Her skin began to ripple like water, and then her features flowed into something else entirely. I blinked to see Loki writhing in the throes of a giggle fit.

His boobs jiggled more pleasantly than Santa's belly. "Your face was perfect!" he gasped. "You should've seen it! All serious and then..." Loki mimed pulling Marius's face into his breasts and exploded in fresh laughter.

While my boss continued to chortle himself purple, Marius seethed. "I did not come here to be mocked!"

"Didn't you?"

"Wow," I stammered. "That was...just... I don't even."

My flabber was well and truly gasted. I'd seen Loki pull his shape-shifting tricks before, but nothing had left me as dumbstruck as the god's familiar, angular features atop "Candy's" lithe body. This was taking drag to a whole new level. Before my eyes, he took both those breasts roughly in his hands.

"I am Loki of Asgard!" he bellowed. "And I am burdened with a glorious rack!"

I buried my face into one of the sofa pillows and giggled. Apparently, Marius didn't appreciate the reference, because when I looked up, he was on his feet, fists at his sides.

"Are you quite finished having a laugh?" he boomed.

"Sorry," I lied.

"Jesus Christ." Loki pushed up from the floor, the jiggle of his tits quite distracting. Without bothering to cover himself or shapeshift the rest of his body, the self-proclaimed Bane of the Aesir sat beside me on the sofa. "Is he always this way or has he just spent too much time around Bitchcakes?"

"Eris does have a knack for sucking the life out of people," I admitted. I reached out a wary hand and poked one of the massive mammaries on Loki's chest. "Wow, they feel real," I whispered. I groped him, enjoying a heaping handful of the god's boob. "Do you moisturize?"

"Fantastic, aren't they?"

"Seriously, they're petal-soft! How do you do that?"

"Excuse me!" Marius interrupted.

I jerked my hand back and folded it with the other in my lap. Loki stared at Marius with equal parts intrigue and mischief. "Well, well, well. If a satyr has stopped being able to enjoy an amazing set of breasts, then I suppose it's good for Marius that he's finally rid of Discord."

Marius paced like a panther, stalking from one side of the room to the other. "Catherine told you, I take it."

"Hell no." Loki snorted. "I've my own sources, and they tell me your name is being passed from countless lips to many a god's ear. You have gotten yourself into a mountain of trouble, Marius. So tell me... Was it worth it?"

"Was what worth it?"

"Come on, old friend. No one stays with Eris for as long as you did out of the goodness of his heart." As Loki spoke, his form shifted. Limb by limb, cell by cell, "Candy's" body was replaced with the form I'd come to see most often. Loki sat with one long leg folded over the other in jeans, a T-shirt, and flip-flops. As if transformation were nothing more complex than breathing, Loki continued, "Unless you've become a masochist of epic proportions, you had another game going. Something you wanted from her. Did you get it?"

Marius's face fell. His eyes sparkled, and for a moment, I thought he might shed a tear. When he spoke, his voice was raw. "No."

For a long moment, the god's ice pick stare pierced the satyr. The chill of silence seemed to cover even the strains of music thumping the club floor. My throat went dry and my palms grew damp as I waited for someone to say something. Hell, I was tempted to jump up and start dancing myself just to break the tension. Should I make a case for Marius? Should I ask Loki to take him on?

No. This was between the two of them. I was just Marius's ride, his employee referral. From here on, I had to stay out of it.

"I'm going to go downstairs," I said.

Loki produced a crisp bill from the pocket of his jeans, and passed it to me. "Get yourself a drink on me."

Considering I could've ordered drinks for half the club with that one bill, I stashed it and promised myself some top-shelf whiskey. "As you wish, Boss."

I gave Marius a parting glance of encouragement. As I shut the door behind me, I saw the satyr sitting on the sofa with his head in his hands.

I had two thoughts as I walked down the hall: how much had changed, and how far had he fallen to be so vulnerable before one so powerful as Loki?

I took to the floor during an intermission. There were no dancers on the stage, but every plush, blue seat in the house was packed. A bachelor party toasted itself loudly as I drifted past. There was a queue at the bar about three deep, but being small—and female—I managed to slip up to a stool with little problem. The bartender nodded to acknowledge my presence, said he'd be back in a minute, then fluttered off to make drinks. I made myself comfortable on a stool and admired the shrine to whiskey.

Beside me, a coarse man pissedly held court over the Vegas night-life. "—drink and food," he said, his accent from somewhere in the United Kingdom. "And the women! Christ, a man could get distracted by the local flavor."

I chuckled, shook my head, and went back to waiting.

He sniffed at the air, then turned his attention to me. The man's stare was a weight of appraisal, a caress on the cheek, and a smack on the ass. "Speakin' of local flavors," he drawled in that accent, "you look positively delicious, love. Skin as milky as ice cream and a cherry on top." He ran a hand over my hair. "I could devour you for days and never get tired."

I shifted uneasily, pulling away from his touch. Otherwise, I ignored him. The bartender arrived, and I picked my poison. "Rusty nail," I said. "And make it with Johnnie Walker Blue, if you please."

"And she knows how to hold her drink! A glorious body, a taste for whiskey, and a gorgeous face," the drunk said, somehow managing to add an extra syllable to the last word.

I gave him a glare guaranteed to shrivel the sac of mortal men.

The DJ announced the next dancer, and as the music flared, the crowd let out a collective whoop. The drunk beside me added his voice to the chorus, and I stole a moment to take him in.

Tall and broad, wearing an offensively purple button-down top, he looked familiar. His dark-brown hair fell past his shoulders in tight, frizzy curls. Blue eyes glittered beneath thick brows. Pale face, with booze-blushed cheeks, a narrow nose, and full lips.

The bartender returned with my drink. Before I could pay, the loudmouth slammed his pint on the bar. "Her drink's on me. And when you're done with that," he added, "I'll show you a real good time."

"No, thanks," I said sternly.

"You don't really feel that way, do you now?" he asked, his voice taking on the texture of dark chocolate. Leaning forward, he closed the space between us to an intimate distance. His hair fell from behind his ear, casting a dangerous shadow full of neon-red promises.

The man's eyes filled with a deep, glowing indigo. His unspoken proposition burrowed into my mind, filling it with sordid whispers, crimson images of sweat and steam...

Bare, slippery flesh against flesh. Limbs twined in tight knots with mine. Swollen lips over my belly and smooth hands up my thighs...

I gasped as desire flopped just below my stomach and spilled warm tingles through my whole being. "It's you," I whispered groggily. "You're doing this..." My voice trailed off.

As the air around us began to bend and shimmer, his lips spread into a familiar leer. "Come on, love," he said. "Let's you and me pop out of here for a nice, long taste of fun."

Taste of fun.

Those words echoed in my mind, and the world vanished.

My mouth opens to his, and I fall into the bliss of his embrace. Oh, those lips—so full and plump. I take his lower lip between my teeth, and he growls his approval. Another kiss, another taste. He is whiskey and song, chocolate and spice.

My senses returned, but still, I heard his voice like a low, constant drone. Without a thought for my drink or anything but the explicit images writhing in my mind, I slid off the barstool and inched closer to the stranger. That abyssal gaze traced up my throat, a touch hot as a brand and moist as breath. His scent—fresh grass clippings and spicy cologne—enveloped me, and I shuddered. Soft, dark curls tickled my cheeks as he bent over me. His tongue flicked over my earlobe, sending shocks of current along every nerve. I drew in a sharp breath as his teeth nibbled gently.

"I can't wait to worship you," he purred, "like the goddess you are."

Though distantly I knew I should probably say no, that I was supposed to be doing something, my whole body went rigid with anticipation. I wished my clothes would melt off, that he would throw me up onto the bar and have his way with me.

His mouth curled. "Come on, love," he said. "Let's you and me find a shady spot."

I slipped my hand into his.

SEVEN

"BLUE POWDER"

With a low whistle, a translucent shape cut through the air and smacked the stranger in the head with a resonant *thwack*. His eyes rolled out of focus, and the world rippled like shadows on a pond. I could still hear him whispering naughty invitations in my mind.

A hand gripped me, and it felt as if flames scalded my wrist, burning away the image of the stranger sliding over me, hands and lips exploring every inch of my body with gusto. The sudden touch doused my desire, leaving me cold and my head full of steam.

"Catherine," Marius barked.

As if waking up, I blinked him into focus. His stare blazed like angry, emerald fire as he held my wrist in an iron grasp.

"Jesus Christ!" the stranger yelled. He rose from the bar holding his head, red staining his fingers. "You son of a piss-swilling whore!"

I was dimly aware of a scuffle. The chains at Marius's hips jingled over the low sounds of grunting. With an arctic blast, awareness flooded me, and I lurched forward and yanked Marius off the other man. As they came apart, both tossed their dark manes and snorted as if ready to lock horns. Literally. The nubs of Marius's horns poked out of his glamour on either side of his forehead. A matching set appeared on the bleeding head of the stranger.

"She's not for you, Malcolm," Marius seethed.

"Oh? Why don't you ask her who she fancies, eh? She and I were just 'bout to pop out for a lovely bit of scrumpin' when you had to put your poncy face in where it isn't wanted."

"I wasn't going to go anywhere with you," I shouted. Marius's arm fell around me. "You were using your...satyr mojo bullshit." I flapped my hands uselessly as I groped for words. "And that doesn't count!"

"No?" The strange satyr—Malcolm, was it?—smirked. "That's why you're pleasantly moist and ready to ride me like Godiva, is that it?"

"I'm not!"

Marius leaned over and murmured in my ear. "Darling, I could engrave diamonds with your nipples right now. Unless you're suddenly quite cold, you might want to shut up before things get worse."

I looked down, and sure enough, my body betrayed me with twin points of interest. With a self-conscious gasp, I wrapped my arms around my chest.

Malcolm winked at me appreciatively. "You should see what I could do if that shirt weren't in the way. Pesky clothes always ruinin' me fun. Not unlike some cheeky bastards I know," he added with a glare for Marius.

"Not yours," Marius growled. His hand was a firm, hot presence on my hip as his arm curved around the small of my back.

"Come on, Marius!" Malcolm whined. "I'd be willing to share. We've done it before. You take one end, I'll take the other, and we'll meet up in the middle. How's that sound?"

"Marius, who the hell is this?" I asked, pushing away from him.

"No one," he growled.

Affronted, Malcolm blinked in horrified surprise. "Are you 'shamed of me, Marius? Your own flesh and blood?"

"Yes," Marius said bluntly. "I thought we'd established that ages ago."

I gaped, somewhere between confused and offended. "You two are related?"

"I'm 'is brother!" Malcolm's voice was high with offense.

"What you are," Marius simmered, "is a blight on the bloodline."

"Oh aye, that's rich comin' from the likes o' you. Which of us went prancin' off to play with the boy-lovin' Greeks? Y' know, Marius, I think that's turned your head if you're not willin' to go halvsies with me and shag this one six ways from a month of Sundays."

Marius's fingers curled into my belt loops, and I actually heard him give a guttural, possessive rumble. "She's not for you, Malcolm, and that is final."

Marius turned me and nudged me back toward Loki's private room, but Malcolm followed. I looked over my shoulder at him, and he gave me a knowing glance. He wagged a finger at his sibling. "You'll no'ice he didn't say nothin' 'bout my guess that he's gay."

—⚉—

Back in the Leprechaun Lounge, I found myself alone in a strip club with a pair of satyrs. Loki had stepped out for a moment, a phone call taking his attention away from Marius's plight. So there we sat—me on the sofa next to Marius, and Malcolm in a chair opposite us.

Malcolm slid a tumbler of whiskey across the silver coffee table, winking at me with an exaggerated nod. I wrapped my fingers around the glass, but before it could make the trip to my lips, Marius replaced it with a sweating pint of ice water.

"Like you need it with him putting salacious thoughts in your head," I heard him mutter. Marius tossed back the whiskey, his face twisting as the burn swept down his throat.

I sneered. "What are you? My mother?"

"My brother's keeper," he said. Regarding the satyr sitting across from us, his lip curled with derision.

Malcolm took a sip from his own drink. "I need no such thing. And, might I add, you're a shit host. You've not even introduced me to your lovely friend here."

"Malcolm," Marius rumbled. It was both warning and statement. "This is Catherine. And as far as you're concerned, she is off-limits."

"Nothing is off-limits to me, brother mine."

The air shifted again, and Malcolm's face swam in my mind. Though his lips didn't move, I heard his purring words in my ears. The lurid pictures flooded my imagination again.

Malcolm's hair falls in curls on either side of eyes that smolder like arctic fire. His face all taut muscle and smooth skin. Those decadent lips meet mine, and his tongue darts into my mouth. Habanero hot and sugar sweet, his kisses are drunken pleasures, luxuriant treats to be sampled and savored.

Pain shot up through my left foot as Marius stamped on it. I hissed, roared in protest and slugged Marius in the shoulder. "Quit that!"

Still, Malcolm's images dissipated. The whispers went silent, and the world returned to its normal upright position.

"Stop it, Malcolm," Marius barked.

Though he slipped his booted foot away, Marius pressed his thigh against mine, a constant presence. I shifted uncomfortably, but his knee followed the movement and held the contact.

Taking deep breaths and sipping at my water, I tried to convince my body that my mind was full of shit. But desire still coursed beneath my skin, and I wondered if I'd have to resort to pouring the whole pint of water over my lap. No matter that Malcolm's stare went straight to my pink parts, I'd long since vowed to avoid romance with the nonhuman types.

"So," I said, "this is...fun? Is this what satyrs usually do on holidays? Have family time at the nudie bar?"

"I'm not here for a reunion." Marius glared at his brother. "What do you want, Malcolm?" he spat.

"You need to come home, *Marius.*"

Though it flashed quicker than a snake's strike, fear stung my friend's eyes for an instant. When he spoke, his voice was hard and dry. "Why?"

"Father's request." Malcolm flicked his eyes to me, then narrowed his gaze. "*Family* matters."

I looked from one brother to the next, trying to read the air between them and figure out what the hell was going on. Marius tightened his fingers around my wrist, his grip fierce and damp.

Marius was incredulous "Father's request?"

"Is he ill?" I asked.

Malcolm waved me off. "Nothin' like that, love. The man might be as ancient as the missionary position, but he's spry as ever."

"Then what is so urgent, Mal," Marius said, "that he would send you to fetch me?"

"How the fuck should I know? The old man said to collect you, and that's what I'm here to do. You might've run off to play with your Greeks, but I stayed near the homestead like a good son."

Marius began to protest, but the other satyr struck again. "When was the last time you bothered to so much as call your own father? I know you've no love for me, and that's fine, but to turn your back on the man that sired you is lower than shit. He needs you to come home. Does it matter why? Don't ask. Just do as the man says."

And I thought my Thanksgiving dinners were guilt trips from Hell.

With a heavy sigh, Marius pinched the bridge of his nose as weariness drew lines across his face. "Fine," he conceded. "But I've got some business to tie up here first."

Malcolm leered at me. "Do you need help tyin' her up?"

"No one is tying me up," I said sharply.

"Are you sure?" Malcolm asked. "'Cause I can promise you a night of delectable sex. A few strands of silk in the right places and you're powerless. All you can do is lie back and enjoy as I devour you...slowly. Pleasing you. Tasting every inch of you. And I won't stop until your legs are shaking and each and every single one of your neighbors knows my name."

I blinked, weighing the offer. "Now why didn't you ever try a line like that with me, huh?" I chided with a hard glance at Marius.

He rolled his eyes. The door opened, and a very male, very pissed-off Loki entered the room

"Just once," he simmered, "I'd like a day when nothing goes wrong. And here I thought Miss Sharp would be my lucky charm where that was concerned."

I snorted with laughter. "I never said I was *good* luck."

"No shit." He flip-flopped his way to the coffee table and retreated to a sofa with an entire bottle of vodka.

Malcolm lifted a finger in protest. "I was going to have some of that."

"You weren't," Loki snarled. "You were going to leave before I rip off your nutsack and use your balls for ice cubes."

Malcolm hopped up from his seat and bounded for the exit. "Meet you downstairs, brother mine."

The door clicked shut behind him. With a sizzle and a gleam of glittering fractals, frost climbed the bottle of vodka. Loki took a long, hard gulp. "Marius, I can't help you. Not in the way you want."

"More good news," my friend muttered. "And why not?"

Loki's scowl darkened. I tried to scooch away so that I wouldn't get hit by the inevitable lightning bolt, but Marius maintained contact with me, inching over to compensate for the most minuscule of my movements.

"What do you possibly think you can offer me?" Loki asked.

"What I've always offered and willingly given: Theft. Inside information on other factions. Protecting your various—" his voice trailed off as he turned his eyes to me "—interests."

"That was all well and good when you weren't on every pantheon's most-wanted list. What made you so valuable before was that only a scant few knew the reach of your sticky fingers. How do you expect to be an infiltrator of any sort when everyone knows they can't trust you?"

"Use me as an assistant, then," he said. The edges of Marius's calm had long since worn away, so much so that his voice began to tremble and rise as he continued. "Eris did it for quite some time. I've got contacts all over town—mundane and otherwise—and I can make certain that—"

"That no one ever trusts me," Loki interrupted. "Really, Marius, you're smarter than this. You know the way this town works, the way *I* work."

"I'll lie low for a bit. Toss a good glamour on me so I'm out of sight. Let all the hullabaloo die down, and then I can come back better than ever. No one need know I wear your mark until you're ready to make it known."

Loki slammed the bottle down. "I have no use for you!"

Thick tension snapped in the room with electric ferocity. Even the sound of the club seemed far away as Loki's anger flared. His gas-flame eyes held no mirth, no joy or mischief. Fury ebbed off him in frosty waves.

Beside me, Marius went stock-still, every muscle tensed and poised for action.

"You were good," Loki simmered. "One of the best spies around. Your greatest gift, though, was your ability to fly under the radar without anyone suspecting you were more than just a hedonistic, lecherous satyr. You blew it."

"I didn't—"

"*You blew it!* You got greedy. Sloppy. You let something cloud your judgment, and you fucked up. You spread yourself too thin, and she caught you. And now the whole game is ruined. You are too great a risk to be a piece on my board."

Marius's shoulders sagged, and his head fell forward. Those luscious waves of black hair tumbled around his face like a dark curtain. My heart lurched. I wanted to reach out to him, to comfort my friend. I wanted to smack him, too, but that was normal for our state of affairs.

I did neither. Instead, I looked to Loki with a silent plea.

"Don't you start," he warned. "You've gotten yourself involved in his mess, and now I stand to lose two of my greatest assets in one move. Eris couldn't have planned a better coup if she'd tried."

I opened my mouth to protest, but the god silenced me with a hard look. My mind raced, looking for another option, any way that Loki would see Marius as a boon rather than an unholy burden. But at every twist, I came up to a blank wall. Loki was right. Marius had been skilled at subversion, at aiding tricksters in their grand machinations. He no longer had the luxury of anonymity, though. The satyr was in the spotlight and no longer any good for subterfuge. All the credit Marius had built over the centuries had crumbled like a house of cards.

"Are you going to turn me in?" Marius asked, voice humble.

Loki leaned back and took another drink. "Believe me, I've thought about it."

I gasped. "What? You can't!"

"It's the only way I gain anything in this clusterfuck," he admitted. "But no, Marius. I will not hand you over. Sure, your head would probably fetch a lovely bouquet of favors, riches, and secrets to add to my personal stash, but there are a few problems with that solution, as well. The least of which," he added, "is that my personal ace in the hole would never forgive me. Isn't that right, Cat?"

I narrowed my gaze. *Ace in the hole?* Now what the hell was Loki planning for me?

"No," Loki said after a long swig from the vodka bottle. "I can't do much to protect you, my friend, but I won't turn you in. I do that and Eris wins. That's inexcusable."

I snorted with appreciation. "Give her hell, Boss."

Loki ignored me. "I am, however, in an awkward position. I can't help you two directly—to do so would be to declare a side and open myself up to scrutiny or even outright attack. I have to keep myself neutral where Marius is concerned.

"As for you," he continued, jabbing a finger at me. He started to speak but choked on his anger. His lips worked, his jaw tightening as he tried to choose his words. Finally, he just let out a frustrated grunt and dragged a hand through his strawberry-blond spikes. "Fuck, Cat, why did you have to get yourself involved in this?"

Now it was my turn to hang my head. Why couldn't I have been like Flynn? Why did I have to give a damn about what happened to Marius? When we found him on my doorstep I could've just kicked the bastard in the shins and stepped over him rather than take on all this bullshit.

"Look." Loki sighed. "The city is going to start filling up with your enemies very quickly, Marius. You've got a short amount of time on your side to retain some small glimmer of surprise. It won't last long, though. Enough people know your connection to Cat that she'll soon be drawing attention of her own while they look for you."

"So we'll get out of town," I offered.

Loki shook his head. "They'll follow."

"Do you know of anyone who might be willing to take him on? Someone who can protect him?"

My boss laughed ruefully. "Sure! The Morrigan is always looking for a fresh body to throw into battle."

I winced. I'd heard of the goddesses, but I'd been lucky enough to never set eyes on the Morrigan before. A trio devoted to war and strife, they were a bloody business.

"I'm no soldier," Marius spat. "Nor am I a sacrifice."

"Those are your primary options at this point, my friend," Loki said.

Marius rose to his feet. "I think it's time I was on my way, then. Thank you for taking the time to see me, Aesir."

Loki waved off the ceremonial title and swung the bottle to his lips. "Fuck off, Marius. And take her with you. She's the best thing you've got going for you right now. And the worst."

"Hey!" I stood up, hands on my hips and ready to argue.

"Don't get my technomancer killed," he warned Marius, "or I will skin you myself."

Marius gave a weak salute and started for the door.

"Cat," Loki barked after me, "don't forget your birthday present."

He tossed me a large jewelry box. "If this is your idea of a proposal," I said, eyeing the black velvet, "it sucks. The rock is probably huge, though." I popped the lid, revealing a silver cuff bracelet. It was about as wide as my thumb. The plain metal gleamed in the light.

"Wow," I said, genuinely surprised. Delicate, yet striking, the bracelet was just my style. I slipped it over my wrist where its cool weight felt perfectly at home. "Thanks! Oh, by the way, since I'm going to be helping him, I'm going to need some time off from the day job."

He pawed at the air lazily, his hooded eyes drifting away from me. "You're fired. For two weeks. With pay. Now get the hell out."

Marius breezed past me and opened the door. He looked back at me. "You coming?"

I waved to Loki. "Later, Boss."

Loki's form melted, and Candy draped herself over the sofa. His hands lingered over those ginormous boobs before he gave me a wiggle of his fingers. "Ta, kiddies."

Marius slammed the door and stalked away. I stood gaping at the closed skybox. "Gods are weird."

EIGHT

"Easy to Crash"

When I caught up with Marius downstairs, he was brooding. Again. His dark eyes swept over the booze-soaked crowd. Sapphire's patrons enjoyed the floorshow from their plush armchairs clustered around tiny tables, the indigo atmosphere split in incoherent patterns of bright white and illicit red. Music thumped and pumped, drums driving against pealing guitars in an industrial orgy of sound, fury, and lust. If I let my senses relax into it, the life of the club would seep into each of my pores and coax me to the same sinuous motions demonstrated on the stage. Sapphire was alive and spoke to me in primal ways.

Near the stage, the bachelor party I'd seen earlier let out a series of particularly canine whoops. Wolfish whistles pierced the air as a lithe, silver-clad dancer lowered herself onto the lap of...

"There's the bastard now," Marius sneered.

Malcolm had ingratiated himself with the partiers, sitting among them as if he were not a stranger but the guest of honor. They seemed to love him, and why wouldn't they? With his satyr skills, money was no matter. A cigar in one hand, a small glass of amber in the other, and a gyrating woman in his lap, Malcolm was the picture of hedonistic joy.

I followed Marius as he cut a chilly path through the audience. Malcolm threw his head back with raucous guffaws of laughter. When he opened his eyes, I thought for a moment that they reflected the pervasive blue light of the club. As I stared, though, I could see that the blue of his irises was too deep. The air around him shimmered and twisted as his spell reached out and around the girl in his lap. The dancer rocked with the music, her lips parted in a pout as she rode the satyr. The men around him lifted their voices in a chorus of congratulations.

"Mal!" Marius barked.

"Right here," he said, never taking his eyes off the stripper. "Come on over, Marius, and I'll buy you a round before we go."

As I neared the table, the air felt thicker, and not just with the density of body heat and energy ebbing off the audience. I could feel Malcolm's magic spreading out from him. Tendrils of desire slid up my skin, and I sucked in a breath.

Those ultramarine eyes flashed to me. Illusory tendrils became groping fingers, silken whispers in my mind. Just listening to his inaudible suggestions left me quivering and glistening with sweat.

Malcolm's lips curled into a wicked promise. "'scuse me, lads," he said as he shoved up from the table. "I'll leave you to your appetizers. I'm off for the main course."

Marius snatched my hand. "No."

"Whatever. I'll have a shag with this one sooner or later. You'll have to leave her alone sometime, brother mine. I don't see why you're so against the idea, anyway. Clearly you've no interest in her; otherwise you'd have tagged her already and I'd be no threat to you."

"Hello!" I said with a wave of my hand between their faces. "I'm not deaf, dumb, and blind, so you can both stop being asshats. You," I snapped at Malcolm, "will not be having a shag, or anything else, with me. So quit it with the Jedi Mindfuck before I junk-punch you right in the man business."

Softening my voice, I turned to Marius. "And you." I wrenched my hand free of his. "Quit playing the white knight. I hate that shit, and it doesn't suit you."

"You don't know him," Marius protested.

Mal slid closer, his whiskey-laced breath hot on my cheek. "But you could *know* me. That's an invitation."

I palmed his face and shoved him away. Putting my back to him, I pulled Marius down so that he could hear me over the pounding music. "So now what?"

"Now what?" he snarled. "Loki wants nothing to do with me and my bastard brother has turned up."

"And is trying to fuck me with his satyr mojo," I added helpfully.

Marius rolled his eyes. "Please, he does that to everyone."

"Way to make a girl feel special."

Ignoring me, Marius continued to spiral into a misanthropy that would've made Eeyore look downright giddy. "As if there wasn't enough going on, now Father sends Mal to collect me and I have to keep him out of your trousers. What next? Perhaps I should just walk outside and let the nearest hellhound tear me apart."

I tugged his hair hard enough to make him wince. "Will you stop with this shit? Did some of the goth from Flynn's hand-me-downs seep into your blood or something?"

"I'm being realistic."

"You're being a whiny little bitch."

Marius hissed and looked away, but I knew I had him on the ropes. I grabbed his face in both my hands and forced him to look me in the eyes. I didn't break my stare when someone tapped me on the shoulder.

"Come on, Marius. Think. You had to know that Loki might turn you away. I know you. What's the plan?"

For an instant—no longer than a flash of the spastic lights—fear and sadness gleamed in Marius's eyes. Then there was rage. "I don't know," he growled. "I don't know what to do or where to go from this goddamn club, all right?"

I softened my grip on his cheeks and tucked a lock of hair behind his ear. "You don't get into a situation without plotting at least three ways out. What were you planning to do after this?"

Marius closed his eyes and swallowed hard. His forehead creased, and deep furrows appeared around his mouth as he concentrated. I kept my hands on his temples, a gentle, constant touch to help ground him. I felt his weariness like a leaden gray shroud over my own soul.

"I'm scared," he whispered. Over the din of the music and crowd, I almost missed it, but the words were there. Again, the fingers tapped my shoulder.

Without taking my attention from Marius, I snapped, "Not now!" Lowering my voice so that only the satyr would hear me, I said, "I'm scared, too."

He opened his eyes. "Really?"

I nodded.

"What are you afraid of, Catherine?"

The familiar dread and panic flexed around my sternum, squeezing the breath from me and closing my throat. From the moment I met Marius, I had feared him. He was part of that strange, horrifying new world of treacherous faeries and sadistic goddesses. Marius was *other*, inhuman. When I had learned his nature, I'd steeled myself against him, suspicious that he might sap my will with his slippery magic. Over time, though, those fears had changed. I didn't worry that he would seduce me, but that my own heart would betray me and throw itself on his sword. I was terrified not that he would leave me in the heat of battle again, but that some dark creature from the bowels of Hell would swallow him out of my world forever.

Worst of all, I was petrified that he might find out. Maybe it was time, though. Maybe this was the only time.

"With you?" I asked, my voice a weak husk of itself. "Everything."

His lips hitched in a timid grin as he tenderly stroked my cheek. "Something else we have in common, I suppose."

"So what do we do?" Once more the fingers tapped on my shoulder. Annoyed, I wheeled around ready to slug Malcolm. "What?!"

Mal's face protruded from the circle of a beefy arm larger than some monster truck tires. As my eyes traced up—and up, and up—the monolith, I began to wonder if this guy's lineage included a bulldozer. The T-shirt he wore practically screamed for mercy as he breathed. Corpsegray skin stretched like thick, taut leather over muscular arms, and when my gaze reached the summit, I found eyes like oil drops glittering with gleeful malice.

My mouth fell open.

The mountain's face split into a craggy smile, all black and jagged teeth. Gravel crunched in his abyssal voice when he said, "We trade."

Blinking my way to coherence, I took a step back and bumped into Marius. His warmth was a drab of comfort, but it did little to assuage the icy dread coursing through me.

"This is bad," Marius murmured to me.

"No shit."

How could it not be when every cell in my body told me to run before this giant decided to squash me between his toes?

"Mage," he said thickly. The mirth had fled his face. He glared at me with disdain and warning. "I make you offer. We trade."

"Trade what?" I asked.

"One satyr for other."

I glanced from Marius to Malcolm. The former eyed me warily while the latter wiggled in the giant's football hold. I gave Marius's hand a reassuring squeeze and took a step forward.

"That's all? Look at him," I snorted with a flippant gesture to Mal. "Why would I trade the perfectly good one that I have for...that?"

"Oi!" Malcolm called from his headlock. "I'll have you know that I am—"

The brute squeezed, cutting off Malcolm's protests. I winced.

"We trade," the mountain said again. "One for other. And you have allegiance of Grote for span life, Mage."

I had no clue who or what a Grote was, nor did I know if its allegiance would necessarily be a good thing. What I did know, however, was that this thing wanted Marius. Also, patrons were beginning to take notice of our odd conversation. Quizzical stares flicked to me, and my trepidation grew. The bachelor party was on its feet, and one of the larger revelers stalked over to us.

The situation was worsening rapidly. We had to get out of here. Mustering all the easygoing charm I could, I caught the monolith's attention. "Hey, you know, why don't we go conduct our business outside? Privately."

One of the bachelor buddies approached. "You want to let go of my friend," he slurred.

"Aw, bless you, mate," Mal croaked. "When I get done, it's the finest lap dance for you."

With the rumble of two fault lines humping, the Grote thing eyed me warily. His gaze narrowed and his arm tightened around Malcolm's neck. The satyr began to flail and tap at the bulging forearm. Veins stood out on his purpling face as he fought for air. I saw the faint shadow of his horns appear. His glamour was failing.

"Let him go, man!" cried the bachelor.

The mountain moved with ferocious speed. With one arm, he back-handed the partier and sent him flying back to his friends. The sounds of breaking glass, surprised squeals, and general property damage signaled the start of an all-too-familiar song.

I sighed. "Here we go."

Chaos erupted in the middle of the strip club, and I stood at ground zero. I rooted my feet in a strong, defensive stance. Marius darted past, and he drew a gleaming blade out of the ether. A sword forged by a god, he'd once said, and it appeared at the satyr's will. With the saber in hand, Marius lunged for the brick wall of a creature in front of me. Grote threw Malcolm to the floor and began to fend off my satyr with one hand and puny drunk mortals with the other.

For a split second, I thought of the panic button in my pocket. We could have run, blinked out of the strip club and returned to the safety of YmFy. But I didn't know if this Grote could follow. Nor was I certain I could get to Malcolm in time to drag him with us. Mostly, though, I didn't want to run. I'd done a lot of running away in the past, and while Marius was better off hiding, I was itching for action. I couldn't just bolt, and I couldn't simply stand there looking pretty.

I stretched out both hands along my sides and inhaled. To the common bystander, it probably looked like I was practicing yoga or tai chi or something, but as I drew in breath, I sucked in power. The energy of this place—the gloriously schizophrenic lights, the televisions in the skyboxes, the thrumming sound system—all of it appeared to me in liquid filaments and streams. I drank it in, called it to me, and let it fill me. A soft nimbus formed around my fingertips, and I brought my hands together as if I held an invisible ball. Still pulling power, I squeezed that ball tighter, making it smaller.

Cell phones and tablets died in their owners' pockets. The music petered out. The crowd screamed as Sapphire plunged into darkness. I held all the club's energy in a tight circle of white fire between my palms. With a guttural roar, I wrenched it apart and my hands were wreathed with twin orbs of light.

In the steady burn of my power, I saw Malcolm gaping at me from the floor. Marius slashed at the monolith again, and Grote just glared at me.

"Decision is yours. I take him."

Grote reached out his gnarled fist, but before he could clamp it around Marius's neck, I whipped my left hand up in a blocking motion. The light spooled out from my fingers, the orb reshaping itself to form a crescent blade. When it connected with Grote's wrist, the light opened a wound that bled black ichor. Before he could counter, I wrenched my right arm in a wide arc. A similar light blade hacked across Grote's massive chest.

The towering creature held a hand to his wounds in disbelief. Had such a tiny fly cut through his thick hide?

"Walk away now," I warned.

The thing towered over me, clearly outweighing me by about fifty tons. He snarled, balled his fists, and let out a fierce noise, something between the blare of a freight train and an earthquake ripping apart continents.

"Or not."

When he lunged for me, I began to dance. At least that's what I always thought the kata looked like. I set into a flow of martial steps—a blend of capoeira, mantis-style kung fu, and water bending I'd seen on a cartoon. My fluid arm motions stirred the light and sent it out in jabs and pops. I leaped and ducked, dodged and swept through the air between me and Grote. The power of Sapphire and its patrons followed my moves and whims, lashing out here or shielding me from Grote's fists there. The light opened up fissures in his stony flesh as I whirled like a dervish on speed. What can I say? Red Bull gives you wings.

In my peripheral vision, I could see patrons huddled behind their chairs, under the tiny tables. Dancers were clearly violating the "no touch" rule as they burrowed into men for cover. Bouncers stared slack-jawed, uncertain if they should join me in fighting off the problem child or if they had fallen into some other world. Marius didn't need an invitation, however. He joined the dance with me to draw the thing's focus.

The satyr's saber flashed wickedly in the glow of my magic as I found an opening in Grote's flank and thrust my power in. He let out a keening wail of pain and frustration. Marius and I slashed down with our blades in tandem, each taking aim at the mountain's heels. Like Achilles of old, the mountain was weak at those tender tendons. Grote crumbled to his knees, and I took aim at the broad expanse of his back. As my light speared into it, Marius's sword made a twin strike.

I didn't wait to see if Grote would fall. I released the flow of power coursing through me, grabbed Marius by the collar, and ran. In the darkness, I tripped over people who'd dropped to the floor, pushed past groping hands, and dodged the velvet ropes.

I burst out into the sweltering Las Vegas night and pounded pavement toward my car.

"What the hell? What the bloody hell?" I heard Malcolm babble. "What the fuck was that thing?"

"Grootslang," Marius answered. "Cave dweller. Not too bright. Seen by the gods as an abomination. Not unlike yourself, Malcolm."

"Less talking, more running away," I called over my shoulder.

I reached out my senses, and a whisper of will popped the locks of my car. I was behind the wheel and starting the engine before the passenger-side doors opened. With the two satyrs loaded, I peeled out of the parking lot and joined the traffic on Industrial.

"Me bike! You've gone and left me bike!" Mal whined.

I ignored him. "Be my eyes," I commanded Marius. "We being followed?"

"Nothing yet," he answered.

I careened down the street, sliding from lane to lane and putting as much distance as possible between us and Sapphire. In the backseat,

Malcolm cursed and gasped for air. On a particularly fast lane change, he tumbled off the seat and squished onto the floor behind me.

"The fuck are you doing, woman?"

"Saving our asses."

"Still no tails," Marius said, his words clipped.

"Excellent."

After a few more blocks of weaving and bobbing like a shadow boxer, I hooked a right on Tropicana Avenue and pulled into the lot at Charlie Frias Park. Only when I'd cut the engine and lights did I let out the breath I'd been holding for what seemed a year.

"So," I said. "That was fun."

NINE

"ALPHA BETA PARKING LOT"

"Oi!" Mal burst out with a smack to Marius's headrest. "Just what the sweet fuck was that all about, eh?"

Marius turned in his seat and cuffed his brother. "Keep your hands off."

"Or what?" Mal tested the waters by giving Marius a swat to the cheek.

Marius blocked it and shoved his sibling's hand away. "Don't touch me."

"I almost had me head popped off back there." Malcolm socked Marius, and the two began slapping at each other in what was best described as a sissy fight. While they tussled, Malcolm kept taunting. "Poncy twat. Is this what you've got? Or are you gonna have a go at me with that shiny sword of yours? No, you're not because you left it back at the joint with my bike!"

"Are you sure about that?" Marius's voice was smooth and serious as the blade that appeared beneath Malcolm's chin.

Mal's blue eyes widened.

"Uh-uh," I said sharply. "Not in here. I just got a new car and you're not going to ruin this one."

Marius rounded on me. "Like you destroyed my Mercedes?"

"That was years ago," I admitted sheepishly.

"I rather liked that car."

I smiled. "I destroyed nothing. The *wakwak* did that."

"A what what?" Mal asked.

Marius's moustache lifted with his sneer, but I saw the slightest hint of mischief in his green gaze. "Ah, yes, the *wakwak* that tore my shoulder open, wrecked my car on the Strip, then tore out the beating heart of a faerie. I'd say you owe me at least a bit of torn upholstery for that fiasco."

Peripherally, I saw Mal's expression turn to horror. With almost being choked by Kilimanjaro, racing away, and now being drawn down by his brother, I'm sure he was beginning to wonder what in the name of all things raunchy he'd gotten himself into.

Holding in my giggles, I gave Marius a level stare. "No bloodstains in my car."

I kept my gaze infused with authority and trained on my satyr. He didn't let me down but matched the intensity, playing the moment for everything it was worth. Just about the time I was about to lose control and bust out laughing, Marius broke away.

"All right, then, Malcolm. You heard the lady. Out of the car."

The sword disappeared, and in the blink of an eye, Marius stood outside in the balmy air. A gust of desert wind buffeted the chains at his hips and ruffled his hair. How could he look so out of place in Flynn's clothes, yet still so damn good?

While he opened the door and pulled Malcolm out of the backseat, I caught myself entertaining too many of Malcolm's earlier suggestions with Marius in the starring role and had to tear my eyes away from him.

No. Not going there.

The brothers scuffled. They were noisy but harmless. Like puppies or polar bear cubs learning to sharpen their teeth on one another. Adorable in animals but laughable in grown-ass men.

I got out of the car to ground myself. I've learned a lot in the few years I've been working with technomancy. One of the most useful tricks is the ability to recoup after heavy magical lifting. There used to be a time when turning on a disconnected machine would leave me drained and dusty, but Flynn and Karma had coached me on the finer points. Apparently, it's not uncommon for the mage to have a sort of empathy with her work, which can be exhausting. Say I'm working with a computer system that hasn't been turned on for years. Someone wants his or her files from a decrepit old Commodore 64 or something. Well, I can give that computer life, retrieve the files, and go about my merry way...for a price. For a while after I work the mojo, I will feel just as old and rickety as the Commodore. I'd make Mrs. M look young and spry.

In the instance of drawing in the power of an entire fucking night-club and every electronic device contained therein, my body felt like it was on the most insane caffeine buzz of all time. My limbs were jittery, my pulse as rapid and driving as a bass drum. Every nerve was alight with the overdose, craving more, demanding attention or sordid release. If I didn't put a lid on it, I'd soon get scrappy with Mal and Marius just to burn off energy and mess with their heads. Or worse, I'd entertain some of Mal's offers.

Thankfully, though, my coaches taught me to redirect some of that energy exchange. Call it grounding, call it meditation or finding my center, but it works.

I sat lotus-style on the hood of my car, closed my eyes, and began.

Deep breath in. Visualize. See the energy inside of you in streams of color.

Threads of light appeared in my mind's eye. White. Blue. Pink. Twining with one another, wrapping like veins and twisting together, the lines raced with arcs of power, pumping and thumping in my body.

Exhale. Divide. Separate the cords.

My power always manifested as a pure white light, and I imagined myself picking up those strings and setting them to the side. The blue and pink strands—the borrowed energy—I untangled and set in their own bundles.

Inhale: pick and pluck a strand.

Exhale: lay it down with its mates.

Inhale again. Disperse. Pour the energy into another vessel.

Since energy cannot ever truly be destroyed—contained, shifted, absorbed, transferred, yes, but never eliminated—I picked up the bundle of blue light. It writhed between my fingers, pulsed with a siren song that called to my blood. It urged me to swallow it, to let it course through me and carry me into a primal dance. *Thank you,* I thought to it, *but no.* Slow breath out: I offered the blue essence to the earth, directed it down, down into the power lines and cables running beneath the asphalt.

The wan pink light fluttered in my hands as I drew it up next. This was the lifeblood of a device, a power that desired only to be of service. Granting its wish, I poured it into the reservoir beneath the hood of my car. (There's a reason I bought a hybrid.)

The last bundle of power—the white—I kept for myself. This I'd need to restore the energy I'd used in the brisk but intense fight. I drank it in, and it flowed through me like cool water.

Slowly but surely, the residual power from Sapphire had been shunted out into various outlets. I felt refreshed, rested, and luminous.

When I opened my eyes, Marius and Malcolm were trading jabs and swipes with each other. Still.

"Seriously?" I said to no one in particular.

Marius flicked his wrist and held his saber to Mal's chest. He wasn't threatening so much as keeping his sibling at bay. "Yes, Catherine?"

Malcolm smacked Marius's wrist aside but didn't pursue their fight further. Instead, he stalked in a feral circle, not unlike another satyr I know. "Bastard," he mumbled.

Marius didn't bother to face Mal, but muttered nonchalantly, "And proud of it. As you should be." With his attention back on me, he once again stowed his sword in some unknown pocket of the world and lowered his hand. "Something I can help you with?"

"Are you two finished?" I asked.

Malcolm saw an opening and lunged at Marius, arms outstretched as if for the tackle. Without so much as a sideways glance, Marius swung his fist. The punch connected with Malcolm's jaw and sent him pinwheeling and flailing to the concrete.

"More or less," Marius answered, ignoring the grunts and epithets coming from near his feet.

I shook my head. "Christ, you two are hopeless. Anyway, what's next?"

"Getting rid of him," he said with a hook of his thumb. "He's a liability if we are visited by more friends."

"Oi!" Malcolm complained. "I'm standin' right here."

Marius curled his nose. "Much to my dismay, yes."

"You'll not be gettin' rid of me anytime soon, brother mine. Not until you and I make for home to see the old man."

Marius sighed and rolled his eyes. "Fine. Catherine, would you care to accompany us, or do you have more pressing duties here?"

"Where would we be going?" I asked warily.

"Across the pond," Marius said. "So shall we have an adventure? I believe you'd expressed an interest in leaving town."

My stomach fluttered. I'd been on business trips with Marius before when we both worked for Eris. I'd never been to Europe, though. I fought back the urge to dive in headfirst and pack my bags, but only barely. "With or without random attacks from huge beasties?"

"No way to know, but isn't that part of the fun?"

Something lounged in his eyes that I hadn't seen in a very long time: wicked merriment. The fight in the club had certainly gotten my blood pumping. Maybe that's what had dislodged Marius's melancholy. Or maybe it was seeing his brother and wrestling with him. Regardless, Marius radiated a playful spirit begging to sprint off and dance across clouds toward the second star to the right.

And it was contagious. "When do we leave?" I asked, smiling.

Marius held up a finger. "As soon as I grab a few of my personal effects from the storage unit, we'll take leave of this wretched city." Turning to his brother, he said, "I'll meet you back at home, shall I, Malcolm?"

Mal fidgeted with his hair and shuffled from foot to foot. "About that... I was actually hoping you could give me a lift to the homestead."

A crease formed on Marius's brow as he glared at Malcolm. "Why?"

"Well..." His voice trailed off, and once again Malcolm's eyes darted to me with a secretive glance. "Well, I've gone and, um...lost me keys, so to speak."

"Lost them?"

"It's not my fault," Malcolm said, backpedaling for his life.

Marius's voice rose to a roar. "Lost them?!"

"What's the deal?" I asked. "It's just a set of keys."

Marius held up a hand. "It's not just keys, Catherine. These are special, rare, and magical items. And this moron has gone and lost his!"

"I've been roamin' around town," Mal explained. "No proper place to stay, right? So I must've lost them between one bed and another. As long as you've got yours, I can get back home easy as you please."

Marius pinched the bridge of his nose in frustration. "Christ, Mal," he breathed. "Nothing's changed with you, has it?"

"Come off it, you high and mighty twat. Just let me borrow yours."

"No."

"We'll pop home, and I can grab the old man's. What's the problem?"

Feeling more and more like an intruder, I stuffed my hands in my pockets and tried to ignore them. I wasn't all that successful.

"No, Malcolm," Marius growled, "and that's final."

"Oh, what, so you can teach me a lesson, is that it?"

"I don't have mine!" Marius spat in his face.

Malcolm backed off, struck dumb as if he'd been smacked. "You don't have them?"

"Not with me, no."

Marius stalked to me and urged me toward the car. From behind him, Malcolm called, "Now how the hell am I supposed to get back? And you take the piss out of me when you've gone and lost your own keys?"

"I didn't lose mine, Mal. I know right where they are."

"Back with Eris?" I guessed.

He shook his head. "Never trusted them near her. They're in my storage unit on the other side of town."

"You sure the unit is safe?"

Marius nodded. "Under a dummy name that no one could associate with me. Cash only, that kind of thing. I made sure to keep something no one would ever find but me. What I keep there is far too valuable to let Eris get her claws around. Would you be up for a drive? The sooner I get my things, the sooner I'll be rid of this bastard."

"Brilliant!" Malcolm said. "But first, I want me bike back."

"Why?" I asked. "It will be faster if we just go straight there."

Mal shook his head. "I'm not going to be in the car with you if that thing comes chasin' up behind us. I don't know what you've done, Marius, but I want no part of it. Take me back to my bike, and I'll follow you there and keep me pretty face where it belongs."

"Wonderful," Marius said. "Let's go."

TEN

"STICKSHIFTS AND SAFETYBELTS"

After dropping Mal across the street from Sapphire so that he could retrieve his bike, Marius gave me the cross streets of the self-storage lot. For the first few miles, the satyr sat simmering in the passenger seat. The cyclops-like high beam of Malcolm's motorcycle was a constant in my rearview as we wound across Las Vegas.

"So," I said, cutting into Marius's contemplative silence, "you have a brother."

"You sound surprised."

"I just never really thought of you as having a family or anything."

"What did you think? That I burst fully formed in all my glory from the stars?"

I snorted. "More like writhed up from the mud where your goat mother dropped you."

"My mother was quite human, I'll have you know."

"Wow. You learn something new every day." I tapped on the steering wheel, waiting for the light to change. "I guess it's inevitable that you'd have siblings, though, with all the scrumping satyrs do."

"It's actually quite rare. Not the shagging, mind," he added quickly, "but the spawning. Satyrs aren't the most fertile creatures. For one of our kind, breeding is so difficult you'd think that the stars had to align and end in a perfect eclipse. Malcolm and I are especially unique."

"Why is that?"

"Well, my father was rather prolific in his affairs. I could fill libraries with tales of his exploits."

I couldn't help but smirk. "Come on, how many are we talking here?"

"Darling, my father is old enough to have seduced Mary Magdalene. All those years, all the women he could find, and with his grandiose appetite? I don't know the actual number, but you know that line about over a billion served?"

"Yeah?"

"Father would be competitive."

"Wow," I said weakly. The light changed, and I drove on.

"Even with an exorbitant figure like that under his belt, fewer than ten of father's lovers gave him children. Only two of those were sons."

"So you have sisters, too?"

"Had," he said. "Long ago. I only ever met one or two of them. The last one died, I believe, somewhen around the French Revolution."

"Died? How?"

"Females born of unions with satyrs will be mortals, and none of the good stuff comes through for them. I mean, they might be tomcats in the sack. Personally, I've never shagged one of my sisters, so I wouldn't know. But males born to a satyr's lover will always take after the father. As far as I know, Malcolm and I are the last of our line."

"I'm sorry," I said.

"Why? Mortality happens, Catherine, even to the best of you. When you've been around as long as I have, you get used to watching people die."

"Cheerful thought."

I took a left and chewed on my lip, trying not to think of myself as just another mortal in his collection. It made sense now—his aloof and selfish nature. If I knew I was going to lose everyone I knew I'd probably avoid making any lasting connections, too.

Marius seemed to like talking about his nature, though. As he kept on educating me on satyr genetics, I wondered how long it had been since someone gave a damn to ask. I guess immortality works both ways.

"So you and Malcolm, you're from different mothers?"

"Yes. My mother was from London while the hag who birthed him was a chav from Newcastle. We're only a few years apart, though, so we were raised together. Father prefers to roam and spread as much of himself over the countryside as he can. He's made it a stone bitch to find a woman in the entire United Kingdom. I'm surprised Malcolm still calls it home."

"I don't understand," I said.

"Once a woman has mated with a satyr, she cannot be claimed by any in his bloodline. Not by magic, anyway. If I tried to shag any of Father's former conquests, it would have to be by sheer merit and cunning. No amount of spells would break the hold Father's blood had on her. I find it difficult to believe Malcolm would have any sort of sport if our father is still in action. Which reminds me..."

Peripherally I saw Marius paw through his hair. He grunted, and when his hand came away, he had a lock of black hair pinched between his fingers. His hands worked deftly, braiding the strands in his lap.

"What are you doing?" I asked.

"Cockblocking my brother," he muttered tersely. "The last thing I need is for him to liquefy you the second you get out of the car. I don't want him to distract you."

I smirked. "And what if I want him to distract me?"

He shot a fearful glance at me. Marius scanned my face for any sign that I might be bluffing. For fun, I popped my eyebrows at him.

"Don't be ridiculous," he said, turning his attention back to the braid. "He's a despicable creature with about as much sense as a spoon. He's got no class, no style, and is lousy at holding his drink. No appreciation for the finer things in life."

"I don't know," I taunted. "It might be fun to climb your family tree."

"You'll do nothing of the sort, Catherine," he warned. "I need you focused on the real world, not on whatever sordid fantasies Malcolm was putting in your head."

"He's easy enough on the eyes..."

"Wouldn't happen," he scoffed. "I'll grant that he might be pretty enough to rouse a bit of interest, but once he opens his mouth, it's all over. He's dumb as a stick, and everything he says proves it. Besides, I know you. You'd never be content with a fling with someone as selfish and careless as my little brother."

"That's rich," I laughed, a slight bitter edge slipping into my tone. "You're calling him selfish?"

"Malcolm doesn't give a damn about anyone other than Malcolm."

"Does that run in the family, too, or is it a coincidence?"

He whipped his head around to face me, stricken. "Is that really what you think of me?"

The pain in his eyes stripped the smile off my face. I'd actually cut Marius with my words. I opened my mouth to speak, but he waved me off.

"Forget it," he said. "I don't think I want to know the answer."

Focused on the lock of hair in his hands, Marius went mute for the rest of the drive.

When we pulled up to the maze of self-storage units, he got out of the car and keyed in a passcode to open the gates. I drove along behind him as he walked through the rows of lockers. When we reached unit 871, I parked and got out of the car.

Malcolm's motorcycle lurched to a stop behind us. He pulled off the canary-yellow helmet and tossed his wavy hair. Immediately, sparks of delight flared in my nethers and those crimson pictures flooded my mind. Malcolm's voice was a whisper in my head: *Forget anything he says. You and I are going to have fun. I'm going to worship you for days.*

Marius put his body between mine and his brother's. "First things first," he said.

He leaned forward and gently brushed my hair back over my left ear. As he pulled me into his arms, fingers playing with my hair, the steam of Malcolm's spell dissipated. No seductive whispers. The air didn't writhe with sexual magic. There was only Marius. He smelled like my kiwi-and-strawberry shampoo, like whatever detergent Flynn used for his laundry, and like, well, Marius. A heady spice like ginger or clove mixed with his natural musk. Something about that specific blend felt like home, and I wanted to rest my head on his shoulder, bask in the safety there. My eyes fluttered closed, and I was about to indulge myself when he pulled away.

"There," he said. A small smile crept onto his face. "Ginger and black. You look rather like a tiger, Catherine."

I checked the mirror and understood. He'd tied the braid of his hair into mine. I twisted the mingled strands between my fingers. "What is this?"

Marius nodded and dropped his voice to a whisper. "A charm to ward off Malcolm's advances."

"Ah, the bloodline thing?"

"As much as I'd prefer to claim you the old-fashioned way, this will have to suit. Leave it tied there until he's gone, all right?"

"Okay."

Malcolm was off his bike now and coming closer. Marius rolled his eyes. "The sooner we send him off the better."

I felt a strange throb in my temples, a pulse like a knock on a door. Out of the corner of my eyes, the air bent and flashed, then immediately righted itself. Whatever magic Malcolm had tried to send my way had stopped short.

"Oi!" Malcolm said. His face screwed up with frustration. "What the bloody hell did you do?"

Marius brandished one of his signature smirks. "Problem, Mal?"

Malcolm looked me up and down, searching. When his blue eyes landed on the charm in my hair, understanding spread over his features. He gaped at his brother. "You cheating twat! That's not fair. It's not like you can just plant a flag and claim her as your own."

"I can, and I have."

"It's a waste of a fine woman, if you ask me."

"I don't believe I did. Now maybe we'll get some work done if you can stay focused."

"I was focused," Malcolm complained. His eyes drifted down my body again, hungry. "Can't help meself wondering if there's salsa on the taco."

"Excuse me?" I rounded on him, drawing power into my fist.

"The carpet. Does it match the drapes?" Malcolm ran a hand down over my hair but stopped just short of touching the braid.

I jerked away from his touch, took a step back, and lashed out with a white-hot whip of power. It slashed a warning at his cheek, tossing his hair.

His eyes went wide. Rather than backing down, however, he took on the manner of a child begging for a new toy. "Come on, love," he whined. "Take that off. You and I will pop 'round the corner for a quick one, and he won't be a bother anymore."

"No, Malcolm," Marius chided.

"I didn't ask you," Malcolm snapped. "You're just upset that five minutes will make her forget all about you."

Marius leaned back, his expression one of amazement. "You're up to five minutes now? Good for you. I see practice makes mediocre."

"Shut your face!" Malcolm's fierce mane framed an attempt at a charming smile as he turned toward me. "What do you say? Just an appetizer?"

"No," I said.

"No?" He sounded as if he'd never heard the word before. Then I thought of his magic, the scintillating story his lust had told my body. Yeah, the word *no* was probably as alien to him as a greaseball bacon cheeseburger was to a supermodel.

I shook my head the way I would to a confused kindergartener. Slowly, deliberately, and with every ounce of bitchcraft I possessed, I informed Malcolm, "No tacos tonight. Sorry."

Dejected, Malcolm trudged back to his bike and fiddled with his things, muttering darkly to himself the whole time. I joined Marius at the door to the storage unit right as he gave it an angry kick.

"What's wrong?" I asked.

He jiggled the large padlock. "Guess what I left in my other trousers."

"When you ran from Eris you left everything behind, didn't you?"

"Everything except what's on the other side of this sheet of metal." Marius ran his hand covetously up the orange door. "And now I can't get to it."

"Christ, you're such a drama queen sometimes," I said.

I shouldered him aside and gripped the padlock with both hands. Instantly, the inner workings of the mechanism appeared in my mind, illuminated blue on black. Springs coiled, holding the tumblers in place against the brass cylinder of the lock. The white light of my will was whisper-thin as it slid sinuously into the keyhole and swirled within. Dancing through the tumblers, it filled the nooks where the matching key should go. Another drab of power to turn the lock and my work was done. I yanked down, and the lock opened. With the hook of the padlock looped over my finger, I offered it to Marius.

He grinned. "Confidence looks good on you, Catherine."

"Um, thanks?"

He kissed my forehead, then took the lock. "Thank *you*."

Without another word, he wrenched up on the handle and the door clattered open.

From behind us came the sound of a road flare sparking to life. "Right, then," Malcolm said. A glowing orb the same size and color as a lemon drifted from his palm. I'd seen Marius do something similar years ago. If Mal had the ability to tap into magic—and not just the seduction mojo—why hadn't he used it 'til now? Was this simple trick his limit?

Malcolm barreled his way past us and into the storage unit. Save for a layer of dust and a veil of shadows, the locker was empty.

"What's this about?" he asked, brows knit closely together.

Marius shook his head sadly, but the corner of his mouth betrayed the hint of a smug smile. "Oh, little brother, how much you have to learn."

Malcolm raised two fingers in response. "Sod off."

"Don't trust your eyes," Marius mused. He dragged his slender fingers over the air, searching for something. When he'd found the illusory—and still invisible to me—*it*, his fist tightened and he yanked at the ether. As if he'd tugged a sheet, the darkness rippled and whipped away from a glass-top table. Now that he had a grip on the glamour, Marius reached for the rest of it. Like a mime tugging at nonexistent ropes, he went hand over hand around the room until the veil had been pulled down and his possessions were visible.

I couldn't help but smile. Marius's magic was subtle, elegant. "Nicely done," I complimented.

He gave a slight bow of appreciation.

Malcolm's mouth hung open. "Where did you learn that little trick?"

"Oh, you know, all that time I wasted with those 'boy-loving Greeks.'"

"Poncy twat," Malcolm growled, waving off his brother's snarkasm.

While Marius dusted off his hands, Malcolm turned in circles, taking in the detritus of a life interrupted. Along with the glass-topped dining table were two matching end tables and a few chairs stacked on top of one another like some depiction from the Kama Sutra. The shape of a tall floor lamp cut the gloaming, its bowl top the overlarge head of a skeletal scarecrow. There was also a leather sofa, and in one corner of the unit, three cardboard boxes formed a weak pyramid.

"There's hardly anything here," Malcolm said. "At least it shouldn't be hard to find anything."

"Not difficult at all," Marius agreed. In two long strides he was at the back wall. The boxes went tumbling away, empty, as he kicked them. He stomped the concrete with his booted foot, and a rectangle of emerald-green light burst open in the floor. As Marius reached down into the portal, I could smell the metallic sweetness of a freshwater stream, could hear the gurgle as it flowed and the birds singing in harmony with the rustle of leaves. The springtime light danced over Marius, as well as the wooden box he withdrew from the secret space.

"What is it?" I asked.

Marius looked up at me as the ground sealed itself. "A safe place."

Malcolm only had eyes for the box. Roughly the size of a shoebox, the wood gleamed in the citrusy light from Mal's orb. Vines of Celtic knotwork wound around its beautifully carved surface in twining designs.

"It's been a long time since I saw one of Grandfather's pieces," Malcolm said, his voice uncharacteristically reverent.

"Made from the trees near his temple," Marius added. He slid his hands over the invisible seam of the box and opened it.

A set of a dozen reeds had been lashed together with leather. Gently, as if handling the oldest scroll or most delicate artifact, Marius lifted the pan flute out of the box. A silver charm dangled from the largest end and winked in the wan light.

"Pipes?" I asked.

"Some of the finest Grandfather ever made," Marius said, hushed with the wonder of a pilgrim.

Pan pipes. Named for the King of Satyrs himself, the instrument of his legend.

The realization struck me in the solar plexus, nearly knocking the wind out of me. "Oh shit," I breathed. "Pan."

Marius lifted his eyebrows. "Yes?"

"Pan is your grandfather?"

Marius rolled a shoulder in a half shrug, but the way Malcolm puffed up his chest screamed of pride. Neither of them needed to say a word to confirm or deny it. All these years I'd thought of Marius as just some spawn of a random goatfucker. I had no idea that he was one generation removed from a deity. Just when you think you know a guy...

Malcolm, visibly humbled, shook his head with futile disdain. "Lucky bastard. Why do you always get the nice toys?"

"Next life you should try being the first born of a first born," Marius intoned.

I punched Marius in the shoulder. "Keys? Why didn't you just say what you were looking for? Melodramatic sonofabitch."

"These *are* keys, Catherine. Play the right song and these will carry you home. Easier than traveling by mortal means. Safer for us, too, at the moment."

"Home." Malcolm moistened his lips, his eyes full of utter longing. As he stared at the pipes, I wondered what he saw. The satyr's jaw worked, swallowing a lump of palpable homesickness. Then the moment was gone, and Mal slugged Marius in the other shoulder. "Right, then. Hand 'em over so I can be on me way."

Marius swatted him away. "Didn't that baseborn whore you call a mother ever teach you manners?"

"Don't you be takin' the piss out of me mum!" Malcolm thrust himself into Marius's space, chest to chest and nose to hooked nose.

"Or what?" Marius asked, his voice as cold as steel.

"Or I'll smash your pretty face in, rip that charm out of the girl's hair, and fuck her cross-eyed while you watch."

"Hey," I burst in. "No one is fucking me cross-eyed!"

"More's the pity," they said in tandem.

The corner of Marius's mouth slid up with a slight hint of approval. He gazed at the pipes with longing, but something flashed in his eyes. A sort of reminder of the moment.

"You'd better bring your car in, Catherine. And shut the door."

"I'll get me bike," Malcolm said.

After stashing our rides in the unit and closing it up with the three of us inside. The lemony light from Malcolm's orb fluttered over us, casting odd yellow shadows over Marius's features. Sliding the ornately carved box under his arm, he caressed the reed pipes. He brought them to his lips, inhaled, and coaxed a few notes from the instrument. At first, the reeds gave off a dry, dusty moan, but Marius closed his eyes and gently pushed more air over them. Soon, the pipes began to sing.

The melody itself was simple—long, languid notes tracing up and down a traditional scale. What Marius breathed into them, though, turned that easy tune into a song that ached with nostalgia and longing. The notes twisted through the air like thick vines, spreading out in the ether and unfolding their leaves for the first rays of morning. I closed my eyes and let the music carry me to a place as lush and green as his ivy song. Like a reed, I swayed lazily on my feet. An impossibly cool breeze splashed over my face, tossing my hair and bringing the slightly metallic scent of freshwater. If I listened closely to Marius's tune, I could hear the bubbling of a stream or spring lapping over smooth stones, the gentle sounds of tall grass whispering in the wind.

Beneath the chaste beauty of his song, however, was a sweet sorrow, a melancholy that would not wash away. I realized then that this was his treasure. This exquisite sadness that he kept boxed in by snark and cynicism was just as heavily guarded as those reed pipes. It poured from his heart and into the melody, leaving bare a soul so scarred and mournful.

My poor satyr.

The last notes tapered off into a tremulous breath that hung in the air, an unanswered plea.

The spell broken, I opened my eyes. To my genuine surprise. I found myself standing not in the musty storage unit, but ankle-deep in soft, spongy grass beneath an indigo sky. Golden shafts of light streaked the horizon as the sun rose. Silhouetted in the dawn was a massive hill, its grassy flanks appeared to ripple with the spiral path carved into the tor. At the top, a stone tower caught the sun and sent spears of light over the valley. The earth rolled with lush hillocks, and wildflowers glistened with dewdrops, waiting to open to the sun's first kiss.

"Your aim is a bit off," Malcolm sneered.

"It's been a long time…" Marius's voice trailed off. "I'm surprised Father has stayed here all the while."

"He hasn't," Mal said as he set off down the slope. "He roams. A month in Tuscany. A year in Morocco. That sort o' thing. Old man always ends up back here, though."

Marius nodded and made to follow his brother. As he passed me, I caught him by the chain at his hip.

"What is it?" he asked.

"What the hell?"

"I'm afraid you'll have to be a bit more specific."

I gestured to the impossible landscape. "Where are we?"

"Glastonbury."

"Glaston— The same Glastonbury that's in…in England?" I stammered.

He aimed a finger toward the stone tower to the east. "That's the Tor. Priestesses from Avalon walked there millennia before the Christians came and insisted that the Lady of the Lake was a harlot. The abbey and spring are a bit off from here, but it's all the same for the most part."

"So we're actually in England?"

Marius smirked as he stowed his pan pipes in their lovely casket. "Yes, we are. Do you see why I prefer traveling my way as opposed to Flynn's vomit-inducing trip through space?"

Gobsmacked, I nodded and turned in a disbelieving circle. To the west, mist curled along the ground, shifting with the slightest breath. Hills rose to the south, and Malcolm trotted northward.

"Oi!" Malcolm called, his voice echoing eerily in the serene morning. "Are you coming?"

Marius laced his fingers through mine. "Come along, Catherine. Let's not keep my father waiting."

ELEVEN

"SAD SONGS AND WALTZES"

If you'd asked me before what I figured a satyr's home looked like, I probably would've conjured up some sort of immaculate playboy apartment with plenty of expensive toys. Maybe an overgrown frat house full of booze, sex, and secondhand furniture. Or a brothel. As daylight cleared the last of night away, however, I saw just how wrong I was.

We ambled up the dirt path toward Casa del Satyr—a charming stone cottage blending the best of pastoral quiescence and hobbit-inspired architecture. A low wall of mossy limestone circumscribed the squat building. Like the hilly landscape, the house rolled from low to high ceilinged. Even at this early hour, smoke wound up from the tall brick chimney.

I'd lived in the desert of Las Vegas for so long I'd almost forgotten what it was like to see full, lush trees. Oaks older than Mrs. M surrounded the small cottage, and birds chirped from their boughs while wind rustled the leaves. Walking beneath an arbor full of ivy and twining wildflowers, we passed a little gray cat slumbering on the wall.

I stopped in the garden and stared at the house. Swatting at Marius, I said, "Seriously, if this is some illusion or trick of yours, I don't want to know."

He smiled. "Like it?"

"I love it."

Marius stepped forward, but I held him back. Sotto voce I asked, "Is it safe?"

He leaned in and spoke quietly so Malcolm couldn't overhear. "There are reasons I haven't come home. Chief among them is keeping this place sacred. Like my pipes and heritage, there are things too dear for me to allow Eris or anyone else access. My father and his home are indeed as safe as I can make them. Sad as I am to say it, Malcolm may have just been useful by buying us some time."

I relaxed a bit, muscles unwinding, as we moved toward the door. It was a perfect circle of wood painted hunter green. A thick iron knocker had been fashioned in the face of the Green Man.

Malcolm lifted it and let it fall with a clank. Marius rolled his eyes. "Come on, Mal, do pretend to care," he said.

Marius gave a knock with the back of his hand—three quick, syncopated raps.

A muffled voice came in answer. It was singing. "...*les sanglots longs des violins de l'automne...*"

The door swung open to reveal a gray-haired man in a pair of horn-rimmed glasses, flannel pajama pants, and a Guinness T-shirt. Barefoot, eyes closed, he swept out into the morning, still singing merrily. Malcolm shook his head and stepped into the cottage. The old man paid him no notice. He swayed a moment, humming a few bars before reaching out and taking me by the hand. Lifting my arm over my head, he spun me around before pulling me against his chest.

"...*blessent mon coeur d'une langueur monotone...*" he crooned as we danced. The older man sent me into a spin then lowered me into a dip.

"Good morning, dear," he said in a weathered voice. His accent was subtle and soft. There was no doubt in my mind that this was Marius's father.

As suddenly as he'd scooped me into his arms, he set me right and turned in perfect time to the tune in his step. Then he opened his eyes and set them on Marius. Widening his arms, he said softly, "My son."

"Father," Marius said with genuine fondness.

The old man caught Marius in a viselike embrace, his voice ringing out with jubilation. "My boy! My boy has come home!" he cheered through hearty laughter.

"It's good to see you, too, Father."

Holding Marius at arm's length, Papa Satyr surveyed his son over his spectacles. Something stern furrowed his brow. "Next time, perhaps you should make it home sooner."

"It has been a long time."

"A long time?" he chuffed. "No, a year or two is a long time. The last time I saw you, Marius, we were on a week-long bender with Toulouse-Lautrec in Montmartre! To a father who hasn't seen his firstborn son, that is an eternity." He gave his son an approving smack on the shoulder and nodded. "But you're here now, aren't you?"

"As you requested."

Papa Satyr squinted behind his glasses, his eyes drifting from Marius and landing on me with no small amount of scrutiny.

Marius's gaze followed, flicking to me. "Pardon my rudeness, Father," he said with the same respect he usually reserved for deities. "Allow me to introduce you. Catherine Sharp, please meet my father, Llyr."

The older satyr fixed me with his gaze, then turned a cheerful smile to his son. "Oh, you are in trouble, Marius." With two jaunty steps he popped to me and took my hand in his. Bowing low, he brushed his lips over the backs of my fingers. "*Enchanté*, Miss Sharp."

"Good to meet you," I said, returning the grin and the squeeze on his supple hand.

From within the house, Malcolm bellowed, "Oi, Dad! Where's your special brew?"

"Children," Llyr sighed. "Welcome to my home, young lady. Please come in and tell me all about yourself and how you plan to break my son's heart." He put an arm around me, the other around Marius, and guided us into the cottage.

"Nothing like that, Father," Marius said as he shut the door behind him. "Catherine is—"

"I didn't ask you," Llyr interrupted.

I gave Marius a knowing, taunting grin laced with threats that I would blab all to his father. I had a sudden urge to embarrass the shit out of my satyr in any way I could. Did baby pictures of Marius even exist for me to paw through? Probably not. Probably for the best, too.

Llyr led us into a perfect country kitchen—wooden countertops, a deep porcelain sink, and ginormous windows that captured the morning light. An antique phonograph played a languorous tune full of crackles, pops, and French ennui. A teakettle atop a wood-burning stove began to squeal. As he passed the butcher-block table, Llyr slid out a heavy chair and gestured for me to sit. Marius took the seat opposite me and folded his hands on the table.

Still dancing to the music, Llyr shuffle-stepped about the kitchen gathering the kettle and a handful of teacups. He placed them on a tray before spinning around Malcolm, who stood gaping into the icebox, one arm propping the door open. Llyr withdrew, his hands clasped around a small crock of cream.

"Do you have nothing to drink, Dad?"

"It's dawn, Malcolm. Take some tea before you get knackered, would you?"

"It might be dawn to you," Mal protested, "but I just left the beginnings of a decent night out in Sin City."

Llyr prepared a plate of fresh fruit and bread. "Las Vegas, then? Is that where you landed, Marius?"

"More or less," Marius replied. "I was paying Catherine a visit when Malcolm arrived and said he'd gone and *lost his keys*."

Mal slammed the refrigerator door shut. "Oi! No need to be tattling tales."

"Again?" Llyr asked wearily. His eyes moved from his task to his eldest son, then to me. Though his mouth quirked in a very familiar smile, those blue eyes studied me with careful distrust. "So you're from Las Vegas, are you, dear?"

"Not from there, but I've lived there for more than a decade at this point."

"I didn't know anyone could actually live there, let alone for so long."

I shifted in my seat, uncertain how much Llyr knew about Marius's life and choices, unsure how much I should reveal about myself. "It wasn't the plan. Just sort of happened that I stuck around as long as I have."

"I've never ventured there," Llyr said as he carried the tea tray to the table. He began pouring tea into each cup. "Truth be told, I haven't been stateside in at least fifty years."

Malcolm joined us at the table, a dusty brown bottle of ale hitting the wood with a resonant *thunk*. "You're missing out. The food is plentiful, the music is loud, and the women are delectable. For example..." He gave a flourish of his hand toward me.

With identical motions, all three men lifted their drinks to their lips and eyed me across the table. Looking at them together, it was impossible to deny their kinship: they shared the same face shape. While Mal was stockier and broader of shoulder, Llyr and Marius were equally lithe. Llyr stood just tall enough that he could look down his nose at Malcolm but was short enough that he had to tilt his chin up to see Marius eye to eye. Llyr's moustache matched Marius's—albeit iron gray—and his bare, round chin mirrored Malcolm's. Along with the satyr blood, the father had given Marius his aquiline nose. To Malcolm, he'd donated those sky-blue eyes.

Three men—father and sons—older than I'd care to count, each capable of charming the scales off Lady Justice herself. And now all of them were staring at me. Malcolm's leer was full of dark promise and envy as it lingered over the charm in my hair. Llyr's gaze fell to my left arm, and I saw the slightest flinch as he caught sight of my tattoo.

The elder looked away, focusing on buttering his bread. "So what is it that you do, Miss Sharp?"

"Tech support. And call me, Cat, please." I gestured to the bowl of fruit. "May I?"

Llyr nodded. "Please."

Malcolm's leer widened. "Cat. And what a pretty pus—"

"Stop right there," I snapped, "or so help me, I will end you."

As Llyr snorted with undisguised laughter, Malcolm sulked into his drink. Pushing away from the table, the younger satyr shambled out of the kitchen and off into the house somewhere. On his way out, he grumbled something about "twat brothers" and the tempers of redheaded women. I looked up to see Marius smiling at me with amusement.

"What?" I asked. "What is that look for?"

He shook his head and sipped his tea, but otherwise didn't answer.

"Now, Cat," Llyr said, "how long has my son been courting you?"

China clacked as Marius dropped his teacup. "Father, I assure you, my relationship with Catherine is purely professional."

I scoffed. "Right. You're always so professional, Marius. Like that time in Belize..."

With a groan, Marius threw back his head. "Don't start with that again."

"...when I caught you going through my clothes at the hotel?"

"I was merely—" he squirmed in his seat and tried to hid behind his teacup "—searching for any...untoward devices..."

"Same trip," I said smartly, sitting back on my stool. "The mistletoe?"

"Festive decoration to ease the fact that we were imprisoned during the festive season."

"Im-imprisoned?" Llyr asked incredulously.

Playfully ribbing Marius, I carried on. "Or how about the time a few years ago when I woke up without pants?"

"To help ease the swelling of your knee." Marius leaned forward, his elbows resting on the table as those lovely green eyes bored into mine. "And as I recall, I saved your life that night. And other nights, as well, or are we conveniently going to forget that?"

Llyr's eyebrows climbed up his forehead. "Saved her life? Marius?"

I scoffed at my satyr. "You were saving your own ass. If something happened to me, then you couldn't get your—"

Marius poked a hole in my fun with a single harsh glance, and he cut me off with a subtle but stern shake of his head.

I coughed into my tea to cover the awkward moment. "Paycheck. You couldn't get paid without me. That time." I took a drink and stuffed a fat strawberry into my mouth before I could shove my foot in it.

Llyr searched the air between us, as if trying to divine the unspoken truth. "Has my eldest son gone and become a mercenary?"

"Not as such, Father."

"I didn't ask you," he said with a wry smile. "Cat?"

I shook my head. "*Mercenary* is a harsh word. More like...indentured servant of fortune?"

Marius's moustache twitched.

Llyr poured himself another cup of tea. "Well, I still fail to see how a lovely woman such as yourself came to be in the company of my son. Do tell me how the two of you met."

Marius shifted uneasily on his stool. "Don't we have something to discuss? Malcolm said you needed me to come home, so what—"

"Never mind that," Llyr interjected, that same distrust from earlier creeping into his gaze. "It's been ages, Marius, and I want to hear all the things about your life that you refuse to tell me. Cat? Don't skimp on the details, dear. I demand to know every embarrassing thing my son has done in his attempts to rouse your interest."

"That won't be necessary," Marius said helplessly.

"I didn't ask you," Llyr countered. "Cat? Please."

As Llyr had asked, I regaled him with the story of how I met Marius. I left out a few of the less savory details, like how my soul had belonged to Eris at the time because Dahlia, my Fae ex-girlfriend, had fucked me over in ways I wouldn't understand for years to come. I also tiptoed around the unfortunate fact of Marius's curse. Without these points of interest, the story of our meeting flowed into one about our first assignment together, which led to a tangential explanation about a Christmas celebrated in Belize looking for the lamp of a very angry djinn. Before I knew it, I'd spent a few hours recounting our highlight reel. Llyr's cheeks were red with his laughter and Marius's crimson with embarrassment. Mission accomplished.

"Well done, Marius," Llyr said, clasping a hand on his son's shoulder. "Not only have you had some entertaining adventures, you also seem to have found the one woman on this planet who can take your shit and sling it right back at you." Llyr stood and opened his arms to me. "And you are quite welcome in my home anytime, Cat, my love." His embrace was tight and warm—everything the hug of a father should be.

Marius yawned and pinched the bridge of his nose. "Christ, is that the time?"

"Ah yes," Llyr said with a quick glance for the clock. "I suppose the time difference has left you a bit jet-lagged. Marius, if you need a bit of rest, your room is just down the hall where you left it."

"How about you?" Marius asked me, voice slurring with weariness. His eyes were already at half-mast.

"I'm good. Go. Crash."

With little more than a sluggish wave, he padded out of the kitchen. He'd probably be asleep before his head hit the pillow. For a few moments, the only sounds were the birds chirping outside and the younger satyr's footsteps on the hardwood floor. Then I heard a guttural noise that was either a very angry bull being accosted by a chainsaw or...

"Malcolm," Llyr said. "The boy's snores could rattle the windows of a lesser house. He's a bit rough on the edges, but the lad is an easy read. As I'm sure you've noticed," he added as he collected the teacups.

I began helping him clear the table and chose my words carefully. "Mal does seem to be a man of simple needs."

This elicited a loud bark of laughter from Llyr. "That's one way to put it. Another is to say that as long as he has good food and bad women, he'll go to bed content. Unlike Marius."

"He is a bit more unnerving, yes."

"You know what they say about misery and company. He's never been content or complete in his whole life, that one. Even as a child." Llyr went quiet as he scraped away a crust of bread and a rind of cheese into the garbage. Those blue eyes drifted through time for a moment, and I wondered what he saw.

He made his way to the sink and began to wash up. "Marius always needed more. More freedom, more variety, more knowledge, more... anything. Everything. It's why he left."

I took up a towel and dried the dishes as Llyr washed the teacups. I didn't know much of Marius's life before we'd met. Sure, I knew the stories he liked to tell about his friendships with various Greek gods and his run-in with the Hindu pantheon. But really, I didn't know how much to believe. Everything I knew about Marius resided in the hindbrain, that place of instinct and primitiveness. I couldn't tell you something like his birthday or favorite color—though he did have an expressed fondness for port wine—but I could tell you the exact shade of green of his eyes and how they changed with anger or laughter. I knew the wrinkles of his smile and the notes of his voice, the cadence of his step and speed of his wit. Over our many years together, I'd memorized *Marius*, not random facts about his life.

That morning, however, I realized that I wanted to change that. There's something to be said for trivia.

"Is that when he went to Greece?" I asked.

Llyr nodded, his faraway gaze still trained on something past the froth and dishrag. "He wanted to know more about our roots. He only got to spend a short time around his grandfather—my father, that is. Marius was so young at the time. Peas in a pod, they were. Anyway, my father passed on, and when Marius grew older, he said he wanted to travel. See the world. Learn. He thought that if he couldn't visit his grandfather directly, he could at least see the Temple of Pan in Arcadia. I'd never begrudge a man his wanderlust, even if that man is my son, barely old enough to grow his first beard."

"I didn't realize Pan was gone," I said softly. "I'm sorry."

Llyr regarded me with a hint of surprise. "He's told you, then? Of our lineage?"

"Just before we arrived, actually. Until then, he'd kept that quiet for ten years."

"I see." Llyr bobbed his head, then went back to his dishes. "My father decided to give up his power and sleep. Can't blame him, what with his age and politics and bureaucrats. It was his time. He left a vacuum, though, in the heart and on his throne."

"Did his role not pass to you or another of his sons?"

Llyr's grimace was bitter. "I've no interest in godhood, dear. As to any of my siblings, well, time has claimed most of them. The result is the same: none has assumed Pan's seat, and the satyrs have been without their god for more than eight hundred years."

I dried the last of the dishes, stowed it in the rack, and then folded my towel. Down the hall, Malcolm let loose with another ripping snore.

"I'm sorry," Llyr said with a hesitant laugh. "If my boys are tired, you must be exhausted."

I shook my head. The infusion of power from Sapphire and the meditative restoration after had left me refreshed. I could probably go on for hours. "No, actually."

"No? Cat, would you care to join me on a walk then? Get away from their snoring and continue our chat?"

"I'd love that."

—⟋⟍—

After Llyr changed out of his pajamas and into a pair of jeans, a fresh T-shirt emblazoned with a Union Jack, and a brown blazer, we set out. He carried a gnarled walking stick polished to a gleaming shine as we strolled together along the winding dirt path. At a fork in the road, he gestured to the east with his stick.

"That way you'll find the ruins of Camelot. If you know where to look," he added with a wink. Stretching west he added, "And that way lies Avalon. If the mists are just right, you can step from this world to the other without difficulty and lose yourself in the sacred orchard. Fantastic apples there. Amazing wine."

We ambled along, speaking occasionally. He'd tell me about a particular wildflower or expound upon the history of Glastonbury. Mostly, though, Llyr and I shared a comfortable silence.

"It is good to see him," Llyr said after a time. "He's a grown man, of course, but that doesn't stop me from worrying about him. To tell you the truth, I'm relieved that he has left Eris."

Unease tingled at the base of my skull, and I retraced our conversations. Neither Marius nor I had told Llyr that Eris had released him. Out of some unspoken agreement, we'd casually "forgotten" to mention the danger Marius now faced.

"I didn't know you knew about that," I said quietly.

"I knew. Just like I always knew no good would come of his partnership with her," Llyr continued. "She brings nothing to this world but sorrow and heartache. Spiteful bint. To this day I don't know why he struck that deal with her, or what she had over him. I suspect you do, though."

Kicking at stones on the ground, I dragged my feet and chose my words carefully. "She never told me."

"Of course she wouldn't," he chuckled ruefully. "What about him?" After a few moments of listening to birdsong, Llyr smiled at me. "*Do you know why Marius took up with Eris?*"

Yeah...that. The curse that kept Marius from being able to enjoy anything. I was pretty sure that Llyr didn't know and I intended to keep it that way, so I just said, "I do."

"You're not going to tell me, are you?"

"'Fraid not. I promised."

"I see," he said with a nod. "Did he at least get what he was looking for out of their partnership?"

I sighed. "No."

Llyr planted his walking stick firmly in the earth and stopped walking, eyes trained on his boots. "Cat, what does Asgard want with my son?"

I pulled up short. "I'm sorry?"

"I rarely had so much as a phone call from Marius in more decades than you've been alive. I occasionally get word from someone that they've seen him here or heard a rumor about him there. Now he arrives without the golden apple on his wrist, but with a woman." He turned, lifting his head and then his eyes to meet mine. His voice was hardly a whisper as he stepped close to me. "And that woman wears the mark of an Asgardian."

Llyr picked up my arm, his fingers gently stroking the rune on my forearm.

"So I ask you again: what does Asgard want with my son?"

"Nothing. I tried to arrange it so that Loki would take Marius, but he refused."

"Refused. Why?"

"I don't know," I lied.

"I think you do. I can't be sure of what you are," he said, his fingers tracing my hairline, "but I see it in you. Mortal frailty. A life lived with the knowledge that your world is finite. Yet, while your form is mortal, you are anything but normal. You hold great power. Knowledge.

Just as you're aware of what bound my son to Eris, I suspect you know precisely why I hear tales of demons and monsters from the abyss searching for Marius. Why is it that an emissary of Crom Cruach—one of the oldest, bloodiest gods of Ireland—came to my home and hissed warnings that if I give shelter to my own kin I will make an enemy of the gods?"

I jerked and took a step away from him. The voice that had been so gentle before now seethed with a quiet anger. The ferocity in his eyes reminded me of what I'd seen many times in Marius, only more potent. This was the source, the master.

"You know?" I whispered. "Is that why you called him home? Why you sent Malcolm to fetch him?"

He shook his head angrily. "I can't expect an emissary of chaos to be honest, but I implore you to tell me. You know exactly why Loki refused him," he said. "I'm glad of it, to be honest. I want my son out of this role he's found himself playing for so long. I grow weary of watching his life run by the whims and machinations of petty gods. You say Loki turned him away, and yet you are here. With him. Are you part of this hunt? Are you watching him for your employer?" Llyr's face was stern but lined with sadness and disappointment. "Tell me, Catherine Sharp, have you brought trouble upon my son?"

"I'm trying to help him!" Fear and frustration caused my voice to crack, the words to come out more harshly than I'd intended. I moved away from Llyr. "He showed up on my doorstep covered in blood, nearly dead, and on the run from droves of supernatural bad things. Including Eris, my former employer. Who, by the way, hates me," I added.

Llyr's expression was one of shock. He just stared at me as it sank in.

"Did *I* bring trouble on *him*?" I spat. "He brought it on himself. He dove into it and swam until his fingers got all pruny. That's why Loki refused him. And me? I'm here because I promised to help Marius. I *promised*."

Llyr's jaw hung open, those blue eyes growing dark and exhausted. "It's true, then? He's in danger."

"Quite a lot," I answered.

"Is it—" He paused, searching for words. I may as well have just told him his son had cancer. Could satyrs get cancer? The creak in his voice yanked me back to him. "Is it *bad*?"

I gave a simple nod.

Llyr dragged his gnarled hands down his cheeks. For a moment, he resembled a lethargic basset hound, with his sad eyes and drawn face. As he had in the kitchen, he let his gaze drift to something in the middle distance. "What did you do, Marius?" he breathed.

I said nothing. Llyr shoved his hands through his gray hair and tried to pass me a weak smirk. "I knew," he said, tears bubbling in his eyes. "I knew something was wrong. He doesn't tell me anything about what he does with or for Eris, and I like it that way. To be frank, I don't want to know what he's done to put himself in such a corner." He swallowed loudly. "Tell me, do you have children?"

I shuddered at the very idea. "None that I know of."

Llyr gave the slightest of chuckles. "Of course you wouldn't. You're too young, I suppose. Do you know what parenthood is, love? It's worry. It is fear and terror every second of every day that passes."

I laughed and shook my head. When Llyr asked why, I said, "It's just funny. I guess I always thought of satyrs as the love-'em-and-leave-'em types. Didn't exactly think that one would stick around to be a father."

"It can be this way," he confirmed. "Gods know that I was certainly useless to my daughters. What could I possibly offer them? And knowing that I'd watch them die before so much as a single wrinkle appeared on my face?" He shook his head. "No. I wasn't there for them. But my sons... I could raise them in the faith, so to speak. From the moment I saw Marius kicking at his swaddling clothes, I felt this weight in my chest, this unbearable joy and terrible, remarkable burden of responsibility. You wear your heart outside your body when you're a parent. And that never stops. Not when they're old enough to cross oceans without you, not even when they're centuries old. Marius might be a grown man, but he's still my son, still learning to walk on his own."

Llyr took my hands in his and squeezed fiercely. "Promise *me* something, Cat. Swear to me that you will help him through this. Even when he makes it impossible just by being his damn self, promise me that you will stick with him. Please? Protect my son."

"I'm trying," I said. "And I'll keep doing exactly that."

The old man brought my hands to his lips and placed a hard, fervent kiss on them. "Bless you," he whispered.

We ambled silently for a time as Llyr collected himself. "So," I started eventually, "parenthood is nonstop worry? And you've got two of them?"

He pawed at the air. "Malcolm is different. He doesn't give a damn about gods or power. If it weren't for the fact that he walks the Earth beneath a glamour and has a particular skill to set him apart from others, Malcolm is no different from the average mortal."

"He doesn't seem to use magic much," I noted. "Not like Marius."

"Malcolm never wanted to learn anything beyond the basics. Wiles for ensnaring women. Simple tricks. He never connected to the earth magic like Marius did. Never felt the call to the Temple. He is innocent." When I raised a questioning eyebrow, he grinned and reconsidered. "Blissfully unaware."

"Must be nice." The words came out before I could stop them.

"How long has it been since you were innocent, Cat?"

I flapped my lips. "More than a decade. Since the night Eris claimed my soul."

"But not so long ago that you can't remember who you were before that night. *That* is who Malcolm is. Not a care in his world. And while I might occasionally be concerned for his safety if he has a pint too many or goes home with the wrong man's wife, I don't have the same worry for him as I do for Marius."

"The guy who goes running around the world pissing off deities, djinn, minions, and Kennedys apparently."

Llyr sighed. "And they're looking for him."

I bobbed my head.

"If you're here, they won't be far behind."

"If this is precisely what you feared, why call him home?"

He pressed his lips into a thin white line. After opening his mouth and closing it again without speaking, Llyr took up his stick and began walking back toward his house. "Better put the tea on if we're going to have company."

We were coming up the path, the little cottage peeking from the curtain of leaves around it when Llyr stopped me again, this time with a gentle touch on the wrist. "For as much as my son keeps close to the chest, it is very clear how he cares for you."

I snorted. "Marius? No, he... No. We're just—"

"Cat, I'm an old goat, but I see many things. That boy of mine adores you."

Sadness tugged at my heart as I remembered the secret to lifting Marius's curse. The secret was love. If he felt that for me, he wouldn't be cursed. And if he was still cursed... Well, I had proof that Llyr was wrong.

"We're friends," I admitted sadly. "It's odd, but that's what it is."

Chuckling to himself, he brought a finger to his lips and kissed the tip before stroking Marius's braid twined in my hair. "Friends?"

Fixing his pointed blue stare on me, he gave the slightest shake of his head. Without another word, Llyr turned on his heel and strolled up to the house.

TWELVE

"WAR PIGS"

When I walked into the cottage, the walls were shaking with the sound of bagpipes and cacophonous drums. Somewhere deep in the house Flogging Molly kicked out of a pair of speakers. Either that or the band had been invited over for a private concert. Turning a corner into the living room, I was slightly disappointed to find that the music was coming from an overamped MP3 player. Malcolm's one-man mosh pit slammed out a rhythm on his chest as he belted out an off-key chorus.

Normally, a single bar of Flogging Molly is enough to send my blood into a frenzy and get my ass dancing. Just then, though, my body was weary. I glanced at my phone to check the time. Sure enough, it was well past last call and this little girl should've been sound asleep—infusion of power or no. Just thinking of my bed made me ache for a soft pillow. Then I remembered that my pillow was across an ocean and covered in satyr blood.

I bumped into Marius. I hadn't even seen him walk up to me.

"Did you get any sleep?" he asked.

I shook my head. "Wasn't tired until now."

He put an arm around me, steadying me. I gladly let him bear some of my weight. "Malcolm!" he called over the music. "Turn it down."

"If it's too loud, you're too old, mate."

Llyr took the room in a handful of powerful strides. With a jab on the MP3 dock, he cut off the music. "Show some respect, son. A lady deserves that and more."

Chastised, Mal gave a sheepish look to his father. "Aye."

"Now, boys, we have things to discuss."

I cowered a little under the weight of Llyr's parental authority. Impressive, given he wasn't even my dad. But I also had an inkling that he was going to get down to brass tacks about the danger Marius was in, maybe plan a course of action. And then hopefully we'd find out why Llyr had gone to the trouble to fetch his wayward son.

"Cat," he said on a long breath, "would you do me the courtesy of staying awake a bit longer? I may need your insight."

I nodded, my head heavier than it should be. Llyr motioned for me to sit on the couch, and I gladly obliged. Marius sat beside me, his arms stretched wide over the back of the sofa. Malcolm took a seat in the rocker by the window, his hands still beating out a tight jig on his knees in time with the creaking of the chair's motion.

Pacing, Llyr cleared his throat. "Marius, it's not that I'm unhappy to see you, but you've never been one to drop in. Why are you here?"

Marius glanced at me, then let his eyes settle on his brother. "Other than the fact that you asked? Because Malcolm lost his pipes and needed a lift back."

"Oi!" Mal called from his rocker. "I didn't lose them. I mislaid them."

"And that makes how many sets that you've *mislaid* exactly?"

On either side of me the war of words began, each of them goading the other with increasingly loud voices. I drew my knees up under my chin and let my head fall forward.

"That's not the point, now is it? You shouldn't go 'round spreading tales, Marius!"

"Boys!" Llyr called. I looked up. Once again, all mirth had drained from Llyr's face. He was serious as a coiled rattlesnake. "Pipes are not the point right now. Mal, you'll make another set if the elders see fit to let you into the grove." He gave a dismissive wave of his hand, then eyed Marius. "Tell me what is happening, son."

I swayed again. I was so weary. The warm weight of Marius's arm fell over my shoulders. With his fingers, he used the slightest pressure to coax me into letting my head rest in the crook of his arm.

"It's nothing, Father. Don't worry yourself over me."

Llyr's smile was amused but sad. "Too late for that, Marius. What trouble follows you?"

Listening to the rhythm of Marius's breathing, of his heartbeat quickening, my eyelids fluttered closed.

Marius's voice became cool and defensive. He squirmed. "Mal said you wanted to see me. Poor timing on his part, but the message was received. I'm here."

"And is that such a bad thing?" Mal protested. "Taking a few minutes of your time to visit the man who raised you? Or are you too good for us?"

"Did you lie to me, Mal?" Marius said through his teeth. The muscles of his chest tensed beneath my cheek, and his hand clenched over my shoulder. "You said Father needed me to come home. Did you lie?"

"After a fashion," Llyr said.

I opened my eyes, a cold weight having just taken residence in my stomach.

"Of course I haven't." Mal swore rather loudly while Marius simmered quietly beside me.

Llyr drew a breath. "Malcolm, I never sent you to collect your brother."

The temperature in the room dropped about thirty degrees. Marius's shiver rippled through me, and I looked to Malcolm.

Stock-still, jaw hanging to his lap, Mal stopped rocking in the chair and gaped at Llyr. "What are you talkin' 'bout?" Mal asked. "Of course you did!"

Llyr shook his head. "No, son. No, I didn't."

"You did! You sent me a text while I was down at the pub. Said to go fetch him."

"A text?" I asked. Llyr—the man listening to World War II–era French music on an antique phonograph and living for centuries in the pastoral English countryside—didn't quite strike me as a texting sort.

He confirmed my suspicion by asking, "How many times have you known me to text you?"

"I thought it was important..." Mal said, sad confusion dragging his voice down.

I gave Marius an intent look. "If they know about your dad and your brother and went to the trouble to manipulate texts, they're going to know we're here."

Marius and his father shared a terrible, pregnant look.

"Bugger," Marius hissed.

He was off the sofa in one swift movement and then stalking down the hallway.

Malcolm shot off the rocker. "What d' you mean? You told me to go get Marius. That you needed to tell us both something important. That it was a family matter and it might be the last time you'd get both of us together!"

Llyr dragged his hands down his face in a perfect impression of Marius and took Mal by the shoulders. "Son, I know you didn't mean to do it, but you've fucked up. There are people after your brother. People with powers of deceit and guile. Someone pulled one over on you, and you led Marius straight to them."

"I don't..." Mal's face fell, clearly still confused. "What have I done?"

The floorboards groaned as Marius returned to the room. "Cheer up. We've never held it against you before when you've completely bollocksed something up." Marius took my wrist and hauled me up off the couch. "Come on, Catherine. We've got to be off before the trap springs."

Someone knocked on the door.

"I'm afraid it already has," Llyr said.

"Will someone please tell me what the bloody hell is going on?" Mal whined.

Ignoring him, Marius and Llyr sprang into action. Marius darted into the kitchen, the blade of his sword glinting in the summer sunlight.

Llyr took my hands in his. "Cat, I think it might be best if you weren't here."

I shook my head. "Can I borrow that MP3 player?"

His eyes narrowed. "I don't think this is the time!"

"Please? Just trust me."

Confusion marked his face. Finally, though, he said, "Of course."

With a few uneven steps I stood at the mantelpiece and plucked the player from its dock. A flick of my will and the power in the player began to flow into me. I may as well have popped the top off an energy drink. Though my eyes still felt scratchy and raw, the leaden feeling in my limbs slid away and the fog in my mind cleared. I wasn't about to run a marathon, but I could handle what was on the other side of the door.

Probably.

"You," Marius said from the living room doorway. "In the back of the house."

I tossed the MP3 player to Mal and smoothed my hair. "Nope. What are we looking at?"

"Catherine, depending on who's out there, I might be able to talk this out, but if it turns ugly, I can't guarantee your safety."

I gave Marius the cocksure grin I'd seen him wear a thousand times. "Like that's something new? Let's take care of you and your dad. Get this place back off the map, okay?"

"What about me?" Mal protested. "Why's she the one who gets to hide?"

"Because she's the one that's mortal," Llyr snapped. "Malcolm, make yourself useful. Go into my room and fetch me the leather bag from the hook."

"But—"

"Now, boy!"

Malcolm stomped past and did as his father bade him. The visitor knocked a second time but no more insistently than the first. Marius grimaced and took to the foyer.

"Dad, I've got it." Malcolm burst back into the room, a satchel of supple leather dangling from his fist.

Llyr held my eyes to his for a second. He gave a quick nod, then turned away. Taking the bag from Mal, he looped it across his chest, and with his left hand, he withdrew a crude blade made of flat stone.

Seeing the old man readying for battle galvanized me into motion. I met up with Marius in front of the door. Tendrils of acrid yellow smoke wafted from outside. A familiar tang of brimstone and bile stroked my nostrils and made me gag.

The visitor knocked again.

"Who is it?" Marius sang.

"He that would have words with you." Though his voice was muffled by the thick wood of the door, the stranger's voice was both melodic and gruff, a lulling bass marked by precise yet slow syllables.

Though Marius's grip flexed over the hilt of his sword, he feigned gaiety. "Any words in particular, or shall we just blather on about nothing?"

"You seek to yoke yourself with a new master. I require your vast knowledge. Perhaps," the visitor hissed, "we might be of use to each other. Will you parley with me?"

I chanced a glance at Marius. He raised an eyebrow in a question, and I shrugged.

Moistening his lips, Marius called, "A lot of people would say such a thing only to have my head when I open this door. How am I to trust you?"

A snort of laughter and the mist dispersed. "You should not. But be assured, I am no bad wolf, thief. Let me in and I shall ease your mind."

"You could ease my mind by giving your name."

"My name is worthless."

"Not very reassuring, that," Marius mused.

The stranger grumbled. "You misunderstand. I am the ruler of this world, the Angel of Hostility and Destruction."

Marius's face fell, true fear glazing his eyes.

"I am he," our visitor continued, "that came last. He that spawned the darkness. My name is Worthless. *Beli-ya'al.* And I bid you grant me entrance, satyr."

Beli-ya'al? I reached out for Marius and raised my hands in the universal sign for *What the fuck does that mean?*

My satyr's skin had gone ashen and pale. His jaw hung slack. Mortified, he whispered, "Belial."

THIRTEEN

"Take It All Away"

In the second after those syllables were spoken, the world plunged into another ice age. My heart stopped, blood frozen in my veins. If I listened closely I could hear my stomach squelching onto the floor.

Belial. One of the princes of Hell.

Not long ago I ran into a crew of mages that had a collective hard-on for Satan's right-hand man. By the end of that little fracas, I'd swiped the relic they were trying to collect, thus thwarting their plan to capture the Almighty Himself. Oh, and I'd lured Belial's pet doggy to his eventual murder at the hands of my employer, Loki.

And now he stood inches away from me, belching sulfuric smoke, listing his credentials, and offering my satyr a job.

Oh shit.

Llyr's steps echoed like war drums in the hall. Eyes wide with shock and terror, I shook my head.

"My door opens for no one from the Abyss," he said, voice strong and confident.

"Ah," Belial purred, "the elder." Something scratched along the other side of the door. I imagined a crooked, gleaming claw stroking the wood, seeking a weak point. "Is the other son there? I must thank him for taking my missive so seriously and bringing his brother here."

"That was your doing?" Marius asked, his tone still jovial. "You needn't have gone to such measures if you wanted to speak with me."

Belial ignored his words. "And just who else is cowering there beside you?"

My guts turned to water. Could Belial see through the door? I wasn't sure, but at that moment, I felt like a hobbit caught in Sauron's gaze. Closing my eyes, I gulped down a bilious lump of abject fear.

"There are prices on your head and wagers for your soul, satyr," Belial rumbled. "Align yourself with me and I will pay those debts."

"With what currency exactly?" Marius asked.

I shot an incredulous look his way. He couldn't possibly be entertaining the idea.

"Nothing with which to concern yourself. You would live with all the protections and extravagances a prince can provide. In exchange, I ask you to share with me what you know of my enemies."

"Any particular enemies? It would be a pity for us to strike a deal only for me to discover that I've traveled in the wrong circles."

"Your knowledge is vast. Some of those I seek are quite close to you."

Another scrape of claws on wood. This time immediately above my shoulder.

Shitshitshitshitshit.

I clamped my eyes shut and swallowed hard, trying to make myself small, my breathing shallow. My knees shook and my heart jackhammered in my chest.

Belial's voice filled the air. "This is my bargain, satyr. What say you?"

"Could I telecommute or must I move to the Abyss? I don't do well with dank pits and firestorms, you see."

A low growl like thunder served as a warning. "You are well-known for your insolent tongue, but beware, Marius, for you try what little patience I was born with."

"Just trying to get a feel for the working conditions, Your Highness."

"Be gone," Llyr spat. "You are not welcome in my home, and I'll not have you threatening my guests."

"Guests?" Belial asked, his sibilants exaggerated. "Why, who else could be there but the fugitive and his sluggard sibling?" There came a pecking on the door. Again, I imagined a talon, razor-sharp and ready to gut me. "Could I be so lucky as to have found both of you?"

"Leave!" Llyr shouted. "None here will have your business."

Belial ignored him. When he spoke, the prince's voice was lustful, hungry. "The thief *and* his woman? The mortal that makes play with gods and dabbles in meager parlor tricks. Are you there, mageling?"

I didn't trust my voice not to come out a quivery bleat, so I tightened my jaw and flashed a look to Marius. Unbidden, the memory came. An image of my satyr racing toward me with that same saber drawn. Running past me, grabbing what he thought was a holy relic, and sprinting away. The sight of his back fading into the murk of an abandoned foundry. Would he do it again? Here and now? Would Marius take this deal with a devil to save his hide, to hell with me? And Llyr. And Malcolm.

Marius lifted a finger to his lips, then gave me a cocksure smile. He didn't realize I could see the beads of sweat forming like pearls around his hairline. Usually so quick on his feet and ready to slither free, he was afraid.

"Her fear," Belial purred. The yellow smoke flowed out of the house as the prince inhaled deeply. "Its bouquet is exquisite. I cannot wait to feast on her."

"Your Highness," Marius said, his voice tight, "there will be no feasting, I'm afraid."

"You seem to think that the matter is up for discussion."

"Not with me, perhaps, but I'm certain you know her master."

"Too well. I fear neither his impotent wrath nor his simple conjuring. No, if I desire it, I will have my vengeance and spend centuries devouring her flesh."

"Oi!" Malcolm called as he entered the hall carrying a shotgun, its barrel aimed at the floor. "If anyone'll be devouring Cat for centuries, it's me."

Before anyone could stop him, Mal raised his arms. After a teeth-shattering bang and a muzzle flash, my ears popped as the round zoomed by and splintered the wood. In a blink, I found myself on the floor beneath Marius and Llyr, the two of them shielding me with their bodies. My ears were ringing, and when Llyr's mouth moved, I couldn't hear him.

Marius was off me and making a beeline for his brother. Mal held the shotgun across his chest and pumped the action. The two of them argued like characters in a silent film. Marius punched his brother in the shoulder. As the gun fell to the floor, I winced. Mal's arm went limp, his face twisted with pain, and I thought I saw his mouth form the word *recoil*. Llyr patted down my arms, tilted my head this way and that as he inspected me for wounds.

"I'm fine," I said, my voice modulated oddly through my bones and ringing head. But was I? I couldn't really tell. I felt numb all over, and my senses were all fluffy and fucked up. I looked myself over. No blood. No pain. I started coughing, though. Here, on the floor, I was face-first in the noxious vapor that had been slipping between the cracks of the door.

I turned my head, bracing myself with my arms as I retched. Through watery eyes I saw sunlight pouring into the dark little foyer. Llyr dragged me up to my feet and steadied me, but I couldn't tear my gaze away from the door. The shotgun blast had hit the wood boards in such a way as to take out a chunk the size of a Magic 8 Ball. Dislodged from its frame, the door swung in an idle breeze. Sinuous, amorphous shadows writhed through the hole.

As the ringing in my ears slowly abated, a low buzzing took its place. It took a second or two for me to register that noise as a voice, another second to understand words.

Llyr grabbed me by the shoulders. "Cat, listen to me. I can only be of so much help to you. Take the boys and run away from here. Run home. Then find the Sileni. It's very important that you remember this name. Do you understand?"

"Wait, what are you—"

"The Sileni," he repeated. "Tell Marius. He'll understand."

Releasing my shoulders, Llyr faced the door and kicked it down with wordless roar of fury.

Belial stood a few yards away beneath the arbor, the grass at his feet black and steaming. My knees went weak at the sight of him. To call him *imposing* would be like calling Everest *tall*. Belial was more than seven feet if he was an inch. Meaty bulk hung on that large frame, concealed somewhat by the jeans and the T-shirt covering his massive chest. Veiny muscles bulged in arms that were the sick, bloodless white of a fish belly.

A long, narrow rectangle formed the structure of his face. His forehead was broad, his brow flat and low. The dome of his bald head was smooth as a marble gravestone. Licking his colorless lips with a dark tongue, he stared at me down his nose with ember-red eyes.

"Hello, mageling," he purred. "I've been looking for you."

His fists flexed at his sides, and I saw black fingernails that hooked like an eagle's talons.

Legs wobbling coltishly, I took an instinctive step back and bumped into Marius. With one hand, he grabbed onto the belt loop at my back.

"Steady," he whispered softly.

"Satyr," Belial belched, "let this be our bargain. In a display of your fealty, bring the woman to me."

Marius's grip on me tightened, but I panicked. He was taking a little too long to think this through. Breathing like a trapped rabbit, I squirmed against his grasp and looked over my shoulder.

"Don't," I snarled through my teeth.

The satyr's features were placid, his green eyes cool as he asked, "I give her to you and I'm protected, you say?"

"No one will dare collect on their bounties when you are in the employ of a prince of Hell. You will be well kept with all that which will satisfy your many appetites."

Marius's moustache twitched in a weak, derisive smile. "Has no one told you, Belial?"

"Told me what, satyr?"

Marius gave a lighthearted shrug. "I'm insatiable."

He lifted me off my feet and whirled me around, shoving me into the waiting arms of his father. Llyr caught me and pushed me behind him.

"Run!" he roared.

Marius drew steel once more. I saw Belial's hand cut a broad arc through the air and a flaming whip appeared in his hand, curling and coiling as if alive. The prince's flesh rippled and shifted. Dark circles formed beneath his eyes, and coiling horns bursting out of his skull.

"Run, girl!" Llyr repeated.

But run *where*? Where could I go that Belial wouldn't follow? And how could I just leave Marius? Every quaking cell in my body screamed to fly, to vanish. I couldn't move. Rooted to the spot, I could only watch as Belial transformed. Flesh gave way to scales and spines the color of granite. Mundane clothing turned into armor slick and black like the chitin of a beetle. A tattered cape the shade of dried blood tossed in the air behind him.

"So be it, satyr. All of you step aside and you need not feel my wrath."

"You will not sully my home," Llyr commanded. "Nor will you endanger those I call family."

Llyr's eyes fixed on me, and my heart swelled. *Family?* No, running wasn't an option. I had to stay and fight with them.

Belial dipped his chin and snarled. "I will take that which is mine—vengeance, blood, and destruction." He cracked his whip, setting the arbor ablaze.

Llyr raised his hands, and the earth began to shake. Tree roots ripped from the earth and lashed around Belial's ankles. When Marius punched at the air a second later, vines shot up from the grass, stretching around the prince's torso.

Belial's whip twisted into an enormous circle around his body. With a burst of heat, the arbor fell in a flaming heap, blocking the path out of there with its rising wall of fire.

Something in my mind snapped, a door slamming on all the horror and screaming in my head. Thinking clearly now, I stretched out a hand, fingers splayed, and sent out a bolt of white power. The lightning struck the prince's chest but couldn't penetrate his armor. Smoke rose from him, partially obscuring his wide, sharklike sneer.

"Fight me, mage," he rumbled. "I've bent and broken those like you since the dawn of time. Conjurers, sorcerers, and wizards have fallen to me by the legion. What makes you think you will fare better than they did?"

I swallowed my pride. I had no witty comeback, no confident retort.

"You have stolen from me," he continued. "You are an accomplice to the murder of my vassal Moloch. Now, little mortal, you will pay with your pain."

He lashed out with that wicked whip. As the flame drew near, I ducked and rolled, coming up an arm's length away from Belial's bulk. Forging a blade of light, I lunged, swiping at the armor just beneath the behemoth's whip arm. As quickly as I closed in on him, I backed off, narrowly missing a swat of his obsidian claws.

Blurs of green, brown, and black flew past me. I heard my name being shouted, warnings and commands to stay back. Marius, his eyes ablaze with verdant fire, took up the flank with Belial. The saber slashed at the prince's thick gray hide. My heart fell, though, as even that enchanted sword didn't score so much as a paper cut. Marius retreated, bringing the blade up to parry a blow from Belial's spiked bracer. I used the opening to take another poke at him with my power. The beast's carapace sizzled and boiled at the contact.

The whip blurred. With a searing pain, my heels rocked. Despite what I'm sure was graceful flailing, I landed on my ass hard enough to make me yelp. Damn Belial had swept my legs right out from under me. My Chucks were singed, the soles smoking and sticky.

I glared at the prince of Hell.

Digging my fingers into the soil, I called to the power lines that flowed through the area. Internet. Telephone. Cable. Electricity. Anything I could find. Out here in the country, the well was shallow, but it had a source, a greater pool of energy. My senses searched at the speeds of light and thought until I reached a burning core. Like poking a straw into a juice box, I connected with that blazing well and drew it into myself in practiced sips.

With an amused, arrogant smirk, Belial lashed out at Llyr and Marius as the two tried to take him on from either side. He squatted down, compressing his girth into a tight ball. His armor glowed red a second before a concussive blast of heat came out of him in a cacophonous roar.

Llyr and Marius went flying with the shockwave, one falling to the grass just a blink before the other. Smoke rose from both of them. I even caught sight of a tiny flame in Marius's hair.

As if I needed another reason.

My gut was now a cauldron. I directed the flow of power into the pit of my stomach and poured in my anger, rage, and fear. I moved into a crouch, bringing both arms around in a low arc, and let the white lightning flow out of me in a scimitar of fury aimed at the prince's shiny boots.

Belial skipped backward, dodging my attack, but his head whipped up. I'd surprised him.

I met his red eyes with a challenge. "Don't fuck with my Chucks, asshole," I growled. Taking another draught of power from the Glastonbury grid, I shot up off the ground with a snap of ozone and kicked out at Belial's ugly, arrogant face. My foot connected, that's for damn sure. Pain traveled up my toes, rattled through each of the tiny bones in my ankle and up to my knee. When I hit the ground, I tucked into a roll. My foot went numb.

Note to self: Never kick a prince of Hell in the skull.

I needed more power. I drank from the well in ever-increasing gulps. Using a few techniques Karma had taught me, I was able to set my bones to healing with the borrowed energy. If I hoped to put a dent in Belial let alone fight him off, though, I still needed *more*.

Belial rounded on me, hatred heaving from his breaths, glowing in his bloody eyes.

I threw my hands up in front of me, and a dome of light encased me, pulsing and humming with white and gold. Belial swung a black-clad fist and struck my shield. Lightning crackled along the dome, but it otherwise stayed intact.

I bared my teeth, relishing this small victory. Sparing glances to either side of the lawn, I saw Llyr just beginning to stir. He brought himself up to hands and knees, Malcolm at his side. Marius lay motionless on the grass, crumpled in a heap of borrowed clothing. (Flynn was going to kill him for those scorch marks.)

"Get up," I whispered.

Belial struck the shield again. The concussion drilled through my connection with the dome and jangled my teeth.

"Come on, Marius," I shouted. "Get up!"

Belial's smile was a terrible promise. "Is that how to hurt you, mageling?"

He turned on his heel and stalked over to Marius, where he picked up the satyr by the scruff of the neck. Dangling from the prince's large fist, Marius looked like a bedraggled kitten.

That was enough for me. I reached into that pool of energy, that burning well of power, and let it flow over me, consume me. I drank and drank, filling myself until my veins hummed with static crackles and buzzed with a thousand channels of activity.

I felt it all. I felt the power grid of Glastonbury. Every landline, every radio tuned into a soccer match or rock station. Every Internet connection and MP3 player. Every video game and lightbulb. If I reached out a tiny sliver of my awareness I could touch satellites.

My hair fanned out in a copper nimbus. Like an aura of fire, a halo of pure gold glowed over my skin. Buoyed by the magnetic field of a few billion electrons, I felt myself levitate off the ground.

"Put him down!" I yelled. Within the shield, my voice took on a queer mechanical modulation. The sound reminded me of Flynn—the real Flynn, when stripped of his mortality.

Belial eyed me. Gone was the placid mask. First, astonishment washed over his face—a brief ripple—before being replaced by a grimace of rage. "This light? Why did he bestow it upon you?"

I lowered my arms, maintaining the spherical shield with mental focus. With a breath of will, I glided across the grass. Stopping to hover just out of Belial's reach, I repeated myself. "Put. Him. Down."

Marius jolted into consciousness. He brought his hands up to Belial's wrist and began to kick and squirm in the prince's grip. Then his gaze flashed to me. His eyes widened, and his jaw fell slack.

"Catherine?"

Belial tossed Marius to the ground. My first instinct was to zoom in front of him, to protect him from the next attack. And as go my whims, so goes my body. I flew to Marius, putting myself between him and Belial.

The prince gritted his teeth. "Tell me! Why has your master given you this gift?"

"Leave," I said, savoring this power.

"I take orders from none, mortal."

Belial lunged forward and whipped the back of his fist through the air. This time he cut through my shield as if it were made of tissue. His fist connected with my cheek.

The power bled from me, snuffed out like a candle. I went limp and began to fall. Less than a heartbeat later, I came to a jarring halt as one of Belial's massive hands closed around my throat.

"Puny creature," he spat. "Irksome. Frustrating." He lifted a hand to tenderly stroke my face. "You could have thrived with my aid, mage. But—" he snarled, claws digging into my scalp and tightening around my hair "—you have chosen to yoke yourself with the wrong fallen son."

Feeling him tearing out strands of my hair, I screamed in pain. Jerking, struggling in his fierce grip, my limbs felt wobbly and pitifully weak. The air around me shivered with a soot-stained aura.

"Look at them," Belial purred.

He allowed me to tilt my head just enough to see Marius, Llyr, and Mal in a scrum. Time had stopped. Marius was suspended in mid-stride. Llyr's mouth gaped as he held an incoherent syllable.

"Sad little goats. I could end you in any number of ways before they blink. Do you understand that, mage?"

Time churned sluggishly into being again. I watched as one millimeter of movement seemed to take hours. As Llyr and Marius made their ways forward, Mal stood his ground. His hand moved a fraction of an inch toward something at his belt. I saw the butt of a pistol there.

"What shall it be, Catherine Sharp?" Belial asked as he forced my attention to his face. "I could fling you through sky, sea, and existence. Let you float in the Void until your being implodes upon itself from the crushing weight of Naught. Perhaps I should throw you to the ground. Pulverize each of your bones. Or treasure the feeling of your life ending between my fingers as I crush your windpipe." The prince licked at the air with his black forked tongue. He shivered with delight. "When your body is broken, the feast will begin. I will take you with me to the Pit and devour your fear and soul over the course of thousands of years."

His grip loosened, and I looked at the trio of satyrs. Time still meant nothing outside this little sphere.

Belial's laughter was a guttural sound that churned my stomach. "No, none of that, I think. There is a better way to watch you die. I will bask in the exquisite pain of these, your final moments."

That tongue poked out of his mouth and licked up my cheek in a long, slimy stroke. Sickened, terrified, I gagged and quivered.

"I will see you quite soon, mage. Hold on to this fear, bring it with you when you pass through the veil and enter my kingdom. This terror shall be the last you know."

Still gripping me by the throat, Belial took a large step backward. I turned away from him. Marius's face was one of stony determination as he focused on the ether where I had been just a moment before. Malcolm's hand clasped the pistol now.

Belial released me, and in a puff of acrid, yellow brimstone, the prince disappeared.

Time rushed back to full speed. What had it been like for them? One moment they'd seen me hanging above the earth in Belial's grip, the next I stood alone.

The satyrs had been too close to alter course. Marius and Llyr blurred past me, but Malcolm I saw quite clearly. He had already raised the pistol. Had already pulled the trigger before his ice-blue eyes went wide and white as the full moon.

The shot was strangely quiet.

"Catherine!" Marius yelled.

I glanced down to see a red stain blossoming on my T-shirt. Shouldn't it hurt? Shouldn't I feel...something? Or was this the plan?

Confused, I looked up to Mal. Horror filled his face, and he started running toward me. Belial reappeared behind him, smirking. Shadows swarmed around the prince before carrying him away from this world.

Dizzy, I stumbled backward and fell into a pair of warm, strong arms.

"Catherine? Catherine!" Marius cradled me just above the ground. Hair mussed, face drawn with terror and anger, eyes obscured by tears. And still...lovely.

I reached up to touch his face but didn't feel his skin beneath my fingertips.

"I'm cold," I said.

Shitty last words, if you ask me.

FOURTEEN

"WORLD OF TWO"

The afterlife was a warm embrace. Nestled in a blissful darkness, I drifted in a bleary haze. That unfettered rest reminded me of every Sunday morning of my life rolled into one lazy stretch. No obligations, no need to rush or roll over. Not even the temptation to open my eyes and disturb the perfect balance of comfort, peace, and luscious sloth.

This must be Heaven, a faraway part of me remarked. *Hell would be hotter, right? Not nearly so pleasant as this.*

I shoved the thoughts away, reminding myself that I didn't believe in either Heaven or Hell, and burrowed deeper into the euphoria.

Tranquility smelled of mossy trees and cool water. I drew in a long breath, taking in that natural-spring sweetness and earthy musk. I imagined that I was lying beneath a tree on spongy grass, the boughs above me swishing and whispering in the softest of breezes.

Like the trees surrounding Llyr's cottage...

No. I didn't want to think about that, either. I wouldn't. That was over. Life was over. Perhaps I was a caterpillar, and this serene darkness was my cocoon. Or I could be something out of a fairy tale. I could sleep on the soft earth while the moss grew over me, vines and flowers sprouting through my hair and letting the sunshine clothe me. Only when I was ready would I rise, a woman made of flowers and meadowsweet, and take my place in legend.

With a languid purr, I stretched. My hand came to rest on a patch of gossamer, and I let my fingers twirl and trace, enjoying its downy texture. A breeze buffeted against my bare skin, brushed my hair away from my cheek, as the sunlight caressed me, pulled me into itself and shared its warmth. I lay there, enveloped in the velvety glow of bliss.

A century or a second later, I recognized a pattern in the rise and fall of the earth beneath my hand, my head. It coincided with the rhythm of the air passing through the trees above me. The world around me breathed in a slow, easy cadence. In and drowsily out. I bobbed on its surface like a boat over ocean waves.

Like a splinter, thought kept meddling with my calm with its reminders of life.

Why does the ground breathe? Why do I sense the things around me as if I still have skin?

These pebbles of thought were the beginning of a landslide. That heavenly delight of floating, of being made of little more than air and light, drifted away. My limbs grew heavier and more solid. I became aware of a hundred tiny aches and pains, including a knot in my hip and a dull, insistent thud in my chest.

Details came to me sluggishly as my brain—so quick to analyze—couldn't quite wake up. I had a body. A body that had been in the same position just a little too long. I wriggled around and stretched legs that felt a million miles away. My toes touched something fleecy. Clothes on my legs. My chest bare. And cold. My nipples were at attention and brushed against something as if huddling for warmth. And warmth there was. It embraced me, just as it had moments or years before. It curled around my back, draped over my side, and rested heavily on my hip as it held me pressed against it.

Beneath my hand, the feathery patch of earth still rose and fell with a delicate rhythm, but there was more now. The warmth came not from a sunny radiance but from the flesh beneath my fingers.

I opened my eyes.

No lush green meadow or sunshine here. Just a dark room with little more than a bed and a table. Glancing up, I saw a sphere of wan amber radiance. Embers or feathers of light dripped down from the orb, extinguishing before they could land on me. I blinked and swallowed, my throat dry as kindling. When I tried to moisten my lips with a sandpapery tongue, I tasted blood.

A subdued snuffle drew my attention. I let my eyes peer through the shifting shadows just enough to see that I lay with my head pillowed on someone's shoulder. My hand lazed on the dark tuft of his chest hair. Weak, my head filled with lead, I turned my chin. Marius snored gently, eyes fluttering as he dreamed. With a light touch, his hand stroked my hip.

I gasped and scrambled to my knees, covering my bare breasts. Marius's hand fell limply to the sheets—my sheets, I realized—but otherwise, he remained sound asleep.

Looking at him, my heart hurt. The delicate, orange light fell over his form as easily and beautifully as paint caressing a canvas. Shadows deepened around the muscles of his arm, the lines of his face. He stirred, the arm that had been holding me now stretching over his head. A white bandage dotted with crimson was wound around his left palm, and bruises bloomed over his cheeks. A series of gashes marred his shoulder.

My poor satyr.

I reached out to touch his hair, so glossy and thick, but stopped just short. My stomach twisted, and my mind roared with confusion. We were in my room at YmFy. But this wasn't right. Nothing was right. Sure, that was my closet, my table, and my bed. Marius snoozing away in it, no less. But how the hell...?

Hell.

With a jolt, I remembered everything. Pitching forward with horrified nausea, I began to cry. The tears streamed down my face, and I fought against the anguished moan swelling beneath my skin. Clamping a hand over my mouth, I eased out of the bed as quietly as I could and padded to my bathroom, closing the door behind me.

I gave into the shakes and sobs. Images boiled in my mind: Belial's distorted face, his words a fetid mist on my cheek. Llyr shouting, his home burning. Malcolm holding the gun. The shot that landed home. And Marius...crying. My knees trembled, and I slid down into a squat, my hands still gripping the basin.

There were things I remembered then that no one could see, mysteries revealed that I could never unknow. Things I couldn't put into words if I sat down with every dictionary and thesaurus of every language ever spoken. Shapes and voices in the Void. Love. Such heartbreaking, soul-filling love. And peace in its truest sense. A world as serene as fresh snow, yet warm as springtime.

And it was gone. I'd been cast out. Pushed back into a body with aches, pains, and questions. Back into a world with strife and screaming uncertainty. The pristine solace had melted away leaving intangible, unspeakable truths burned into my being. No way to purge them, no way to explain or give them voice. No one to ask or share with. Just this horrible burden and this inadequate form. This goddamn human body with its unique and beautiful existence.

I was alive.

And I wasn't sure if I should be grateful or not.

FIFTEEN

"I WILL SURVIVE"

After crying myself dry and sobbing on the bathroom floor for a while, I crawled to my feet and stepped into the shower. As I cleaned myself, I let all thought wash away with the old skin. I kept my eyes closed the whole time. I didn't want to look at my body, didn't want to see. I just let my hands slide over the familiar curves of flesh and bone that I'd known for my own personal eternity. And if I didn't look at my body, I couldn't see the wound. I could still imagine that maybe none of it had happened. Or maybe I could try to salvage that anchorless warmth from the meadow...

None of that worked, though. When the water ran cold, I was still alive. Still human.

Joy.

Drying myself, I dared to look in the mirror. My stomach flopped at the sight of the bullet hole and all the terrible truth it represented. Just above my breasts and to the left of center was the dime-sized blemish. The outside of the circle was an angry red while the center was comprised of pink, puckered tissue.

The red ring of death, I snickered to myself.

A quick turn revealed that I had a matching wound on my back. I gave the skin on my chest an experimental poke. Beneath the first layer or two of skin, white lines of light appeared and flashed out of sight beneath the healthy flesh. Another jab and I saw the pattern of the lines—circuitry like a microchip.

This answered at least one question. I'd been saved—yet again—by one of Karma's cybernetic implants. But like the hydra of old, cutting off one line of questions just birthed two more. And none of them would get answered naked in the bathroom.

I opened the door and peeked out into the room. Marius was gone, his amber sphere with him. Someone had turned on my bedside lamp, though, so the room was not entirely dark. I peered around. Satisfied that I was now alone, I stepped out and went about the mundane routine of getting myself ready. I didn't bother with jeans. I'd just died and been ripped out of the afterlife, for fucksake. If I had to be in this body, I was going to revel in comfort as long as I could. Pink flannel pajama pants and a baggy black T-shirt would suffice. The silver cuff that Loki had given me clung to my wrist with a cool, easy weight. Slipping into a pair of fluffy slippers and twisting my hair up into a clip, I looked like exactly like Cat Sharp should.

Now if I could just feel like her again.

I shambled out of my room and down to the common area without any idea what day it was or who I might meet along the way. The kitchen, though, had chai, and chai was what I wanted almost as badly as I needed answers.

I found Flynn waiting for me in the kitchen, two steaming mugs on the table in front of him. When he saw me his face lit up, a smile spreading from ear to ear.

"She lives," he sang.

"More or less," I said, hoping the bitterness didn't seep into my voice.

He winced. "You sound like hell." He pushed one of the mugs across the table to me and, with his foot, shoved out a chair, indicating that I should sit.

I stood rooted to the spot. Checking over both shoulders, I avoided looking at Flynn and asked, "What time is it?"

"About two thirty."

"Morning or afternoon?"

"Afternoon. Monday, in case that was going to be your next question."

I sat down and blew out a long sigh. Curling my hands around the hot mug, I let my eyes drift in the middle distance as I sussed it out: I'd lost a day between Glastonbury and YmFy.

"What happened?" I asked my chai.

"I'm hazy on some of the details," Flynn said, "but the quick of it is that you got shot. Marius used your fob to teleport the two of you here. We worked fast and furious, got one of Karma's implants into you, and..." His words trailed off.

I looked up into his face. Flynn chewed on his lip, his eyes trained to the floor as he mulled something over. When he felt the weight of my stare, his eyes darted up.

"We almost lost you," he whispered.

I ground my teeth.

I should be grateful. I should be throwing my arms around him and thanking him tearfully, not wanting to scream at him that he was wrong.

When I opened my mouth, all that came out was a hoarse, "Almost."

"What do you remember?"

"Enough."

"Care to fill me in? Marius wasn't exactly talkative after he... Well, after you two got here."

Shaking my head, I avoided his question. "Where is he?"

"Took off awhile ago."

"What?" My head shot up, and hot panic flooded my whole body. "He's gone?"

"Said he had to go make sure the others were okay," Flynn explained.

"What others?"

"He can't have just left." My heart jackhammered with true fear. My stomach felt knotted, yet empty. Incomplete. "Not without saying anything. And without me? Is he stupid?"

Flynn's voice hardened. "Well, yeah, but that should hardly come as a surprise."

"Shut up!" I screamed. I wiped tears out of my eyes with the heel of my hand. "Gah, I'm sorry. I have to go."

"What? Cat, you can't just—"

"I need to." I sprang up from the chair and sped down the hall back toward my room. While my mind mentally packed my bags, words spooled out of my mouth. "I need to get back to Glastonbury and make sure Llyr and Mal are all right. Well," I said, after a quick thought, "maybe not Mal. He shot me. He can fuck off."

"Glastonbury? Nothing you're saying makes any sense. Will you just slow down?"

I rounded the corner, barged into my room, and made a beeline for the closet. I started tossing things onto the bed and continued thinking out loud. "I'll have to reverse the teleporter to get back. If I can. Not like I've got pipes to get me there. Dammit, Marius, why did you leave without me?" I fought back more tears—and my building anxiety—by focusing on what I needed to do. Pants. A few shirts. A jacket. "It's July. I don't need a damn jacket," I growled to myself. "Teleporter. Reverse that. Assuming it's still charged, that is. If not, I'll have to spend the time charging it, but then that shouldn't be too hard really if I just give it a bit of my own juice."

Flynn grabbed my shoulders, spun me around, and shoved his face up to mine. "Cat, stop this and talk to me!"

"You wouldn't understand."

His hands went limp, and I easily broke out of his hold.

"Wouldn't understand?" he asked, clearly wounded.

I ignored him, focusing on stuffing things into my bag.

"This is me, Cat. *Me*. What the fuck makes you think I wouldn't understand?"

How could he? Even with his infinite knowledge and ages of experience, how could he understand *this*? This ache in my chest, this crazed need to be somewhere else. This bitter hatred that he'd brought me back from...

"Glastonbury?" he asked, exasperated. "Llyr? Mal? I don't know what any of that means because you won't tell me what the hell happened."

"Hell," I snapped. "That is exactly what happened. Be—" His name caught in my throat, and I coughed with dry heaves. I pitched forward—hands to the mattress—and tried not to vomit. I looked up and saw a bloody stain on my sheets.

"Is that mine?" I asked soberly.

"It's not mine," he said, his tone grim. He pawed through his spikes. "We didn't move you after we got you patched up. Not exactly a priority to make the bed, you know."

I nodded, numb. I eased down on the mattress and drew my knees up to my chest. Flynn sat beside me, waiting for me to explain.

I blew out a shaky breath and began. "Loki wouldn't take Marius."

For the next half hour or so, I reviewed the trip to Sapphire and the revelation that Marius was not an only child. I told Flynn about our trip to Glastonbury and meeting Llyr. When I told him that the old satyr had begged me to protect his son, Flynn laughed.

I narrowed my gaze at him. "What's funny?"

He shook his ginger mop. "Don't worry about it. Go on."

"Anyway, while we were at the cottage, we received a visit from a certain prince of Hell."

Flynn's eyes darkened. "Belial?"

I nodded. After giving him a summation of the very one-sided fight with the prince, I shrugged. "You're going to have to fill me in from there," I said.

Flynn bobbed his head. "Well, the teleporter went off and I came to check on you, make sure Marius hadn't gotten you into trouble. And I found..." His eyes went out of focus, face drawn with remembered horror and anguish. When he spoke again, his voice was raw. "Christ, it scared the fuck out of me. I show up in the doorway and Marius has you in his arms."

My stomach flopped with a dull ache at the memory of waking up being held by Marius.

"You were limp, Cat. And pale. Well, more than usual," he added, trying to inject some humor into his voice. I gave him a half-assed smirk. "He was freaking out. There was blood everywhere. I grabbed one of Karma's implants while he got you to the bed, and...well, you know how that part works."

I did. The previous year, my life had been saved by one of her cybernetic gadgets. A bit of blood from a willing donor, a bit of power, and the circuitry would meld with the body, healing it. Karma had explained the specifics to me, but I still didn't quite grok it all, like why something that was going into a wound would need blood from another source to do its thing. Such was Karma's magic, though. And it was damn effective.

I took my hair out of the clip and let it fall just so I could drag my hands through it in frustration. Flynn circled me with his long, lanky arms and planted a kiss on top of my head.

"Don't scare me like that again, okay?"

I nodded and let him squeeze me. The longer he hugged me, though, the more my insides squirmed and rebelled. And don't think I didn't feel guilty. Flynn was my best friend, but at that exact moment, I felt... lost. I found no solace or comfort in his embrace. No gratitude that he and Marius had brought me back from death. I didn't want him to hug me. I didn't want him near me telling me how wonderful it was that I'd lived.

I wanted to go back to the serenity of the meadow, the blissful weightlessness. But I knew that path was closed to me now. With the same searing knowledge gained from being well and truly dead, I knew that I could not seek out that place. If I saw it again, it would not be on my own terms.

I ached for it, though. I craved peace, and if I couldn't have the real thing, I wanted to be in the crook of Marius's arm. Safe. A piece of that tranquility here in the land of the living.

But I couldn't have that, either. For so many reasons.

What a life, eh?

Fresh tears welled in my eyes, and I trembled with the force of them. This only made Flynn tighten his hold around me. I choked down another wave of my own anguish. Rather than fill the emptiness in me, my sadness only expanded it.

Gently, I pushed against him and broke the moment. "I have to go back. To Glastonbury," I added, although the clarification was more for myself than for Flynn.

"Why?"

"Why not?" Marius sang from the doorway. "It is glorious this time of year."

My eyes shot up at the music of his voice. He lounged against the door to my room, a smile on his face and his gaze sparkling. Fully intent on rushing to the door and wrapping myself around the satyr, I launched to my feet. Though relief buoyed me, fear lay heavy in my stomach like a lead weight. This push and pull left me standing stone-still.

"Hey," I squeaked like a lame eighth grader. "You're back."

"So are you." Marius's smile faded as his eyes drifted down and focused on my chest. As if he could see through the T-shirt, his mouth twisted with disgust. His throat tightened visibly, and his next words came out bitter and hoarse. "Up and about, I see. Feeling all right?"

"More or less," I said.

Seeing him there... Oh gods, a part of me stamped my feet that I was not allowed to need him or rejoice in his return. But him standing in the room restored life to this bone-weary soul. Some of the sadness ebbed away simply by being near him.

Marius looked more like himself in a pair of faded jeans, a green shirt, and a pair of Birkenstocks. I tilted my head with a question. "More of your threads, Flynn?"

"Pan's balls, no," Marius answered. "While I appreciate the earlier loan, I don't feel comfortable in another man's clothes. I popped to a shop on my way back from Father's house. He sends his regards, Catherine, and says he's glad to see you'll live to torment me another day."

I smiled, genuinely relieved. "He's okay?"

Marius nodded. "Not a scratch on him. Some fire damage to the front of the house. Needs a new door and a good breeze to clear away the stink of Hellspawn, but otherwise the old homestead is just fine. More than I can say for Malcolm."

"Why's that?" I asked with perhaps too much venom in my voice.

"Father nearly flayed him alive. First time I've ever seen Mal remorseful about anything, honestly."

"I should fucking well hope he feels bad for nearly killing Cat."

Marius sobered. "You weren't there, Flynn. You don't know what we saw." For a moment, his lovely green eyes swam out of focus. "One moment Belial had her by the throat. The next she was standing alone.

Mal had pulled the trigger before he realized who he was shooting. Stupid bastard was trying to help her, but Belial outsmarted him."

"Doesn't sound difficult to do," Flynn snarled.

"No one ever accused Malcolm of being the ripest grape on the vine," Marius said with a shrug.

"Really? A satyr that's just a pretty face? Who'd a thunk it?"

"He's okay, but not super hot," I assured Flynn. "You'd think he'd pick a better glamour."

"Not how it works," Marius told me.

I cocked my head at him. "What do you mean?"

He started to explain, then cut himself off. Eyes drifting to the ceiling, he gestured with his fingers and hands, as if trying to pull an answer from the ether. "It's... We look the way we look. The glamour a satyr uses is a minor bit of magic meant to conceal the horns and furry legs that people seem to take issue with. Some satyrs exaggerate their better features to make themselves more attractive, but on the whole, what you see is what you get."

"So a short and fat satyr can't make himself look like Flynn?" I clarified.

Marius snorted. "He could. But it would be quite an effort. In case you haven't noticed, we tend to be a bit of a lazy lot."

Flynn crossed his arms over his chest. "So why haven't you changed how you look to hide from the beasties that want to get you?"

"Why hide one's light under a bushel?"

I giggled. Flynn rolled his eyes.

"Vanity aside," Flynn said, "shouldn't you at least try? Wouldn't that help?"

Marius raised an eyebrow. The air around him shimmered and blurred. As I watched, his eyes went from a deep green to a piercing blue. His cheekbones paled, and his beard winked out of being. The hair falling past his shoulders lightened from black to brown. As his face rearranged itself, I gasped. Within seconds, I was staring at Mal in Marius's clothing.

Flynn grimaced. "That's the best you can do?"

"It's his brother," I explained. "That's Mal. Almost."

The satyr nodded. Marius's voice came out of Mal's mouth. "Flynn doesn't know what to look for, but Catherine, you've seen him. This doesn't convince you at all, does it?"

I waved my hand back and forth. "A little. I mean, it's close, but there's something wrong."

"It's hard work to maintain and shift. The worst part is that there are spells and relics made specifically to see beyond a glamour. Most deities are so powerful they wouldn't be fooled in the slightest. Assuming they're bothering to do a visual search and not a magical one, that is."

"Is keeping it together really so difficult?" I asked.

His answer came in the beads of sweat pearling on his forehead. Marius's appearance changed again. The long locks of brown shrank up into his scalp where they formed unruly ginger spikes. His skin lost most of its color, and Marius's eyes flushed to a golden hazel. His face lengthened, his features becoming more gaunt and pronounced. Tattoos formed on his arms in a perfect mimicry of Flynn's.

"I hate you," Flynn said to his new twin.

My giggles were quickly silenced by the stony look Flynn shot me.

"Take off my face, Marius, before I knock it off you."

Not-Flynn smirked just before melting into another form. This time I could tell that Marius was concentrating hard. I don't know if Flynn noticed, but I could almost see the real Marius beneath the glamour as he worked to morph his appearance. His hair spooled out from his head in a lush ginger mane. His cheekbones rounded, features softened, and his eyes turned a muted shade of green.

My jaw dropped. She was a little taller than me, curvier and prettier than what I usually saw in the mirror, but there was no mistaking it. Cat Sharp stood across the room from me.

"Oh, now that's just fucked up," I said.

Marius leered down at his—my—chest. He copped himself an admiring feel. His voice came out of my mouth. "How do you manage to leave the house?"

"Stop that," I snapped. "Those aren't yours."

"Technically they're not yours, either," Flynn said with a shrug.

"You're not helping."

"Go back to the first one," a bubbly voice said. "He was cute!"

In a single instant, many things happened. With a snap of power, Flynn sparked to life, arms aglow with orange light. Marius's glamour of me dropped, and he stood wearing his own face and brandishing his sword. I whirled around, already reaching out to the well of energy within YmFy, and found a dead girl sitting in lotus position about three feet above my bed.

"Polly?" I gasped.

SIXTEEN

"SHUT THE FUCK UP"

Her chestnut hair was pulled up into a little bun on each side of her head. She hovered, the sheer white of her gown flowing around her as if in a current of water.

"Impossible," Flynn said.

She lifted a perfect hand and wiggled her fingers. "Hi!"

"Polly?" I repeated. "Polyhymnia?"

She flapped her lips. "Not even close, sister." Unfolding her legs, she stood on my bed and bounced a little before stepping to the floor. She was shorter than Polly. The more I looked at her, the more differences I could see. Like the pert nose, smattering of freckles, and radiant dimples. But the resemblance was uncanny.

"And *sister* is the answer to your next question," she sang.

"You can't be here," Flynn snarled.

Her toes barely skimming the floor, the woman floated across the room and licked Flynn's nose. "And yet here I am, Copper Top."

"Muse," Marius said with a reverent bow of his head. "You honor us with your presence."

The Muse glided over to Marius and offered him her hand. He bowed over it, letting his lips graze her skin.

"No, you don't," Flynn protested. "*We* don't. There's no honoring here."

She gave Marius a curtsey before glaring over her shoulder at Flynn. "At least someone knows his manners around here."

"What are you doing here?!" Flynn roared.

"Bleebie bleebie bee," she said, her face pulling into a mocking frown. The Muse rolled her eyes and turned her attention to me. Extending a hand, she said, "Charmed. I've heard a lot about you, Cat."

129

I shied away from her. "Really?"

"You solve my sister's murder and you think I'm not going to hear about it?"

Shaking her hand, I asked, "So which one are you?"

"Who am I?" The Muse spun, the gossamer of her gown flying wildly about her. As she whirled, her feet came off the ground and an ephemeral pink light poured from her skin. When she spoke again, her voice echoed with strength. "I am she who would tease out tears from your soul. She who would pluck the strings of your heart until you melt into a weeping puddle. I am the reason Meryl Streep has won so many fucking awards. I am Melpomene."

"The Mistress of Tragedy," Marius intoned.

"And you beg for it every time."

In a movement faster than I could blink, Flynn caught the hem of Melpomene's gown and yanked her to the floor. His eyes blazed down at her, and she returned the heat of his stare tenfold.

"How did you get past my wards?"

"Oh, those were supposed to keep me out? How cute."

"How. Are. You. Here?" Flynn demanded.

"I am a thought, you clueless bastard! And since that is supposedly your thing, I had no trouble slipping right in through your front door. It was as easy as coming home."

Melpomene got to her feet in a huff. Though she was a head shorter than Flynn, her presence filled the room. She lifted her chin proudly and squared off against my friend.

Flynn seethed. "Impossible."

Melpomene lifted a gentle palm to his cheek. When he flinched, the Muse tilted her head, her eyes soft and pitying. "Oh, dear Recluse... Have you forgotten so much in your time away from your kind?"

Flynn smacked her hand away. "I have no kind."

The Muse coughed, a noise that sounded remarkably like "bullshit."

"You'll have to forgive him," Marius said. "He's gone and left his manners with his sense of humor."

"Up his ass and three doors to the right?" Melpomene sniggered.

"Somewhere in that neighborhood, yes."

"Excellent."

"Why are you here, Muse?" Flynn bellowed.

"Ah!" She lifted a finger then dug in the folds of her gown. Soon her hands came up around a small silver disc—a pitch pipe. She blew into it and coaxed out a high note. After she cleared her throat, she sang, "I am your singing telegram."

The white of her billowing dress exploded into a wreath of black smoke and bloody light. Her face, so beautiful before, now appeared gaunt and withered. The sclera of her eyes melted to a glistening jet black.

"The Recluse will hide no more!" she called, her voice deep and twisted with the screams and sobs of children. "We see him, a bright star among lights in the desert playground. He will come forth. He shall deliver the traitor, or we will purge him from the sanctity of this puny demesne."

"Like hell," Flynn snarled. Power coalesced beneath the skin of his fists, and he made to lunge for Melpomene.

Marius put his hands to Flynn's chest. "She's but the messenger."

"I can send a message right back!"

"Messengers are sacred to their gods. A Muse, doubly so. Don't you know anything?"

I flinched. Marius had no clue about Flynn's true nature. Flynn—a deity of thought and intellect, a creature of technology and insight—knew the sum total of all. But he had been in hiding so long. He'd been masquerading as a technomage-bartender hybrid. Had he forgotten so much about the trappings of godhood?

The Muse's terrible voice cut through the air again. "Come forth! Embrace that which you have forsaken. We see you!"

"What is she going on about?" Marius asked, not taking his attention off Melpomene.

"And you!" Her gleaming eyes shot to Marius. "The price of your blood tips the scales. Soon your skin will hang from the halls of Hades while your shade wails for mercy. Your soul shall know only everlasting despair."

The cacophonous gale that swirled around and through the Muse abated. The shadows melted into the ether, and she floated back down to the ground. Restored but winded, she said, "Love and kisses, the lords of Olympus."

Marius pondered this, his eyes darting back and forth between Melpomene and Flynn.

"All right," Flynn snarled. "You've said your piece. Now get the fuck out of my home."

As she caught her breath, Melpomene's face twisted in an unimpressed grimace. She didn't get the chance to say whatever she'd wanted to, however. Instead, orange light flared around her and the Muse's being dissolved into citrine bubbles and sparks.

Marius gaped. He pawed through the orange haze where the Muse had been a second earlier, then wheeled on Flynn. "Do you have any idea what you've done?"

"She's fine. I just sent her back to where she belongs." Flynn turned his back on Marius, but the satyr clamped down on his shoulders and yanked him back around.

"Before we could find out exactly who sent her! What's more, you've insulted a Muse and potentially the beings she is working for. Are you really that dull? What are you to them, Flynn?"

Flynn jerked himself out of Marius's grip. He paced the room, simmering with fury, but he didn't speak.

"He's a god," I said.

My friend shot me a glare of sheer contempt, but he made no attempts to deny my words. He simmered, the orange light on his tattoos shimmering and twisting.

As Marius studied Flynn, his lips moved and his fingers danced in the air, as though he were adding up a great sum. Marius—so quick and smart—was a voyeur. He was probably remembering every interaction with Flynn and holding them up against this new revelation like a slide against light, trying to divine what it all meant.

When he'd reached some sort of conclusion, Marius addressed me. "But he's not an Olympian. I know most of them. He's not of their pantheon."

"Not of any," Flynn growled. "And now they're looking at me. I feel them, Cat. I feel their fucking eyes all over me. And he's the one that drew their attention." He jabbed a finger at Marius. "I want you gone. Now."

"What?" I asked.

Flynn stalked up to Marius and looked down his nose at the satyr. "I want you gone. I don't care where you go or what you do, but you are not welcome here. Do you understand?"

"Flynn!" I protested.

"Gone. You have one hour."

"Come on, Flynn." I followed him as far as the door, but an orange force field zapped into being inches in front of my face. When my breath splashed across it, the light pulsed and flared with the snap of power. I didn't dare touch it.

"Dammit," I muttered. "Sometimes he can be such a whiny, emo son of a bitch."

"And that bright ray of sunshine has all the power and trappings of a deity? That's what you're saying?"

I nodded.

Marius pondered that a moment. I could almost see the questions flowing through his mind. Rather than ask, he just chuffed out a breath. "He's going to get himself into worlds of trouble if he doesn't learn diplomacy."

"As long as I've known him, he's only ever learned anything the hard way."

"Something else the two of you have in common, then?"

"I guess."

I shuffled over to my bed and stared at my things thrown over the sheets. The clothes and necessities I'd meant to pack before Marius had returned. I'd been about to do anything to get to him and now that we were alone together... My mouth went dry along with any well of words. What was I supposed to say?

He seemed to be thinking the same thing. Marius stood just inside the door, hands in his pockets. The longer the silence, the deeper the lines on his forehead became.

What was he thinking about? Why was his stare so dark and intense?

Marius cut the silence with a single syllable. "Why?"

Of all the questions either of us could've asked, I hadn't expected that one. And I wasn't certain what he even meant. "Why what?"

"Why did you put yourself between me and a prince of Hell?" he asked, his voice creaking.

The reason clamped over my chest in that familiar tightness beneath the breastbone. The troublesome affection. The four-letter word. The words bubbled up into my throat but stuck there. My vision blurred with tears as I said, "I keep my promises."

Marius frowned. "Yes, you do."

In quick strides of those long legs, Marius was across the room, sweeping me into a viselike embrace. His arms locked around my shoulders, one hand cupping my head to his chest. As fiercely as he gripped me, I clutched him. I let the tears fall, let him stroke my hair.

"So stupid," he muttered as he planted a kiss on the top of my head. "So bloody stupid."

"He was going to kill you," I protested, my voice muffled by his body.

He pushed me away only far enough that he could fix me with his stare. "So you should let him kill you instead? No, Catherine. Not for me." His voice wavered as he pulled me back to his chest. His whole body tightened, and I felt his hot tears slide over my scalp. "I thought he would...you know. I thought, 'This is it. I'm over.' And I was ready for it."

I stepped back, lifting my head so I could watch him speak.

"Then I looked up and I saw you." He stroked my hair again, his expression softening with admiration. "Like a radiant, vengeful goddess coming to smite her enemies. You were beautiful. And terrifying."

That's when I remembered the golden sphere around me. The aura of light and power. Flying. Being filled with energy and life. My voice a fuller version of itself as I squared off against Belial.

"What did you do, Catherine? How?"

The memory of holding that kind of raw energy hit me, and I swayed on my feet. Marius steadied me. If I reached out now, here in Las Vegas where the well seemed infinite, could I draw that kind of power to me? I didn't dare try.

"Magic," I said.

Marius's half smile soaked into his words. "Does Flynn know?"

I shook my head. "I didn't tell him that part."

"Probably for the best. Your little trick knocked out the power all the way to Bristol. You don't do things by halves, do you?"

"What?"

He smiled down at me, eyes glistening. "Blackouts for a thirty-mile radius. Father said it took six hours for power to be restored, but otherwise, everything is fine."

"And Llyr," I asked, "is he really okay?"

"Finer than Chinese silk." His hands traced up and down my arms, massaged my shoulders. "I'm glad you're all right."

"Thanks," I said weakly. "Flynn says that if it weren't for you I'd be..."

"Ah, and just what did Flynn have to say on that subject, then?"

"That you used my key fob and got us back here. Good thinking on your part," I added.

He let out a long breath. "It was nothing. Just did what you'd have done."

"What I should've done," I said on a sigh. "I could've ported us back here the moment Belial knocked, and it would've saved a lot of heartache."

His fingers were feather-light as they drifted up over my collarbones, down to my chest. He paused just over the bullet wound.

"Heartache," he whispered. "Is that what this is?"

My belly quivered with a thousand puking butterflies. The distance between us, though little more than the width of a hand, was too much. If I couldn't find a home in the circle of his arms, I thought I might shake myself to pieces. While part of me longed to dive into him and never leave the safety of his embrace, another part of me argued that this was *Marius*. Could waking up next to him erase all the sins he'd committed? What did it matter if he was an arrogant, lecherous, smug bastard if just being near him made this terrible sadness ebb away even a fraction of an inch?

I opened my mouth to speak, but he shushed me with a gesture. When he spoke his voice was insistent but gentle. "No. Before you say anything, I need to tell you..." He let out an uneasy laugh. "I don't see why it should be difficult, and yet I don't know that I've ever truly said it. And certainly not to you. I... Thank you, Catherine. You've given me more than I deserve." His hand lingered over the hole in my chest. "Too much."

His gaze dropped to the floor, and his jaw worked.

"What aren't you saying?" I asked.

He blew out a long, tense breath. "We're done."

SEVENTEEN

"MULTIPLY THE HEARTACHES"

It would've hurt less if Marius had whacked me in the stomach with a sledgehammer. The breath flew out of me, and I deflated. His hand fell away, and he turned his back to me. That's when the wound began to sting.

"What?" I growled. "What did you say?"

His shoulders hunched forward. From the other side of the chasm between us, his voice was soft, gentle, and sad. "We're done, Catherine."

"Just like that?"

"Yes," he said, turning to face me, not bothering to wipe the tears from his reddened eyes. "I'm ending our agreement. You..." He swallowed something and took my hands. "You go your way, and I'll go mine. You owe me nothing."

"Bullshit," I simmered.

"Go home."

"Bullshit!" My voice was shrill and echoed off the low ceiling.

Marius flinched.

I tossed his hands away and paced my own angry circle, dragging my hands through my hair. "You think I'm supposed to just, what? Walk upstairs like nothing happened? Maybe have a drink with Flynn and make my way home. Feed the cat. Fix a computer. Then what, Marius?"

He wheeled on me, his eyes blazing green fire. "Live your life! The one that almost ended because I was stupid enough to drag you into my problems."

"Oh no," I said. "You aren't going to pull this shit. We had a deal."

"That was before..."

"You need my help."

"And just how will your death help me? Did you plan on sprouting wings and becoming my guardian angel or some bollocks like that? Why are you so keen to fight me on this? My idiot brother shot you after a prince of Hell came to collect my head."

"My head, actually, or were you not paying attention?"

"*Loki* killed Moloch. Not you."

"And I helped! A lot! For fucksake, you're not the only one with problems. This is what people do, you know? They help one another. They take risks and get the job done, not because of deals or some scorecard but because they care."

"Stop," he hissed. "Don't lecture me."

"Apparently you need one. Do you think that right this second I care about what I may or may not owe you? Or what you owe me?"

"I can't watch you die!" he shouted. The room became still as a coiled snake. Marius looked to the floor, and I pretended not to watch tears trickle over his cheeks and into his goatee. "Remember what I told you about my sisters? How they were mortal and it was just part of my life to watch them grow old and fade away? I can't... I've never... Look, most of the time, I deal with others like me. Immortals. At the very least creatures gifted with longevity. They all want something. They all have designs or ambitions. I have partners and business contacts. And then there's you."

My chest tightened, and my cheeks flushed with heat as Marius pinched the bridge of his nose. Still avoiding me, he sat on the bed. His stare was fixed on the crimson stain of my blood.

"Stubborn. Smart. Witty," he went on. "You have the ears of the gods and you've probably never even thought about asking any of them for something like a better apartment or car, money or fame. No, none of that means a damn thing to you. Because you're different." His fingers grazed the dried blood. "In your short, stupid little life you've had *more* than I have had in too many centuries. More friendship, trust, joy, and..." His voice trailed off as he measured his words. "And just when I realize what I've got, you go and try to die on me. Quite literally *on* me. It's one thing to ruin my clothing, but Flynn's now, too?"

He let out a weak laugh, but I couldn't. Shaking, I stood rooted to the spot. What was he saying? What was he keeping from me? He composed himself, that terrible honesty deepening the shadows of his face.

"I've found something in you that I've never had before. Lovers? Conquests? Partners and contacts? None of them are like you." He met my eyes, and my blood began to boil. There was something there, something unsaid. He went back to worrying the damn sheets. "I know you find me repellent and tolerate me on the best of days, but I...I've found..."

Heat rose to my cheeks and with it came an inability to breathe. He was on the verge of saying it. Whatever secret he'd been trying to keep, it was almost to the surface.

"What have you found?" I asked.

"A friend."

I winced. *Friend.*

"It's bad enough to know that even if you go the rest of your days without a single problem—which is impossible, because you're *you* and always find trouble—I'll still live to watch you die. I can't stand it, Catherine. I can't stand to see my friend put herself in such dire jeopardy for me."

I blew out a long, disappointed breath and dragged my hands through my hair. "Jesus Christ, you're a moron."

Marius blinked at me, mouth working but not saying anything. Score one for me for rendering him speechless, if only for a moment.

"I'm sorry?"

"You're a goddamn idiot, Marius. Yes, I'm mortal and my life is short. News flash, asshole: I've known that the whole time!"

He hung his head. The satyr looked weary, wrung out. I padded over, squatted in front of him, and balanced my elbows on his knees.

"Hey," I said, giving him a poke. "Let me put it to you this way... Do you really think that it would be any easier for *me* to watch *you* die? Hmm?" With one finger, I lifted his chin so that he had to look at me. I shook my head. "Not really."

Taking my hand into his, Marius laid a kiss on my palm. Closing his eyes, he drew in a deep breath and let it slowly out. His shoulders relaxed, and I knew I'd won.

"So what's next?" I asked. "What do we do now?"

"We," Marius mused to himself. "Odd word, that... Right. Flynn wants me gone, so I should make myself scarce."

I motioned to my bag. "It'll take me less than five minutes to be ready to blow this place. You have a destination in mind?"

"Greece."

It felt like my blood drained from my body. "Isn't that... Aren't there people hell-bent on killing you in Greece?"

"Let's face it. There are people hell-bent on killing me everywhere. Our visit from the Muse left me with a few questions, though."

"Such as?"

"How many of the lords of Olympus were signatories on that little telegram? I have a friend or two in that pantheon, and I'd like to know whom I can trust. Flynn was too hot on the trigger. I didn't get my answers."

"Can we find a safe spot?"

"If my ally is where I left him, yes. Are you sure you want to take this risk with me, Catherine? I'll not deny that what I'm about to do is foolhardy and could end very badly for me. You don't need to come."

"No, I don't," I admitted.

And it was true. I didn't. But I couldn't let him go alone. I couldn't turn away someone I'd come to l...like intensely. I needed to be near him. For my own sanity, I needed to be close to Marius, to his warmth. I needed to know that he would survive, and if I could be a part of ensuring that he made it through this gauntlet, I'd go to Greece with him just as easily as I'd gone to Glastonbury.

But I couldn't tell him that. The words wouldn't form.

I dragged my hands down my face, feeling utterly exhausted. "All right. To Greece we go. Any clue as to how we're traveling?"

He fell back on the mattress. "Bugger, there's that to consider. I'm not going Flynn's way, I can tell you that much."

"Tummy trouble?" I snickered. He lifted two fingers in response. "As much as he wants you out of here, I doubt he'd help with that anyway. There's my fob, but it will only get us back here. What about your pipes?"

"Not a particularly viable option at this point. I can use them to get us to a very specific place on the mainland, but then we'd be stuck in the middle of nowhere without a way to get to the islands. Mortal transport is out, too," he added.

"Why's that?"

Propping himself up on his elbows, Marius gave me a level stare. "Most of a day spent in a fragile tin can, the majority of that time suspended over open water when there are several deities and minions hunting me? What could possibly go wrong?"

"Noted. Well, what does that leave us?"

He fell back again. "There is one other way, I suppose, but I'd rather not rely on it."

Frustrated, I snapped, "Running out of options here."

"I know, I know. It's just that it comes with its own set of problems."

I indulged myself in stroking a hand through his glossy hair. His shoulders tensed, and he gasped, a shudder rippling through his core. I softened my tone to one of affectionate, playful mockery. "Well you're involved, so yes, there are problems."

He scrunched up his face at me, but I tossed him one of his cocksure smiles and raised an eyebrow in challenge.

"Fine. Pack your things. We're going back to the storage shed."

We hitched a quick cab ride home to feed Linux and ask Mrs. M to make sure he was taken care of for a few days. Then we hopped back in the cab and made our way to the storage unit across town. When we hauled up the door to the shed, I was pleased to see that my car was still there, if occupied. Malcolm sat on the hood, his knees up to his chest.

"There you are!" he called.

"How did you find me here?" Marius asked, clearly defensive.

Mal slid down to the pavement and swaggered toward us. Bruises painted the right side of his face with dark purples and wan yellows, and his right eye drooped.

"Blood calls to blood." When Marius tossed his brother a *Tell me no bullshit* stare, Mal said, "D'ya think I'm a complete twat? I knew she'd have to come back for her car at some point."

"Wow," I said. "Not as dumb as you look."

He stuffed his hands in his pockets and dropped his eyes to the ground. "I deserve that," he said sheepishly. "I just want you to know that I'm sorry. I didn't mean to... I mean, I wasn't aiming for..."

"Skip it," I said. "I know what happened. Just one thing... A shotgun for the door? A pistol that got me? Where the hell did you get the guns?"

"Ah." He bounced on the balls of his feet and tossed his hair. "Right. That would be a long story involving me and the IRA. I'd be happy to tell it to you over dinner some time."

"Fuck no."

"Didn't think so," Mal muttered. He flashed me a smile and a cheeky wink. "Can't blame a bloke for tryin', though."

"I can," I said, voice hard.

"What are you doing here, Mal?" Marius asked.

"And what the hell happened to your face?" I added.

Marius leaned close and murmured, "He was born like that."

Ignoring the gibe, Mal explained, "Ah, well, Dad was a little upset with me, as you can imagine. What with mistaking a prince of Hell for him, and luring you two into a trap, and the fire, and blood, and... Well, we were all there, weren't we? Let's just draw a veil over that. Anyway, he sent me along to apologize and offer my help in any way you might have need of me." He turned those icy-blue eyes on me. "And I do mean *any* way you need me, Cat."

"You'll be the first one to know, Mal," I said drily.

"I know something you can do," Marius said, a smile rippling over his face. "Perhaps you can give us a ride to Greece."

Mal snorted. "Are you kidding me? Dad sent me here with the sole of his boot. I'm on me own as far as getting home and anything else."

"Damn!" Marius kicked at the floor.

"Can't you just use your keys?" I asked.

Marius shook his head. "They would take me to the Temple, and I'm not certain that's a wise choice of destinations at the moment."

Mal nodded. "Aye. Where were you thinkin' of puttin' down?"

"Santorini," Marius answered. "I've got a friend there who owes me a favor."

"I thought you said you had a way to get there," I cut in.

Marius hemmed and hawed as he strode to the back corner of the storage locker. "Yes, about that," he said. "Mal, be useful and make sure we've not been followed, then close up."

While Malcolm silently obliged his brother, I followed Marius to where he stood. He passed his hand over the floor, and once again the rectangle of verdant light opened in the concrete. The gurgling sound of water and the birdsong reminded me of the sweet solace I'd known just before waking up in my room below YmFy.

Don't, I admonished myself. *Don't think about that. You can't go back.*

As Marius sealed the portal again, I was left with a feeling of cold longing. I felt like a hole, empty and alone.

"Need to make it quick," my satyr ordered tersely. "If I'm going to do this, it's going to need to be fast, lest Eris show up and ruin an otherwise lovely day."

He breezed past me, a bag on his shoulder and a cloth in his hands.

I put a hand on Marius's arm. "What are we doing?"

He unfolded the cloth in his hand to reveal...well, the only word for it is *bling*. A braided gold chain sporting an ostentatiously large amulet. Diamonds on it spelled out *Player*.

I cleared my throat to stifle my laughter. "Um. Flavor Flav called."

"Disgusting, isn't it?" He flipped the amulet over, and I saw Eris's mark—the golden apple. "It's one of her more overt insults."

"What is it? I mean, other than gaudy with a capital *Oh My Gawd*?"

His lip hitched into a half smile. "You know how Eris used me as a thief and a spy? Well, do you think she would send me hither and yon by mortal means?"

"That cheap bitch? Hell no."

"Precisely. And I certainly wasn't about to let her know that I had pipes created by Pan himself. The less she knew about my bloodline the better. So this," he said hefting the necklace, "was something she concocted for me to get from Point A to Point B quickly and without detection."

"And the *Player*?" I asked, suppressing a laugh.

"It changes over time to be as embarrassing as possible."

With the jarring sound of metal against stone, the locker closed behind us. Mal peered over his brother's shoulder. "Nice. Can I borrow that sometime?"

I snorted.

"No matter how repugnant I find you, Malcolm, I would never wish this curse upon you," Marius said. He looped the necklace over his head. His eyes darted left and right before focusing on a point in front of us.

"All right," Marius said, steeling himself. He took up my hand and grabbed Malcom by the wrist. "Whatever you do, whatever you see or hear, do *not* let go."

"Okay. What do we do?"

"We walk."

As one, the three of us took a step. Reality swept past us in a blur of buildings, lights, and people. I heard the wail of sirens, the roar of flames, and the squalling of a baby's first cry. The smell of car exhaust and gasoline, and burning rubber reached my nose.

Another step... The muggy air of the bayou clung to my skin, and the swamp pulled at my shoes. The sun was low in the sky, its blood dripping over the horizon. Laughter and an acoustic guitar met my ears only to be replaced by the meaty smack of fist against flesh.

Another step... Velvety night. Perfect darkness except for the waning moon and the Milky Way. Salt spray on my cheeks and waves beneath my feet. I looked down to see I was walking on starlight. At least that's what it looked like as the water shifted and reflected the jewel-encrusted sky. The head of a whale peeked up through the foam before exhaling a plume of mist.

Another step... Firelight and golden dunes. Footsteps in the sand. Camels lowing in the night. The crack of gunfire and the peal of a hundred voices being raised in triumph.

Another step...

The strange whip of motion and sound stopped abruptly. The three of us stood on a beach now, the water reaching up to caress the black sand in rhythmic teasing strokes. I felt the ebb and flow in my own blood. In a matter of seconds, my breathing matched the steady in and out of the ocean.

Though it must have been nearly midnight, the beach was awash with golden light. Torches lined a path along the strand, and a series of resorts rose up behind us. Like a thousand fireflies, windows glowed with the soft flickers of candlelight.

"Damn," Marius hissed. "I forgot about the time difference."

Mal's face was pale, his eyes wide and haunted. "What... Where are we?"

"Santorini, Greece," Marius explained.

"How did we get here?"

"We walked." When Mal and I both gaped at him for further detail, Marius added, "You know the term *Godspeed*? Well, congratulations. You just experienced it. God-stepping is not easy on the mind, but it gets the job done." He yanked the chain from around his neck. "Do you have that key fob with you?"

"Yeah," I answered. "Why?"

"Making sure I'm not about to burn our ships." Marius whirled the necklace over his head and flung it out to the sea. He watched the gold amulet sail into the night and fall into the water, his face grim. When he spoke, his voice was heavy and dark with loathing. "Let her stew on that for a bit."

"What are you talking about?" I asked.

Marius turned on his heel and began trudging up the slope of the beach toward the resorts. "Well, if she's breathing, Eris is going to know I used her charm. She will also know where I am. But in coming to Greece, I leave her to wonder why I would dare do something so foolish. What's more, I've just left the amulet in a very, shall we say, strategic place."

"And so now she's wondering if you've found an ally and would use her necklace just as a *fuck you*," I guessed.

Marius's smile was a lupine promise. "Or worse. Did I just set a trap for her?"

I imagined Eris sitting in her office—or whatever dank pit the bitch called home—and fuming because her Spidey-sense was atingle. I hoped it burned. Knowing that right at this moment she might be squirming or tugging at her own mousy hair with frustration made me happier than I'd been since I'd died.

Looping my arm around his, I pressed up to Marius, unable to suppress the gleeful laugh. "Oh, I love this. Can we keep fucking with Eris while we're here?"

"All in good time," he said warmly.

EIGHTEEN

"THE DISTANCE"

As it turned out, we'd arrived on the volcanic island of Thira—now commonly called Santorini—sometime around three in the morning. When we strolled into the lobby, a very groggy-looking concierge greeted us in Greek. Without missing a beat, Marius responded in kind and a melodic conversation began. The concierge's fingers flew over the computer keyboard. A couple of smacks on the space bar and he turned his dark eyes up to Marius, his expression contrite.

"I have rabid badgers in my pants," he said.

Well, okay, that's not what he said. Probably. I have no clue what Marius and this guy were saying to each other. It sounded pretty, though, and the concierge seemed friendly enough as he lifted his hands in the international gesture of, *There's nothing I can do.*

Marius flashed his signature smirk and held up a finger, urging the young man to hold on a moment. My satyr fished through his bag and came up with a black credit card. He slid it over the counter, and the concierge's eyes widened. Staring at Marius as if he'd just found himself standing in the presence of royalty, the concierge gaped, his mouth working like that of a drowning fish.

The young man's eyes darted between me and Mal as his fingers beat out a furious rhythm on the keyboard. When the computer answered him, the clerk reported his findings to Marius. He nodded, and the clerk swiped the credit card.

"Care to enlighten the savages?" I asked.

Marius kept his cool, aloof demeanor as he turned to me. "I asked them for three rooms, but it turns out they have only two left. Mal and I will share one. You can have the other."

I shrank a little, and even as I did, I yelled at myself. I didn't want to share a room with Marius, did I? Even if I did, no good could come of it. Stupid Cat.

I bobbed my head and stepped back, letting Marius finish up. Soon, the concierge handed Marius two key cards. Indicating one of them, he pointed down the slope to the left—back the way we'd come. Marius asked a question, and when he approved of the answer, he put the key card into his pocket. My satyr gestured to me with the other key and said something to the clerk.

"Of course," the concierge said in accented English. "I'd be happy to show your lady friend to the suite."

"Thank you," Marius said. He turned to me and pressed the plastic key card into my hand. "Go get settled in. Mal and I are in villa number three. If you need anything, Andreas here will take care of it. I'll be by in a bit, all right?"

I glanced at the desk clerk. He stood a few feet away, his hands clasped at his waist. He gave me a slight bow and an unassuming smile. I nodded to Marius. "All right."

"Excellent." Marius brushed a lock behind my ear and placed a kiss on my temple. His fingers lingered a moment over my hair before he stepped away. "Come on, Mal. We're this way."

Mal eyed us, his thick brows shoved together with consternation. Rather than pick whatever fight was brewing in his mind, Mal shrugged and followed his brother out into the warm predawn. As I watched them leave, my stomach twisted. I didn't want Marius out of my sight. What if something happened to him? What if Eris showed up and I wasn't there?

The concierge cleared his throat, jarring me back to the moment in a world where people didn't know about satyrs being real or needing to run from vengeful goddesses.

"This way, Miss," Andreas said with a subdued wave of his hand.

Andreas led me outside, around a winding path, and up a tight stone staircase. Soft amber lights dotted the ground, their glow bouncing off the white walls like torchlight. This resort, I soon found, was not like anything in Vegas. I was used to layer upon layer of identical rooms reaching in a tower to the sky. Here, though, the suites climbed the slope of the volcano in a hodgepodge arrangement. Where the casinos on the Strip kept everything under one roof, the resort basked beneath the open dome of the night. Each suite was its own tiny dwelling. Looking around, I noticed a balcony with a private, jewel-bright pool. To my left was a terrace with simple furniture and umbrellas, which were folded for the night. Even at this hour, lights burned on the patios and cobbled walkways.

Andreas opened a small, thigh-high gate and gestured me through. "Your suite, Miss."

I nodded gratefully and took the few remaining steps to the door. Andreas's soft footfalls receded into the darkness as he returned to his post.

I let myself in, throwing the security lock behind me. When I switched on the light, my breath caught in my chest.

The room was the lovechild of a spa retreat and a honeymoon suite. An oval-shaped desk sat to one side of the room. Above it was a flat-screen television. Across the stone floor was a squat plush chair. Unlike the furnishings in Vegas, this actually looked *comfortable*. The queen-size bed—an inviting square of fluffy white pillows and pristine coverlets—stood in its own alcove behind a sage-green curtain drawn to one side.

The crowning glory of the suite, however, lay beyond the sliding door. Sheer curtains brushed past me in the light, sea-scented breeze as I stepped out onto my private patio. A chaise lounge with a mountain of pillows upon it reclined a few feet away from my private Jacuzzi. Its gin-clear water sparkled and beckoned me to sink in and rest my weary soul.

Glancing up, I took in the view. Santorini lay within a volcanic crater, and we were on the inside of the bowl. Other resorts climbed the slope of the crater. And down below it all, far beneath the ocean surface, the volcano slept. Rather than curl up on the chaise and glut myself on the spectacular scenery, I hitched my duffel bag on my shoulder and took it into the bedroom where I started unpacking. I was almost finished when a knock came on my door.

"Coming," I called.

When I opened the door, Marius stood smiling down at me. "All settled?"

"Just about." I flopped my arm as an invitation that he should come in.

Hands in his pockets, he turned in a circle and took in the room. "Quaint little retreat," he said. "Surprised you're not out there partaking of the hot tub."

I sighed and swept back to the bed "Didn't think to pack a bathing suit."

"Shame you'd let that stop you," he said, his voice giving an appreciative purr.

I snorted. "Yeah, right. Not out there for the whole island to see." With the slam of a drawer, I stowed the last of my things in the bureau. Finally alone with Marius again, I had a million questions, but all the big ones got stuck in my throat.

"So," my voice cracked, "who are we meeting? Please tell me it's not another family reunion."

With a sidelong smile, he sauntered out to the balcony. The Mediterranean breeze tossed his hair from his face. He closed his eyes and drew in a long breath. "Not family. Well, not by blood, anyway. We had good times together, though. Damn, it seems like so long ago..."

"Please tell me you're not banking your life on this guy's sense of nostalgia."

"Of course not." Marius's laughter was a lazy melody. Low and easy, unforced. Honest. "No, Hephaestus knows all too well what it's like to be an outsider without a tribe."

"That's great, but can we trust that Heph— Wait." I waved at the air, trying to make sense of what I'd just heard.

Hephaestus, God of the Forge of Olympus?

The myths said he was gruff, lame, and quick to anger. So great was his mythical wrath, that his tantrums rumbled up from his volcanic demesne in the form of catastrophic eruptions. And we were going to meet up with him and ask a favor?

Despite run-ins with gods, angels, and princes of Hell, the prospect scared the shit out of me. I gulped down my fear. "Hephaestus? The god? We're meeting Hephaestus?"

Marius nodded. "Already sent him my calling card, so to speak. Just waiting for him to respond."

I stomped to his side, suddenly very afraid that we'd made a huge, suicidal mistake. "Are you crazy? You heard the Muse! She said the lords of Olympus sent that love note. You know that part about your skin hanging from the halls of Hades? How can you want to visit one of them?"

"Heph has no love for most of his brethren," Marius said, casually adding, "especially after he and Aphrodite split up. I am confident that he had nothing to do with that little message."

"And you know how to find him?"

The satyr gave me a capricious smile and turned his gaze out to the ocean. "That's his home. Deep beneath the waves in the belly of the crater."

"And you're sure we're safe here? So close to him, right in plain sight of a shit ton of people who want you dead?"

"Eris will know we're here, but she'll be scrambling to suss out Heph's motives, as well as mine. If I'm wrong about him, if Hephaestus calls down judgment, I need you to take Malcolm and use the fob."

"And just leave you?"

"If I've lost my ally in Hephaestus, there will be nothing to stop Zeus from taking me straight to Hades."

Marius kept his gaze fixed on the sea. Leaning forward, he rested his forearms on the patio wall. His shoulders slouched, and his face relaxed. He closed his eyes and took in the scent of the Mediterranean, seeming to savor it.

Starlight painted bluish streaks in his lush hair as he beamed at the moon, and for the first time since he showed up at my apartment, Marius looked truly carefree.

Frustrated, I swatted at his arm. "How the hell can you be so calm?"

"This is my home," he answered, awe in his voice. Sparing me a glance, he added, "Oh, sure, I was born near Glastonbury, but I never felt like I belonged there. I needed to see more. Do more. Know more. I felt like I was too young to put down roots like Father had."

"Or like Mal?"

He bobbed one shoulder in a half shrug. "Mal—for all his foibles—lives a decent life, I suppose. It's simple. He needn't question things around him or work too hard for his pleasures. And it's enough for him."

"Whereas you're insatiable." I smiled.

He gave a light laugh. "In every possible way."

I sidled up beside him so we stood arm to arm. His body was a warm, golden hum against me. "So you came here?"

"Well, not at first. I traveled the Continent for a bit. France, Spain. Spent a fair amount of time in Italy. When I came to Greece, though..." Marius's eyes went out of focus as he searched for words. "Before I'd been so restless, so frenzied. But here... For the first time in my life I felt...calm."

My belly quivered. I knew what he meant. I knew exactly how he felt. Had been wrestling with that same awkwardness since I woke up at YmFy earlier that day.

"It's like there's all this background noise in life," I said. "Fear and to-do lists, all the what-ifs and buts. Right? And then there's this one perfect place where it all just stops."

Marius's stare met mine with an electric snap that shot through my core. "There's silence."

"Peace."

"Yes," he said, voice little more than a soft breath between us.

"I know what that's like," I said.

"Do you? Where does your soul feel at peace, Catherine?"

Despite the fact that my guts were fluttering with nerves, I smiled. Maybe I could explain what it had been like to die, to wake up safe in his arms. Maybe I could confess that my Fortress of Solitude couldn't be found on a map but in another person.

As I opened my mouth to tell him, fear clamped on my stomach and all that came out was a weak cough that quickly morphed into nervous laughter. "YmFy." The half-truth oozed out of me easy as any lie I'd ever told. "I found it at YmFy."

The sparkle of anticipation drained out of his eyes. "Ah." He stood upright and turned his gaze back to the ocean. As I watched, he seemed to slip back into his glamour. Not the spell that masked his satyr heritage. No, his hardened, aloof exterior. For a moment I'd been granted access to the soft, *real* Marius.

I wanted to reach past that barrier, to peer into him a little longer. "Where's yours? I mean, is it just Greece, or is there a specific place?"

"There is a place," he murmured to the sea. "It's on the mainland in Arcadia."

"Tell me about it?"

As he stared into the night, Marius's voice took on a reverent tone I'd rarely heard from him. "The Temple of Pan is in the woods there. Its door is carved into a cliff side. Not too far downslope, a small tributary of the Neda River pools to form a lagoon. For a long time the only ones who knew about it were the satyrs and nymphs. We'd play our pipes and the dryads would dance.

"The water," he continued, "is cool and crystal clear. Sweet on the tongue. In some ways it was better than wine."

"Wow," I said, genuinely impressed. "Water better than wine? To you?"

"Amazing, isn't it?"

"Go on."

"Sometimes I'd go there alone. The nymphs would have been off, other satyrs lazing in their homes or the fields. Very rarely would I get the place all to myself, but when I did, Catherine, it was like...something holy. Sacred. The wind would whisper through the trees, shaking blossoms down into the water, and the flower petals would ride the tiny waves created by the waterfall.

"And there used to be this boulder covered in moss. I'd sit upon it and play my pipes. It was in those moments when the questions stopped. Those noises, as you say, vanished. I knew peace."

His face was drawn with longing. He pined for this pool in the woods, yes, but I saw a sadness in his eyes that wished for more. Perhaps the simplicity of that time long ago when the world was nothing more than music, sex, and a serene lagoon.

"Can we go there?" I asked.

He winced ever so slightly. "As much as I would like to visit Grandfather's temple—pay my respects, as it were—and play a few notes by the waterfall, I don't think it would be wise."

"Why?"

He blew out a breath. "The Sileni."

Those four syllables triggered something in my memory, and my intestines pitched.

The scent of brimstone, a muffled ringing in my ears. Fear, acrid and bitter in my mouth. Llyr's eyes flashing a warning. "Take the boys and run with them. Run home. Then find the Sileni. It's very important that you remember this name."

As if I were clawing my way back up from the abyss of Hell itself, I gripped the balcony wall and willed myself back into the moment, to the cool Grecian night. Like a relic of my trip, a burning souvenir, the word came out of my mouth in a hoarse whisper.

"Sileni."

Tell Marius, Llyr had said.

I'd opened my mouth to do just that when Marius growled, "Murderers."

"What?"

He brooded there, smoldering, his jaw tightening with anger. Before he could go on, there was a knock on my door.

Mal's voice was muffled. "Oi!"

Marius gave me a wan, half-assed smile and said, "Never mind." He pushed away from the balcony wall and stalked across the room to let his brother in.

"Mal, I told you I'd be back in a bit," he said as he whipped open the door.

The younger satyr stood there looking very much like a contrite puppy. "I know, and I'd be in me own bed dreamin' of loose women and tight clothes, but he said if I didn't give y' this, he'd have me hide. And I've had just about enough of getting me face punched in so I didn't want to wait for you."

"Who said what now?" I asked.

"Big bloke. Dark. Didn't catch his name but he gave me this. Said Marius would know what it meant."

Mal held up a small metallic sphere no bigger than a billiard ball. Its surface gleamed, casting back warped reflections of the room. Something about it called to me, plucked the strings of my strange senses.

I took a step forward, reached out to stroke the smooth silver. "What is it?"

Marius stilled me with a gesture of his hand. He plucked the ball from Mal's hands and examined it. "That was fast," he whispered.

His breath fogged the nearest side of the orb, and the enigmatic thing melted. A small flame erupted above Marius's fingers with the scent of ash and molten metal. He jerked away, and as he did, I thought I saw a grinning face within the fire. A *whoosh* of air and the fireball snuffed itself out. The smoke dissipating in thin wisps and tendrils, and the room filled with a man's low, jovial laughter.

Mal's eyes were wide as saucers. "Can't a bloke go five minutes without all your hocus pocus bullshit? I'm done. I'm going back to me room where I can drink m'self senseless."

"Coward," Marius called as the door slammed shut behind Malcolm.

"And that was...?" I prodded.

Marius dusted his hands over his jeans. "That was an invitation. Up for visiting the Forge?"

NINETEEN

"LONG TIME"

When someone asks you if you're up for meeting a god, you say... well, you should probably say no, because nothing good ever comes of that. Me, though? That ship had long since sailed.

Marius and I walked down to the beach. The sand, dimpled by our footsteps, shone silver beneath the light of the moon. The night was still, eerily quiet save for the peaceful respiration of the tide and the water lapping gently at our feet.

"Where are you, old friend?" he mumbled to himself, eyes casting out to the open water.

"Playing hide-and-go-seek, Marius?" a voice asked from behind us.

Her voice was like nails on the chalkboard of my soul, grating to the point of nausea. It had been featured in more than a few of my nightmares—real and imagined—over the years. I would know it anywhere.

Eris.

Marius's mustache twitched with a similar reaction. Then he closed his eyes, resigned, and turned slowly in the sand. I followed suit, and when I looked, the shadows rippled to reveal Discord's lupine smile.

"Lady," Marius said, his tone bitter and cold.

Eris's lips spread wide over her too-white teeth as she stepped into the moonlight. The goddess hadn't changed in the past few years. Her skin still clung to her bones in pasty wrinkles. She wore a black caftan belted at her waist. Rather than form a figure, the garment only emphasized her withered physique. The Mistress of Strife resembled the skeleton of a mountain range—craggy, sharp, and brittle.

She tilted her head with birdlike curiosity. "Expecting me, Marius?"

He shook his head. "But I'm not surprised to see you."

"Pity. The look of shock on your face when I removed your mark was simply delicious. I was hoping for another serving."

Marius glowered at her, but the goddess only smiled.

"And Catherine Sharp," she said cheerfully, bringing her hands together with glee. "It's been an eternity if it's been a day since I set eyes upon you."

Meeting her golden stare, I felt a snarl building in my throat. "And what truly glorious days those have been."

"You've not missed me? Not even a little?"

I snorted. "I've missed you like a woman misses a pap smear."

Marius's hand was a warm warning against my wrist. "Catherine," he said gently, "mind your tongue."

"Pay him no heed, Miss Sharp. I'd love to hear what you'd say to me. Now that I have no sway over your soul, surely you have a few choice words you've been aching to unleash for a long time."

Boy, did I...

How do I loathe thee? Let me count the ways.

"She is baiting you," Marius whispered in my ear. "Do not let her."

He was right. Loki might hold the deed to my soul, but Eris still had her own power. I would be a fool to forget that. I drew a breath and tried to will my malice into the sand.

"What do you want of us, Lady?" Marius asked with trepidation.

Her wintry laughter cut over the ocean, jarring the serene Grecian night. "Of you? Oh, satyr. It is enough for me to know you suffer. Both of you," she added, piercing me with her glare. "In your own time, you've each made a fool of me. And for that, I wish you nothing but sorrow. I relish the thought that Catherine will meet the same fate as you, Marius, seeing as she's yoked herself with you. The pair of you torn apart by those who crave vengeance. Two naughty birds with one stone."

An electric hum brought the hairs on my arms to attention. I squinted at the goddess. Her golden eyes shimmered queerly, and the ether around her quivered.

She's drawing power, I realized. I inhaled some of the energy pumping through the resorts, preparing my own defense.

She must have sensed it, because Eris raised both hands to her chest, as if she were holding a ball. Black lightning arced between her clawlike fingers.

At the same moment, we attacked.

I stomped one foot, and a wall of sand flew up between us. The goddess's lightning struck my flimsy barrier, and with a flash of greenish light, the sand transformed to glass. It hovered there, and I punched the air, sending out a pulse of my own power. The glass shattered and propelled forward into the goddess's ugly face. She screamed and brought up her sinewy arms to shield herself. I pressed my advantage. Bringing both hands up with a sweeping gesture that mimicked the ocean's rolling waves, I gathered more energy. As the movement crested, I thrust my hands at Eris. A gout of white light and seawater shot toward her as if I'd unleashed all the fury of a fire hose, but she dodged it.

I blinked. *Water? That's not supposed to happen.*

The moment of hesitation cost me. Quick as a viper, Eris lunged for me, teeth bared in a hungry snarl. I groped for the singing electricity of Santorini, and the island answered immediately. Power flooded me, and I didn't even have to say please.

The next strike came not from Eris and her outstretched claws but from the side. Marius's body barreled into mine, sending me off my feet. I tumbled to the sand, the power ebbing away and flowing out with the tide.

"Son of a bitch," I hissed.

Marius had drawn his sword. He whirled the blade, snagging Eris's flowing caftan. This was no more than a puppy nipping at her heels, but she followed him, turning her back to me. Eris seethed, shoulders hunched and hands flexing as if imagining what it would feel like to take the satyr's throat in her hands.

I slowly moved to get to my feet. A hand reached out of the night and pressed against my shoulder, the weight of it heavy as the world. Instantly, the touch dampened that glorious, heady sensation of drinking in power.

"Be still, girl," said a low male voice.

My gaze searched the area, but I could hardly make out the features of the newcomer. He wore the night like a second skin. Then the shadows shifted and I caught a glimpse of his other hand, fingers splayed, aimed at Marius.

"No," I choked out.

"Hush now!"

Intent on working some badass-fu and getting this guy off me, I grabbed the hand pressing me down and gasped. Cold and solid as rock, each digit was as large as two of my own. Whoever he was, the guy was a landmass.

In an instant, his features lit up—a hint of silvery eyes and a rugged jaw—illuminated by orange fire. I jumped and turned my attention to the sudden ignition. Marius's saber blazed, flames caressing the blade. In all the times I'd seen him fight with this particular sword, I'd never witnessed this. Marius's eyes widened only slightly, and it was that brief expression that told me he hadn't expected to see his sword do that, either.

Eris, however, could not hide her surprise. She went stock-still, her face a mask of horrified confusion.

Beside me, the night stirred with a barely audible laugh.

"Something vexes thee, Lady?" Marius asked coolly.

"Marius," Eris said, her voice thin and high with fear, "have you gone and learned a new trick?"

When he spoke, his voice was as hard and unwavering as his stare. "Oh, this?" He indicated the flames wreathing his sabre. "Just something I picked up somewhere."

Slowly, the two stalked each other in a tight circle with the deadly ferocity of jungle cats. Eris recovered her wits, and with a malicious smile, she reassumed her poker face. Marius—oh, my Marius—regarded the goddess with stony resolve. The fire licking up from his sword cast his features in ever-shifting shadows and patterns like war paint.

"And what of you?" Marius asked. "This is rather out of your character."

"Is it?"

He was right. Eris was rarely one to go on an outright attack. She preferred to strike through others—like me or Marius—and watch the fallout. What was she doing coming at us full frontal?

"Do you see?" the hulking mass to my left whispered. "Her spell is weak."

I tried to focus but couldn't suss out what the stranger meant.

"Doing your own dirty work for a change, Lady?" Marius asked. "That is rather unlike you."

"A few lashes here and there are rather fun for me, vermin." Eris stopped her wary circle and fixed Marius with her cold stare. "Could it be that you've found another benefactor? And so quickly."

"Perhaps you were simply too quick to dismiss me," Marius sang.

"I dismissed you for far too long, satyr." Her tone was charred beneath the heat of her loathing. "I believed you to be nothing more than a wastrel, a fool. No one betrays me and goes unscathed."

She lashed out, her fury arcing in the night like a whip made of that black lightning. Marius parried the strike with his blade. Her power sizzled and cracked at her side as they continued their dance.

The weight lifted from my shoulder. The sand beside me was empty, save for a large impression where the stranger had been. Turning my attention back to Marius and Eris, I slowly got to my feet and put my back to the ocean.

"There is no one," she said finally, resuming her pacing. "Is there, Marius? This flash and dazzle is a parlor trick, not a divine gift from a new master. You've found nothing but a fool." She spared me a wicked glance. "A meager mage."

"An ally," Marius countered, cutting a tighter arc in his circuit. He was closing in on Eris and drawing her away from me. "Someone who knows exactly what it's like to be tethered to a bitch like you."

Pride swelled in my chest. I'd never heard him openly insult Discord before.

She lashed out again. He responded with another a swipe of his sword, batting away the crackling power she wielded.

"You're no closer to a safe haven than when I cast you off. Your bridges are burned, satyr, and soon your skin will curl in the flames of vengeance. I assume Asgard's son refused you," Eris said. "That's why you went to *her*, isn't it? To beg Loki to take you into his confidence?" Her golden eyes twitched to me. "What did this one tell you, Miss Sharp? What lies did he spin to gain your trust *this* time?"

I could feel her spell worming its way into my mind like a barbed vine. As she spoke, the tendrils of distrust thrust out, seeking purchase. With the same kind of clarity I had when it came to technomancy, I understood Eris's magic.

She plants the seed in fertile ground. Discord blooms in its own time.

With an effort of will, I shoved back, purged it from my mind. After letting out a slow breath, I stared a challenge at the goddess. "Nice try."

Eris arched an eyebrow. "Perhaps the mage isn't as weak as I suspected."

"You were wrong about him," I said. "You're wrong about me. You know, for a deity, you totally fail at the whole omnipotent thing."

"Mortals," she spat. "So headstrong. Always forgetting how fragile they are."

Again, Eris's power snaked through the night. It moved past Marius and straight toward me. As he spun on his feet, kicking up sand, Marius called out. Eris's toothy grin—that was her tell. That's how I knew she had no intention of harming me. Not when she could cause so much more pain. It was the same dirty trick Belial had pulled.

Eris let the lightning whip go slack and pursed her lips. A puff of air, a flash of amber light, and the flames on Marius's blade leaped to the sleeve of his shirt.

"No!" I shouted.

I thrust out my hands, intending to send a blast of light into Eris's ugly face. Instead, with a gurgling roar, the ocean behind me rose up. Like an enormous hooded cobra, it struck, dousing Marius, his sword, and the goddess.

When the steam dissipated, there was only a sopping wet satyr.

Eris was gone.

The night became still. The waves washed in and slowly out like the breath of a slumbering giant. Santorini was just as it had been moments before Eris had appeared. I inched forward, alternating between examining Marius and my hands.

"Where did she go?" I asked. "Did I melt the bitch?"

Marius, his sword now sheathed in the ether once more, dragged his hands through his thick, wet hair. He squeezed the ponytail, water dripping to the sand, and sighed. "No such luck. It seems she wasn't actually here."

I gaped at him. "Could've fooled me."

"You're in good company. She had me convinced, as well."

"Well if it wasn't her, what the hell was it?"

"A sending. A sliver of her awareness was here with us while her body was elsewhere. It's an ability all gods share."

I nodded. "The answer to the old question, 'How can God be everywhere?'"

"Precisely. It's the magic of their kind."

"So what just happened, then?" I asked.

Marius slipped out of his shirt. Moonlight glistened on his skin, and my stomach flopped with heat and desire. "Water," he answered, wringing out the tee. "It nullified the spell."

Again, I bobbed my head with understanding. "Cleansing."

"Doubly so with seawater." Marius smiled. "That was quick thinking on your part. I had no idea you'd taken up another form of magic."

I stared at my hands. "I haven't," I whispered. "I don't know how..." I stopped mid-sentence, and for a moment, I pondered our large visitor. Had he cast the gouts of water, just as I'd assumed he had empowered Marius's saber? No, the power had been mine. The release of energy, the flow and connection, it had come from my hands. My will. How, then, had I ensnared water magic?

When I looked to him for an answer, Marius had—much to my disappointment—put his shirt back on. Damn.

"What about you? I've never seen your sword catch fire."

His smile was broad, eyes glittering with mercurial humor. "That's the beauty of visiting the maker from time to time. Upgrades."

I thought of the low voice in the night. "Hephaestus?"

He nodded. "He's got to be around here somewhere."

I did a slow 360, searching for the owner of the voice that had been in my ear. A few feet from Marius, something metallic caught the starlight and winked. The shadows rippled, and a behemoth stepped into view.

My stomach twitched, fear and awe tugging at my guts. He was as tall as Belial and broad as a barn. Shirtless, his chest and shoulders bulged with muscles of comic-book-hero scale. His skin was as dark and impenetrable as a black hole. His eyes—dear gods, he should've been blind!—were pure silver. No irises or pupils, just solid silver casting back the light. His hair hung in moss-colored naps down past his shoulders. His lips split to reveal an ivory smile and one gold tooth.

He raised an arm. The amulet—the charm Marius had used to grant us Godspeed—dangled from his gargantuan fist.

"You've dropped something," he said, his voice deep and musical. "If you wanted my attention, you could've called rather than leaving a flaming bag of dog shit on my doorstep. It attracts flies that I'm not fond of." The god indicated the wet pool of sand where Eris had stood.

My satyr's face glowed with relief and a genuine happiness. "Hephaestus."

Wincing, I watched as Marius was swallowed by the giant's hug.

Hephaestus grunted pleasantly. "It's good to see you again, my friend."

"The feeling is mutual," Marius replied. He smacked the god's back in that way men do. The resulting sound was that of flesh slapping a slab of marble. "Time's been good to you."

Though he could've palmed Marius's head—and probably torn it off with little effort—the god's hand on the satyr's shoulder was gentle. "And to you. But you seem to have found yourself in a bit of trouble."

"Trouble fancies me."

Though his unblinking eyes gave nothing away, I felt Hephaestus's attention flash to me. "So that's her name? Trouble?"

Marius remembered me. "I'd like to introduce you to Catherine Sharp. As you saw, she's quite the talented mage."

"Indeed, I *see*," the god rumbled. Hephaestus draped his arm over Marius's shoulders and guided him toward me. "Come, my friend. You've been gone too long, and we must talk."

"Of many things," Marius said, a pointed glance in my direction.

As he passed me, Hephaestus reached out his free hand and stroked my wrist. I blinked, and when I opened my eyes, I was no longer standing on the sandy beach of Santorini but in what I could only assume was Hephaestus's sanctuary.

I'm always intrigued to see what constitutes a home for magical beings. Of all that I'd seen up to that point, Hephaestus's abode—though not quite humble—was the one I liked best. We were in cave with cathedral ceilings and smooth obsidian floors. Orbs of amber light provided a steady glow bright enough to read by, but not too hard on the eyes. Porous stalagmites rose up from the ground to form end tables. Tunnels burrowed deeper into the earth, presumably leading to other rooms. Every piece of furniture—chairs, a sofa, an ottoman—was huge and squishy, covered in Riot Act–Red suede. Nooks in the rocky walls held books, knickknacks, and tools. I recognized the haphazard placement from my own apartment—a multi-tool placed on the shelf as I walked by while tinkering with this object or that. There were posters on the walls, too. Most of them were movie ads—*The Lord of the Rings*, superhero flicks. Big-budget, special effects stuff.

The air quivered with mirages. Though it wasn't uncomfortable, the room radiated an intense, dry heat.

The transition from shore to cave had been seamless. "That...was smooth," I said, awestruck.

"See? Traveling his way is much better than Flynn's, too." Marius snarked.

I rolled my eyes. "Baby."

Hephaestus emerged from one of the many tunnels that branched out from the cave. He clutched two bottles in one hand, and a stein the size of my laptop in the other. He held up the bottles in an offering to Marius and me. "It's not the Elysian wine I know you prefer, Marius, but it's a good lubrication for catching up with an old friend."

Seeing the god in full light rendered me speechless. Breathless, even. He was incredible. That dark skin—cold and hard to the touch—was truly like marble. Here and there, white veins shot through the stone of him, providing muscle definition, a pattern along the chin that resembled a goatee. His dreadlocks were made of aged copper. Most of the locks appeared dark, but what I'd earlier mistaken for moss I now understood to be verdigris.

Again, there came the eerie sensation of his attention as he turned his sightless, steel eyes to me. He flashed me a gold-toothed grin.

"And a new friend," he added, voice as deep as a bass drum and twice as resonant. Concern replaced the joy in his expression, the stone that comprised his face shifting just as easily as flesh. "Something wrong, girl?"

"Just a lot to take in," I said.

I dragged my hands through my hair and crossed to one of the plush chairs. Well, for someone of Hephaestus's size, I suppose it was a chair. I was able to curl my whole body between the arms and melt into the soft folds. Yeah. He and I shared similar tastes in furniture and décor, not to mention a propensity to tinker and build. He'd barely spoken and I knew that Hephaestus was a kindred spirit.

As he leaned against the arm of my chair, Marius passed me a dark, unlabeled bottle. I took it but didn't drink. I was too interested in the way Heph was studying me.

"Really?" Hephaestus asked. "I should think that one connected with Loki would be used to anything."

"How did you know I work for Loki?"

Heph leaned back, resting his tankard on his knee. He lifted one mammoth finger. "Your bracelet."

"Aren't there, like, a billion silver bracelets in the world?"

"Of course. But I never forget one of my creations."

Stunned, I gaped at the bangle on my wrist. "You...you made this?"

"Long ago. Centuries before this one—" he lifted his chin to Marius "—was a gleam in his grandfather's eyes."

"Christ," I said, amazed. "You remember making this of all things?"

Heph nodded. "Every piece I make carries a piece of me. I would recognize myself in that bracelet among a thousand that look just like it." He took in my amazement and smiled tenderly. "How did you come by it?"

"Loki gave it to me just a couple of days ago. Birthday present."

"Only a few days, hmm? Then you've probably not had the opportunity to see all that it can do."

My jaw dropped. "It doesn't happen to manipulate water, does it?"

His laughter was the shifting of tectonic plates. Heph answered my question only by shaking his head, bringing his tankard to his lips and drinking.

"Speaking of your creations, old friend," Marius said, "what exactly happened to my sword back there?"

Hephaestus brought one marble foot to rest on a squat ottoman. "I made it, so I can change it," he said simply. "How is your arm?"

I noticed that, except for his hair, Marius appeared to now be dry. Either Hephaestus had worked that magic in transit or the ambient heat of the room was sufficient to suck the moisture from his sopping clothes.

Marius looked down at his shoulder. The fabric of his shirt was scorched, the skin beneath it an angry red. "Bugger!" he hissed, poking at the hole in the tee. "Just like old times, I suppose. It's not a night out with you unless someone's clothes have burned off."

TWENTY

"Palm of Your Hand"

By the time sane people were waking up, Hephaestus had gone spe-lunking in the depths of his tankard, and Marius had finished both our bottles of brew. I sat back in my comfy chair, enjoying the tales they told. The stories gave a glimpse of Marius's past, his days before Eris and his damnable curse.

Heph leaned toward me. "Now, Cat, you have to understand, in those days one did not just walk up to Aphrodite. No one but Zeus him-self was allowed that privilege. If she bothered to look down her perfect nose at you, fine. You could bow and scrape and plead your troth to her until you were blue in the face. But striking up a conversation with Love and Beauty was a surefire way to find yourself without your skin."

Marius pinched the bridge of his nose, face glowing with a jovial humility. "Gods, you're not going on about this again, are you?"

"Shut up," Heph barked. Turning back to me, he dove back into the story. "She's standing there next to an enormous yellow tent. And there's Marius, sauntering over to her with that smug, suave smile on his bastard face."

"You know, I think I'm familiar with that smile," I said, passing Marius a tormenting grin.

"Marius calls out, for all to hear, 'My Lady! Dost thou fuck on the first date?'"

Abashed, Marius hid his eyes behind a hand. That did not, however, hide the crimson crawling up his cheeks.

The laughter began to build in Heph's voice. "And then...the yellow tent...turned around!"

"Oh shit!" I covered my mouth to stifle a laugh.

"*Ares*, his enormous bulk stuffed into a yellow tunic, turns around. His face was red and angry as a star! The Lord of War raised his fist, and in an instant, Marius was on the ground."

"I would think so!" I said. I looked to Marius. "You're lucky you didn't die."

"Luck had nothing to do with it," he said, still clearly embarrassed.

"Then what did you do?" I asked.

"I said, 'Thank you, milord,' and let Heph peel me off the ground!"

Marius's laughter was drowned out by the hearty blasts coming from the god. When we'd all caught our breath, Marius gestured to Heph with a lazy hand. "If I'm not mistaken, that was the night *you* began courting Lady Aphrodite."

Heph's good will ebbed away and his attention turned to his tankard. "Don't remind me," he rumbled. "I'd just as soon forget that time."

"Weren't you two married?" I asked, recalling my high school mythology lessons.

"Briefly. Aphrodite and the other gods of Olympus took pity on me. Wasn't that nice of them? When I found out that I was little more than a public relations move to make her look even better, I kicked her out."

"That was a good night, too," Marius mused. "Get anything nice in the divorce?"

"Only what she left behind. Trinkets and baubles from suitors. I'd always planned to melt it down in the Forge, but it's all still in a box somewhere."

My eyes began to cross. It had been a fun evening, but I was fading fast. After all, I had died about twenty-four hours ago. A little postmortem-and-resurrection lag was to be expected, I suppose.

Marius must have noticed, because when he spoke again, he tone was tender. "I suspect I shall have to get Catherine back to her bed soon."

Heph smiled appreciatively, then placed his tankard on a stalagmite. "In that case, old friend, we must be about our business. What brings you here—of all places—when you've a price on your head?"

Marius shifted uneasily in his seat. "Heard about that, have you?"

"I hear everything. What are you looking for?"

"Hoped to hide in plain sight. Pay you a visit. And see if you might know where I might find a benefactor."

"You mean a sucker?" he teased.

"An *employer.*"

"Hoping someone will pay off your debts and protect you from the raging mob with their torches and pitchforks?"

Marius bobbed his head. "Something like that. Know of anyone who might have need of a satyr's skills?"

The god's lip lifted in a smirk. "Depends on which of your skills you hope to market. Who are you trying to be, Marius? The fop with a winsome smile? The satyr who won the affections of Zeus's favorite nymph? Or the beguiling thief who angered Discord? Those are different men with different paths."

Marius's face darkened. "I'd forgotten how philosophical you can get when you're drunk."

"It doesn't make me wrong, though. Do you know who you wish to be?"

The ambient heat in the room coupled with my weariness to blur my vision. I blinked and tried to see Marius clearly. His green eyes met mine for an instant before he went out of focus again.

Reply hazy. Try again.

I'm not sure if I nodded off or not. The darkness was cool on my eyes. The sounds of the room grew muffled. A moment later, I heard Heph saying, "I am not the employer you seek, friend. You know that. I hold little power over the lords of Olympus, and with them allied against you, I am not enough to protect you or your interests. Not alone."

I opened my eyes.

Marius sagged in his seat. "I had a feeling you'd say that."

"I'm sorry. Ask anything else of me and I will do it."

Waving him off, Marius said, "You owe me nothing."

"It's not about a debt, Marius. You're a friend. Friends help one another."

"Funny," my satyr said with a pointed glance in my direction. "I've heard that a lot recently."

Then I caught myself nodding off again, my head jerking as I woke up.

"I should get her back to the surface," Marius murmured.

My limbs were limp and felt miles away as Marius slipped his arms beneath me and pulled me up to his chest. I let my head fall against his shoulder. Taking in the rhythm of his pulse, the scent of him, I sank into a blissful peace. I let myself drift, too tired to join in their conversation.

"There is one thing," Marius said. "The amulet. Could you alter it, by chance, so that Eris cannot track me with it?"

There was a pause. "Probably," Heph drawled. "Her enchantments are difficult to break, but it's not beyond my skill."

"I would consider it a favor if you could work that magic."

"I'll see what I can do and contact you soon. In the meantime, I'll use what I have to shield the island. Give you and Cat some time and protection from outsiders."

"Eris will be blaring the word out that we're here," Marius complained.

"But Santorini is still my domain. That is good for more than lip service. You will have time to rest and breathe, my friend." Hard stone brushed over my forehead. "I'm sorry I didn't get to learn more about this mage. She is strong. One of my ilk."

"Another time soon," Marius promised.

"Stay close. Stay safe."

TWENTY-ONE

"UP SO CLOSE"

A wareness flooded me as cool air blasted across my cheeks. Opening my eyes, I saw Marius and I were back on the shore. The salty wind tossed my hair and invigorated me as the sunrise cut the sky open until it bled red clouds.

"Good morning," Marius said quietly.

I rubbed my eyes. The surface air—clean and downright brisk compared to the Forge's heat—was enough to wake me up.

"Shall I carry you up to your room and put you to bed?" Marius's eyes twinkled and his smile hitched.

"I'm good," I said. "Put me down. I'll walk."

"As you wish."

I wobbled as my feet met the sand, but after a few steps, I knew I could make it to the room.

Intrigued, I asked, "So that's your buddy, eh?"

He stuffed his hands in his pockets and gave me a lopsided smile. "What do you think of him?"

"Not at all what I'd expected," I admitted, pawing through my hair. "The myths all say he's lame and ugly. But he's not. Very much not."

"You have to remember what the Greek ideal was at the time—pale, perfect proportions, not too tall and not too short. You might notice that Heph doesn't fit that description. He has, therefore, always been the literal dark sheep of the family."

"No shit. And to be made of marble and metal? That's a pretty cool trick."

One of my satyr's hands gently slid down my spine, coming to rest at the small of my back as we mounted the stairs, closing in on my bungalow.

"It's what he does," Marius said. "The stories downplay his skills, likening him to a mere blacksmith. Truth be told, the man is much more like you—using magic and technology—than a typical god."

I tried to process that, but my head felt full and fluffy. "So that's what he meant by saying I'm one of his ilk?"

"Yes."

As I keyed open my door, I turned to Marius. "I would invite you in, but all I'm going to do is fall down face-first and sleep for a year."

"The past few days have been..."

"Yeah," I said with a weak laugh. "They have been."

He took my hand in both of his and brought it to his lips. "Thank you, Catherine. For everything. I don't think I can say that enough."

The kiss was a half shot of espresso, making my eyes widen and my heart race.

He stared at my hand in his, thumbs caressing my knuckles. "I wanted to ask you," Marius's voice was thin and breathy. "That is, if you don't have any other plans...would you like to have our date tomorrow night? Or, well, tonight I suppose," he added with a nod to the sunrise.

My stomach twisted, and excitement seeped into my blood in hot bubbles. Taking my hands from him, I fidgeted with my hair. "Our date."

A warm smile went all the way to his leaf-green eyes. "Yes. *The* date," he reiterated with emphasis.

I laughed. "The one I still owe you for saving my ass a few years ago."

"That would be the one," he said, rocking on his heels.

I tapped my fingers on the doorjamb and pretended to think about it. "I don't know. If memory serves, back at YmFy you were trying to get rid of me. You said I'm free of that. I don't owe you anything."

Marius lifted his eyebrows. He leaned his elbow on the open door and reached out to stroke my hair with his other hand. "So I did. That was terribly stupid of me, wasn't it?"

"A little bit, yeah."

"Then allow me to amend the request." He pushed away from the door and stood at full height. His expression soft but his eyes commanding my attention, he spoke. "Catherine, I would very much enjoy it if you'd do me the honor of joining me tonight as my date. No magic or coercion. You of your own accord."

I giggled a little and dropped my gaze. "All right," I consented. Mustering a bit of the same decorum he'd put into his words, I looked up and asked, "And what shall we do?"

"Well," he purred, "I was thinking that I would like to cook for you. I've got a kitchen in my suite. I'll send Malcolm out with an extensive shopping list, then kick him out of the room and you can come by around sunset. Just the two of us."

"I'd like that," I said, voicing the most incredible understatement of the century. The thought of spending an evening alone with Marius... And with Heph's protection, maybe things would actually be calm. The possibilities of a night like that swirled in my mind. What adventures could we have, just us two, in a room alone?

My musings got a little too real, a little too scintillating. To cover with a bit of humor, I asked, "Black tie or casual?"

"Whatever you like," Marius answered with an indulgent smile.

All the things I would have liked rose up in my mind, heart, and body like clamoring voices aching to be heard. I fought the urge to grab him by the shirt, pull him to me, and take him up on the offer right then and there. But I wouldn't. The stupid curse of his meant that Marius and I could be nothing more than this. An odd kind of friendship with all sorts of paths that were off-limits. And even if he could, how much between us would be unrequited?

I shriveled at the idea, my stomach sinking. The last of the wind left my sails, and I sagged against the door.

"Go rest, Catherine," he said, placing a kiss on the top of my head. As he backed away slowly, I saw his eyes sparkle with happiness. "I'll see you tonight."

"Sleep well, Marius," I drawled with exhausted joy.

I closed the door and shuffled across the room. Falling onto the mattress, I sighed and sank into darkness. While all the *what-ifs* and *can't-haves* swirled in my thoughts, the bitch of Pandora's bunch—hope—lit my way to bed.

—⚹—

I woke up to my heart pounding in my chest with panic. The dark velvet of dreamless sleep had slipped off somewhere in the night, leaving me vulnerable to the cold, gnashing teeth of nightmares. Ancient beings snarling with rage. Lightning and brimstone. Thick fingers around my throat. Marius's back as he ran away. And the faces. Patchwork skin wrenched in a grimace. Dahlia's exquisite features glaring with haughty disdain. The gray, scaly hide of a prince of Hell. So many faces leering hungrily from the shadows.

Dragging a hand across my forehead, I wiped the fine layer of sweat away and shivered. As I caught my breath, I put that same hand to my chest, as if I could still my manic pulse with the touch; however, the only thing I accomplished was to further punctuate my fear. My fingers grazed the bullet wound, and beneath my scarred flesh, I felt the fever-hot wires of the implant that had saved my life.

A piercing trill rang out and I whipped a fist toward the sound. Only when the plastic shattered around my hand did I realize the noise had come from the hotel phone. I sighed, embarrassed that I'd been so jumpy that I'd just smashed the phone to splinters, and I flopped back to the pillows. I let my mind wander and reacquaint itself with reality.

I'd fallen into bed around sunrise, and the clock said it was sometime past noon. I was in a posh resort off the coast of Greece, and I'd met a wicked-cool god. Eris knew we were here, though. Which meant there were probably other factions on their way searching for Marius.

In other news, I'd reached for technomagic and come up with water. How the hell had that worked? I'd seen Marius use elemental magic—bending air, water, and earth to his whims—but I'd never done that myself. Heph had said that the bracelet Loki had given me had powers but that the ability to play with water wasn't one of them. Could it somehow be a result of the implant? I made a mental note to call Karma and ask her what other side effects it might have, since I was going to be living with it and all.

The more I pondered it, the more I didn't loathe the idea of being alive. That burning ache, that horrible feeling of being ripped away from paradise, had abated somewhat. While I still felt like a piece of myself had gone walkabout, I didn't hate Flynn for bringing me back from the Great Beyond. That was a step in the right direction.

My stomach let out a volcanic rumble.

Oh yeah. I hadn't eaten since before I died. And I'd just destroyed the phone that would make room service happen. Great. Then I remembered something else.

I've got a date with Marius tonight.

Oh shit.

Before I could have my second panic attack of the morning, someone knocked on my door. I vaulted out of bed and met with a young man at the door. He wore a cream bellhop uniform and a gold name tag that read "Miklos." His black eyes and coal-dark hair gleamed like coffee. My stomach lurched again. I needed to get something to eat with a quickness.

"Good day, Miss," he said, his accent light. He offered me a folded piece of paper. "I have a message for you."

"Did you try calling?" I asked sheepishly.

Miklos's smile was easy and courteous. "Yes. Several times."

I winced. "Um, I've got a problem with my phone. It seems to be... broken."

"I will have it replaced right away. Is there anything else I can get for you, Miss?"

"Room service? I'd do horrible, naughty things for a cup of coffee, a short stack of pancakes, and a few strips of bacon right about now."

He bowed his head. "I'll put in the order myself. Have a pleasant day, Miss."

Miklos the Awesome turned on his heel and took to the path at a jaunty, purposeful pace. I shut the door and unfolded my note. A slanted hand had written:

Word from our friend H this morning says multiple visitors have tried to come in, but have been turned away. He put out a rumor that we are bound for the Far East. Dogs have stopped knocking on the door, but you might want to keep your head down today. Also, I've changed my mind: the dress code for tonight is now formal. No blue jeans allowed. If you've need of anything, let Malcolm know and he'll take care of it. Or charge it to my room.

Sunset. Bungalow 3. Bring your appetites. -M.

I read the note a few times over, my stomach flopping with a nervous joy I'd not felt since...well, too long. My step light and my head in the clouds, you'd think I'd have just gotten a note in study hall from my crush asking me to prom. *Circle yes or no.*

Ridiculous. Next I'd be dotting the *I* in Marius's name with little hearts.

Breakfast arrived soon thereafter, along with a new phone and a brochure of all the resort's amenities. I took my food and the pamphlet out to the balcony. Santorini by sunlight was even lovelier than I'd expected. Turquoise water lapped at the sugar-white sand below. Colorful umbrellas dotted the beach. Sunbathers lounged in chairs, and in the distance I saw boats sailing to the center of the crater.

When my belly was full, the sting of my nightmares abated. I closed my eyes and let the sea breeze toss my hair. For a moment, I could relax.

"Good morning, Cat," Heph's deep voice chimed.

I jumped. When I saw him smiling at me from the path a few feet away, his steel eyes hidden behind sunglasses, I hissed. "Dammit, don't sneak up on people!"

He laughed, a sound like a merry foghorn. "I was wondering if you'd assist me today."

"Me? How so?"

"Working with Marius's amulet has proven to be irksome."

I nodded. "Par for the course. Eris and Marius both have a knack for that."

"Truer words," Heph said, gold tooth peeking out from his smile. "It's Eris's magic that I am having trouble unraveling. Then I remembered that Marius had said you once wore Discord's brand."

"Sadly, yes."

He eyed me over his shades, mischief playing at his expression. "Care to hack through her spells?"

I glanced at the spa pamphlet. A hot-stone massage would be amazing, but... "Will it piss her off?"

"Absolutely."

"Where do we start?"

His titanic hand was cool and gentle over my wrist, and in a blink, the balcony was gone and I stood in his volcanic lair again.

"Seriously," I said. "That's smooth."

"I've had time to perfect certain things," he said humbly.

I followed his lumbering form down one of the obsidian tunnels toward a flickering amber glow. The deeper into the cave we walked, the heavier and more oppressive the heat became. I suddenly remembered every documentary about volcanoes ever filmed.

Shouldn't my pants be spontaneously combusting right about now?

"Um, do I need a fire suit or some other protective gear or something?"

With a shake of those verdigris locks, he called over his shoulder, "No need. You are my guest. That is all the protection you will require. However, a word of caution: do not touch the fire."

I laughed. "I think I can manage that."

The cave opened onto another vast space like the one we'd lounged in the previous night. In one wall, the stone gave way to form a circular window larger than a two-car garage. Beyond that hole, a river of molten lava churned and flowed. The black rock walls and floor shone like glass, reflecting the gold-and-orange glow of the volcano's beating heart.

My breath caught in my chest.

Hephaestus's smile painted his voice. "It stirs you, too, doesn't it?"

I nodded, mute with awe. My gaze danced over this sacred space—the very seat of Hephaestus's power. Rough-hewn ingots of metals were strewn about in massive blocks. Tools hung from racks along the walls. Some I recognized—tongs, hammers, and spikes. I saw crucibles of varying sizes near the Forge itself. And an anvil. The unmistakable shapes of swords and axes lined the farthest wall. I saw helmets, breastplates, and other pieces of armor. Wheels and axels. Silver spheres. A marble urn.

Carefully, reverently, I crossed to this collection of Hephaestus's creations. "Amazing," I breathed.

I felt his presence behind me. Pride radiated from him like heat from the furnace. "Some of these are commissions that have yet to be picked up. Others are things I will never give away. Or cursed objects that must be destroyed. Then there's this," he said, his black stone hand caressing a rectangle of silver about the size of a shoe box.

The thing had the shape of a treasure chest, but if it was one, where was its lock? Its lid? There were no hinges or lines. The otherwise-perfect surface of the thing was marred by a single charred glyph.

"What is it?" I asked.

"Pandora's box."

I blinked in astonishment. Despite the fact that I was standing in a volcano, gooseflesh prickled over my skin and my hairs stood on end.

"*The* Pandora's box?" I muttered.

"The one and only."

I reached out a hand and let my fingers glide over its smooth surface. The metal was solid and cool. With the same sense I used to pop locks or fix computers, I felt the structure of the box. There was a hinge inside. A groove. A divot. The mechanisms of the chest were cleverly concealed. Power thrummed through my arm as I examined it. A heat beneath my fingers. Then something rattled furiously inside the seamless chest. I jerked my hand away.

"And now you see why I cannot destroy it," Heph said. "To throw it into the fire is to kill all hope. But to open it... Well, that way lies folly."

"How...? How could Pandora open this?"

"Pandora was the first of your kind."

"The first woman, yeah."

His face split into a grin, those strange, sightless eyes taking me in. "The first mage with the ability to commune with machines." When

I didn't speak, just gaped at the box with a mixture of reverence and temptation, the god went on. "There is a little bit of her in every one of your kind. The same fire that burned in her cast sparks into creation. One of those embers burns in you, Cat."

For the first time in my life, I felt like I was part of something greater. Oh, sure, I knew that I was part of an exclusive circle, being a techno-mancer. But this...this was special. There was a magic to knowing that somehow Pandora was a sort of ancestor.

I straightened my spine, full of pride. "You said you needed help with that amulet?"

Heph's easy smile widened as he gave a sweeping gesture toward his Forge. "This way."

The god led me to a long worktable made of the same glassy stone that formed the rest of the place. Numerous projects were strewn about in various states of completion. Marius's ridiculous necklace glinted in the firelight, and next to it was a black sphere. This one had a visible hinge and seam. The hasp had been popped, and I could see a golden shimmer coming from inside.

"How much experience have you had with Eris's magic?" Hephaestus asked.

"Other than being on the receiving end of a bitch slap or two, not much. Well, and her brand, if that counts."

"It might." He slid the amulet over to me. "Look and tell me what you see."

I opened my mind and gazed with that *other* sense. The gold neck-lace illuminated with filaments of dark energy that resembled Eris's lightning bolts. These black threads of power undulated with purplish light, making the spellwork look like a pulsing bruise. Beneath that sickly web, a holy white light gleamed with steady radiance.

"There are two kinds of magic at work here," I said. "Hers is encas-ing the other."

"Very good. The spell that allows Marius to god-step is permanently affixed to this object; however, Eris has woven two strands of her own work around it. One of them allows her to change the appearance of the talisman."

"Let me guess, the other is a tracking spell."

"Correct."

I stared intently at the snarl of Eris's spells. "Can't you just snip them off?"

Hephaestus took a seat next to me and shook his head. "Her magic is alive."

My eyes widened, and I stared at him incredulously. "You're going to have to help me with that one."

"Think of it like music. When you play a single note, it is over in an instant. Yet, if you record that note, you can listen to it again and again. Manipulate it, shape it, repeat it. So it is, too, with magic."

"So the original magic of the talisman is the single note?"

"Yes. It is a permanent, immutable moment. It endures over time, but—"

"—but it just *is*," I finished. "That's why the light doesn't flicker. The spell was cast and done."

Heph nodded.

"But Eris's spells appear to change because they are fluid."

"Precisely. Which is one reason we can't just, as you say, snip them off. They are slippery, constantly in motion."

"What's another reason?"

His silver eyes narrowed. "That kind of magic has ways of defending itself. Also, it tends to bleed when cut. It will leave...stains."

I looked back to the pulsating fibers. My lip curled. "Ick."

"Quite."

I closed my eyes, willing away my techie sense. Opening them again, I saw just a simple, tacky necklace. "Okay," I muttered to myself. I circled the table, pondering this particular puzzle. "The magic will bite back if we just try to cut it, so it's not a simple matter of red wire-green wire like in the movies. On the one hand, that's good news, because it opens up our options. But we've got to get Eris's cooties off without getting the pretty white light dirty."

Heph said nothing. He just watched me, a hint of amusement on his face.

"We've got to separate it from her somehow, like a dam," I said. "Block the current from her to the spell."

"To what end?" he asked. Now he was a teacher questioning the student.

"Well, once we do that, the spells might wither and die. Then we'll be able to cut them away, easy peasy."

"Eris is quite old, Cat. And Marius has carried this for a long time. For the spells to atrophy could take centuries."

I sucked in a breath through my teeth. "Okay, maybe not." I tapped my forehead, an old habit that manifests in my more pensive moments. I ran through a few ideas, shooting down the lame or impossible ones. (*No, Cat, chocolate will not help. Nor can we just take Eris's head off her bony-ass shoulders.*) Right about the time I started rehashing movie plotlines, rifling through them for ideas, I wondered what Flynn would do. And that's how I got to "Trojan rabbit."

"Pardon me?"

Christ, hasn't this guy seen any Monty Python? I shook my head, clearing away the extraneous thoughts so the solution blazed in my mind. "Okay, so, it's like a closed-circuit feed. Eris pours juice into the spells on this thing, and it sends signals back to her. Right?" When Hephaestus nodded, I continued. "So, what if we intercept one of those signals?"

"I think I understand your meaning. Go on."

"We catch the current coming from Eris and—using the trace elements of her magic already in this thing—we send dummy messages back to her, so she doesn't see someone tampering with her spell. Then, with the spells completely cut off, we can sort of...transplant different signals into it. We bleed out her magic while filling it with our own."

Heph nodded. "And from there we can either alter the enchantments or break them entirely."

"Yes!" I said, hissing with excitement. "And when we're finished, we throw Eris a false signal that Marius is somewhere in Tibet or something and sever the link. Then the bitch is confused and beaten."

Hephaestus bared his teeth. "Clever plan. I offer one small adjustment."

The god laid his hand over the black spherical container. The hinge protested with an ominous creak as he opened the lid. Gold flared with brilliant light. My guts churned, and my skin prickled as a slimy, sticky energy reached its tentacles into the air. As Hephaestus drew his hand away, I saw what might easily be mistaken for a golden ball. Except for the small stem and gilded leaf sprouting from the top, that is. Greek symbols were etched into the side.

My jaw dropped. "Is...is that...?"

"The one and only," Hephaestus rumbled. "The Golden Apple of Discord."

TWENTY-TWO

"SHADOW STABBING"

Staring down at Eris's actual, factual Golden Apple filled me with a new kind of spine-melting dread. Its tangible surface glittered in the amber glow of the Forge, those carved symbols darkening with the shifting light. Beneath that surface, however, was bad juju. I didn't dare open my senses to it. I didn't have to. The dark chaos of Discord slithered within, a ball of vipers pressing against my senses. The thing hissed into my brain, its icy scales writhing over my mind. At the corner of my vision I saw bared teeth dripping venom. A flash of anger. A wail of rage.

I closed my eyes. "I can't look at that."

"I won't ask you to, Cat," Hephaestus said soothingly. "There may come a day when you must look at the maw of madness and deceit, but this is not that day."

I heaved a sigh of relief. "Thank you. So what do we do?"

"Exactly what you said. Only instead of sending those dummy messages, as you put it, from the amulet, I will use the Apple to direct power away from the talisman and back to Eris. This carries her signature, her purest power. I can harness it and manipulate it as you work with the electricity and technological power of the amulet."

I pondered how I might set my plan in motion. Like pulling strands of energy apart to fuel my car, I could mentally focus on the amulet and the spells braiding about the bauble. I searched the worktable for tools, a tangible object I could use to focus my will on the spells twining about the amulet's white core. I found tweezers, a needle, lock picks—the only things that would fit my small hands and allow for the delicate work.

"So I take the amulet and do the work on it while you use your Olympian mojo on the Apple to keep her off our scent?" I glared at the Apple, weighing the options and trying to come up with some alternative. "If she finds out, she'll be pissed."

"Of course. And if your hand is not steady, you could unleash potent magic. The recoil could be strong enough to crush your sanity, if not kill you outright." He paused. "No pressure," he added, his grin soft and reassuring.

Seriously? Those were my choices? Succeed on the first try, piss off Eris (more), die (again), or be left a dribbling idiot?

I worried my lip for a moment. "And this will help Marius?"

He nodded. "You will buy the satyr valuable time and forge a new, strong magical artifact."

I blew out a breath, rattling my lips. "Let's get to work, then."

Hephaestus beamed with pride and merriment. "Take off the bracelet and any other enchanted objects you carry. Their magic might interfere."

Slipping off the silver cuff, I did a mental pat down of my person. "Um, I've got these implants, but I can't exactly take them out. And there's Loki's mark."

"Those are part of you. They will not hinder."

"Good to know."

Hephaestus took up the Apple and stood facing the Forge, his back to mine.

"I'm ready, Cat. Are you?"

Hovering over the necklace, I let the magic become visible. Taking up the tweezers and one of the lock picks, I licked my lips. "Let's do this."

Behind me, Hephaestus did something that unleashed that unsavory magic. The vipers were released, shrieking and crying out with their reptilian screams. Beneath their hissing and wailing, I heard Eris's voice. What was it Marius had said about the sliver of a person in her magic? A bit of Eris herself had been woven into each of those snakes as if they were tentacles slithering away from her. I drew into myself, cowering at the idea that she might be able to see me here. Hephaestus, however, dampened the goddess's energy with a force of his own. I wondered for an instant what his magic would look like, but I didn't turn around. Couldn't. My all-too-reasonable fear kept me facing the damn tacky amulet.

"Now, Cat."

I pushed the sounds out of my mind. I had a job to do. *I'm pulling an* Ocean's Eleven. *I'm hacking her security feed and Heph is replacing it with his own false feed while I bleed out her power and sneak in with my own, unnoticed.*

I bent down close enough to the necklace that the minute force of my breathing blurred the lines of Eris's magic. I squeezed the tweezers over the black bands of her energy and mentally pinched off her power. I waited for a terrible moment, expecting the switch—the Apple for the amulet's signals—to fail.

"I've got it, Cat," Heph assured me. "Get to work."

The deep purple of her web—now cut off from her—began to ebb, colors lightening. Using the needle and lock picks, I made the tiniest of tears along one of the strands.

A drop of oily ichor bubbled up like blood from a pinprick.

"Shit," I hissed. Careful not to drip or apply more pressure, I lifted the pendant and quickly held it over the black box that had previously contained the Apple. The box caught the spell's life as it spilled away.

Okay. No stains. Just let it bleed out and replace it. Right?

That was the plan.

I spent the next eternity bending in odd positions, blowing hair out of my face, making magical incisions, and letting my own power seep into these strange filaments. Not too much or the spells would burst. Not too little or the slime of Eris's power would still have a hold. I knew this somehow. Like information in a dream, I just *knew.*

When the fibers grew white with my own energy, I whispered purpose into the dribs and drabs I sent into the talisman.

Protection. Keep him hidden. And for the love of all things holy, please look better than this piece of shit.

"Are you almost finished?" Heph asked, the slightest strain in his voice.

"Two shakes."

With the innate ability I had for fixing things, I mended the holes I'd pricked into the spellwork with patches of my own energy. Between my hands, all I could see was light—pure, white, and perfectly still. The ooze of Eris's power formed a stagnant pool in the black case.

I let out a breath. "Done."

I sagged, drained, as I felt the energy of the Apple close behind me. My muscles shook and my head swam with dizziness, as if I'd just come off an Everest-sized adrenaline rush. A cool glaze of sweat had risen to my skin, and I wiped my forehead.

Heph turned to face me. The Apple came to rest on the worktable with a too-heavy thud, and Heph's touch on my shoulder was incongruously light for someone his size.

"Well done, mage. Flynn has taught you much, but you are a spectacular talent in your own right."

I blinked at him. "You know Flynn?"

His marble brow furrowed as he considered his words. "I know the Recluse as the fire knows the ember. Besides, you sing his song when you work."

I chewed my lip. Humming while I worked on computers was one thing. Endearing, even. But after singing techno-hymns while working my magic in the past, well, I'd learned that could be dangerous. I'd outed Flynn with my singing, and I didn't want to do anything like that again. Most of the past year I'd been trying to break myself of my singing habit.

"It's all right, Cat. Rest. I will get you some water."

I crumpled into the stool beside me and rested my head against the workbench. The necklace had transformed. No longer a gaudy piece of bling, the talisman had reformed itself into a platinum disc engraved to look like a poker chip.

"Oh shit," I said, stomach plunging into my shoes.

"Something wrong?" Heph asked, returning with his tankard.

"It's a poker chip. Did I screw up?"

He gazed at the disc, those steely eyes seeing more than just metal. "Quite the contrary. This is subtle work but well done."

"Then why is it a poker chip?"

"Does that have meaning for you?"

I blinked numbly. "Um, yeah."

"Then that is why. The magic is yours. Not hers. Fear not."

Hephaestus passed me a cup of water, and I drank thirstily. Some of the trembling in my blood and bones began to subside after a few draughts. I slid my cuff bracelet back on and dragged a hand through my hair. "So will this help keep him off the radar for a bit?"

The god blew out a mammoth sigh. "Only for a short time. What Marius needs is not a benefactor to protect him, but to take the initiative and fight for himself."

"That's all well and good," I countered, "but how is he supposed to do that? He's a satyr. There are deities after him. Plural. With dogs and sharp, pointy, nasty teeth."

"There is a way. Tell me, Cat, are you familiar with the Sileni?"

I bristled with a cold anger and uneasy interest. "I've heard the name. Marius's father told me to go to them. But then Marius said—"

"Ah, yes," he interrupted. "He would not turn to them if he were on fire and they held the only bucket of water." The slightest of laughs laced his words. "But they are the key."

"Who the hell are they?"

He leaned forward, balancing his elbows on his ginormous knees. "Are you acquainted with Marius's bloodline?"

I nodded.

"Then you know it is divine. The Sileni are satyrs not of this blood. They are common."

"Muggles," I offered. He regarded me with curious confusion, and I shook my head. Seriously, Heph needed to get out a bit. "Go on."

"In the oldest of days, satyr-kind gathered around the root of Marius's lineage, a one of their own blessed by Dionysus called Silenus. Silenus was granted with magical powers, divine gifts of body and mind that set him apart from other satyrs. The bloodline of that species split into two factions: the offspring of Silenus, and a baser, more crude form of half goat. These lesser beings took to worshipping Silenus as their own god. And when Silenus stepped down, a group of worshippers took his name—Sileni—and honored his offspring."

"Pan," I breathed.

Heph nodded. "Pan was lifted to the seat of godhood left vacant by his father, Silenus. The Sileni—satyrs with no magic or claim to divinity themselves—changed over the centuries, however. Mortal and malleable, they took their cues from other churches. Devotees turned to cult-like acolytes. Acolytes turned to power-hungry zealots. Pan gave up his throne and chose a life of seclusion and mortality. Since the Merry One left this Earth, the Sileni have been left without a deity to follow. They hunger for one to sit before them—one of Pan's lineage. Know anyone who fits that description, Cat?"

"Wait," I said, putting down the cup. I started snickering at the idea of Marius in golden robes and on a plinth. "Yeah, right."

"He is of the sacred bloodline. Llyr turned aside the birthright. It falls to Marius as the eldest scion of Silenus."

I shook my head, sobering. "He'll never take it. He calls them murderers. You said it yourself—if he were on fire, he wouldn't ask them for water. And he's pretty close to being on fire right now."

Hephaestus bobbed his head sadly. "But if he takes up the mantle, the game will change. He will be safe. Otherwise, he will just be buying time, postponing his death for a later date."

Date. Shit!

"Oh gods. What time is it?"

He closed his eyes. "It is half past five."

"Fuck. Fuck! I'm supposed to meet Marius at six, and I'm all..." I gestured to myself. It's not like I was covered in filth, but this was definitely not how I'd like to look on a date. And clothes! "Shit, I was supposed to go get something nice to wear tonight! Dammit, dammit!"

As I buzzed around the room having a total meltdown, Hephaestus stood up and rummaged in a pile of scraps. He came up with a wispy cloth. With its seemingly endless yards of shimmering fabric, it reminded me of a sari.

"You will wear this," he said.

"It's...it's lovely, but—"

"Trust me. This is armor I made for my wife. *Ex*-wife," he corrected himself. "She was so picky about her clothing, never practical. I created this so that it might take the form of whatever she wished to wear but would remain as strong as my finest plate."

Hephaestus draped the cloth over my arms while I gaped like a fish.

"I can't accept this," I said humbly.

"You can, and you will." Hephaestus smiled, that gold tooth winking as his steely eyes squinted with merriment. "Consider this my birthday gift to you. Oh, and if you would please make it something red. Marius can't resist a woman in red."

I didn't have a chance to protest. I blinked and found myself back in the cool confines of my hotel room. The strange fabric in my arms had gone from smoky and sheer to a shining silk the color of Asian poppies.

"Okay, now this is cool."

I dropped the dress onto the bed and sped to the bathroom to get ready.

A half hour later, I studied myself in the mirror. The silver cuff gleamed on one wrist; Loki's mark winked on the other. These were my accessories. A messy cascade of ginger curls spilled out of a clip, leaving my neck and shoulders exposed. The knee-length halter dress looked better that way. The red silk flowed over my form with a graceful, flirty sway. It looked good on me, but then, something made for Aphrodite damn well better. The magic even extended to my feet, turning my Chucks into strappy sandals. Who needs a fairy godmother?

My eyes lingered over the wound in my chest. I worried at it self-consciously.

"Stop it, Cat," I admonished myself.

As I toyed with my hair, I realized something was missing. Marius's braid, the charm to shield me against Malcolm's advances, was gone. Trying to figure out when I could've lost it, a flash of brimstone tore through my memory. The snap of Belial's fist, the feeling of hair being ripped out. He'd taken it. By whim or design, Belial had the braid.

Well, shit.

Nothing I could do but see what played out.

I took one last look at myself and grinned at my reflection. I was actually excited beneath the nerves. I shut off the light, grabbed my room key, and headed out the door before I could talk myself out of it.

TWENTY-THREE

"PERHAPS, PERHAPS, PERHAPS"

A few minutes past six, I knocked on the door to Marius's bungalow with a shaking, sweaty hand.

The door opened, and Malcolm's blue eyes widened. "Jesus Christ on a jet ski! Cat, you look delectable."

I beamed and let out a breath. "Thanks, Mal. Still not sleeping with you."

The satyr gestured me in, his stare doing laps of my form. I didn't feel his presence trying to get into my head—or my pants—so that was a good thing. As he closed the door behind me, I took in the main sitting room. It was similar to mine in design and color, but larger. I stood between the sofa and chairs and noticed a small kitchen next to the door. The space had clearly seen some use but remained tidy. I caught a deliciously murderous whiff of cooked meat and a mixture of spices— rosemary, onion, and garlic. My stomach moaned appreciatively, and my mouth began to water.

"I was just on me way out," Mal said. "*Someone* wanted the place to himself tonight." The satyr waggled his thick eyebrows, and I felt the color rise to my cheeks.

"It's not like that," I said. "Won't be." *Can't be.*

"Well, save yourself for me, then, won't you? Just a nibble?"

From behind me, I heard Marius's familiar grumble. "Not on your life, Malcolm."

I saw him just as he stepped through the sliding glass doors. He leaned against the doorframe, and I drank him in. Gaiety twinkled in his eyes, and his mouth hitched up in that lopsided smile he wore so well. His thick, glossy locks spilled down over his shoulders. Against the black of his hair, the crisp, paper-white shirt he was wearing all but gleamed. An emerald-green tie drew a line down his chest toward his black pants.

Damn, he looked good. Better than good...

My heart sped up, and my lips spread with pleasure. Marius's gaze met mine with conspiratorial excitement.

"Come on, Cat," Mal said in a failed attempt to draw my attention away from his brother. He slid into his leather jacket. "You sure you don't want to pop on a bike with me and ride around the mountain? Leave this sorry twat to 'imself?"

My eyes continued to feast on Marius's lithe form. "But he got all dressed up. I should at least humor him."

"Bah. Right, then. I'm off."

"We knew that," Marius said blithely.

The door shut, and we were alone. Unbidden, the memory of waking up in his arms slammed into me. I shuddered, goose bumps prickling over my flesh at the thought of our bodies touching, his naked skin against mine.

"Catherine, you are staggeringly beautiful this evening. You wear red as easily as a rose."

His gaze traced temptation up my body—glacially slow, yet warm as a flame. Fighting the urge to smooth my skirt for the millionth time, I coughed a nervous laugh. "Thank you."

He pushed himself away from the door and crossed to me, extending a hand. "Come. Dinner is waiting on the veranda."

I slipped my hand into his, strangely relieved to feel his palms were as clammy as my own.

"Care for a drink?" he asked as he led me outside.

"Yes, please."

While he busied himself with a bottle, I took in the scene that awaited me. A table for two was bedecked with candles and crystal glasses. Steam drifted up from dinner: pan-seared steak, roasted potatoes, and green beans plated with the precise beauty of any top chef.

If the view from my room was breathtaking, the sight of Santorini from this vantage point was majestic. We were higher up the slope of the crater and able to take in more of the crescent. It wasn't quite sunset, but as the sun drifted toward the horizon it bathed everything in a golden wash. The ocean below reminded me of Hephaestus's Forge, its surface a fiery reflection of the sky. The waves rippled and glittered like diamonds.

The sound of a popping cork drew my attention back to the patio. Marius had lit several candles along the ground, some of which climbed the steps to his private hot tub. Like mine, the water shone jewel-bright and inviting. Flower petals floated on the surface.

As Marius poured two generous glasses of red wine, I padded to the table. "You went all out, didn't you?"

"Who's to say when I'll have the honor again?" he asked, pulling out my chair. He bowed his head, a gesture urging me to sit. When I did, he slid the chair under me.

Marius took the seat opposite me. Drawing in a deep breath, it seemed he inhaled me right along with the steam drifting up from his plate. When his eyes fell to the small scar on my chest, his smile faltered.

"Take some wine," he said. "And eat while it's still warm."

For a short time, there was only the sound of silver on china as we ate. I hadn't noticed it earlier, but music was playing from a set of nearby speakers. A random mix—some Chopin, some Clapton, even a few songs with a more electronica feel—served as a quiet counterpoint, no more intrusive than the sea breeze.

We passed idle chat about Santorini's weather, the way the sky darkened to indigo in the east and the sun bled in the west. The food had been cooked to perfection. The potatoes had just enough crunch to them. The green beans were buttery, yet still crisp. My eyes rolled after a particularly delectable bite of beef melted in my mouth.

"Dear gods, Marius, this is amazing."

He beamed. "I'm not without my uses, you know. Glad you like it."

"No, no. *Like* doesn't quite cut it here. This is incredible."

When I looked up from my plate, I saw his eyes were once again fixed on the healing bullet wound in my chest. His face grew dark as he stared. Turning back to his dinner, he said, "You're just saying that because you've had a near-death experience. I could've bought you McDonald's and I'm sure it would've been just as delightful."

I shook my head. "Hell no. That's not food." I cut another slice of beef. "I will admit, though, that since your idiot brother shot me things feel different."

"How so?"

My thoughts snagged on their way to my mouth. How could I explain the changes? The way light and power flowed more readily at my whim. The way the world hummed at a new, more potent frequency. The way I looked at him.

I took a drink of wine, hoping to lubricate my mind and shake loose all those things I didn't know how to say.

"Colors are brighter," I said. "The breeze on my skin doesn't just feel nice, it feels divine. And yes, the food tastes better than anything I've ever eaten. Even this wine! I don't usually go for wine, but this is fantastic."

I swigged a bit more wine to slow down the rambling of my chatter.

Marius wrinkled his nose. Appalled, he asked, "Who on earth taught you to drink?"

"Excuse me?"

"You're not enjoying one drop of the wine that way. You're barely tasting it. This isn't some rotgut you shoot back and wince at from the burn. Nor is this some cordial you drink for a candy-flavored buzz. This," he said, raising the glass in his slender fingers, "is a full-bodied, well-aged Bordeaux."

I tilted my head. "I've never heard you talk about drinking as if it's an art."

"Well, it is," he countered. "Wine—good wine—is meant to be savored and experienced with every sense."

Marius tilted his wineglass so that the candlelight shone through the dark liquid. As he spun the stem of the glass between his slender fingers, the deep red shifted and swam with the dancing light of the flame, throwing shadows of deep orange and burgundy over his features.

"It starts with the eyes," he intoned, his words soft and reverent. "Like a fine dress on a lovely woman, the color of the wine is a subtle promise of things yet to come."

Thumbing the red silk strap of my gown, I raised my eyebrows, incredulous. "Oh really?"

His eyes sparkled. "She may bare all or blush. Or like this, she may cover herself in the deepest crimson. But there are glimmers of her spirit in the color she chooses. Lighter reds, hints of daring darkness. Just looking at her, your imagination begins to churn with ideas of what may lie beneath. *What will she taste like when I finally have her?* I wonder."

I shifted in my seat, heart fluttering. His stare smoldered from across the table.

"Then the bouquet," he said. Marius swirled the glass beneath his nose and inhaled. He closed his eyes, and his face relaxed as he breathed in the wine. "You've already entertained hopes about the wine. Desire her. Even if you put down the glass and walk away, taking nothing, the scent of her will tickle at your mind and lure you back. That scent will lead you on, tease you until you can't hold back any longer. You have to have her," he said, the slightest of growls punctuating his words. "And so you drink."

He offered me his glass, and I took a sip of the rich wine.

"But this isn't the end," he cautioned. "Hold the wine in your mouth. Savor each flavor—the light sweetness, the bass notes of the grapes that went into the barrel all those years ago. Let them explode like decadent fireworks that sizzle and pop on your tongue."

I closed my eyes and saw pictures of his words, fat, juicy explosions of purple, black, and gold.

"You hold on to it so that you might know her entirely, for this may be your only opportunity."

I swallowed, the wine sliding down my throat in warm tendrils of languid joy.

"Even after the drink, the wine is still being experienced. It becomes part of you. A blush to your cheeks, a warm breath on your skin."

I opened my eyes lazily.

"That, my dear, is how you drink wine."

Marius brought the glass to his lips and stole a fleeting but practiced sip. Watching the colors of his skin and eyes deepen and the candlelight dance over the black silk of his hair, I felt the wine settle somewhere just south of my stomach. Desire stirred with a feline stretch. As I'd taken a few moments to just enjoy the wine, I spared an extra moment savoring the sight of Marius. I wondered if I'd ever just appreciated the angular slant of his jaw or the fullness of his lips. My gaze slipped over his hands, those long fingers holding the crystal with little more than a whisper. The same careful touch of his hand that had been on my waist that morning.

I shivered with the remembered closeness, the ignited desire. For a moment longer, I entertained all the things that might be if it weren't for Marius's impairment.

"You certainly do know about pleasure, don't you?"

He passed me a weak smile. When he spoke, his voice was almost raw with... Was it bitterness? Sadness? Or did he just need another drink? "It's in the blood."

The mention of blood led me to thoughts of his lineage, of the things Hephaestus had revealed about the Sileni. Turning my attentions back to dinner, I said, "Marius, what if you don't need a bigger fish to help get you out of this mess?"

"What do you mean?"

"Well, your bloodline. Grandpa was a god, right? Can't you make something of that?"

He dabbed his mouth with a linen napkin. "Who've you been talking to, Catherine?"

I wrinkled my face at him. "Seriously?"

"You've no poker face. You cannot lie to me or even try to squeeze something past. You've got something specific in mind, so just come out with it."

Caught, I rolled my eyes. "Hephaestus. Your dad, too."

"Ah. And what did they have to say on the matter, then?"

"They both think you should go to the Sileni."

Marius pressed his lips together as if biting back anger. "Do they? And when they offered these opinions, did either Hephaestus or my father educate you about just who the Sileni are?"

I nodded. "Satyrs without a god, essentially."

"More like a Catholic church without a pope. They are corrupt. They are greedy and power hungry. But they want someone at the center, someone of the old line to serve as some sort of conduit. Their avarice drove my grandfather to weariness. As far as I'm concerned, they are the reason Pan is dead. They pushed him. Pulled at him until he had nothing of himself left."

"But if they can help you—"

"They might not even know I exist. And I'm happy to keep it that way. I've not been to the Temple since before Zeus's judgment. I don't know that I can go back."

He looked away, eyes falling to the candle's flickering flame. I thought of what he'd told me the night before, of the area near Pan's temple being his soul's own home.

"You must miss it."

"So much," he whispered, squeezing his eyes shut.

My heart broke for him. How long had Marius dreamed of going back to his grandfather's temple? To the pool with its waterfall? But as much joy as it might bring to go home, how awful would it be to go only to feel nothing? I could understand why Marius stayed away.

"I'm sorry," I muttered. "I shouldn't push."

"No," he said with a shake of his head. "You mean well. I just don't... I don't think I can. If the Sileni are still hungry for an avatar, they will bleed that soul dry. I'd rather not put myself on their altar if it can be avoided. Can that be the last we speak of it?" he added, eyes pleading.

"Sure."

Guilt twisted in my belly. I took another drink of wine in hopes that I might drown it. The music shifted from a sultry tango to something old, crackly with vinyl. A lovestruck guitar played by a slow hand. I looked up to find Marius's ivy-green stare fixing me with a question.

"Shall we stop talking for a bit?"

He pushed away from the table and offered me his hand. With a smile, I took it and let him lead me away from the table. We stood in a shadowy, bare space on the veranda—the perfect size for two people to dance. The sun had slipped beneath the lip of the crater, twilight hanging low over Santorini. The only light came from Marius's candles, the glow of the hot tub, and the waking stars.

Without a word, Marius slipped one arm around my back. I curled a hand around his shoulder, while the other remained safely in his gentle grip. Slow and languid, like reeds on the breeze, Marius and I swayed together. As he traced up and down my spine, temptation flowed through my blood, and I let my head fall against his chest.

As we fell into a comfortable rhythm, his arm tightened around me. He brought our entwined hands up to his lips and laid hints of kisses on my fingers. I smiled, soaking in bliss. As much as the truth of it terrified me, I understood that this was my home. This space in the curve of Marius's arm where I could hear the tender beat of his heart, feel the warmth of him all around me—that was my place of peace.

Lulled by the gentle rocking of our dance, by the silky touch of his hand against my back, my mind wandered into dreams of waking in his arms as I had just the day before. Skin to skin, safe and vulnerable. I craved another morning like that...every morning. My thoughts drifted to what it would be like to enjoy Marius, to not just bask in his embrace but dive into his passion. To be the object of his desires when there were no curses between us, no barriers or fears. Just the moment.

But we wouldn't have that. He couldn't. And if we didn't find an out for him soon, his trouble would only grow deeper.

I sighed, willing away the cold realities and exchanging them for warm fantasies.

"Penny for your thoughts," he said softly.

My eyes fluttered open, and I looked up to find him staring down at me with mild amusement. Embarrassment rose to my cheeks, prickling over my skin. "Nothing," I lied.

"Nothing? Again, Catherine, you are rotten at fibbing."

I buried my face in his chest, hoping to hide the fresh wave of heat and fickle shame flooding my features. He playfully rocked me faster, letting go of my hand and looping both arms around me.

"You blush spectacularly. Some people just redden a little, but you get this soft glow about you that is really quite fetching."

The compliment only fanned the flames. "Stop it," I said, avoiding his eyes. I looked out to the ocean, the smile on my face betraying everything.

"What is the wine telling you? She's singing to you, isn't she?"

"A siren song," I admitted.

"Really?" he asked with interest. "Do tell."

"I'm not listening."

"Pity, that. If you'd give it half a chance, you might find that you like the tune."

"Oh, I like the tune."

"Then why not listen and let yourself enjoy the chorus?"

I chewed on my lip. Couldn't he understand? Didn't he know better than anyone why I—*we*—couldn't just enjoy this? I opened my mouth to explain, but the words caught in my throat.

Understanding dawned on him, and his eyes widened. "You're scared."

I dipped my chin, unable to meet his gaze. *Of course I'm scared! You're every bad decision I've made embodied in one person, but you make me feel like I'm finally home!*

When I dared to bring my eyes back to his, the expression on his face stopped me cold. The wrinkles at his eyes deepened as he gaped at me. His lips quivered with subtle astonishment.

"What?" I asked. "What is it?"

"You're scared," he repeated. "Afraid that if you let go you will be vulnerable. Weak."

My heart pounded against his chest as he read me like a neon sign.

"Terrified," he continued. "Worried that if you let the moment swallow you up, you will disappear into it wholly, completely giving up all that you are for one taste. Afraid you will drown in that one, blazing moment."

I nodded mutely.

"Everything you've ever believed screams at you to turn the other way and run. Just ignore the luscious song and all the promise it offers. Run and remain free. And yet..."

We stopped moving with the music and stood, just peering into each other as if all the answers could be read in the other's eyes. My nerves strung as tightly as a damned violin, I waited, aching for completion, for the next note.

"Yet?" I prodded.

His hand glided up my spine and sent waves of sweet torment through my body. I gasped and quivered beneath his touch. He stroked my cheek. "And yet you jump in headlong," he purred. "Even though you know the fall is going to hurt like hell."

His thumb tipped my chin up as he brought his lips down to mine. I drew in a breath—the gasp before the plunge—and opened my mouth to his. Ecstasy—dark, silken, and rich—poured through me. He tasted of sweet wine and fire as his tongue glided over mine. Sparks shot through my core, and I gripped Marius with need, grinding against him.

As his hands roamed, I arched to meet him, desire escaping me with an urging growl. His fingers twisted in my hair, held me close as his mouth explored my throat. I hissed, another bolt of need rocking me as his teeth nipped at my skin. Heat flared over my flesh, my pulse raced, and delicious shudders exploded through me.

He moaned, my name burst out on his breath, flashing hot against my neck. I relished the velvety sensation of his kisses as they glided down my throat, over my collarbones only to land on the spot above and between my breasts. Marius hesitated over the bullet's mark, but not for long. He took my back in both hands and pressed himself to the scar, tonguing it lightly. A chill bit into my blood, and my nipples shot to attention. He cupped my breasts, his thumbs flicking at a tantalizing angle.

Boiling with desire, I ran my fingers into his mane and guided those smoldering kisses up, up, back to my lips where I could devour him. Savoring the taste of him as I had the wine, I wrapped my arms around him, stroked through the luxury of his hair.

My satyr, I thought. *Mine.*

Like a grain of sand, the name of his nature burrowed beneath my passion. Marius wasn't like me. He was something *other*. A satyr with divine lineage. Though I tightened my grip around him, doubt swirled in my mind. A list started to form, a long list of all the reasons why this couldn't be happening, why I couldn't throw myself into Marius without looking. Hadn't I done that before? Hadn't it ended in a glorious train wreck that cost me everything?

Reality crashed over me in a cold, sickening wave.

Nothing good could come of this.

Though my body screamed and ached for pleasure—for Marius—I pulled back on the reins of my desire. Drawing away from his lips was like trying to pry myself out of the sweetest of dreams. As my fantasies dissolved, I stared at my satyr, trying to come back to the world. His lips brushed mine. Face blotchy with color, pupils dilated, he fixed me with a drunken gaze. The horns on his brow glowed in the wan light.

"Yes?" he asked breathlessly.

Those full, luscious lips beckoned me. *Just one more taste.*

And then what, Cat? I snarked to myself. *Back to dinner?* Every cell in my body craved him with a thirst that could not be slaked.

If I fell, if I let myself get caught up in this raging tide, I would drown in Marius's kisses. But no more could come of us. His curse. His past. His tenuous future. That path held only madness and heartache.

"I...I need..." I said.

His forehead burned like a fever against mine. I could feel his pulse racing in a sympathetic rhythm to my own.

"What, Catherine?" he rasped. "Tell me what you need."

If I finished that sentence with the truth, I'd be sucked under. I chose the lie. "I need to go."

I broke the circle of his arms but not the spell of his kisses. Drowsy, burning with this deep, throbbing ache for him, I moved sluggishly back into the room and picked up my key. Before I could talk myself out of it, I opened the door.

I heard him call my name as I moved down the path. I sped up, the world blurring past me as I practically teleported back to my room. I had done the right thing. I had to believe that or I would fall to pieces.

TWENTY-FOUR

"Is This Love?"

I slammed the door to my bungalow with a little too much force. The fire in my blood that only moments ago had been singing for Marius turned into anger, bitter and ballistic. I tore off the dress and tossed it to the floor where it resumed its smoky, glittering formlessness. What next? Would the room turn to a pumpkin at midnight? I yanked the clip from my head and let my hair fall around my face like a furious mop of flames. Gripping the cuff, I slipped it off my wrist. When I hurled it across the room, the metal elongated, lashing away from me like a long, silver tongue. The whip struck the phone and sent pieces of plastic flying all over the room.

Again.

I gaped for a brief moment. Frustration won out over curiosity, and I just shouted, "God dammit!"

I pulled on pajamas and stomped out to the patio. Seething, hands gripping the side of the hot tub, I closed my eyes and tried to count away my anger. I pushed the boiling tension out through my fingers. The water began to bubble and gurgle as if I'd turned on the jets. And shit, maybe I had with my particular skill set. But no. This was different. I stared at the churning water, dumbstruck and curious. Remembering how I'd called the ocean to douse Eris the night before, I reached out a hand and lifted it through the air. I whispered my will into it as I would when calling electricity to my control. A column of water rose from the hot tub.

I gasped and let go of the energy. The pillar collapsed, and the choppy water slowly ebbed to a sullen froth.

Backing away, I retreated into the hotel room, just staring at the water. I'd never worked elemental magic. How was I suddenly doing this? Furthermore, I had punched through a phone like it had been tissue paper earlier that morning, and my own technological powers were coming more easily. What was happening to me?

I snatched up my cell phone and plopped onto the bed, dialing the one person I thought might have some answers. Besides, I needed a friend at the moment.

Karma picked up on the second ring. "Oh my god, girl, why didn't you call me sooner? I've been dying to hear what happened the other night!"

"Things have gotten a little...crazy. Tonight's the first time I've felt like I could breathe. Maybe."

"Tonight? Where are you?"

"Greece," I answered sheepishly.

"What the hell are you doing in Greece?"

"It's a long story. Look, I need to talk to you about your implants."

"They are not implants," she said hotly. "They are natural. And fabulous, I might add."

I snickered despite myself. "Ha. Yes, they are. But that's not the point. Anyway..." I gave my fellow technomage a quick and dirty rundown of the past few days up to when Flynn had to use one of Karma's cybernetic devices to bring me back from the dead.

"Damn, girl," she said heavily. "I'm glad it worked. You doing okay?"

"Yeah. Grand. Better than okay. And that's what's got me freaked out."

I imagined her forehead wrinkling during her pensive pause. "Why?"

I explained the changes in my strength, my ability to manipulate water. "So, these implants," I pressed. "No reason I should have super-strength or suddenly be a goddamn water bender?"

"Nope. Well, not because of the implant itself," she said.

"What do you mean?"

"My piece is made to take the blood of one person and use the life energy in it to heal another. That's it. But the blood used might affect you in some way. If the donor had magic powers, you might be getting something that way, but I'm not sure."

That wasn't much help. Nor was the fact that my thoughts kept drifting back to kissing Marius.

"Christ, Karma, it's just been so nuts. And the date with Marius sure as shit didn't change that any."

"Whoa!" I could hear the record scratch in her thought process. "Wait. *What?*"

"Yeah, I— Look, the past few days have been really full. I've died, seen Pandora's box, been in three different countries in as many days. It's been fucking crazy, okay?"

"Crazy enough that you went on a date? With Marius?"

"Just now, actually."

She sputtered on the other end of the line. "Holy shitballs, Cat! Dish. Now!"

I rolled my eyes but was grateful for the chance to talk to someone in the know about my issues dating nonhumans. I fell back against the pillows on my bed and spilled my guts, babbling like I was back in junior high. I told her about how he'd gone to the trouble to make dinner, how amazing it was. The music, the candlelight, the view. Heat flared through me, and I felt my limbs go rubbery just at the memory of his lips.

"And shit, Karma, the kiss..."

"Why the fuck did you leave?" she shouted at me.

"Because! This is Marius! You know I don't date nonhumans. Not since Dahlia."

"You're full of shit, Cat."

I rocked back as if she'd smacked me. Stunned, I said, "Excuse me?"

"This whole hang-up of yours is total bullshit. And you know it," she added pointedly. "Seriously, you don't have some righteous mad-on for anything non-vanilla-mortal. If you did, would we be friends?"

"That's different."

"How 'bout Flynn? He's— Well, he's different, too." I started to protest, but she cut me off. "Or Loki? You're pretty chummy with him."

I let out a choked laugh. "This is ridiculous."

"Face it, sweet cheeks, you're not vanilla. You're just as inhuman
as Marius, only in a less overt way. Besides, do you really think you'd
be happy with a normal guy? Or gal? You'd be bored out of your mind.
You'd have to hide the things about being able to talk to machines, or
your direct line to actual gods, or the fact that you've now seen Pandora's
box. Just so we're both clear, was that a euphemism?"

"No," I said with a roll of my eyes.

"Do you really think you could keep a relationship with someone
who didn't play in the same pool as you? I don't think so. You might be
able to fool yourself into believing that line about how Dahlia screwed
you over and now you will never trust another nonhuman again, but
fuck that. People get hurt all the time by other people without some
supernatural kink in their DNA."

Tears streamed down my face as the ache in my chest became palpable. "I'm scared," I whispered.

She sighed with pity. "I know, boo," she crooned. "We're all scared."

I let out a long breath. "So what do I do?"

"Get back over there and jump him. Tear off his clothes, hop on the
good foot, and do the bad thing. A couple of times."

I laughed out a snotty bubble. "I can't. Not tonight. I just... No."

"Well, then I don't know what to tell you, Cat. But you can't keep
trying to bullshit yourself out of happiness, okay? You're not with Eris
anymore. Loki? He's good to you. You no longer have an excuse to keep
living some sad and dreary existence. And you know I'm right."

I didn't say anything to that. We both knew she was right. I wiped
my eyes with the heel of my hand and sighed.

"Hey, I gotta split, boo," Karma said. "I've got a real job to get back
to."

I shook myself out of my thoughts. "Shit, I'm sorry. I forgot what
time it was there. Thanks for talking. I heart your face."

"No worries. Hey, can I ask you a question before I take off?"

"Shoot."

"Do you love Marius?"

The question punched me in the chest. My throat closed up and my blood went cold with a sick, slow dread. I knew the answer to that question. And I didn't like it. The answer terrified me more than princes of Hell and monolithic beasties.

With my free hand, I gripped at my hair. I couldn't say it. Not to Karma. Not even to myself.

"Look," she said quietly, her voice soothing. "I know you're probably going crazy about this right now, but for what it's worth, I think you need to tell him. If he's in as much trouble as you say he is, this might be the only shot you've got. Take it while you can."

"Thanks, Karma."

"Have fun in Greece and bring me something shiny."

"Will do. Later."

Karma's voice belted out a pop diva's song, "Teeeell hiiiim!"

Laughing through my tears, I hung up on her silly ass.

—m—

My dreams were full of steam and whispered secrets. When I woke up, Marius's name was on my lips. With the clarity that comes the morning after, I realized I had been colossally stupid to leave the satyr's room. He'd gone through a lot of trouble to make our night together a glittering, delicious affair, and I'd gone and ruined everything.

"Dumbass," I spat at myself. Freaked out by a couple of kisses... Spectacular, mind-numbing kisses.

My head swam with just the memory of his hands over my skin, the hot flush of need brought on by his mouth pressed to mine. An echo of that desire throbbed in my chest.

Karma was right. It didn't matter that he was a satyr. I'd been using that bullshit excuse on myself for years, and as she pointed out, it no longer held water. It was okay for vanilla-mortal Cat to go through life hating nonhumans because she'd been dicked over by one treacherous faerie and a goddess, but I'd entered a whole new category when

Flynn and I had broken the binding that had kept my technomagic inert. Vanilla Cat had used her xenophobia as a flotation device after everything crashed a decade ago. But now, I wasn't just bobbing along anymore, was I?

The old rules didn't apply; therefore, I couldn't cling to the same fears.

I lay there in bed thinking about all this, fingers dancing over my lips, lightly tracing the lines left behind by Marius's kisses the night before.

Tell him, Karma had said.

But...

But what? Karma would ask. She didn't know about Marius's curse or his stubborn belief that love was for crazy, deluded humans. Those thorns were a very important part of reality in this case, weren't they?

At the end of the day, though, what mattered was the twisting in my chest and the pangs of emptiness I felt when Marius and I weren't together. Curse or no curse, I still wanted him, still craved his presence.

It didn't matter if Marius couldn't feel pleasure, or even if he didn't reciprocate, did it? Any moment now some big bad nasty could come scoop him up and drag him away and there would be this thing dangling between us, the chord that wouldn't resolve.

With a flutter in my tummy and a hot splash of fear, I gave myself the order: *Tell him. Now.*

As if I were watching myself on television and not living the whole thing, I saw myself stand up from the bed and move around the hotel room.

Holy shit. She's going to do this. I'm going to do this.

I didn't bother with breakfast. I doubt I could've kept anything down anyway, what with the elephants sumo wrestling in my stomach. My hands shook as I brushed my hair, and then sweat beaded on my forehead, and my palms went damp as I walked up the path to Marius and Malcom's shared bungalow.

I stood at the door trying to rehearse my words and gather the courage to say them. And I realized I was smiling. My body felt light and almost giddy as I realized that as terrifying as this confession would be, it would also be liberating. I could share my secret, and then I might also be able to confide in Marius just what had happened after Malcolm shot me. That I'd truly died. That I knew so much of the peace of the next world that it made coping with this one difficult. And if I explained that...then maybe Marius would understand why I needed to be near him. He'd finally know why I couldn't let him just run headlong into danger on his own.

Then what?

With a strange sense of déjà vu, I knocked. Malcom answered. The nubs of his horns poked through the unruly coils of his hair. His face was drawn and weary, eyes bloodshot. The funk around him smelled of cigarettes, booze, and a floral perfume.

"Cat," he drawled. "Haven't we done this before, love?"

My nervous smile stretched. "Morning, Mal. Looks like you had quite the night."

Mal opened the door wider so that I could come in. "Damn near perfection. Only thing missing was you."

As I stepped in, I saw that Mal was shirtless. And...well, a half-goat. Black, sleek fur covered his inhuman legs. A pair of Superman boxers, saved me from getting an eyeful of Mal's bits, though. The signature *S* was emblazoned on his ass.

"Damn, you're smooth," I said sarcastically.

As his hooves clicked across to the kitchen floor, Mal rolled a bare shoulder with feigned embarrassment. "I know. What about you? You're beaming like sunshine, but he's been pissy all morning."

"That's...complicated," I said, sucking air through my teeth. Mal padded into the kitchen and plucked some food from a plate. The cold remnants of our dinners were piled unceremoniously in the sink, and Mal grazed on them. The glasses were empty, and I saw at least two empty bottles of wine. Pillows had been tossed around the room, disturbing the neat and quiet order of the bungalow.

My heart shuddered. Something told me this wasn't the aftermath of a wild rumpus.

I should've stayed.

"Where is he?" I asked quietly.

Mal's face stretched in another yawn as he scratched his furry belly. He shook like a dog and made a similarly canine barking sound in his throat. Without opening his eyes, he pawed limply toward the sliding-glass doors. "Out there somewhere."

I'd already put my back to Malcolm and breezed out the patio door before I remembered to mumble a halfhearted thank-you. My satyr wasn't there. Whatever whirlwind had torn through the sitting room had spared the outside. In fact, all I found out there were the waxy puddles of candles. Marius hadn't bothered to snuff them out. The rose petals, darkened and shriveled, floated in the hot tub in a reminder of what might have been.

Guilt gripped me by the throat. A small gate was ajar so I passed through and followed a twisting, tile path down the slope toward the beach. I caught the scent of Marius's cologne as a sea breeze tossed the air. Prowling for my prey, I quickened my pace.

The path merged with a wooden boardwalk as land joined up with sandy beach. Though it was heading into midmorning, the day was overcast. Thick clouds threatened rain, and the sea rolled with large, choppy waves. Apparently, most people were enjoying other parts of the resort because the beach was quiet. Practically vacant. A man played Frisbee with a black dog, stopping only to admire the slender, bronzed woman jogging past them.

I found Marius plodding through the foam. He wore a white T-shirt that was loose enough to be comfortable but tight enough to show off the lines of his muscles. His white linen pants were rolled up to avoid the spray. A pair of thong sandals hung limply from two fingers as he stepped along the shoreline, his bare feet leaving imprints in the moist sand. Hoof-shaped ones. If anyone else noticed, they wouldn't have a chance to confirm any suspicions before the waves washed away all remnants that he'd ever passed by.

Sadness radiated from him, dragging the clouds around him like a dark shroud. And yet, from beneath his cloak of melancholy, something primal blazed in his eyes. Something without pretense. That's when I understood: this Marius was real. Sure, there was the standard glamour hiding his satyr's features. Beyond that, however, was Marius. *Just*

Marius. This was my satyr at the most vulnerable I'd seen him—well, when he wasn't bleeding on my doorstep. That was something different. That was trauma and danger. This was a man having a moment to himself, wrapped in thoughts and unaware of anything else.

I didn't go to him then. I stood on the boardwalk, leaning against the railing and watching Marius. Just watching, enjoying the sight of him. Any moment he would feel the prickly sensation of my eyes on him. He'd look up, catch me staring, and...well, whatever happened would happen.

Until then, though, I'd savor this scene of him away from the eyes of the world.

A particularly strong gust of wind blew in from behind him. His black locks whipped around his face. He stopped walking and turned to face the wind, giving me a view of his profile. He closed his eyes. As he had a night or two ago, he seemed to relish the feeling of the Grecian air flowing over his skin. The wind rippled over his clothes and through his hair, and as it did, some of his sadness melted away. Frothy waves lapped at his ankles, and he spread his arms, welcoming this cleansing.

Maybe things can change, I mused.

This was a different man than the one I'd met all those years ago in Eris's office. Marius had changed so much. We both had. And if my own contempt for him could shift into this warm, terrifying affection, could his? If the two of us could go from bitter enemies to whatever *this* was, perhaps even more would be possible.

Maybe, just maybe, we could love each other.

The wind died down a bit, and as it did, Marius lowered his arms. When he opened his eyes, he looked as though he'd come to some understanding with himself. Or the world. Or both. His gaze tracked over the horizon, and the barest of smiles dimpled his cheeks. Not a smirk. An honest smile.

My stomach quivered. Just that simple shift in his features transformed his morose beauty to something heartrendingly attractive. Speechless, I melted in awe of my satyr.

Mine.

A smile of my own warmed me.

Now, I nudged myself. *Go to him now.*

Since moving to Vegas I'd learned a thing or two about gambling, and now was the time to take a risk. To scream and leap into the unknown, come what may or hell to pay.

I took a few steps toward him, my feet sinking into the deep sand. "Marius!" I called. I was surprised at the joy ringing in just those syllables.

He followed the sound of my voice and found me, his stare mimicking the surprise I felt. Confusion furrowed his brow. As the moment came closer, that moment of spilling it all to him, it seemed the world slowed down to take notice, as well. The man throwing the Frisbee stopped his game, the disc floating past Marius and landing out somewhere in the surf. The dog bounded along the shoreline, jaws open. And growing.

Marius's face changed then. The confusion darkened, his features sharpening with alarm that soon morphed into true horror. The dog leaped, its massive black form eclipsing the perfect white of Marius's clothing.

I didn't understand.

Not until I saw the red stain flowing out with the tide.

TWENTY-FIVE

"AIN'T NO GOOD"

Even though I was still a good twenty yards away, the rank stench of brimstone was strong enough that I gagged. Choking on the memories that stink evoked, my stomach churned and threatened to heave.

I'd never seen a hellhound before. The already-large dog had doubled in size, its coat shifting from sleek fur to wisps of shadow that absorbed the light. Its teeth dripped with sulfuric venom, and its eyes glowed red as coals. Waves pounded the pair. Gigantic paws pinned Marius to the sand, scraped at my satyr's chest. As the water ebbed away, Marius sputtered and coughed, his face contorted with agony as his fresh wounds were doused with salt.

He roared in pain, the gashes on his sides bleeding into the water. He held the hound at bay with one strong arm and the blade of his saber, drawn from its sheath in the ether. The steel was buried to the hilt into the dog's body, but the twisting shadows refused to split or bleed.

As I ran, I screamed Marius's name. My voice, thin and shrill, sounded a million miles away. My feet slid as I pounded down the dune. Goddamn sand! Every step seemed to take me farther from him. Every second jerked through time too quickly, skipping precious nano-moments that could make all the difference between... Oh gods, I couldn't think of that.

Twenty feet away now.

I began to pool power in my fists, preparing to punch the dog so hard I'd send the mutt flying out into the crater and down to Heph's Forge.

Fifteen feet.

At the end of the tunnel that served as my field of vision, Marius thrashed in the surf, the hellhound's jaws snapping at him with gleeful ferocity. His arm—locked under the beast's shoulder—trembled from the effort of holding its bulk. The hound dug its back paws into Marius's thighs.

Ten feet.

My satyr roared with pain again. This terrible warble was drowned out by the next wave, a huge swell that swept over both Marius and his attacker.

I plunged into the whitecap and unleashed my power. Water exploded in a plume, and my legs went out from under me in probably the least graceful face-plant ever. The water I'd just sent skyward fell right about the same time I got tossed by the next wave crashing in. I couldn't see, couldn't breathe, and I couldn't find Marius. Groping with outstretched hands only brought fistfuls of water or silt. As the waves receded again, I got my feet underneath me and shot up from the water, gasping and ready to tear that hellhound's face off.

But it was gone.

Disoriented and dizzy, I searched the nearby shore. No dog. Worse, no Marius.

What I thought might be a scrap of his shirt was nothing more than a broken shell. The stringy flotsam was sea grass, not his hair. Nothing of Marius remained but a pink tinge to the sea foam.

"No," I said, the waves pounding my back.

On my knees, I flailed, shoving at the water as if I could somehow part it. If I dug a little deeper through the wet sand, maybe I would find the satyr there. As my desperation mounted, my splashing became more feverish. I threw clumps of sand, fought the tide as I trudged up and down the shore looking for him. I called his name over and over.

He never answered.

No one did. The beach was so desolate I may as well have been on the moon.

Another behemoth wave threw me off my feet. I came down on my hands and knees, and as the water washed over my back, I felt all hope ebb away.

"No," I moaned, mouth dripping with seawater. My guts rolled as I entertained the horrible notion that the salty taste on my lips was my satyr's blood.

He's gone.

Terrified, I tried to quantify what that could mean. All manner of horrors played out behind my eyes. As the terror took over, my lip began to quiver. Deep in the pit of me, something roiled and quaked, threatening to burst out of me in the most hideous wail. I clamped down on it, biting into the sides of my mouth to keep from erupting.

"No," I said again, this time through a thick bubble of despair.

Another wave and I crumbled beneath it like a sand castle. Rage tore through me, and I punched at the earth. I thrashed and kicked, sending up sprays of water. Fighting didn't bring him back. It didn't give me mystical insight on where he'd gone, nor did it tell me if Marius was alive or... I pitched forward, nauseated at the very thought.

The place where he'd been, the patch of sand he'd occupied just moments before, had already been smoothed to perfection. Not so much as an imprint of him remained.

My satyr.

Gone.

I let out a wordless, ululating howl of despair that left me feeling cold and weak. Sputtering, shivering, I crouched on my hands and knees.

At that moment, of all the things I could think of—all the hideous torments I could imagine—I could hear Llyr's voice.

Promise me, he'd said. *Swear to me that you will help him through this.*

Tears flowed down my face, adding their salt to the sea. I closed my eyes, but it didn't stop the vision. Llyr's careworn face swam up in my mind. Those old blue eyes questioned me, accused me.

Please? Protect my son.

The weight of it all dragged at me, clung to me like hoarfrost. I'd tried to help him. But somewhere between dying in England and dancing on a balcony in Greece, I'd gotten swept up in my stupid feelings. I'd lost sight of the very real danger.

And because of that, I'd failed.

I'd lost Marius.

TWENTY-SIX

"IT'S COMING DOWN"

I don't remember how I got back up to the hotel room. I only know that one minute I was sobbing on the shoreline and the next I was sitting on the floor of a steaming hot shower. My fingers were pruny, so gods only knew how long I'd been sitting there. My hair was clean, though, and the deep chill I'd felt down to my soul had seeped away.

I stood, and as I turned off the water, I heard voices from my room. Almost immediately, the low sounds cut off. My mind didn't begin the process of deducing who might be there and what they might want. No, I was too numb to feel something like panic. Too hollow to think.

I drew energy into my right hand as easily as one picked up a towel. Friend or foe, it didn't matter. I padded forward, ready to meet what—or whom—ever might be in the room.

There came a light knock on the door. "Cat, it's me," Loki said. There was a pause laden with any number of rote responses he could offer, and it was that silence that told me that he knew about Marius. One of the reasons I'd grown to respect Loki, though, was that he didn't do rote. He spit in the face of propriety and scripted social responses. At that moment, though, the gap between his words told me that he was sorely tempted to go easy on me.

"We should talk," he said finally.

Without letting go of the power in my fist, I said, "Sure. Who's with you?"

"Hephaestus."

Again, Loki paused. Something about his reticence annoyed the shit out of me. I knew that kind of silence. It was the same brand everyone used after a huge trauma, like being told you have cancer...or the sudden death of a friend. It was a silence that didn't know what it would take to be filled.

"Your clothes are drying on the terrace," he called through the door. "Is there anything you'd like me to bring you?"

I scanned the bathroom, and sure enough, my clothes were gone. There were towels on the rack, and a white robe hung on a hook. I slipped into the terry cloth robe and opened the door. Loki was slouched there, hands braced on the doorjamb and head bowed. He lifted his chin just enough to bring us eye to eye. Emotions crowded his face, each vying for the top spot. The trickster's brow creased with pity. From beneath a blossom of dark-purple welts, the god's arctic eyes flashed with confusion. Blood dried on his swollen lower lip as his mouth parted in subtle surprise.

I didn't have the energy to question why he looked as if he'd been rumbled for his lunch money. I shrugged deeper into the robe and answered his earlier question. "I'm fine."

Loki met my stare, studying me, searching for clues as to my mental state. Had I been in a better mood, I'd have probably enjoyed the hell out of making a trickster god wonder if I was speaking in layered riddles. As it was, though, I didn't give a shit either way. Perhaps it was the bond we shared through my soul, the mark that branded me as his vassal. Or maybe I imagined it, but it seemed that Loki hung there trying to decide who I was and how he would treat me. In what capacity should he act—boss, friend, or master?

I took the decision out of his hands. Stiffening my lip and straightening my spine, I asked, "How can I be of service to Asgard?"

He held my gaze a moment longer, marred jaw working as he weighed his options. With a resigned nod, Loki let his hands slide off the jamb and stood to his full height. "Follow me," he said coolly.

I padded into the hotel room behind him, hands in my pockets.

As we passed the overstuffed chair, Loki motioned with one finger that I should sit. I curled up in the seat, knees drawn to my chest. Across from me, Hephaestus took up most of the sofa with his bulk. Loki slithered into the narrow space between Heph and the arm of the couch. Pale and slender tucked in next to the obsidian land mass. It was damn near comical.

"Hephaestus," I said curtly.

"Cat," he rumbled. Heph's quicksilver eyes were impossible to track, but it felt as if his attention swam around the room, seeking anything to rest on but me.

I sighed. If neither of them would open the wound, it might as well be me. "I take it you both know about Marius."

Heph winced, his massive shoulders hunching at the sound of the satyr's name. After another gaping chasm of silence, the blacksmith nodded, his stare trained to the floor.

I passed a question to Loki. "You?"

"Heph told me."

"I see. Is that why you're here?"

"More or less." In the full lamplight, the shadowy bruises on Loki's face looked even darker than they had before. At the collar of his Ramones T-shirt I saw what looked like scorch marks, the skin at his throat red and puffy.

"What happened?" I finally asked. "Did you get rolled by a hell-hound, too?"

"More or less," he repeated. "Look, Cat, we need to talk about your future."

I couldn't suppress the irreverent scoff. "What are you, my guidance counselor?"

"I'm serious. Even though Marius is— Well, even though you're not—" Loki shook his head and looked away from me, searching to see if his next line was written on the walls. Maybe the carpet. Nope. Not there, either. "You're still in danger, Cat."

"Are you new here? I'm always in danger."

"It's different now. You've got several sets of eyes on you, and I don't think I can protect you from all of them."

I glared at Loki icily. Parting the thick folds of the robe, I revealed the bullet hole in my chest. "You don't say."

"Don't be a smart-ass, Cat. You're good at the snark, but with me, you're grossly outclassed."

I put away the wound but not the attitude. "Sure, Chief. So it's suddenly news to you that I'm an endangered species?"

"It's not like before," he warned. "You had the attentions of a few factions—some with power, some trying to gain it back. And ever since your little dance with Moloch, more of my colleagues are aware of you. Allowing you to step out with the satyr was possibly the stupidest thing I could've done. I'm sorry."

"I probably would've done it anyway."

"And that also would have been incredibly dumb."

"Yeah, well, can't take any of it back..." I shrugged. I could think of far more idiotic things I'd done in the past twenty-four hours. My mind lingered on that kiss. And my exit. When I spoke again my voice was raw with regret. "None of it."

"No shit. Now anyone who ever had a beef with Marius—or Eris, for that matter—is watching you, sizing you up. They want to know who you are and how you can be used."

"Against who? You?"

"Anyone. But if it's names you want, your pal Flynn jumps to mind."

That hooked my attention. Would hellhounds go knocking at YmFy next? Or worse, would Belial show up there?

Loki pressed his warning deeper. "And if they find you can't be used, Cat, they'll be working out the best way to bring you down."

I sighed. "And just what do you propose I do about all this?"

"Hide."

I blinked at him. "Are you serious?"

"As Ragnarok. You need to make yourself scarce. Heph here has offered to shelter you at the Forge for a week or two until I've got something better worked out."

"Wait," I said.

But Loki spoke over me. "You'll need to disconnect from Vegas for a few months at least. A year or two would be best. Cut your hair. Dye it. I'll have some alter egos for you to play with."

"Wait a minute," I repeated.

"Heph, we'll need some armor."

"I've already given her Aphrodite's," the blacksmith rumbled. "If you'd like, I will work with her on packaging some cloaking spells if you'd be willing to provide them."

"Of course. I have a few other ideas we can discuss at the Forge."

I jumped to my feet and let out a snap of white power, like a frat boy wielding a wet towel. "Wait just a fucking minute!"

The gods cut off their plans and gaped at me, Loki's jaw and eyes wide open. The energy still crackled at my fingertips.

"I'm not cutting or dying my hair," I simmered. "I'm not disconnecting from Vegas. I'm not hiding. And as much as I appreciate the offer, I will not be hunkering down at the Forge for the next few weeks. And would either of you like to venture a guess as to why?"

"Because you're a stubborn twit with a death wish?" Loki sniped.

"Because I still have a goddamn job to do. Christ, both of you are here, morose as fuck and plotting to whisk me away like some helpless princess when what we should be doing is figuring out where the hellhound took Marius."

My words floated in the air, a thick miasma that choked the gods. For a few beats, they just stared at me. Heph dropped his gaze, and held his head in his hands. Loki, though, fixed me with his cold eyes. He pawed down his cheeks and steepled his fingers in front of his mouth.

"Oh shit," he murmured. Loki focused on the floor, dragging his hands through his strawberry-blond spikes. "Shitshitshit," he hissed. "Why the hell...? Of all the sons of cursed whorebag foolish fuckwits and..."

"Okay. You go ahead and make up new and exciting swear words. I'm going to get to work."

I hopped off the chair and started for the bedroom. Loki took me gently by the shoulders and guided me back to my seat.

"Catherine, please," he said. He'd used the full version of my name, which was rare for Loki.

Oh gods. What do they know that I don't?

When Loki spoke again, his voice was soft. "We can't go find Marius."

I shut my eyes. He didn't know. He couldn't *know*.

"Cat? Cat, look at me. *Look* at me."

I opened my eyes, but Loki hid behind the quivering blur of my tears.

"He's gone."

"No," I said thickly.

"Cat," Loki warned. I stood up and struggled against the god's bulky arms.

"No."

"Cat, I'm sorry. I'm sorry," he repeated, voice breaking yet loud enough to muffle my protests, "but he's gone."

"No!"

I lashed out, drawing on power, but as Loki clamped his hands over my wrists, the energy drained away. I gasped. I couldn't feel the electric hum dancing in the air, couldn't see the filaments of power or the workings of even the simplest of devices. Somehow Loki had muted my powers. For the first time in years, I was *normal*.

My heart pounded, and though I tried to breathe, to draw in power and air alike, both were denied to me. My ribs shrank in my chest, and I felt as if I were drowning. I pushed and slithered, trying to wrench myself free of Loki's grip, but his fingers tightened painfully around my wrists. I hissed and growled through my teeth, angry and scared as any caged wild animal.

"He's gone, Cat," he croaked. Loki's sadness was a nail in my chest. I stopped struggling and looked him in the face. I saw anger there, mirroring my own. Beneath it, though, I saw anguish. I knew it all too well. Deep beneath some frosty layer of denial, I felt that crushing sadness, too.

A single tear traced down his bruised cheeks. "Marius is dead. I'm sorry."

I bit my lip until I tasted blood, then squeezed my eyes shut. More hot tears spilled down my face. Loki released his dampening hold on me, and a tide swallowed me. Air filled my lungs, power and sensation overwhelmed me. Then despair, my old friend.

Before I could sink beneath the crushing weight of everything, Loki took me into a fierce embrace. "I'm sorry," he repeated, his tenor quavering with the truth of it all. "He was my friend, too. I cared about him."

I shook my head. "Maybe you're wrong."

"Pandora's box," Hephaestus said from the sofa.

Gently, I pushed away, leaving Loki to wipe his eyes on the heel of his hand. The blacksmith hadn't moved. He still sat on the couch with his head cradled in his hands. A lock of verdigris fell into his face.

"What did you say?" I asked.

"Pandora's. Box." His silver stare rose to meet me. "Do you remember what it contained?"

"The evils of the world," I answered. "Vice. Sin. Disease. All that stuff."

"And do you remember what was left when she finally closed it? What remained locked inside?"

"Hope. But I don't see what this has to do with—"

"Has it never occurred to you to wonder why it was in the box to begin with? It would be like putting a virgin in a prison full of rapists and thugs. Why include hope in the same chest as all the vileness the world had yet to inherit?"

After a moment of pondering, I said, "I don't know."

"Because of all the blades a man can use upon himself, hope is the sharpest. It cuts the deepest. It is what you feel right now, a warm tingle at the very center of your heart. The ember."

"But you know him, Heph. Marius is smart. Wily. There could be a chance."

He let out a rueful laugh. "Even now you fan the ember. Take heed: If you breathe it to life, that fire will consume you, Catherine Sharp. Hope will do nothing but kill you slowly."

"You and I both know that the goat-legged sonofabitch loves himself far too much to just—"

I stopped talking as Hephaestus drew a sword. Not out of fear of him striking me with it, but because of the blade itself. The saber gleamed in the light like a sharpened smile. I'd seen that same sword many times.

"How... That's Marius's saber."

Balancing the sword in both hands, Heph nodded.

"But, if you have it..." My brain hurt at all the different ways I could end that sentence. "What does it mean?"

"Precisely what the Trickster has told you. It means our Marius is gone. He is beyond the veil."

TWENTY-SEVEN

"No Phone"

I didn't know what to say. I had no idea if anything could be done so I focused on one thing I could control at a time. First, I stood up. Then I went to the bathroom and brushed my hair. Bit by bit, I put myself together. Clean, dry clothes. Chucks.

By the time I'd gotten dressed, I felt more like myself and my mind started working on the unruly knot of this situation. Though something down to my very blood insisted the contrary, the evidence of Marius's death was irrefutable. The blood in the water. The fact that his sword had returned to its maker. Loki's honest grief.

What a glory it must be when the gods themselves weep at your death, I thought.

The god-forged cuff on my wrist was a cool, welcome weight. As I tidied up around the room, I found the silver poker chip that had once been Marius's amulet. I'd meant to give it back to him, but had forgotten to take it with me when I met him for our date.

If he'd had it, would he have...?

No. I couldn't think like that. Couldn't question every little decision, wondering if he'd still be here if I'd turned left rather than right. *There lies madness.*

I slid the chip into my hip pocket and plodded back into the sitting area. Heph was pacing with the slow tempo of a dirge while Loki slouched on the sofa. I plopped next to the Aesir and let out a long breath.

"I suppose I should tell Malcom," I said quietly. "And Llyr."

Loki nodded. "I'll go with you."

I shook my head. "No. I'll do it alone. But thank you," I added quickly. "I appreciate the thought."

"Let me put it another way, Cat," Loki said. "I'm coming with you." The bruises on his face were dark and serious. So wrong on the God of Mischief.

Heph sat down in one of the chairs. The three of us were silent, numb.

My gaze drifted out onto the terrace. A pall of clouds shrouded the sky over gray and choppy seas. What a strange pair we were, Loki and I. Friends divided by titles like *god* and *mortal*. *Employer* and *employee*. And yet, for all the tales of his lies and trickery, I never doubted that Loki would be anything less than honest with me if I posed a question he was able to answer. It was part of our strange respect for each other, I suppose. It was with this knowledge that I asked a very loaded, very dangerous question.

"Where do they go?"

"Back to the fire," Hephaestus said. "From it we came; to it we must return."

Loki piped up from beside me. "If I'm not mistaken, you've been there yourself. Quite recently."

I hadn't spoken of it to anyone. Loki was the first person to admit that I hadn't just "given them a scare," but that I'd actually died. Though the lessons and truths learned in that other place had already faded to obscurity, like the details of a dream, I would never forget the sense of wholeness that came with death. The memory of the warm meadow, the blissful place of love and light, wrapped me in its sweet embrace.

Of course, this only made me think of Marius and waking in his arms.

With a pang of grief, my heart began to ache. "Is it always like that?"

Loki shrugged. "I'm not sure, Cat. Places like Hades, Heaven, the Nether, Hell...they all exist. They are very real, and very few beings come and go as they please."

"Hell? Is that where you think he is?" I choked out.

"I don't— Cat, I'd rather not know. I'd rather just imagine that Marius is hanging out in Elysium with a nymph or four."

My stomach hitched, and I whipped to face him, angry.

"Sorry, I didn't mean— Fuck." Weary, Loki pawed at his face. The Trickster gave me a weak laugh. "I should just shut up, shouldn't I?"

"It might be best," I said. "But I do have a question for you."

"Lay it on me."

"I died, right?"

Loki surreptitiously stroked his bruised cheek. "Much to my chagrin."

"And yet, here I am." I studied Loki's face, locking stares with those gas-flame eyes. "If I came back, why couldn't he?"

Before Loki could answer, Heph rumbled, "Someone is coming."

Not a second later, there was a knock on the door.

Loki lifted a finger. "Hold that thought," he said, bouncing up from the sofa. He crossed to the door, and when he opened it, Malcolm stormed in.

Ignoring Loki and Heph, Mal marched right up to me. His wild curls were in an unruly state. "Where the bloody hell have you been?" he shouted at me.

"Who is this?" Hephaestus asked.

I sighed. "This is Marius's brother, Malcolm."

Mal had no interest in introductions. "First Marius runs off. Then you. And when I go looking, I can't find either of you about. I understand if you wanted to nip off for a cheeky romp, but come on. Have some manners."

There was a dissonant note in his words. His voice shook, but it was more than that. I took him in. Something was wrong about the set of his jaw. His blue eyes blazed widely, and his skin was pale. His hands trembled.

"Mal, what's wrong?"

"You tell me." He fixed me with his stare. I'd have to have been blind to miss the accusation there. "Where is he?"

I hung my head. How the hell was I supposed to explain what had happened?

"Why don't you have a seat?" Loki suggested. "We should talk."

I glanced up just as Mal violently shrugged Loki's hand off his shoulder. "I don't feel like sitting." He looked as though he was being held together with little more than his anger and a threat.

"You know already," I said softly. "Don't you?"

The young satyr grimaced, lips pressing together in a thin, colorless line. Fury flared in his eyes, and every muscle in his body tensed. When he spoke, his voice was a forced, quivering whisper. "Blood calls to blood."

Heph stepped in close to Malcolm. "You have my sorrow. Your brother was a good friend. I will mourn him."

Malcolm's face twisted with bitterness. "Fuck off with your sympathy, mate. It's not like he's dead."

"Mal," I began.

Loki took over for me, bless him. "I'm sorry, but it's exactly like that."

"You daft twats, I think I'd know if me own brother was dead. He's not. Cat'll tell you."

Mal's desperation called to that stubborn ember of hope, fanned it. "Mal, what do you think is happening here?"

"If I knew, would I be asking you? You went off to find him, then... then it was like he was in my head, screaming at me to protect you. Then he just...he just disappeared. Like—" His face fell.

"Like he died?" I didn't try to hide the tears or stop their flow. "Because he did, Mal. He's gone. I couldn't save him. I'm sorry. I'm so goddamn sorry."

"But he's not dead."

"He is."

"Then why do I hear him now?"

My heart stopped. Did I dare believe? Should I hope?

I glanced to Heph. "Is it possible?"

The blacksmith's brow furrowed with deep creases, silver eyes narrowed as he pondered. "If he crossed into Hades..."

"Oh for fucksake," Loki said. He pinched the bridge of his nose. "They took him where we can't follow."

"Wait." I shoved into Loki's face and forced him to look at me. "What the hell are you saying? Is Marius alive?"

"Of course he's alive," Mal answered. "He's not happy about it, but I can feel him out there. Surely you can, too, love. Can't ya?"

I searched my feelings and found a cyclone. "I can't be sure of what I feel."

Mal snatched my hand. The change was almost instantaneous. My blood flashed hot, and with the heat came a sense of connection. Like a computer plugged into a network, I could feel others sending and receiving data. Mal pinged into being, a fiery light that pulsed hotly. If I followed his rhythm, I could trace other lines. Small tendrils were little more than dull gray filaments. But two of them...two of them blazed in my mind. I let myself drift toward the brighter of the two, a blue sphere. Immediately, I heard French music. Llyr's eyes opened wide where he sat in his home. He'd been worrying his fingers, and his face was lined with despair. He whispered my name, but I pulled away and fixed my attention on the next light. Emerald green, it gave off a wan radiance.

Somewhere I had a body, and in that body, my stomach lurched. My connection wavered as I registered the physical sensations. Tightening my focus, I reached for the green sphere.

It was like swimming through sheets of cool fog. Shimmering fractals of frost climbed rock walls the exact color of lunar dust, and voices echoed in the caverns. Screams, haunted whispers, and panicked animal bleats filled the air. Someone lay on the stone floor, a heap of blood, fur, and shredded flesh all curled in on itself in the fetal position. A hand twitched, flattened against the ground, and pushed up. Slowly, the body drew away from the floor. He lifted his head. And I saw them—a pair of eyes the color of a leaf.

"He's there!" I shouted.

Mal broke apart from me, and I came back to the corporeal world. Loki and Heph gaped at us.

"How did you do that?" I asked, my voice raw.

Mal stared at me, haunted. When he spoke, he sounded like a traumatized child. "He's my blood."

"Mal, I need you to answer me this: was that real?"

His eyes swam out of focus, face pulling into a grimace. He'd seen too much. What was it Llyr had said about him? That Mal had spent so long blissfully unaware of most of the magical world? Those days were gone for him now. The shrieks echoing in that other place, they had heralded the end of Malcolm's innocence, such as it was. And to see his brother as we had?

Too much.

To jar him back to me, I grabbed his face with both my hands. "Was it real?" I asked more sternly, urgently.

"Yeah."

"Yes!" I planted an ecstatic kiss on him. When I pulled back, Mal wore a pleased leer. "You're a genius, Mal."

"Hello, there," he growled.

I whirled to face the gods. "He's alive! Marius is alive."

"You're certain?" Heph asked.

I nodded and explained the vision. "It's him. I know it. He isn't dead."

Hephaestus put his hands on his hips and regarded his fellow deity. "She has described the innermost pit of the Underworld, playground of Hades himself."

"Cat," Loki began, "are you sure you saw blood? A whole body, not just a shade?"

I shrugged, terrified that I was wrong about the vision. "How would I know the difference?"

Heph answered. "A shade is an echo. Think of what you saw and tell me again. Was the blood dry?"

I closed my eyes and focused on the memory. "Some. It oozed out of him and dripped down. It was...fresh," I said, almost choking on the word.

"You are certain it did not float out of him, like mist?"

I nodded. "Positive."

"And did you see his eyes?"

"Yes."

Heph paused, and my heart raced. Hephaestus was fighting off hope himself. I could tell by the intensity of his stare, the way he'd gone still. The air itself seemed charged with possibility. If Heph believed... If he could find an ember of hope...

"Did he see you?" the god asked. "Recognize you?"

Oh shit.

My stomach fell. "He didn't look at me. He was looking around the cave, afraid, and he was making that face—you know, the one he gets when he's trying to get his bearings so he can squirm out of a trap?—yeah, that. But he didn't seem to see me. Is that bad? Please tell me it's not bad."

Loki sighed and stepped back, clearly weighing something in his head. He pressed his fingers to his lips and stared into the middle distance. "Why would they do that?"

Heph's deep bass voice answered. "He is more valuable alive."

"You said alive!" I jumped up and grabbed Mal's hand in what I hoped was reassurance.

Loki ignored me, pensive. Heph watched my boss think.

"What are they doing?" Mal whispered in my ear.

"Being gods, shh."

Loki came to some conclusion. "So they kill him and whisk him to Hades, but revive him?"

"All the better to torture him, my friend," Heph replied with a sad nod. "There will be a line forming of beings seeking to take a chunk out of his hide."

"Right, then," I said. "Let's get him out of there before the line gets too greedy."

With quick steps, I burst into the bedroom and grabbed my bag. I didn't bother actually packing. Just grabbed the few things I might have need of along the way: a stun gun, my panic button, and a few other gadgets. I slid a handful of mistletoe darts into my pocket, too. Loki had given the charmed weapons to me the year before and I found them quite useful.

"Cat," Loki said, "I can't let you go."

"I don't remember asking for your permission."

"I'm not joking."

"Neither am I."

He grabbed my arm. "Do you think this is a game?" he seethed through his teeth. "Do you forget our arrangement?"

"No, Loki, I don't think it's a goddamn game. In games people can win or lose. Me? I'm just trying to get everyone out alive."

"Then why would you run headlong into the mouth of the beast? No. Don't answer that. I refuse to believe that you're that fucking stupid."

I slammed my bag down on the bed. "Unless you have some helpful advice, I urge you to get the fuck out of my way, Loki."

The god's eyes widened. How long had it been since a mortal—one who wore his mark, no less—defied him? I realized in that moment that he could have leveled me, left this resort a smoking crater. But he didn't.

"Cat, you're not the only one charged with protecting someone."

"Then help me get him back!"

"Dammit, woman, I'm not talking about the satyr! You can be so irritatingly dense sometimes, you know that? I can't let anything happen to *you.*"

Then I remembered something Loki had said on more than one occasion. That he didn't own my soul but was its steward. Someone else held the deed. Someone else pulled his strings. And mine.

"Who is it, Loki?" I breathed.

He shook his head. "Can't tell you that."

I took in the bruises and cuts on his face, his swollen and split lip. "Is that what happened to you?"

"Well, you know how deities can get," he sniped. "They're like children, really. Get more than a little testy when you break their favorite toys."

I rankled at that. In my years working with Loki, I'd almost forgotten that I was a piece in someone else's game. Someday I'd be free of this crazy cycle. No more gods or warring factions. No more immortal politics.

"I can't let you just fly off to the Underworld and risk your life, Cat. I need you to stay alive."

"Then help me," I pleaded. "I can't just sit here. I have to go after him. I have to, Loki."

"Why? So you can keep up this futile attempt at finding another backer for him in time? You lost. It's done. Why can't you accept that?"

"Because..." The rest of the answer caught in my throat. I couldn't say it. I locked my gaze on his, hoping he would understand.

Loki's head fell. "Dammit. Of all the brainless, foolish..."

I pulled the pack over my shoulder. "If you're going to try to stop me, Loki, now is the time to do it."

His gaze flicked to my hands. I'd drawn power into them, ready to fight the Bane of the Aesir if that's what it took for me to get to Marius. The Trickster's lips hitched up in a smile.

"So incredibly stupid," he muttered. "But damn, you've got moxie."

From behind my steward, Hephaestus said, "It will serve her well if she is to parley with the Lord of the Dead himself. And if her description is accurate, that is where Marius is being kept—Hades's most inner sanctum. There will be no breaking him out, no daring escape. There will only be diplomacy."

My knees wobbled, as did my confidence. I'd never been great at diplomacy. But for Marius...

Loki and I stared at each other: will against will.

"I need to do this," I whispered. "Please."

Loki spun on his heel and breezed back into the sitting room. Jabbing a finger at Mal, he barked, "You're going with her. And you're going to look after her, do you understand? If anything happens to her, I will take great pleasure in pulling every inch of your skin off your bones and feeding it to the hungriest souls in Hell, do you understand me?"

Mal nodded vigorously, eyes haunted and pallor ashen.

I rushed Loki and threw my arms around him. "Thank you."

He gave me a reluctant pat on the back. "Don't thank me," he said darkly. "I can't go with you."

Hephaestus stepped up. "I will guide her to the Otherworld."

After a grateful nod to the blacksmith, Loki said, "Cat, any glamour I would lay upon you would be rendered null once you crossed over.

Watch your back. But you get in, you get the satyr, and you get your ass out of there, do you understand?"

I bobbed my head. "Snatch and grab. Got it."

"Good. Now go get him. Bastard owes me money."

Twenty-Eight

"Dime"

Hephaestus had urged me against indulging in hope, but that ship had sailed. As Loki took his leave, the flames of hope roared in my chest, and I smiled. This was crazy. Possibly suicidal. As I thought of Marius, though, of all the things we'd been through and all that I had yet to tell him, I knew there was no turning back.

I swept my attention to Hephaestus. He frowned at me. "There is no swaying you, is there?"

"Nope."

"What fools these mortals be," he muttered under his breath.

I blinked, and when I opened my eyes I stood...well, I didn't know where it was. Sure as shit wasn't the posh hotel room I'd just been in. Heph had done his teleporter trick again.

The ground beneath my feet was cracked and parched. It seemed we stood in a dry lake bed, but as I scanned the landscape, it was difficult to confirm. Anything more than ten feet away from me was blurred and twisting. This place lay beneath a thick haze, an odorless miasma that shifted and swirled. The obscuring lens gave everything a silver-yellow tinge. What I could see of the sky was the dark slate that came during an eclipse. If the sun, moon, and stars had any meaning here, they did not make an appearance.

Heph and Mal lingered a few feet away. As I stared at them, the air itself seemed to rob them of all color. It was like watching an old cathode-tube television as the garish orange T-shirt stretched across Mal's barrel chest fritzed and twitched before going gray. His eyes remained piercing blue, too vibrant against the monochrome surroundings.

"Where are we?" I asked.

"The Otherworld," Heph said. "The one that lies beyond your own."

"Is this...is this like the Fae realm?" I shuddered at the thought. I didn't do well with faeries.

"No," the god assured me. "This place is not Fae. It is what lies between your world and Fae. The space between all realms."

My head ached from trying to wrap my mind around the concept. "So there's my place. There's *your* place. And then there's here? In between, like a buffer?"

Heph nodded grimly. "It is a place for dreamers, the dead, and the insane. They are the only ones that would roam this land willingly."

"Not hard to guess which we are," Mal murmured.

I snickered at that thought. In for a penny, right? "So which way to Hades?" I asked.

Hephaestus lifted his hand and the vapor parted to form a quivering tunnel. At the end of it squatted a blackened Joshua tree. Its empty limbs twisted and reached out toward the shimmering ground. Was that water?

"So we're headed toward a mirage," Mal complained. "Brilliant."

"It is no mirage," Heph insisted. "That is your destination. And this is where we part ways."

"You sure I can't persuade you to come with us?" I asked, unease slithering in my gut.

Hephaestus shook his head. "I will not cross into my cousin's realm uninvited. Stay on this path. Go to the tree. All will become clear."

I swallowed my fear and nodded. "Got it."

From the ether, Heph brought up a silver ball. Roughly the size of a large grapefruit, the sphere gleamed with a perfect, unmarred shine.

I tilted my head. "What's that?"

"It is for you. A gift. It might be of help once you are in the realm of the dead."

The sphere was cold and heavy when he transferred it into my hand. Whispers of power tingled in my fingers. Something churned inside, aching to be released. Guts still twisting with anxiety, I turned the ball over in my hands. No seams or hasps.

Hephaestus had given me a puzzle similar to Pandora's box. Though it wasn't the true relic, it bore the same kind of mystery as the chest I'd seen at the Forge. But what lay inside?

"Keep your hope close, girl," he said.

I held up the sphere. "Thank you," I said as I stashed it in my bag.

"Good luck, Cat. Follow this path. Find Marius in Hades's sanctum. Bring him back to us. There are still memories we have yet to make together."

With a shiver, I gave the blacksmith a salute. Tugging on Mal's sleeve, I put my back to the god and started down the path. As we walked, the shapes of other travelers appeared in the haze. Now and again, one of them would step through the shimmering veil and share our path for a moment. Their forms shone like tarnished silver, devoid of any true color. At first, I thought that these people were travelers like me and Mal, lost in the not-fog of the Otherworld. It didn't take long for me to figure out, though, that these were little more than ghosts.

When a little girl ran through the gelatinous barrier between us and the world, she flickered. The light that made up her body flashed and blurred. At one point she disappeared only to materialize three steps back from where she'd winked out of being. She chased something, reached for it with her chubby fingers. Then, with a jolt of surprise, she was jerked up by an unseen force and whisked away. The last I saw of her, the girl's mouth was open in a silent scream.

She wasn't the last such creature we saw. More of them shuffled into our path with eerie gaits disjointed from normal time. Wisps of smoke lingered after them like memories, fragments of their essence struggling to catch up with the rest.

I stayed close to Malcolm, his warmth a physical reminder of reality. We said nothing to each other. His breathing, shallow and quick, spoke of fear. After what could have easily been seconds or hours, we reached the scorched Joshua tree. I turned back, seeking to signal Hephaestus that we had made it, but when I looked, the haze had swept over our path. The way back was shut.

"No way out but through," I murmured.

With a light swat to my arm, Mal said, "I hope you can swim."

Returning my attention to the gnarled, torched tree, I reeled at the abrupt shift of the landscape. Here, it was clear, and the overcast sky gave no hint of night or day. A wan, greenish light illuminated the blackened earth, and jagged, glassy rocks littered the ground and sloped down to the bank of a river. Only this river was like none I'd ever seen. It didn't seem to be made of water but black fire. The flame-like tongues lapped at the shore with an eerie, crackling ripple. Reflections of the silver sky glinted off the dancing surface.

With a gasp, I suddenly realized where we must be. "Styx," I breathed.

"Never liked them, really," Mal said. "Don't favor classic rock."

I winced, physically wounded by his ignorance. "The river, Mal. It's the River Styx. We have to cross it to get to Hades."

Gazing across the river, however, it looked like this would be an Olympic feat. The Styx flowed for miles in every direction. I couldn't make out the opposite shore, only a line of mist. Far beyond, mountains cut the horizon with black spines.

"So how do we get there?" I asked no one in particular.

As if in answer, the sound of the river changed. A low, rhythmic *whoosh* was now punctuated by the tinkle of a bell. From the fog emerged a gondola dark as cinders. A lone, shadowy figure stood at the prow. He lifted a long staff with a broad, leaflike blade at the end, then dipped it back into the river. The motion of his oar brought on that deep *whoosh*.

"Excellent," Mal said. "Let's ask 'im for a ride."

I shook my head. Unlike Mal, I remembered the myths and legends that went along with the River Styx. Though some diverged here and there in the details, the basic gist of Charon the Ferryman remained the same. "He'll expect payment," I warned.

Malcolm patted down his pockets. "I'm skint. You got any change?"

"I don't think he wants money." Just in case, I did a quick check of my own pockets. As my fingers searched at my hips, they fell over the silver poker chip. "Hey!" I called, having an eureka moment. "We don't need him. We can use this."

"Wha's that?"

"Marius's tacky-as-hell necklace. I repurposed it."

Without waiting for Mal to agree, I grabbed his arm and held up the poker chip. I had no earthly clue how to activate the spell so I had to wing it. I focused on what I could see of the far shore and gave a whisper of will into the chip.

"Step on three," I said.

We counted together and put one foot in front of the other. In a breath, we stopped. We hadn't moved an inch.

"Maybe I have to do something else to get us across?"

"Don't ask me, love. I've never been for all that hocus-pocus shite. That's Marius's area of expertise." As he said his brother's name, Mal's face fell. He looked around the desolate shore, and the full weight of our situation settled over his shoulders. He might not have been well versed in all the myths, he might have been shit when dealing with magic, and he might have had terrible aim, but Malcolm knew in that instant that he was on the border of life and death. His brother was in the other country, and we—together—had to bring him out.

I saw this change happen in an instant. When Mal's eyes refocused, his jaw tightened with resolve.

"Maybe you need to think of Marius. Like we did in the room, right?" he asked.

I nodded. I offered my left hand—the hand holding the chip—to Mal. His palm was clammy and cool against mine. Our fingers laced together, the satyr squeezed his eyes shut.

"Blood calls to blood," I heard him whisper. Over and over like a mantra, he repeated these four words as fervently as any prayer.

Images of Marius came in fits and starts, jerking my attention here and there. I guess the Otherworld has bad reception because in the channel-surfing barrage of information, I saw moments from our shared past. Times running through Vegas on this whim or that. A dance shared in a room full of gods. A Christmas spent in Belize. The day we met. I also saw flashes of what must have been his days with Malcolm. Younger versions of the satyrs I knew drinking together, sparring. Laughing. There was always laughing in Mal's memories.

I poured more power into the chip and, without speaking to Mal, took the step.

Again, we hit some sort of barrier. While there was no physical evidence of it, something kept us from reaching the other shore.

Opening my eyes, I saw him palming the air in front of us, seeking the invisible wall.

"What do you reckon?" he asked.

I shook my head in response. I tried again only to be stopped again, like there was some kind of force field. There was no sound, no actual impact, but as I raised my foot something kept me from taking the step.

I let go of Mal's hand and moved back from him. "Try walking into the river," I said.

Mal shrugged but went along with it. He slid his shoe over the jagged rocks. Though the effort and strain shone in his face, Mal was stuck, too. We could go no farther.

Tsk, tsk.

I jumped—and possibly flailed a little—at the sudden sound, looking up just as the Ferryman's gondola slid up onto the shore. The loose stones ground beneath the weight of the boat, and with a thick squelch, he buried his oar in the earth.

Apparently Charon was the only way across this damned river.

He wore a tattered robe that had probably been dark as midnight. Now, though, it was a faded reminder of its former self. His face was hidden in the deep folds of the cloak's hood. Charon raised a skeletal hand and twitched his index finger in admonishment.

Mal nudged me with his elbow. "Go on. Say somethin'."

I sidestepped, moving as close to the gondola as I dared. "I'm Catherine Sharp," I said, voice echoing queerly. "We seek passage to Hades."

Charon's hood tilted. "Do we?"

I'd expected a ghastly whisper, but the Ferryman's voice rang with gentle familiarity.

"Yes."

"I know you," Charon said. "As does my master. He is expecting you, mage."

I swallowed the knot of fear that had surged into my throat, bilious and sour. "Is he?"

"Indeed."

"So you'll take us?"

He stretched out his hand, bones clattering as he opened his fingers. "Cross my palm, for payment is due."

I looked at the poker chip. Of all the things I had, this was the only thing I could part with. Besides, if I was being honest, the idea of using Godspeed again gave me the heebie-jeebies. The chip fell into Charon's hand with a light clatter of silver against bone. With a magician's flourish, he did away with the chip and gestured that I should board the gondola.

When Mal went to follow, Charon stopped him with the staff of his oar. "Payment is due."

Mal tried to contain his panic. "I...I don't have anything to offer."

"No coin? No trinket?"

The satyr shook his head. "Nothing."

Charon wrenched the oar up from the rocky shore. With a nudge, the gondola floated out from the bank, carrying me away from Malcolm.

"Wait," he cried. "Stop! I need to go with her!"

Malcolm's protests were absorbed by the dark hood. Charon didn't care.

Try as he might, Mal could not charge after the boat. He flailed along the riverbank, held at bay by whatever invisible magic worked there. When he gave up, he was almost in tears. He yelled to me, voice ragged. "Cat! Bring him back! You grab that no-good bastard brother of mine and bring him back!"

"I will," I called.

"Be gone," Charon hissed. "Back to the world that spawned you."

Malcolm winked out of sight, and I stared up at the Ferryman. He turned his back to the shore and began to row. I gazed across the River Styx and saw the eerie peaks of Hades, realm of the dead. As Charon parted the black-flame river, we came nearer. One slow stroke at a time.

TWENTY-NINE

"ROAD TO SOMEWHERE"

"Back on my barge so soon?" Charon asked.

"I'm not dead, and I don't plan on staying in Hades any longer than I did last time."

"I did not deliver you to Hades, Catherine Sharp, but to another shore entirely."

Confused, I shifted in my seat to face him. Anticipating my question, he said, "There are more realms than there are stories in the greatest of libraries, child. I took you to the one that suited you best."

The Ferryman's voice was warm and familiar. The subtlest notes of nostalgia played in his throaty purr and reminded me of pipe smoke and peppermint. "You sound like my grandfather," I said. "I mean, you don't use the same words he would have, but your voice is similar."

"Charles Sharp. Airman. Carpenter. With a love for tobacco he pretended to hide from his wife, Phyllis."

Eyes wide as the full moon, I gaped. "How did you...?"

"I ferried them both. Not so long ago."

"Is that why you sound like him?"

He gave a light shake to his head. Though I couldn't see through the inky shadows of his hood, I sensed his smile. "Some require incentive to cross over. Others seek comfort. I take on the aspect of that which will aid them most in making this final journey."

Suddenly I understood all the stories about being met on the other side by those you've loved and lost.

"So you can mimic anyone?"

"Anyone who has passed through the veil. I remember them all."

"Trippy."

I turned in my seat and once more faced our destination. Charon's oar dipped into the black river, eliciting that low *whoosh* with every languid stroke. For all the speed he'd shown in getting to Mal and me, it seemed this circuit was particularly slow. I fidgeted, knees bouncing and fingers twisting around one another.

"So," I said uneasily, "I feel like I'm on one of the gondolas at the Venetian. I mean, there's no music. And it's a little less cheerful here, but I suppose beggars can't be choosers."

Charon gave a chuff of laughter. Then he did something that shocked the hell out of me. The Ferryman began to sing. He'd abandoned my grandfather's voice and slipped into a sweet tenor. I knew that voice, too. Long since murdered, but this voice served as the soundtrack of my life and millions of others. John Lennon.

As he sang, the boat rocked me into a gentle reverie. Absent friends, but in memory still bright. Before I knew it, I was singing with Charon. I don't sing willingly, but at that moment, it was the only thing to do. Didn't matter if I was off-key or fudging the words. I sang. And with each word, I thought of those who'd died too soon. Then those I would leave behind if this whole thing went to shit. My parents and sister. Mrs. M. Karma. Flynn.

"In my life," I finished the song, "I love you more."

The last notes disappeared in the vast expanse around us.

"Wow," I remarked. "Thanks for that. I've never done a duet with a Beatle."

"My pleasure," he said.

I pondered Charon's parroting skills, what it might mean in terms of my current situation. "Wait...you said can mimic anyone you've ferried, right?" I began, letting the question dangle between us.

When he spoke, his voice had changed to something unknown to me—cold, low, and dripping with disdain. "I do not take requests."

"I was just wondering if you could confirm something for me."

"I will not tell you if Elvis has died so that you might go back to your world and tell all. Not that you would be believed."

I giggled. "Nothing like that. I have a...a friend. Someone I'm looking for in Hades. Can you tell me if he's there? For certain?"

He piloted the boat quietly, the darkness of him aimed at the far shore. From within the depths of his hood, he hissed, "Yes, I can. But I will not. I am not a plaything, Catherine Sharp. Nor am I a dousing rod to point you in the direction of that which you seek so desperately. If you wish to hear that voice again, you must find its keeper and coax it out. I'll not give in to your masturbatory desires."

"Hey, I didn't say anything about masturbation."

Charon snarled. "You already know the answer to your question. You do not wish to confirm anything, mortal. You are merely looking for a way to bolster yourself, to feel that your hope is justified. I will not be party to this."

I nodded. "Fair enough."

Was he right? Was this just a way for me to make myself feel good and useful after all the mistakes I'd made?

We passed the rest of the ride in silence, floating into the mist. The fog clung to my skin, gray and cool like the early morning in autumn, and within a few moments, my hair was damp. As the barge scraped up on the sandy bank, I stood.

"Catherine Sharp," Charon said in his own voice. "Be ye warned before you step onto the shore of Hades. Drink nothing, no matter how much you thirst. Eat of no tree or plate put before you. For if you do, your soul is my lord's to keep."

"My soul already has a lord," I snarked.

"All the worse for you, then. Partaking of Hades's culinary hospitality will yoke you to this place, and you will never again be allowed to pass back to the realm of the living. Mark you my meaning?"

"Don't eat or drink anything or else I can't leave. Got it. I don't suppose you could clue me in as to where I might find the big man himself, could you?"

"I could."

"But you won't, will you?"

"There is no need. He awaits your audience in his throne room. The path will make itself known."

For lack of anything better to say or do, I nodded. "Thanks."

I hiked a leg over the side of the boat and climbed out. My feet sank into the sand, which was inexplicably moist considering the river didn't appear to be actual liquid. The soft squish of my Chucks on the earth reminded me of the beach...of Marius.

Good, I thought. *Stay focused on him. Find him.*

"And one other thing, Catherine Sharp." When I turned to listen, Charon continued. "I will ferry you to the final shore but one more time, and from that journey you will not return."

Chills coursed through me. Before I could respond, Charon whipped back his hood. My face stared back at me. My reflection's eyes twinkled with a haunted glee that was evident in the smirk she wore.

With my borrowed voice, Charon said, "Use wisely what is left of your life."

Unable to take my eyes off...well...me, I staggered back. Charon's skeletal fingers wiggled in a mercurial farewell before he once more shoved away from the shore. I watched as the black gondola retreated into the mist. The Ferryman smiled at me until the fog swallowed him. Only then did I put my back to him and focus on Hades itself.

I stood inside a crescent of mountains. To my right, far in the distance, verdant peaks rose to touch the bright sky. Shafts of golden light rained down upon the green mountains. I looked up at the sky but couldn't find a sun. Did Hades *have* a sun? I shook the thought away and scanned my surroundings. The landscape to my left resembled the wastes of Mordor. Black, jagged crags stretched to the horizon like the fossilized spine of a ginormous beast. No sunlight there. Only red clouds and a sickly, sulfuric haze around the tallest peaks.

Ahead of me, the mountains paled, and the world lay under a gray, dusty pall. A city had been carved into the rock, mimicking the elegant architecture of the Greeks with columns and caryatids. Steady, perfect geometry with little embellishment. Rising above it all was a tower. Thousands of feet high, it resembled an overturned goblet. And at the center of the flat expanse that served as its top, a green fire blazed.

Perhaps if I'd seen it without the other two "countries" so clearly visible, I'd have appreciated this middle ground for its stark beauty or simplicity. Instead, I had trouble wrapping my mind around it.

Beside the lush, green scenery, the city resembled a relic like Pompeii. However, when compared to the dark, beastly spine to my right, Hades proper seemed downright cheerful.

Though I was certain I had to head to the tower, the mountains didn't part and give me a straight line to follow. Then, just as Charon had predicted, a path made itself clear. Emerald mist hovered over the sand, twisting a road into the city. I followed it, the mist swirling around my ankles as I wound my way through the stone structures.

It's not that I expected a parade or anything, but no one greeted me in the city. In fact, I saw no one on my trip from the river to the tower. Not so much as a ghost in the shadows. I heard them, their voices breaking the silence with the occasional burst of crow-like laughter.

I walked for what seemed like an eternity. My Chucks were about as useful as tissue paper when walking on the jagged rocks, and the air was dry as Phoenix in June. You could've started a brushfire in my mouth. I swallowed ash and tasted blood on my cracked lips.

Step after step, mile after mile, I trudged to the tower with one thing urging me on: Marius. I might be parched and exhausted, but he was at the end of this walk. I had to bring him home, and once I did, we could drink ourselves into oblivion.

Staggering, starving, and thirsty enough to drink Lake Mead, I finally arrived at the base of the tower. A colonnade stretched before me boasting statues of marble, bronze, and obsidian. Titanic creatures frozen in the throes of battle. Lovers caught in a final embrace. The statues radiated with an icy, slimy power.

As I reached the end of the colonnade, the green mist dispersed and the gray earth shifted. Silvery tendrils wafted up from the ground with sinuous grace. Earth and air merged to form blocky shapes that divided and grew. A head. A large, beastly body. Soon, four paws stamped at the ground and three canine heads tossed and snorted. Thick ropy tails whipped and lashed behind its enormous bulk. One of its eyes opened— acid-green sclera with black irises—and fixed me with malevolent curiosity.

"Why do you seek the Lord of the Dead?" Cerberus asked. Its gravelly voice echoed queerly—high then low—before dissipating.

"He has something I want. I've come to bargain with Hades for the life of another."

"Do you intend to cheat him as you have already cheated death, mage? For if this is your plan, I assure you it will end with naught but your pain."

I shook my head. "I play fair, puppy."

Cerberus snarled. In tandem, all three heads tilted to regard me with cynical disdain. "Then herein lies your first mistake: you labor under the delusion that this is but a game."

Chastened, I folded my hands and bowed my head. "I mean no disrespect."

From above came an unctuous laugh. "I suppose there is a first time for everything, isn't there, mage?"

I looked up. Someone stood at a window high in the tower. From this distance, however, he was little more than a silhouette.

"Master," Cerberus rumbled. "Shall we make quick work of her?"

"No," the voice called. "I've been expecting such a visit. Send her up so that I might humor her."

The shadow retreated from the window, leaving me to stew in embarrassment. Cerberus lowered all three heads to glare at me. Its fetid breath—rank with the scent of decay and blood—stirred the mist and dust as it plumed out of all those nostrils.

"Pity," the dog growled. "I'd hoped to snap your neck between my jaws."

"Sorry to disappoint you," I lied.

"Play your game. Perhaps there will yet be time."

With a sucking vortex, the earth inhaled and Cerberus melted back into the stone. A portal in the seamless tower opened, and green light flickered there. While it brought to mind a merry fire crackling in a hearth, I also thought of dungeons and pits hungry for the wails of prisoners.

"It puts the lotion on its skin," I murmured to myself. Resolve steeled, mind focused on the job I had to do, I stepped into Hades's tower.

I found myself in a small, circular chamber with little more than the torches on the walls and the beginnings of a spiral staircase. I thought

I saw the shapes of contorted faces screaming in the green flames, but they flickered out of sight as the fire burned.

"Come, come," Hades sang, his voice ringing down the stairs.

I started the climb, one foot staggering in front of the other. Up, up, up the winding steps. My weary head soon started spinning, dizzy from fatigue and the constant circles. Somewhere along the line, I started muttering bitter epithets to myself.

"Couldn't possibly foot the bill to upgrade this place and get, oh, I don't know, an escalator or something? Oh, no, let's make the short chick walk all the way across the damn barren wastelands of Tatooine and send her up the world's worst staircase. Fucking bastard gods."

Bracing my hands on the narrow walls, I kept on climbing. I sincerely hoped that the way out of Hades would be something simple. Like teleporting Heph's way. Or at the very least, a slide.

After a while, Hades said, "It's not often that I get to entertain a vassal of Asgard. Shall I make you feel more at home, mage?"

The god laughed and an arctic wind tore through the corridor. The light guttered and dimmed, some of the torches going out altogether. Beneath my fingers, frost formed on the walls. Within a matter of minutes, a thick layer of ice covered the stairs. Each step I took had to be a carefully controlled movement coordinating hands and feet on the slick surfaces, managing joints that creaked and locked. Any moment I could lose my precarious hold on the wall or my shoes could slip out from under me and I'd fall. I could just imagine tumbling all the way down the winding staircase. Or maybe I'd pitch forward and bust my chin on the rocky steps. Fun.

I stopped at one of the few remaining torches and hugged myself for warmth. Quaking with the cold, I brought my face as near to the torchlight as I could without sacrificing my balance. But it was useless. The fire gave off no heat.

I hate gods. And shit like this is precisely why.

My breath a dense fog, I managed to stammer, "Y-y-you do r-r-r-realize that I'm f-f-f-f-from Vegas, right?"

"And?" Hades asked.

"Cold and I d-d-don't exactly get along."

"Is this difficult for you, mage?"

"Now that you mention it," I said with a sharp burst of laughter.

The god's voice echoed in the chamber. "Oh, how inconsiderate of me."

The staircase grumbled as the stones began to shift. Before I could slip and go tumbling down the stairs, I grabbed onto the bracket holding the torch over my head. Not a moment too soon, either. The whole tower swirled with nauseating speed. I tightened my grip, and my dry skin split and bled, chafed by the bitter wind. Faster and faster, the demonic pace threatened to wrench me loose of the wall and send me flying into orbit.

Closing my eyes to ward off the emerald strobe of the torchlight didn't do me any favors. The darkness behind my eyelids wavered with phantom shadows and shapes, ghostly images that quivered. Pressure mounted and my ears ached, skull throbbing and warping like a super-charged subwoofer.

I screamed. A piercing, sandpapery warble that matched pitch with the roaring wind. Numb fingers slipping, I lost my grip on the torch. As I crumpled to the stairs, the hellish carousel stopped. My eyes snapped open just in time to see the wall dissolve into another green portal. Momentum propelled me through the door, and I landed face-first on a polished marble floor. Pain streaked through my jaw with enough force to rattle teeth loose and send blood flowing into my mouth.

At last, something warm to drink, I thought darkly.

"Oh," came Hades's soft voice. "Oh, dear me. Oh my. I've gone and offended. This won't do at all. Not at all."

Gray, spindly fingers wound around my wrist, my shoulders and guided me to my feet. My head still throbbed and my eyes refused to focus. The world was little more than a gray-green blur. Wraiths sent wispy, black tendrils snaking into my peripheral vision, but if I tried to get a fix on them, those shadows disappeared. Always there, just out of sight.

The scent of flowers wafted to me as a figure approached. He reeked of them. Nothing so sweet as roses or as calming as honeysuckle. No, he smelled pungent and spicy. Like lilies. Stargazer lilies. I wrinkled my nose. That was the scent of mothballs, caskets, and wax. Grease paint and polyester. The wretched stink of stargazer lilies and every funeral I'd ever attended.

My gorge rose. I swallowed blood around my swollen tongue.

"Please, mage, let me show you my hospitality," Hades cooed.

With his gentle prodding, I shuffled forward. My vision clearing, I saw that I'd reached the flat top of the tower. At the center of the massive stone disc, a green bonfire blazed with traces of silver and ebony. Faces twisted there, distorted by the dancing of the flames.

As I came back to myself, I took in the view. From here I could see the whole of Hades. Those lush mountains. The crags. The ashen city. Nothing stood taller than this spot. Nothing but the Lord of Death himself.

Hades glided past me with a preternatural grace, his back to me. He wore black robes. The sleeves were trimmed with gold, as was the hem dragging along the ground. His blond hair was cropped short against his scalp, and his skin was the exact shade of gray as a tombstone. His neck was too long and bowed forward, almost as if the weight of his head was too much for his spine to bear.

"Go on, mage," he said, not bothering to look at me. He gave a dismissive wave. "Partake. Warm yourself."

A new scent called to me. The scent of spiced tea, warmth, and solace. I looked down to find a table next to me that I swore hadn't been there a moment ago. A beautifully crafted obsidian mug of chai was steaming before me, begging me to indulge. All manner of treats—from cookies to small red velvet cupcakes—lay on platters. There was even a bowl of piping hot tomato soup.

Comfort food.

My stomach growled, and my mouth watered. I knew that if I could just have one spoonful of that soup, I'd be full and warm. Satisfied. I'd have my strength back to meet whatever lay ahead.

As I reached for the spoon, Charon's warning speared through me with a jolt: *Drink nothing...Eat of no tree or plate put before you.*

Whimpering softly, I heeded the Ferryman's word. "Thank you, but no."

Hades eyed me over his shoulder, showing me the barest hint of his features. His was a profile that could've sliced through bone. His too-long nose threatened to meet the tip of his Wicked Witch chin. Leveling me with an arch stare, he asked, "No?"

I fumbled for something to say that wouldn't get me chucked off the building. "Y-your audience is hospitality enough," I stammered. With a light bow I added. "Thank you, Lord Hades, for admitting me."

His smile hooked up into a sated sneer. "You can be taught. How adorable."

I simmered at his patronizing bullshit but kept my mouth shut. I got the feeling that Hades was all about propriety and manners in some sick and twisted fashion. If playing it up for him got me what I needed, so be it.

Crooking a finger, he beckoned me to follow him. We had reached the opposite side of the fire when he stopped. With a flourish of his robes, he whirled around and sat on a blocky, marble throne. Now, here, I saw Hades properly. With his hawkish, angular features and sickly pallor, the Lord of the Dead reminded me of Eris. Like my former mistress, Hades's lines were all sharp and jagged. From the hooked nose and thin line of the mouth, to the bony elbows and long hands, the resemblance was striking. This realization didn't exactly endear him to me.

Unlike Discord, however, there was a decidedly insectoid air about Hades. Though his body was swathed in black robes, the fabric hung in such a way as to accentuate his skeletal form. His head, it appeared, was too large for the rest of his emaciated body. But like a wasp, this fragility could only be a clever ruse. Hades hid his sting, but I did not doubt his lethality.

He perched in his seat almost delicately, as a spider does in its web. With a subtle, featherlight drumming of those skinny fingers, he caressed the marble arms of his throne.

"Now," he purred, "to what do I owe the pleasure of your company, mage?"

Oh shit. Here we go...

THIRTY

"Bound Away"

My stomach churned with trepidation. I hadn't exactly thought about how to approach Hades once I got in the door. How did the myths go? What was I supposed to say here? My thoughts were still thawing out as I searched the floor for help.

"You told my guardian that I have something you want," Hades said. "That you are here to bargain for a life."

"Yes," I replied. I straightened, stringing together what wits I could and tying them with all the reverence an atheist could possibly show to a god. "Marius. A satyr. Son of Llyr, who is himself the son of Pan."

The thin line of Hades's mouth spread into a torn smile as he steepled his fingers. "I see. And what is it you will offer me in exchange for his pathetic life?"

I held out the cuff bracelet. "This is god forged, from Hephaestus himself."

"Trinkets?" Hades scoffed with a dismissive wave. "If I want something of the Blacksmith, I need only beckon him to my side. What else do you have?"

Well shit. If he wouldn't take the cuff, he wouldn't take the puzzle box, either. Not that I particularly wanted to part with any of these things, but it was all I could offer. I searched the barren space of Hades's tower, looking for some sort of hint, a clue that might help me figure out what I could possibly give to the Lord of the Dead.

Glancing at the delicacies he'd laid out for me, my stomach grumbled. "My hospitality," I said cheekily.

"And what, precisely, is that worth? The hospitality of a mortal?"

"I would be in your debt, Hades. And I'm damn good at what I do. You can ask Eris or Loki."

Hades curdled at the mention of these names. "A word of advice, mage: these outcasts are not references you wish to list on your résumé. Their names are no better than mud, and yours is sullied the longer you keep such company. Pity, really."

"Does my reputation precede me?"

"You do not come here unknown to me, mage. I've heard your name whispered in the halls of Olympus. It drips from the tongues of demons and echoes in the screams of angels. Well," he chuffed, his leer wicked, "at least one."

My belly rolled at the memory of an angel, tarnished and burned— Nate. I'd failed him. I snarled, angry that Hades would use that against me. Fists clenching, my knuckles went white. "What's your point?"

"My point is that you, Catherine Sharp, are a very popular girl with very risky prospects."

"Oh goody," I said, clapping my hands twice. "So nice to know that I'm the belle of the fucking ball."

"Now, now." He lifted a single finger—and his nose—in warning. "You begin to forget yourself. Mind this waspish tongue of yours before it gets you into trouble."

I blew a lock of hair out of my face and let my eyes drift to the shadows beyond Hades's throne. "Wouldn't be the first time."

"But it could very easily be the last." He rose and crossed to the fire. He held out a delicate finger and stroked the lithe flames. In the twisting images there, I saw my face. And Belial's. I saw my final moments play out.

"You've already escaped death once this week," he said slowly. "Do you wish to try my patience? To test me? See if you can repeat your little parlor trick?"

Sobered, I shook my head. I folded my hands in front of me and bowed a fraction of an inch. "Not particularly."

"Good. Now let us focus."

With a flick of his skeletal wrist, the flames guttered. Though the thick, green glow remained, the fire itself was gone. In the gelatinous light hovered a figure, spinning slowly on an unseen axis. Obscured though he was by the eerie luminance, I'd recognize Marius anywhere.

He'd been stripped. Without so much as a stitch of clothing or a breath of his glamour, Marius was suspended in his natural satyr form. The dark fur was matted at his hips and thighs. I saw all too clearly the lashes on his back. As he turned, the wounds from the hellhound's paws became visible. The beast had punctured his chest, gouged troughs through the stayr's rib cage. My eyes tracked upward, and as I looked at what had been done to his throat, I barked a mournful noise.

"This is why you're here, mage. Is it not?"

I closed my eyes, holding back tears. I counted long breaths. Emotion wouldn't save him. Sentiment would not sway the Lord of the Dead. I hardened my heart with ice in hopes that I could remain indifferent.

Yeah right.

When I looked up, Marius's face was in full view. Our eyes met through the fog of verdant light. Though I heard nothing, his lips formed the unmistakable shape of my name.

With a fluttery warmth, I passed Marius a sad smile. He could see me. He *knew* me. Whatever had happened after that wave had taken Marius away, he was still here. I could work with that.

"Here he is, mage. Your prize," Hades said with a note of disgust. "Now tell me what you offer in exchange for his pitiful life."

Marius's eyes grew large with panic. *No*, he mouthed to me.

I raised an eyebrow at Marius. Did he really think I would leave him here? Fat fucking chance.

Without taking my eyes off my satyr, I asked Hades, "What could I possibly get for the man who has everything?"

"That isn't the question, is it? No. The question is what are you willing to part with?"

As if weighing a slew of options—which I most certainly didn't have—I thumped the bracelet in my palm. I had to stall Hades while I drummed up a plan to get Marius out of here.

"Well," I said, "you already know that my soul isn't mine to give."

"For now," Hades purred. "But things can change quickly. That you well know."

If I could reach through the queer, green light, maybe I could yank Marius back and we could run. But I wasn't stupid enough to think that Hades would let us get very far.

"You don't want my life," I said, stating the obvious.

"Don't I? A life for a life is the typical exchange."

"If that's what you wanted, you would've demanded it by now."

Hades's face split into a smile. "She's bright! Bright as a star among the dimness of mortality. You are correct," he said as he pranced toward me, a slight swagger in his step. "I don't care for dealing with lives or souls. Not today."

"Then what?" I kept my voice chilly and hard. "You've obviously got your eye set on some prize where I'm concerned, but you're playing a coy game. What is it that you need for me to offer that you can't just take?"

This soured him. The Olympian's eyes darkened and his already-pale skin blanched. Creases formed between his brows. "Manners, Catherine," he warned.

I rolled my eyes. "Oh, come on. Your little pet down there got all ominous and foreboding, told me that this wasn't a game, but you've done nothing but try to make me dance."

"Poppet," he snarled through his teeth, "do remember your station and behave properly, or I shall take offense. Then what will you have, hmm?"

Hades snapped a finger. Marius's body bowed, stretched back in agony. Every muscle in his body was tight as a drumhead. Veins bulged in his arms, his torn throat, and at his temples. Though I couldn't hear them, his screams echoed through my blood.

"Stop," I hissed. "Enough!"

"Stop what? Manners."

"Stop, *please!*"

And just like that, whatever string was holding Marius let him go. Once more he spun on that ponderous thread. His wounds seeped, the blood black in the odd light. Wisps of his life trickled into the beam that held him, floating like dye in water. Similarly, Marius's hair fanned out in lazy waves as the current caught his locks.

"No more outbursts now or I shall become cross," Hades said.

Keeping hold of my temper was like reining in a comet. I blazed with fury. As Marius came back to himself from whatever torture had been delivered, his features softened. He found my gaze with his and gave the slightest shake of his head.

What would he do if he were in my position? Well, he wouldn't be in my position because he never would have been dumb enough to care so much about someone as to storm the gates of Hades. Beyond that, though, what would Marius do? He knew all about the kind of propriety the Lord of the Dead wanted of me. The satyr knew all these nuances and tricks. He knew the steps to this dance. Marius would play along until the moment was right. Then he would strike.

I'd never been good at patience or politics. I sucked at minding the rules. Maybe, though, this situation needed a little less of me and a little more Marius.

"Forgive me," I said, mimicking the tone the satyr reserved for ass-kissing with the gods. "I'm used to being the big fish in a little pond of mortals. I've forgotten my place, as you said."

Hades's face relaxed. "That's better."

"What would the Lord of the Dead wish of me? If it is mine to give, I will honor that bargain."

"Well," he said, those slender fingers dancing at his lips, "I must admit that you are an intriguing sort, mage. You've yoked yourself with the scum of my pantheon, and that of Asgard, yet you are regarded in high favor by some. To others you are quite the threat. I would know what it is *you* know."

Hades took slow, silent steps across the room, keeping his eyes on the marble floor.

"You want information?" I asked, careful not to add, *That's it?*

Black eyes flashed to mine for an instant before focusing once more on the floor. "Not quite. Not just." He gazed at me from beneath his lashes. "And yet exactly that."

I blinked away confusion. "I don't understand."

"I would know why the Fae want you killed. Why a reclusive god long thought dead would reveal himself to you. Shelter you. Guide you." He stopped, his face a few scant inches from my own. He glared down at me from beneath his hooded eyes. "I would see what is so special about a half-trained mortal mage named Catherine Sharp."

I blew out a breath. "Dude, if I had a nickel every time I asked myself the same question."

Ignoring my comment, he regarded me with genuine curiosity. "What is it about you that has held the attention of the most capricious of gods and satyrs?"

As he reached out to me, I repressed the urge to jerk away. His touch was corpse-cold and clammy. His fingertips brushed back my hair and slid along my neck. My heartbeat quickened with fear, and the god closed his eyes.

"That there," he breathed. "The life in you. The vitality so pure and strong. It races through you like a song."

He stroked my throat where my pulse jumped beneath flesh, and his eyes rolled back with an obscene joy. Those spindly fingers worked in the air as if they could close around my life and take it away. He probably could, too. All it would take was his will. As his touch glided down over my collar bones, his hand fell away. The sensation of his covetous desire lingered on my skin like a slug's slime trail.

Hades leaned in, his breath icy on my cheek. Bile rose in the back of my mouth as his dry lips brushed against my ear.

"I would know the song of you," he whispered. "That is what I want."

Once more, I felt Marius's anguish in my bones. I risked a glance at him there in the center of Hades's chamber. Though his hair still floated with the weak, lazy current, his head thrashed from side to side. His fists pounded at the barrier between us.

"Your consort is jealous, it would seem," Hades said with relish. "And I've not even sampled so little as your lips."

He inhaled deeply, taking in my scent, my fear.

I repeated my earlier question, this time with a sick, sad understanding of the answer. "What is it that you need me to offer that you can't just take?"

He tapped his nose. "Clever beauty, you already know."

And I did. What couldn't a man of manners such as his just take? Consent to use my body as he wanted.

"Ew," I said. Hey, it was either that or give in to the urge to dry heave.

"No," he called loudly.

Before he could admonish me again for my horrible manners, I lashed out with the bracelet. As it had in my hotel room, the metal elongated into a whip. Hades rocked back, and I spun beneath the spidery grasp of his hands. With another flick of the whip, I circled the god's throat. Pooling all my power into the effort, I yanked. He crashed down to the floor with enough force to crack the marble, and green light shot up from the tiny fissures. With some of my newfound superspeed, I knotted the cuff around Hades's wrists.

Squatting over him—one foot grinding into his forearms—I took his throat into one hand and squeezed the desiccated flesh. More angry than repulsed, I got my face right into his and spat, "You still want to know my song? Do you?"

He laughed. Sweet fucking gods, I hate being laughed at. I dug in my heels and squeezed harder. His giggles died beneath my fingers. With a flop of his hands, he signaled for me to stop.

I loosened my hold on his neck.

"Oh my." He gasped. "You live up to your legend. And so hotheaded. It's no wonder you've accrued so many enemies in this short little life of yours."

"So let's make a deal."

"What do you want, precious mortal? The satyr? Really?"

"Really," I confirmed. "Marius and I walk out of here, back to the land of the living, and you don't do a damn thing about it."

"I can't let that happen."

Hades sputtered as I choked him again. "Are you sure?"

He nodded. His hands flapped beneath my foot, this time pointing to the edge of the circle that formed his chamber. For the first time, I noticed others standing there. A small man stroked a hellhound between the ears. There were others, too, that only revealed themselves as pairs of golden eyes behind a veil of shadow.

"What do they want?" I asked.

"The same as you, mage. They've all come for the satyr. And they aren't the only ones. It would seem, my dear, that your consort—like you—is quite popular."

I took in the stares boring into me. What was I going to do? Kill Hades—if that was even possible—then bully my way past these people? Fight off a hellhound? Marius had been taken down twice by such a beast, and he had centuries of experience on me. "Be clever," Hades urged. "Think this through."

And what of those that I couldn't see? What if someone like Belial waited there in the murk?

"Do you really think you can cheat death again, Catherine?"

THIRTY-ONE

"You Turn the Screws"

Golden eyes narrowed at me from the edges of the chamber. The hellhound bared its teeth, panting out a cloud of that sickly yellow venom. Suspended in the beam of green light, Marius begged me to stop with a horrified expression.

Frustrated, I let out a growl and stomped myself upright, releasing Hades in the process. The eyes retreated back into the gloaming. Sinuously, slowly as smoke, the god rose to his feet and offered me his still-bound hands. I yanked the cuff away and slid it onto my own wrist where it remained simply a bit of jewelry.

Hades brushed his robes free of dust, glaring at me the whole time. "Do not think for one moment, Miss Sharp, that I will forget this outburst."

He turned away, cold and indifferent. As he massaged his wrists, he paced back to his throne. "It would seem," he said to the room, "that I have many courting my favor. But who shall I choose? How will I be fair?"

"You want me to sweeten the pot?" I asked ruefully.

With a flourish of his robes, he whirled to face me. "You accept my terms, then? Yourself for the satyr?"

How far was I willing to go for Marius? Stay and offer myself to Hades? That sacrifice was loaded with disgusting promise, a loss of dignity worse than any I'd suffered before. Or leave the Underworld empty-handed, knowing that there was a way I could've saved Marius?

I looked at him through that viscous green fog and tried to find an easy answer, but none existed. My satyr shook his head again, pleading with me. *Not for me*, he'd said. My throat tightened around any response I might have made to the Lord of the Dead.

"I will not be ignored, Hades," came a thunderous voice from the shadows. "I offer more than this piteous mortal could ever muster."

More voices, each just as angry and boastful as the last.

Poised on his throne, Hades clearly pondered the situation, fingers fiddling at his lips. An insect with far too many legs danced about at the hem of his sleeve.

"There's only one solution to this problem. Only one way I win, you see. And that is this…" Hades cleared his throat, and when he spoke again, his fragile voice rang out with all the booming authority of thunder. I imagined that all those in this realm, the Otherworld, and my home could hear him when he said, "There will be an auction for the life of the satyr."

"An auction?" I asked. "What are you going to do, list him on eBay?"

With a pointed glance in my direction Hades continued, "Marius, son of Llyr, son of Pan. In one hour, I will entertain all offers. Those who wish to acquire his life must bring their bid with them."

"But where?" a gruff voice barked. "The place. It must be neutral."

"No," protested another. "We take him to sacred ground. It is the only way my benefactor will be satisfied."

The bearer of the golden eyes stepped forward. He was a satyr but unlike any I'd seen. His head was a goat's, but the hands sticking out of his robes were that of a human. His horns caught the emerald light. "The scion must return to his rightful place."

He must be one of the Sileni, I realized.

On and on the arguments waged. I glanced up at Marius. Once more, our eyes met. What was he thinking? What would he say to me if he could?

"I'll win," I swore under my breath.

Marius shook his head lightly and passed me a sad smile.

"It is done!" Hades called, the echo of his voice rattling my teeth. "An hour hence, all those with an interest in the satyr's future will meet, offerings in hand. He—or she," he added for my benefit, "with the most handsome bid will take home one satyr, slightly used."

"Where?" I demanded.

Hades's smile was full of malice. "The tomb of a dead god. What say you, Marius? Shall we visit the family mausoleum?"

My satyr pressed his eyes shut. Jaw quivering, he hung his head and went slack. Listless and grief-stricken, Marius bobbed in the green glow.

"The Temple of Pan," Hades said sharply, calling my attention back to him. The Lord of the Dead stood and reached out a pale hand. The green flames burst back to life, and Marius disappeared into their twisting dance.

I chewed on my lip, scared. All right, I was terrified. I didn't dare show it in this company. My heart pounded in my chest, and it took all my focus to keep my breathing steady. Across the room, the hellhound gave a doggy smile, its black tongue falling out of its mouth.

Hades folded his arms within his robes. "One hour. Bring your best, mage, if you wish to have your precious satyr again. And a word of advice, though: you will need more than a shiny trinket to compete with the other bids."

I stiffened, fists tight at my sides.

"Now," Hades rumbled. "Be gone from my sight."

Before I could so much as flinch, a cyclone of icy fire swept me up. The sudden cold stole my breath. Struggling to find up or down, to breathe, to scream, I flailed and tumbled at the whim of the tempest. Soon, my head throbbed and ached from the lack of air. My chest felt as if it would collapse on itself. I heard nothing but the roar of the wind. Saw nothing but green flames. With a jerk, I shot upright and spun in tight, ever-faster circles. Just when I thought I might black out, my feet touched solid earth.

The wind dispersed and the flames flickered out, kicking up a gray cloud of dust that lingered in the wavering air. I fell to my knees, coughing, gasping for breath.

"Cat! Cat!" Mal called to me.

One hand on my back, one under my arm, he kept me from falling face-first into the carpet of my bungalow in Santorini.

Wait...what?

"Where is he? Where's Marius?"

Still unable to talk, I shook my head and went back to retching. Mal's fingers slackened with disappointment.

"He's...he's really gone, then?" The pain in the satyr's voice was heartbreaking. "But...he can't be. I feel him. He's alive."

"Not dead," I confirmed between gasps.

Another hand pressed on my back, this one heavy and cool. I looked to see Hephaestus kneeling beside me, those silver eyes fixed on me with worry. "You saw him?"

The coughing subsided, and I was able to breathe, even and clear. The air tasted sweet. As I calmed down, I nodded again. When I spoke, it was in quiet, laconic bursts. "Yes. Hades's chamber."

Loki appeared with a glass of water. "What did Hades have to say on the subject?"

"Doesn't like you." I took a drink and waved away the guys. While I appreciated the chivalry, I had to stand up on my own. And I did. Then I shuffled myself right over to the couch and fell in a heap. Drawing a deep breath, I finally felt like I could talk. I told them the quick and dirty version of my trip through the Underworld.

"We've only got an hour," I said. "Then Hades is holding an auction. Marius goes to the highest bidder."

"Where?" Loki asked.

"The Temple of Pan."

Loki hissed a curse under his breath. "What an asshole."

I toasted him with my glass of water. "Preach."

"Heph," Loki barked, "got any money on you?"

Hephaestus folded his arms. "You know I cannot bid against another Olympian."

"Not what I asked you."

"He may be the original plutocrat, Loki, but my cousin will not settle for something as worthless as money."

"Then what will he accept?"

My eyes widened. In a flash, I was on my feet and standing at Loki's side. "Wait, you'll bid on him?"

Loki shook his head. "You already know I have to stay out of it."

I sagged. "Then..."

"You," he cut me off. "You want him so bad, you will have to go in there and win him yourself. But nothing says I can't loan you the capital to do so."

Hephaestus shook his head. "I have already given her the best I can offer."

I shook the cuff bracelet on my wrist. "Hades wasn't too thrilled with jewelry, either."

"Of course he wouldn't be, the slimy shit," Loki growled. He took me by the shoulders. "Look, I'm going to go pull a string or two, see what shakes out. You two—"

"Three!" Malcolm interrupted.

Loki rolled his eyes. "You *three* come up with something and get to the Temple."

Heph raised a hand, begging for a pause. He closed his eyes, and his attention seemed to fall inward. When he opened his eyes again, his shoulders drooped and his brow furrowed. "I cannot go with you. Not as an ally."

Loki responded with a raised, dubious eyebrow. "You just get word from on high?"

Hephaestus's head bobbed ponderously. "Zeus asks for all the lords to attend."

"Wait? Zeus?" I asked.

Heph confirmed this. "Solidarity or some other such bullshit." To Loki, he said, "I will be there, and I will look after her from my place with the others. That is all I can promise."

Loki nodded in disgruntled assent. "Safe travels."

With a fist to his chest, Hephaestus offered the Asgardian a salute. Then he did his disappearing act, leaving little more than the scent of burning metal in his wake.

"Okay, so—" Loki stopped speaking. His face went blank, and his ears twitched. He was hearing something I could not, but my brand throbbed with cold. I waved a hand in front of the god's face.

Nothing.

"Hello?"

A moment later, he blinked back to reality. "Shit. That was Odin."

My eyes widened. The King of Aesir. The Allfather. Quite possibly the only hand that could ever hold Loki's leash. "You guys have each other on telepathic speed dial?"

Loki grinned. "Something like that. Hades put out the invitation to the heads of other pantheons. Odin just informed me that I, too, must be present. I'm going to go talk to him. See what I can conjure up on that end.

"If I don't get to talk to you before the auction," he added, "here's a tip: don't bid early. It's far too easy to be outspent. Wait until late in the game, when people are bidding desperately."

"But I am desperate," I whispered.

Loki's hand was warm on my cheek, his eyes cool. "Pretend you're not."

"If this works, will he be safe? Or will they just keep coming?"

Loki chewed on my question. Before answering, he drew in a long breath and let it out slowly. "That depends."

"On what?"

"On who wins. And how."

Then Loki knocked me off-balance—figuratively speaking. He kissed me on the forehead. A very paternal gesture that carried with it loads of sentiment that I didn't have the time to decipher.

"Good luck," he said.

And just like that, he was gone. Though I'm sure he didn't take the door, I heard a phantom slamming noise. This jarred me into motion. I grabbed Mal and yanked him out of the hotel room. I still had my backpack, but I knew its contents were worthless to Hades.

"Where are we going?" Mal asked as I dragged him down the path.

"Your room."

"You can't be wanting a quickie. Not now."

"Nope. No sex. I need to go through Marius's things. He had to have something in his storage shed, something he brought with him that would fetch a satyr's ransom."

Once in the room, I began tossing the drawers. Marius had always had an eye for fashion, but as I pulled shirt after shirt out of the drawers, I began to curse his nature as a clotheshorse.

"All right, we need to find something. Something unbeatable." I groaned. "Christ, how many silk ties does one man need?"

Mal let out a nervous laugh as he dumped the contents of Marius's bag on the bed. "That's my brother. Posh bastard more interested in looking flash."

"Didn't look so 'flash' the last time I saw him," I murmured.

Mal didn't meet my eyes, but his hands slowed down as they searched through the random swag on the mattress. His voice was soft and as vulnerable as a scared child's. "He wasn't— I mean, when you saw him, was he...?"

I stopped ransacking the room and took Mal's hands. "Hey," I said calmly, drawing his gaze to meet mine. Tears had pooled in his sapphire-blue eyes. "You were right. He's alive."

The satyr's lip trembled. "The last thing I said to him... Shit, I was a twat. An' I didn't mean it. I didn't know he wouldn't come back."

"Stop," I barked. "He *is* coming back. Do you understand me? We're going to find something here and we're going to go get him." My words spilled out of me in quick waves that couldn't cover the fact that I was crying, too. "And you're not the only one who fucked up. But we'll get him back. And we'll both be able to tell him— Well, we'll make up for those last moments, okay? They won't be the last. Not by a long shot. Got it?"

Malcolm closed his eyes, set his features to stony resolve, and nodded.

"All right. Let's get to looking, then."

I let go of his hands, and Mal moved to the other bedside bureau and searched the drawers while I sifted through Marius's possessions. A silver cigarette case—empty. A sealed, unlabeled black bottle—full, though of what I couldn't tell. One of Eris's poker chips.

"What was it you said?" Malcolm asked, his tone curious.

I set aside a phial of white light. "What?"

"That you wish you could take back. What was it you said?"

"The problem's not what I said, rather what I didn't say."

He tossed aside another damn silk tie, this one gold. "Ah," he said, nodding with a wry chuckle. *"That."*

"Yeah." I dragged my hands through my hair. "I don't know what half of this shit is!"

Clothes stopped flying, and I looked up to see Mal had frozen, his eyes fixed on whatever lay in the drawer.

"Found summat," he said.

Mal dipped into the drawer with both hands. He lifted the contents as gently as he would a baby. The wooden box was carved with intricate vines and beautiful symbols. With excruciating care, he delivered the box to the bed and laid it on the pillow. He thumbed an unseen latch and opened the casket.

Marius's pan pipes gleamed from inside. I remembered the awe in his face when he had taken those out at the shed. How his fingers had caressed them, how his lips had pursed *just so*. When he played them, it had been with the utmost reverence. Of all things—clothes, money, or connections—this bundle of reeds was truly his most prized possession.

I shook my head. "No."

"What?" Mal chuffed. "Why not?"

"You know how feels about those."

"If it's the only way to save him, surely he'll understand!"

"It's not like he can just pick up another set!"

"This is all we've got, Cat," Mal roared. "This is the best chance we have. Pipes made by Pan himself. One of a kind."

"They're the only thing he loves. It would break his heart to lose them. You *know* that."

"Yeah, and the gods know that, as well. They'll take sick fun out of accepting this over anything else because it will continue to hurt him. One last kick in his ass."

Shit. I hated it when satyrs were right.

But Mal knew what he was talking about. I'd been around enough of the high and mighty crowd to know that this sort of dig would be precisely the thing that would turn Hades's head.

"Dammit." I sighed. "Fine. Fine. But this was *your* idea. If this works...just don't blame me, all right?"

Mal moved sluggishly, as if the whole thing was a burden he was not prepared to bear. He reached out to close the box.

"No, don't get too hasty," I said. "You're going to need to use those."

He blanched, real fear striking him across the face. "What?"

"How else do you expect to get to the Temple of Pan in less than an hour? Hail a cab and speed across to the mainland? That is where Marius said it was, right?"

"B-but...I d-don't," Mal stammered. "I mean, I can't. It's..."

"Your birthright. Come on. You can play us there."

"No, I can't. I've never been there."

I shook my head. "Doesn't matter."

"Of course it bloody matters!"

"You're wasting time," I snapped.

"I can't do it!"

"Bullshit, Mal, I know you can."

"And just how do you work that one out?"

I gave him a level stare that would've made Marius proud. "Blood calls to blood."

"Shit," he hissed. Mal paced quickly, like a caged cat looking for a way out. But he knew I was right. Even if he didn't like it, he knew.

Without another word, Mal picked up the pipes. I closed the box and held it close to my chest.

The satyr moistened his lips and played a trembling note. "I dunno if I know the right tune."

"Of course you do," I said, keeping my voice soft and reassuring now. In truth, I was annoyed as hell. We didn't have time to spare. Our hour was almost up. And if Mal didn't know the tune, we were fucked. And not in the fun way he'd like. I reached into myself and pulled out some hokey movie bullshit. "Just focus on it. This is part of your heritage. It's in your blood."

Mal gulped down his nerves. "Right. I'm just as much Pan's grandson as Marius, right? I can do this."

He closed his eyes but didn't relax. His face was a harsh mix of determination and fear as he brought the reeds to his lips again. At first, the notes quivered breathily, like a nervous child singing a solo at a Christmas pageant. Soon, though, Mal found his voice and pushed it through the pipes with every erg of himself he could muster.

The song was light and lilting. Damn near playful. The notes stirred a new cauldron of butterflies in my belly, but these weren't flutters of desire or fear. No, this was joy. Simple, pure joy. A summer breeze wafted in from the beach and tossed my hair. I closed my eyes and let the song touch me, let it seep into my frozen, petrified heart and work a little magic.

THIRTY-TWO

"You Part The Waters"

M al stopped playing.

When I opened my eyes, the hotel room was gone. Rocks of all sizes and queer shapes jutted out of the sandy earth. For a moment, I thought we'd traveled to the Otherworld again. However, this place wasn't devoid of color. In fact, it looked more like someone had taken a paintbrush to the rocky walls of the cliff face before me. Stripes of tarry black mixed with the light brown of fresh-baked bread. The higher up the rock wall my gaze traveled, the more uniform the colors became. Slate gray outcroppings were covered in a dry, brittle grass.

This place looked as if two different cliffsides had been smashed together. To my left, the wall was red as the martian landscape. It boasted a covering of lush, green shrubs that swept off toward the horizon.

Meanwhile, the slab in front of me was pale and parched. Where its neighbor had only been shaped by eons of erosion and exposure to the elements, this side had been carved with hammer and chisel. In a diagonal line following the natural slope of the earth, three alcoves had been cut into the rock. Though weathered, the scalloped details of the arches were still evident. Beneath the highest of these alcoves was a vast archway. Unlike the other carvings, this doorway had no decoration to it, no imagination.

"I've gone and done it now," Mal said, crestfallen. He stared at the barren ruins in the cliff and sighed. "This can't be the place."

The sound of a waterfall glided over the hill, and I thought of Marius's tales of the Temple. Of his lagoon hideaway.

"This is the place," I said. We were alone, but I felt eyes on me from all directions. "Hurry," I whispered, opening the casket. "Stash the pipes before someone sees."

Mal put the bundle of reeds back in its box and stowed the casket in my backpack. And just in time. Deep inside the archway, the cliff quivered and a shape emerged. Whatever it was, its steps clicked lightly on the rocky terrain. I saw the vague silhouette of a short person—well, a biped at least. He wore something on his head that fanned out to either side.

Beside me, Mal shivered. "Oh, bollocks."

The figure stepped into the light, and I gasped. Staring at me with golden eyes was a goat. He was small—shorter than me, even—with limbs as frail as a child's. His fur was a light-cream color mottled with snowy white. He wore a tight braid on either side of his face and had a long white beard. Horns—tortoiseshell and smooth—jutted out of his skull and twisted off to either side of his head. These were far longer than any I'd seen sprout from Marius or Mal.

The goat walked on his rear legs. From beneath the hem of his indigo robe, I could see hooves. He was different from the common barnyard animal, though, in that he had the slender arms of a human. Though stubby and furry, his fingers were just as functional as mine.

"Mage," he said, his voice both nasal and gruff. "I wasn't certain you would come."

I remembered the golden eyes peering at me from the shadows of Hades's chamber. "You were there, too," I said. "Trying to bargain for Marius's life."

He dipped his bearded chin. "Hades called you Catherine Sharp. You are marked for Asgard." He poked forward with one of those nubby fingers, indicating my mark and stating the obvious all at once.

I smiled, but there was little joy in it. "Aw, and here I don't know anything about you."

"I am called Astraios. And I am the high priest of the Sileni."

Malcolm retreated a step, his shaking breaths audible even over the sound of his feet on the gravel.

Astraios fixed those alien eyes on Mal and cocked his head. "Who is this?"

I chanced a glance at Mal. His face had lost all color. Suddenly the weight of all he'd been through these past few days dawned on me. He'd been tricked into finding his brother and luring him into a trap. He'd accidentally killed me—asshole. He'd seen magic and deities and the fucking River Styx. And now he was faced with a very real example of a heritage he'd all but forgotten. He stood in the shadow of the temple to his grandfather. That in and of itself was pretty heavy.

Quite honestly, I'd have probably thrown up by that point. The fact that Mal was staring uselessly, mouth gaping like a cod, was stellar on his part.

"Malcolm?" I asked softly.

Something of the moment must have infused him, for he swallowed hard and stood a little straighter. When he spoke, it was with a little more dignity than I'd heard before. "I'm Malcolm, second son of Llyr, who was the son of Pan 'imself. I'm here to take my brother home."

Astraios narrowed his eyes. "Are you?"

"Aye. And I'll kick the goat ass of anyone who tries to get in me way."

I sighed. Well, so much for dignity.

The Sileni's muzzle curled in a sneer. "I see."

Mal nodded for punctuation. I resisted the urge to pat him on the head. Poor guy.

"We are here to bid for Marius's life," I said, loading my words with respect.

"The Sileni welcome you to our sacred temple," he intoned with a bow. "The auction will begin shortly. Please, come in and join the others."

With a click, he turned on his hooves and motioned for us to follow him through the arch and into the mountain itself. We'd only gone twenty feet into the cave when darkness fell in a pall. Mal's lemon-yellow orb sparked to life in his hand, illuminating the walls with the citrusy glow. Soon, we came to a dead end. Our guide, however, didn't break step. We passed through rock as easily as through air, and as we did, I felt magic shiver around us.

"Is it a glamour?" I asked.

Astraios spared me a glance over his shoulder. "Set on this temple by Pan before his departure."

"Why?"

"To keep out the marauding riffraff. Romans. Christians," he spat with disdain. "Any number who would defile this sacred ground. These days it protects our rites from the prying eyes of tourists. Or worse, scientists. Archaeologists who would take our relics and hide them in museums."

"So outside we see ruins, but it's actually—"

"The ruins are all too real, woman," he snapped. "We veil the cave so that none may come unbidden into our sanctuary."

Amber light swelled, and we found ourselves at the mouth of the tunnel. We'd entered a vast circular chamber. It wasn't exactly a football stadium, but the room was larger than most churches I'd seen. We stood above it all, separated from the floor by a winding stone staircase. Below us, all sorts milled about.

I don't know what I'd been expecting—perhaps a handful of gods or minions bearing gold and myrrh. This? This was just...

"Oh fuckin' hell," Mal said for both of us.

Quite the crowd had turned out for Marius. At least a hundred bodies filled the space below. The churning mass of voices held the electrified excitement of a crowd of sports fans. All that was missing were a few vuvuzelas. Any moment—if given the proper spark—they could turn into a violent mob. A mob capable of wielding magic and biting with sharp, pointy teeth.

Astraios led us down the narrow, unstable stone steps. Though the priest kept his hands folded together in front of his chest with the solemnity of a monk, Mal and I palmed the wall for support. Between this and my experience with Hades's Spiral Staircase of Infinite Suckage, I had a feeling I'd be done with stairs for a good long while.

When I get back to Vegas. I'm taking every damn elevator I possibly can.

"Do you lot live here?" Mal asked. "It's a bit...rough."

Astraios's horns dipped. "We keep rooms in a monastery nearby. Though that is where we spend much of our time, this is our sanctum. Our most sacred place. When our lord returns, these halls will be resplendent with his radiance."

I shivered. Marius. That's why they wanted him. To make him their god.

As we neared the main floor, I saw that some of the visitors were being herded behind golden ropes to keep them pinned closely to the walls. Other Sileni—goats in robes a few shades drabber than Astraios's—worked the crowd like ushers.

"What's up with the ropes?" I asked.

"Spectators. They've no stock in the auction itself but have come to watch Fate play her hand."

"Reality television, Greek-god-style?"

Astraios ignored me. "If you wish to bid," he said, "you will join the rest of the interested parties near the center."

Mal and I followed the Sileni's outstretched hand. Chaos slowly became order, rings of people forming according to their purposes. Far more had turned up to watch than to bid. In the audience I saw all sorts—some I recognized but most I didn't. There were dwarves, elves—looking very much like garden gnomes rather than anything you'd see from Tolkien—and demonic-looking things, all shriven of their glamours. Lovely women gathered in pockets, noses held high as they preened. Some of these women trailed leaves, or seemed to have smooth bark for skin.

"Dryads," a voice purred in my ear. "They have an interest in satyrs."

I whipped around to find Dahlia staring at me. She wore a white gossamer dress, a light sheen of glitter, and her preternatural beauty. Her mahogany skin was flawless, save for the black oak-leaf tattoo at her throat. Even that dark mark added to her allure, though. And she knew it. Eyes like honey gazed at me from behind that perfect, cold mask, and my ex-girlfriend tossed her raven hair.

"What are you doing here?" I asked, unable to keep the tremor from my voice.

"Officially?" Dahlia held up a small velvet bag and shook it in front of my eyes. Its contents made no sound, but the act was jarring enough that I could almost hear my guts twist. "Same as you, I hear."

"You're here on Fae business?" I asked. "Why would either of the queens want Marius?"

"Who says it's Mab or Titania that wants him?" She pocketed the pouch. "I'm bidden to come, and therefore, I'm here. Charged to score one satyr. Slightly used," she added cheekily, mimicking Hades's earlier words.

I didn't see the humor. Slipping into my comfortable loathing for Dahlia, I crossed my arms over my chest. "And unofficially?"

My ex appraised me, her gaze sliding up and down my body, lingering over my wrist, my hair. She drew in a breath and let it out with a hint of sadness. "I wanted to see you."

"You've seen me. Are we done?"

Her full lips spread into a smile.

Oh gods, that smile. I'd been a fool for it one too many times.

"You have no idea." Without another word she glided away, fluttering here and there to offer greetings to other guests.

I shook my head. I couldn't deal with this now. My ex issues would have to wait. Turning back to Mal, I saw that he was staring up at the tall ceiling. He hadn't even noticed Dahlia. Probably for the best, really, but quite a feat all the same.

I tugged on Mal's sleeve. "You okay?"

He jumped, startled. "This is just..."

"It's a lot," I said.

Mal nodded. "You hear stories when you're a kid, but after a while, they're just stories. Things that happened to people who don't have any real connection to you. This, though... This is intense." His gaze drifted around at the assembled parties. "And them... How do you do it?"

"Do what?"

"Stand in the same room with gods and not feel tiny?"

I smiled. Just a few years ago, I'd asked Marius the same thing. I was no nearer to an answer, but I realized that standing there with a purpose, with power of my own, I didn't feel so small. "It gets easier," I said. "Just fake it. Act like you own the place. Which in some weird way, *you* do."

"Right. Family heirloom, I suppose. Bloody hell!" He blew out an exasperated breath. "Who are all these people?"

I took him by the arm and set to acting the part of friendly native guide. "Over there by the dryads? Those are Fae."

"How can you tell?"

"See the oak-leaf tattoos? That's their brand. Most people who serve another deity will wear a mark."

"Like the one on your wrist."

"Right," I encouraged him. "You'll start noticing patterns."

Together we did a slow circuit of the room, taking in the audience first. There were creatures I couldn't name but that I'd seen in paintings. Titans. Demons. An elephant in ornate robes decorated with gold and jade lotuses. A blue-skinned man as fair as any of the Fae held a woman close to his nude body. She rested her head against his chest and let him stroke her coal-black hair.

Padding around the circle we came to a section of proud figures. I recognized Hera immediately. The Lady of Olympus stood with her chin at a regal angle, her curls falling artfully from her head. She wore a sour expression, nose curling as if she smelled something vile. And yet, there was something about her presence that spoke of haughty triumph. And why not? She had it in for Marius for some reason. She wasn't the one who'd cursed him, but she was the one who refused to free him.

Near the Lady of Olympus, I saw Ares and Aphrodite. There were others, all similarly dressed bearing golden pins or seals on their robes. These were the lords of Olympus. Attending them were carbon copies of Polly and Melpomene, the Muses. One of them waved at me with a giddy smile as if we were the best of friends. Standing at a distance from his pantheon, Hephaestus looked like the most stern of statues.

"Oi, that's Heph!" Mal said. Some of the tension left him now that he'd seen a friendly face.

Hephaestus gave an almost imperceptible shake of his head, warning us to not make any contact. I nodded. Over the years I spent with Eris, I'd seen inter-pantheon struggles, and none of them were pretty.

While I wouldn't mind seeing Eris on the receiving end of some of that bullshit, I wouldn't wish it on a friend like Hephaestus.

The crowd in front of us parted to let someone through. That someone, it turned out, was my boss.

With a hopeful gasp, I ran to him. "Well? Did you pull your strings?"

Loki tilted his head and scrunched his still-bruised face. "You could say that."

"What happened?"

"I... Well, I may have accidentally reminded Odin of the time someone stole his eye patch."

"So what's that got to do with—" I wasn't sure how this mattered, but a terrible thought occurred to me. "You didn't..."

"It was just for laughs, okay?" he whispered angrily. "We were drunk and thought it would be funny. Next thing you know Marius is tied up in a Valkyrie's underwear and I'm pregnant with a horse. Again."

He shook his head, as if nursing a hangover, and I gaped at him.

"You're...just. Gah! What does this mean?"

"It means I can't bid. Odin will be doing that."

Odin bidding for Marius? "Is that good? Please tell me that's good."

"Not exactly."

I swatted Loki on the shoulder. "You had one job to do!"

"Will you stop it? You're making me look bad. You're my vassal, dammit." The air around us shimmered, and shadowy wraiths of Loki and I appeared. I couldn't hear what his said, but he roared at me and I quailed beneath his wrath.

"Great. Now they'll all think I'm your bitch."

Not-Loki raised a fist to backhand me. I fought the urge to punch the real one in the stomach.

"What about you?" Loki asked. "Did you find something to bid with?"

I nodded. "I think we've got something that fits the bill."

The illusory copies of Loki and I vanished. My boss stepped in closer. "Good. You're going to have a lot to compete with."

"How does this work?"

"Not like any auction you've ever seen. Everyone's bidding in different currencies. There's not exactly an exchange rate. Basically, you're all going to go up to Hades, make your offer, and he will decide what he wants most."

Mal spun in a tight circle. "What do all these people want with Marius?"

Loki's expression turned dour. "He wronged them in some way. Stole things. Seduced people. Wreaked havoc. Generally, all things I enjoy. But they aren't so sanguine about it now that they know who's behind those crimes."

"Didn't Eris tell him to do most of that?" I asked.

"If that's true, why go after him and not her?" Mal added.

"They don't know Eris commanded it. Your brother—and his former benefactor—are both very good at what they do. Eris covered her own tracks. All these people know is that Marius dicked them over. There's no proof he did so at Discord's command."

Mal pinched the bridge of his nose, suddenly looking very much like his brother. "I don't understand this. I don't recognize any of these supposed gods."

"They're not all deities," Loki said helpfully. He draped an arm over Mal's shoulder and spun him around, pointing out the things I'd missed. Like the broad-shouldered form of Zeus and a rock monster like the one we'd seen at the strip club.

"Those three women up there with the ravens on their heads? That's the Morrigan. Steer clear. They always want new soldiers."

I shuddered. My eyes landed on the red-skinned djinn Na'ar al Afrit. "Shit," I hissed. Then I covered my face and put my back to the djinn Marius and I had tried to steal from.

"And that," Loki said merrily, "is why his reindeer can fly. You're welcome."

My eyes shot up to see a plump, white-haired man in—of all things—a crimson lab coat. He traded words with a bearded dwarf, and when the two laughed...

"It really is like a bowl full of jelly," I gasped, awestruck.

The cavern rumbled with a single note beat against an unseen, mammoth drum. All conversation ceased, leaving only the sound of rushed footsteps as everyone went to their places.

Loki's breath was hot on my ear. "I can't stay with you. Remember what I've told you about bidding. About *everything*. I'll collect you when this is over."

The Trickster swept away to join the crowd behind the golden ropes. All those with skin in the game—so to speak—stood in a wide circle. Mal and I fell in with the nearest arc, putting me a little too close to Dahlia for my personal comfort. Then again, if I had to choose between her and the djinn, well, this would work just fine.

Another hit of the drum rattled my teeth, rumbled in my chest, and all movement ceased. All eyes swept to the center of the circle, ready for whatever happened when a god held an auction.

THIRTY-THREE

"What's Now Is Now"

Hades clapped his spindly hands, a mirthless smile slithering across his face. "My friends," he sang. He glided around the circle, leaving a slimy trail of ass-kissery behind him. "Cousins," he added with a gesture to Zeus. To the Morrigan, he bowed his head. "Colleagues. Esteemed guests. You honor me with your presence this day. Each of you has expressed interest in the fate of a recent...let's say, *commodity* I have acquired."

Hades snapped his fingers and once more that beam of emerald, gelatinous light appeared. Marius, still in his satyr form, hovered within. His eyes widened as he took in his surroundings. His stare blurred past me and Mal, too intent on the assembled enemies. How many of them had he worked for at one time or another? How many had he called friends?

Spectators cast boos and jeers at him, some hissed. A few of the dryads even sighed. Within the circle of bidders, however, a slow, silent anger simmered. Hatred backed by power, lust for revenge, and the endless amounts of time to exact it.

"A thief. A drunken wastrel. A feckless philanderer. The Scion of Pan," Hades called, his voice ringing with terrible authority. Robes sweeping along the floor, he approached the Sileni in their tight pack. "To some, he is potential, the corpse of a god to be revived. To others, he is an opportunity for redemption, retribution. Some of you seek a plaything, a whipping boy. Do with him as you will, for it is no matter to me."

A throne of billowing white smoke appeared behind Hades. "I will entertain all bids," he said, sitting. "Prepare your offerings."

As one, those in the inner circle reached into hidden pockets. Dahlia held her velvet pouch while a pair of tiny elves toted a steamer trunk to Old Saint Nick.

Mal made to reach into my backpack, but I stopped him. "No. We wait."

"Wait? Why?"

I glanced over to Loki. He stood near Hephaestus, but not quite among the Olympians. He nodded, a gesture loaded with commands and advice.

"Divine mandate," I said.

Hades met my stare from across the room. As he took notice of the fact that I carried nothing, he sneered.

Let him think whatever he wants. Play the game like Marius would.

I didn't honor Hades with any more of my attention. Instead, I kept my eyes fixed on Marius in the verdant light. He still didn't look at me. He just gazed at the floor. Something was carved into the stone there, but I couldn't make out the exact shapes.

Without preamble or permission, Zeus marched forward. Slung over one arm was the pelt of a lion, amber shimmering where its eyes should have been. He pushed a woman in front of him, his hand latched around the back of her neck. She wore little more than a trace of moonlight over her creamy skin.

"Oi," Mal whispered. "I'll have a taste of that."

I elbowed him. "Quiet."

The woman knelt before Hades and bowed her head.

"For my cousin," Zeus bellowed, "I bring the pelt of the Nemean Lion, slain by my own son."

Hades sneered. "A pittance." His lascivious stare lingered over the nude, lithe body of the woman. "And...?"

"One of my favored courtesans. A nymph who frequents the pool nearby. Her talents are many."

Hades moistened his lips, barely giving the kneeling nymph a second glance. He fixed me with that lupine leer—so much like Eris's—before turning his graceless smile back to Zeus.

"I shall consider it," he said. "Next."

And so it went. In turn, each person approached Hades with his or her offering. Jewels. Promises of power or allegiance. Enchanted snow from the north. The djinn brought fire from the heart of the sun itself. The pile of riches continued to grow, each object more obscure than the last.

Beside me, Mal grew agitated. He dug into my backpack, and before I could stop him, he ran up to Hades with the carved box. I didn't dare tip my hand that this wasn't the plan. I chewed my cheeks and bit down on my tongue to keep from screaming, from reacting.

Within his cell, Marius gave a languid flail. He tried to stop Malcolm, his gestures as frenetic as the soupy beam of light would allow.

Mal knelt before the Lord of the Dead.

"And just who are you?" Hades asked.

"Malcolm, second son of Llyr, son of Pan."

Marius buried his face in his hands with embarrassment.

"How precious," Hades said. "Is this to be a display of fraternal love? A man begging for the life of his brother?"

Ignoring the snark, Mal lifted the box in both hands. "I offer this. The box was carved by my grandfather. As were these." He opened the box to reveal the pipes.

The Sileni erupted into furious shouts. Mal screamed back at them. "OI! You'll have your chance."

Some of the spectators laughed. I looked up to see Loki glaring. He knew our plan was fucked now that it was in Mal's hands. Beside him, though, Heph was a flurry of movement. He caught my attention and gave a quick wave to make sure I saw him. When I nodded, Hephaestus put both his hands together as if miming a closed book. Then, slowly, he opened them.

The arguing among satyr and Sileni continued.

What? I mouthed to Hephaestus.

He repeated the gesture again. A third time but slower, with more emphasis. His lips formed the word, "Open."

Open? Open what?

"Order, please!" Hades called. "Let us show some decorum in this—" he let out a snide laugh "—*sacred* place. There now, boy, if that is all you've to offer me, go on and wait for me to pass judgment."

Mal rose to his feet, face flushed with ruddy anger. He gave a two-fingered "archer's salute" to the Sileni and stalked back to his place in line beside me.

"How d'you think it went?" Mal asked, keeping his voice hushed.

I stared at him, blinking that he could possibly be so blissfully unaware. "Fantastic," I said, heavy on the sarcasm.

Next, Yama—his skin indigo, eyes flame red—went to Hades with his hellhound at his side. He laid a noose, golden scales, and a single lotus at the god's feet.

"Handsome prizes, indeed," Yama intoned, "for my kindred who works behind the veil."

Hades bowed his head with a shadow of respect. "Indeed. I thank you."

Yama retreated, his dog snarling at Marius.

Hades searched the crowd. "Anyone else?"

Dahlia stepped forward, each step graceful and elegant.

"Ah, a lovely representative of the Fae. How fares your Queen?"

"Mab is well, milord," Dahlia said with a deep bow.

Mal elbowed me. "Oi," he whispered. "Heph. He's tryin' to talk to you."

My attention flickered from Dahlia to Heph. Again, he made the motion and mouthed, *Open*.

I know, but open what?

Heph cupped his hands as if holding a ball.

Understanding hit me like lightning between the eyes. "That's it," I breathed.

I slipped off my bag and found the silver ball Heph had given me. The sphere was a puzzle box, that much I knew. What was inside, though? And would it be enough to win Marius's life?

Hephaestus beamed and bobbed his head.

I nodded feverishly, signaling to him that I understood. Then I got to work. I sent my senses into it. Yes, this was exactly like Pandora's box.

And like that particular relic, this little sphere held something danger-ous. The energy pulsing from it was black and spiky, cold.

Mentally, I pulled away from the object and focused on the silver sphere itself. There had to be a mechanism, some way of popping it open. But how?

At Hades's throne, Dahlia opened the velvet pouch and dropped a tiny light into the Olympian's palm. No bigger than a ring box, it gave off a faint white radiance.

The god's eyes grew wide, and he drew in a long, covetous gasp. "Oh my. Is that what I think it is?"

"Indeed," Dahlia's voice echoed in the chamber. "A treasure any would be blessed to hold—one human heart. Metaphorically speaking, that is."

I squinted, trying to get a better glimpse of Dahlia's shiny trinket. All I could see, however, was the gleam of it reflected in Hades's eyes. "Dare I ask how you or your regents came by such a gem?"

"Given freely," she said. "Unconditional love makes fools of us all."

Hades smiled wolfishly. "And how long have you had it?" he asked.

"Long enough," Dahlia replied. "Its owner misses it, I'm sure. Unable to love fearlessly without it. But that only sweetens the tragedy. Wouldn't you agree, milord?"

He peered into the bauble and turned it around in his hands, tak-ing it in from every angle as if it were a fine-cut gemstone. "Exquisite. Hardly a single flaw. A human heart in this condition is difficult to find. Well done, faerie. Well done, indeed."

Dahlia bowed low and stepped back to her place in the arc.

Hades put the pouch on his lap, patting his hand over it. "Well, if any of you can top this, I will be most impressed."

As the next bidder went forward, I turned away, focusing only on that damn puzzle. I closed my eyes and a picture of the sphere formed in my mind. There were channels carved on the inside that formed a sort of labyrinth. Like dipping a paintbrush into water, I sent my will into one of these minuscule canals. A vibrant ring of lucent power appeared in my mental blueprint. Still, there were other rings to be filled, but I was on the right track.

I stole a glance to see Hades dismissing another courtier. Marius stared at me, his head tilted with concern or confusion. I held his gaze for a moment, hoping he could understand that come hell or high water he would be leaving this temple with me and Malcolm.

Back to work, eyes shut tight, I worked with fluid speed. The rings inside began to spin and whirl around the contents of the sphere. This brought to my mind an image of a white ball encasing a dark orb. What the bloody hell had Heph stashed in here for me?

Hades's sinuous voice pierced my concentration. "Anyone else?"

Faster. Ticktock, Cat.

The rings were full, every last one of them spinning in a gyroscopic orbit and building speed.

"No one's stepping forward," Mal said in a panicked whisper.

Shitshitshitshitshit. Must go faster.

As I thought it, so the rings responded. Now spinning at a dizzying blur, the light began to swell. Brighter and brighter.

"Is that all? Is there no one else that would like to stun me with a bid for this satyr?" Hades asked, a note of surprise in his voice.

What am I supposed to do now? What's the key?

The sphere grew hot in my hands. As the power mounted, the ball vibrated. Any minute now, I thought it might levitate out of my grip entirely. I tightened my fists around it, shoving more of my frustration inside.

Come on!

"No? None of you? As Discord's former servant, this satyr is privy to many secrets. Just think what sins you can unleash from his lips while he's in the throes of agony."

"Come on, Cat," Mal whispered. "If you're going to do something, now is the time."

"I know," I ground out.

Come on! I screamed at the ball. *Open! Unlock! Go web! Please!*

The whirring stopped and the white radiance fused to form a glowing layer of power between me and the object inside the box. Energy flashed in my mind. Surely someone nearby saw something. I opened my eyes and whipped my head from side to side. No one had seen or felt anything. Odd, that.

"Very well then. Going once," Hades bellowed.

The puzzle box dissolved, melting away from the contents. Through the cool, silver mist, I saw a flash of gold. Though the ball was gone, I still felt something solid—and very heavy—in my palms. The smoke cleared, and I gasped.

"Oh shit," I muttered.

THIRTY-FOUR

"Sick of You"

The Golden Apple gleamed in the ambient torchlight. Other than the Greek symbols etched into its surface, it could have been plucked from the most perfect tree in creation. The Golden Apple of Discord. And I held it in my hands.

"Oh shit," I said again.

Dark whispers came from that damn orb and filled my head with pictures. It was like channel surfing through a flip-book of every magazine ever published, every website. Slurs and epithets, vile chants, and sinister promises made the soundtrack.

Too much, I thought. *It's too much.*

But still, the information came. Like downloading the history contained in the Apple, the black, thorny power wormed its way into my veins and coursed through me, slithering in my guts and tugging at my gag reflex.

Then it was done. The rush of data stopped. All specifications had been imported, but I still held Eris's thumb drive. So to speak. I knew her sins, her stories. Looking around the room, I was able to pull up her schemes as easily as clicking on a file.

Yama: Marius ordered to kidnap the water-buffalo companion. Yama blamed Yami. War ensued. Water buffalo later fed to Kraken.

With every face came a name and a plot, most of them carried out by Marius at the behest of Eris herself. The Trojan War. Multiple thefts, at least a dozen murders. Insults and fights that tore families and friends apart. A million little slights between mortals and monsters.

"Going twice!" Hades called.

This was it. I could not only win Marius but I could prove his innocence. I just had to get Hades to understand...

"I have something," I shouted.

I kept my stare locked on Hades's face. In my periphery, though, I saw all eyes turn their focus to me. No pressure, right?

Taking a step forward, I held the apple up for all to see. "I offer the Golden Apple of Discord."

Murmurs filled the cavern with curiosity. Hades steepled his slender fingers and narrowed his eyes. When he spoke, his voice was a purr of amusement. "Do you? And just how does a mortal come by such a relic?"

"I have my methods," I said.

The djinn snarled as I passed him. Clearly his memory of Belize was just as good as mine. "She is a minion of Eris. She and this satyr have conspired together before. I say we take her hide, as well."

I snorted with laughter. "I don't work for Eris."

"She is mine," Loki called from the gallery. "And I'll have words with any that wish to try to change that fact."

Hades didn't bother to face Loki. "Does she do this on your behalf, Aesir?"

He shook his head. "I've no interest in the prisoner. But I like my employees to be happy. If having a satyr for a pet amuses her, so be it."

The djinn moved back with a growl as others continued to chatter about this strange change in events. More whispers and suppositions. Verities and balderdash.

Believe what you want, I thought.

"All of you are so focused on the satyr," I said, "but why?"

This snagged a few ears. As I turned in a circle to take in the room, I caught Loki and Heph smiling. They must have picked up where I was going with all of this. Marius, though, was still puzzling through it. In his cell, he watched me, brow creased with confusion.

"What is he? Oh, sure, he's flesh and blood that you can rip and tear at. He's done all these things to piss you all off. You're not alone. Believe me, Marius is one of the most unsettling, annoying, and altogether irritating beings I've ever met. And I worked for Eris!"

This elicited a rolling wave of polite laughter from the audience. Good.

I bounced the apple in my hand. "Our friend the djinn over there just said I was her minion. While it's true I worked for her once upon a time, I was still just that—a minion. A tool to be used when she had need of me. And that's all the satyr is, too. Just a tool."

"You've got that right," Mal called.

I rolled my eyes. I continued my circuit of the cavern, making my way toward Marius. "He's lied, cheated, swindled, stolen, and otherwise fucked over nearly every being in this room in one way or another. But you've all forgotten that for all his clever wit and skill, he's still just an employee."

When I reached Marius I stared at him through the green light. All I wanted to do was reassure him, but I had to play this to the hilt if this gambit was going to work. I sneered at him. "A charming puppet on a long set of strings."

His expression darkened, jaw working with anger and frustration.

I've got this, I said to him in my mind. I don't know if he heard it, but he continued to glare at me.

I moved to Hades with slow, confident steps. "These are pretty little presents, I suppose. But why settle for them? Why bother with a satyr, *slightly used*," I added sharply, "when you could have his *boss*?"

Stretching out my arm, I offered Hades the Apple.

The Lord of the Dead held his hands close to his chest, fingers dancing in anticipation. "Oh my, mage, you do make a cunning offer," he said breathily. He reached for the Apple, then retreated a moment, almost as if afraid to touch it. I realized, though, that his hesitation wasn't fear but a sort of ecstasy, prolonging the exquisite suspension of the moment.

Before Hades could accept it, however, Zeus bellowed from behind me, "How are we to know that this is the truth? She has been seen in the satyr's company. Perhaps she is trying to trick us to save her lover."

I snorted and laughed. "I'm not."

"It might be a false apple," he added.

"It's not."

"You've seen the real apple, Lord of Olympus," Loki chimed in. "Would you recognize it?"

"Shut up, Aesir," Zeus spat. "Know your place."

Loki gave a respectful bow of his head, but I saw the mischief gleaming in his arctic eyes. Zeus would pay for that one later. Somehow. Possibly through me, even.

Zeus approached me. "I would see the Apple, mage. Hand it over."

I glanced to Hades. "By your leave."

He waved his fingers dismissively. "If my cousin insists."

To ensure this had the best chance of working, I mentally rifled through Eris's files and found a selection of misdeeds associated with Zeus. As the king reached for the Apple, I sent a bit of will through the relic loaded with the details of one of her many schemes. As we both touched the Apple, the current flowed between us, a complete circuit. All evidence of Eris's treachery against Olympus shot into Zeus in one electrifying jolt.

Zeus's broad face scrunched with the impact, eyes squeezing shut. His muscles strained as the thorny magic, the trace of Eris's essence, stabbed into him. He released the Apple and shook like a giant dog.

"That...that bitch," he sputtered. Zeus looked from the Apple in my hand to Marius. "Nothing but a tool," he whispered. "This satyr is worthless to me. I retract my offer, Hades."

The slimy grin slid from Hades's face as Zeus took his woman and the lion pelt off the floor.

"Mage!" Santa Claus barked at me. "Let me see this."

The jolly old tinkerer set upon me, and before I could stop him, he'd grabbed hold of the Apple. With the same jumpstart from my own power, Saint Nick was given a dose of reality, Discord-style.

Soon, they all wanted a bite off the Apple. The djinn, Yama, Odin—though, I had nothing for Odin. Eris hadn't put Marius to work where the Asgardian was concerned. Apparently Marius's slight against Odin really was as Loki had said—just a joke among friends.

The gods and creatures of myth surrounded me, each one touching the Apple and coming away wiser. And each of them rescinded his offer to Hades. As you can imagine, the Lord of the Dead wasn't too pleased with this.

"Wait," he said. "What are you doing?"

They didn't care. The audience began to disperse. Creatures made their ways up the stairs or just disappeared with flashes of fire or bursts of smoke. The stone golems simply melted into the floor and rumbled off.

"Where are you going? This isn't over!" Hades fumed.

"Give it up, cousin," Zeus said. "He's of no interest. He was not the culprit of the greater crimes, nor is he of any use in hurting Eris."

They were packing up and leaving. Even Odin, with his genuine beef against Marius, had lost the will to stick around. Yama sneered silently at Hades. As he led his shadowy beast away, the hellhound's ears drooped with disappointment. Soon, only a handful of us stood in the Temple. In fact, I think the only reason most of the stragglers remained was to see how things would shake out.

"What am I supposed to do with him now?" Hades grumbled.

"You can still get an apple," I said. "My offer stands."

Astraios clicked forward hurriedly. "Turn him over to us, sire. Free him from death so that we may lift him!"

"Lift him?" I asked. "What the hell does that mean?"

"You wouldn't understand, mortal," the goat sneered.

"Oh, now you're just being rude."

He paid me no regard—what with me being nothing but a puny mortal woman, I suppose—but instead bowed lower to Hades.

"Please, I beseech thee," Astraios moaned.

Hades glared darkly from beneath hooded eyes. "Why should I turn him over to either of you? Why should I not just keep him and the secrets he holds in my demesne for all eternity?"

I gave the Apple another bounce. "If it's secrets you want..." I said tauntingly.

"We have waited for so long," the Sileni sniveled, his nose inches from the stone floor. His fellow goats crowded behind him and prostrated themselves before Hades. "Please, we beg of you."

Hades expression held only daggers for me. "It would upset a certain mage I know if I gave him to you, Astraios. I would relish her torment, indeed."

So that's how he wanted to play? "You know, that's cool, Hades," I said. "If you don't want this old thing, I'm sure my boss with have a use or two for it." I walked away, past Marius and toward Loki's open palm.

"Cat, my dear," Loki said unctuously. "For me? You shouldn't have."

I held the Apple over Loki's hand and eyed Hades over my shoulder. "Going once."

Hades's lips curled as if his blood itself curdled—assuming he had blood, of course. Either way, he looked like he'd just swallowed something particularly foul.

"Going twice," I sang.

Hades shot out of his smoky throne. "Fine. Fine!" he roared.

The brand on my wrist flared with Loki's approval. I turned around to face Hades properly.

"Yes?"

"I will," he said darkly, "accept your most generous offer, mage. The Apple of Discord in exchange for the life of this despicable satyr. He is yours."

The green light fell from around Marius, and as it did, he became victim to the laws of gravity. Marius fell, utterly graceless, to the floor. Bracing himself on hands and quite-human knees, Marius coughed and retched. His hair fell between me and his face, but he was there.

"Now," Hades spat, "give me the Apple."

I took my time crossing the room, drawing a long breath and tapping in to a dram of power. When I plopped the Apple into his outstretched hand, Hades shuddered. He cupped it, caressing it with an obscene avarice. Soon, though, confusion rippled over his ugly features.

"What is this? I see nothing. What trickery is this? What have you done, mage?" he raged.

Weathering his wrath, I looked him in the eye. "Nothing."

"Why can I not see Eris's schemes written here as the others did?"

"Maybe you just don't know how to look. Keep trying. I'm sure you'll get it eventually."

Hades let out a visceral yell and lashed out with his hand. Sickly green light crackled from his fingertips—not at me but toward Marius. From out of nowhere, Malcolm dove in and shoved his brother from the magic's path.

THIRTY-FIVE

"WHEELS"

Malcolm's scream was a wail of agony. I reached into my pocket and drew one of my Loki-issued mistletoe darts. Lightning-fast, I sent it flying at the Lord of the Dead. For good measure, I added a chaser of my own electrified power. As the Sileni surrounded Marius and Mal, Loki launched himself across the room and blocked me with his body.

Hades cried out with frustration, his fingers spreading and sending gouts of green fire to the ceiling. My dart had scored a hit in the god's wrist. Green leaves of the mistletoe spread out from the shaft of the dart and curled around Hades's arm. As the vines reached higher, seeking his shoulder, tiny white berries began to burst into being.

"Aesir!" Hades roared. "Stand aside and let me flay that mortal of her pretty skin."

"I'm afraid I can't do that, Dave," Loki said, voice cool and mechanical.

Hades narrowed his eyes at Loki. Some of the mistletoe withered, blackening until there was nothing but a charred mass disintegrating from the god's arm. "I will not be made a fool by you, or worse, a petty mortal bearing your mark."

I'm sure that Loki and Hades were revving up a pretty awesome bout of verbal posturing, but I didn't give a shit. At that moment, another set of screams erupted from the furry scrum of the Sileni. This time, it was Marius's voice echoing in the cavern.

"No!" I called, dashing away from Loki's protection.

The goats had formed a ring around Mal and Marius. When I tried to break through, they tightened their ranks, some actually shoving at me to hold me back. What I saw within their circle, though, made me stop dead in my tracks.

Astraios stood, his furry hands outstretched, palms to the floor. Sigils and linework—like those carved on Pan's lovely pipe box—glowed in the stone. On his hands and knees at the center of some larger symbol was Marius. Once again, he'd been robbed of his glamour. Goat's legs and horns exposed, his body still bore the wounds that had more or less killed him. As I watched, the gash in his throat healed and the slashes on his chest vanished. His hair fell, partially obscuring his face. But what I could see of his expression was pained: eyes clenched tight, mouth pulled in a grimace. He panted, fighting back something greater as if being burned from the inside.

Beside him, Mal writhed on the floor. Hades's spell wrapped around him with smoky tendrils, and his skin looked ghastly gray. Black power illuminated the veins in his neck as he curled in on himself and cried for mercy.

I was dimly aware of Loki and Hades trading insults, but I only cared about the satyrs. "You can't do this," I called to Astraios. "Whatever it is, stop! You're hurting them!"

"I have waited too long," Astraios whispered with fanatical zeal. "I will lift the Scion of Pan to his rightful place!"

As if punched with an intense, magical uppercut, Marius shot upward and levitated just a few feet off the floor. Back arched, he let out another roar of pain.

"No," he called out. "I do not want this!"

"No?" Astraios asked. "I offer you true immortality! Power beyond measure!"

"Not worth it," Marius spat, each word an effort. "Murderers!"

His black hair tossed in the gale of swirling power, and his eyes opened. They were made entirely of emerald light. As I watched, his body began to change. The fur on his legs darkened to match the ebony of his hair. His skin healed of all scars, muscles tightened until he had more tone to his already-fine shoulders, arms, and chest. His horns grew longer, spreading out from his head to resemble those worn by the Sileni.

I stopped struggling against those other goats who protected the rite. I stared at Marius, jaw slack and eyes wide. Even in this dark, terrifying moment, I couldn't help but be in awe of him. He was heartbreakingly beautiful.

"Why do you fight against the mantle you were born to take?" Astraios asked. "This is your birthright! The divine blood of Pan calls to itself within your veins!"

"You wish to grant me this power?" Marius's words came easier now, but they were laced with anger. "To lift me to godhood?"

Astraios shuddered with obscene pleasure. "Yes," he hissed.

"Marius, no!" I shouted. Again, I tried to burst through the scrum, but two of the goats held me back. Even my new-and-improved strength wasn't enough to get through.

I could only watch as Marius stretched out a hand to Malcolm. Wisps of silver-and-emerald power traveled from his fingertips to his brother's broken body. Immediately, Mal's screams stopped. His breaths were shuddering moans, but there was relief.

Marius's face still showed strain. Even as he used the power of Pan, he denied it.

"What are you doing?" Astraios snarled.

"Using my birthright," Marius shouted. "But not for you! Never for you!"

Astraios cried out something in Greek, and with a whirl of his arms, he yanked his focus away from Marius. My satyr fell to the ground and stared at his hands with his normal, leaf-green eyes.

I called his name, but the word was drowned out by renewed horror from Malcolm.

"Stop!" Marius tried to stand but stumbled back to the floor. Without the divine power flowing in him, he was weak as a kitten. He'd fought too hard. Unable to lift a finger to help his brother, he pleaded, "You can't do this to him!"

The sickly pallor of Hades's spell seeped out of Mal, replaced by the same wreath of light that just moments ago had encased Marius. Blue radiance shone from him as he rose into the air.. Back arched, screaming, Mal hovered there. And the transformation began.

Astraios's voice rang out. "I've waited too long! We all have! I will not waste this moment when the Sileni will once again have our prince to worship."

"He won't understand," Marius protested. "He can't!"

"But that also means he can't fight back!"

Rent apart by the magic at work on his body, Mal let out one last peal of anguish.

"Blood calls to blood," the Sileni chanted. "And so the mantle shall be passed on!"

Malcolm spun in the air so that his feet pointed to the floor. He, too, had been stripped of his human glamour. Hooves poked out from beneath his jeans, boots clattering to the stone.

Marius pooled all his strength, and with a roar, he barreled into Astraios. He knocked the goat off-balance and into the ring of Sileni. This distracted the two holding me back just enough that I was able to jostle my way into the circle. I made a beeline for my satyr, pushing him off Astraios before Marius ended up killing the old goat. He and I stumbled together, a tangle of limbs falling to the symbols on the floor as the power and life ebbed out of those arcane sigils.

"No," Marius panted.

"Look at me," I said. "Are you all right? Look at me!"

Relief flooded me as I touched him. He was real, whole. The skin beneath my fingers was supple, glazed with a cool sheen of sweat. Though he was no longer radiant with power, the sight of Marius brought me to tears. I threw my arms around his neck and clung to him in the fiercest embrace I've ever given.

"I thought... Oh gods...Marius..." I said into his shoulder.

Marius shrugged out of my arms, stunned into silence. Confused, I followed his stare.

Bathed in a wash of silvery light, Mal floated gently down to the ground. The clothes he had been wearing burned away in a flash of blue fire that matched his glowing eyes. I could still see Mal in the satyr standing there, but he'd been transformed. The bones of his face were sharper, more like Marius's natural lines. His eyes looked a little wider, and his hair—though still comprised of tight, unruly curls—had more luster. Dark-brown horns formed wavy lines on either side of his forehead. A billy goat's beard drew an s-curve from his once-bare chin.

"Mal?" I asked.

That sharp chin of his cut a stern line, and he fixed me with his gaze. "Is that my name?"

I gasped. His voice... Dear gods. Mal's accent was in there, terrified as a child's, but another voice trampled it, an older voice with immense authority.

The more I stared at him, the more changes I saw. His ears came to an elven point. The slight paunch he'd carried had been replaced with a six-pack that looked hard enough to chip a tooth. The fur of his goat legs was soft and rich.

"Malcolm," Marius moaned, tears in his eyes. He approached his brother with care, padding forward slowly. "I'm sorry. I'm so sorry for this."

Astraios prostrated himself before Mal and bowed low, nose scraping the floor. "My Lord. We have waited long for your return."

The other Sileni joined Astraios in supplication.

Mal stared down at them, his face a queer mixture of horrified confusion and haughty entitlement.

"Malcolm?" Marius asked as he laid a gentle hand on Mal's bare shoulder.

Mal whipped to face Marius, his body blurring with enhanced speed. Marius stumbled, surprised, but stared with terrible understanding.

"Marius?" Mal asked, voice still altered. "What...?" He grabbed his throat. More of that childlike fear quaked out him. "What happened to me?"

Astraios answered before Marius could find the words. "We have lifted you, my Lord. We have raised you to the proper throne."

"What does that mean?"

The Sileni reached imploringly to his newly born god. "Sire, you are now as you were born to be. The sacred blood of Pan—"

"I don't give a shit about sacred blood!" Mal roared, his own voice taking over again. His eyes became human, but the other changes—his beard, the points to his ears, his sculpted body—remained all too real. "Marius, please, just tell me what's wrong with me."

"Oh, Mal," Marius said. "They've gone and made you a god."

One of the prostrate goats rose and approached Mal with a silver robe. Mal went to shrug him off but, instead, backhanded the goat across the room. Mal gaped at his arm, suddenly imbued with more strength than he'd ever known, as if it were someone else's body. And in truth, it was.

"I don't understand," he said. Tears melted down his face. "I don't understand this. I don't want to be... I just want to go home."

"You are home," Astraios intoned. "At long last, you are exactly where you belong."

"Piss off!" Mal bellowed. Dust rained down from the high ceiling.

Astraios quailed. As he tried to pull himself together, he cleared his throat. "Perhaps my Lord would like a moment with his kin."

He and the other Sileni clicked away in a flurry of bows and excited whispers.

"Mal?" I asked. "How do you feel?"

He pawed his hair, felt out to the tips of his horns. "I don't... All right, I s'pose. But...it's like I'm...too big for me skin."

Marius nodded. "And you've never worked with power, really, so you don't know how to control it."

Mal shook his head. "Is this...? Is this what you feel like when you do all that fancy stuff?"

"You get used to it." He put a hand on his brother's shoulder. "With control and understanding comes comfort."

"I'll take that anytime now." Mal's voice shook, but the panic had seeped away. He continued to examine the now-tighter contours of his body. "This is a bit different."

Marius gestured to his own chin. "You've got something. Just there."

Mal grabbed his new beard. "Oh gods," he whined. "I don't like beards. Never have done. Why do I have a bloody beard? Now I look like you, you daft twat!"

"Is that such a bad thing?" Marius preened, his voice unctuous. "I have always had the better looks in the family."

"Have not..."

My satyr was incredulous. "No? They didn't need to rearrange the bones in my face when they were making me into a god."

Mal's hands flew to his own cheeks, feeling frantically at his nose, his chin. "Shut up!"

Marius laughed, sending Mal into another string of colorful epithets, most of which criticized Marius's parentage. Before Mal could get on too big of a roll, though, Marius grabbed him in a tight hug. Minding the extra long horns, of course.

"I'm sorry," Marius whispered.

Mal grimaced uncomfortably. But he returned the hug, eyes closing with something akin to relief. When he pulled away, he took in Marius's nude form and grabbed the silver robe from the floor. "Christ," he said, disgustedly hurling the robe at Marius. "Put something on, would ya?"

"And hide this light under a bushel?" Marius smiled, but he did put on the robe. They eyed each other, each wearing a divine mantle.

"Are you all right?" Mal asked.

Marius nodded. "More or less."

"Cat says it was...that things were rough. But she also said we'd get you back."

For the first time in this whole crazy maelstrom, Marius looked at me. A smile touched his eyes and made my knees weak. "She's too right."

"Oi!" Mal called to me. "How's about a little taste now? Huh?" He gestured to himself proudly, hands lingering down near his hips. "Are you sure you picked the right brother?"

Marius smacked Mal on the back of the head, and the two set to their puppyish bickering.

"Cat," Loki barked at me.

Damn! Loki and Hades!

I'd totally forgotten about them, what with all the deification and shit going on. Turning away from the brothers, I ran to Loki's side. "Where's Hades?"

"Gone," Loki said. "Don't know that he wanted to be around when the Sileni were done. Either way, it didn't bode well for him."

I nodded. "So is this it, then?"

"Marius is off the hook. Well, as much as he ever was." Loki raised his chin to point at the brothers. "This changes things. He'll have some protection if anyone still holds a grudge."

"So...he's free?"

"Who is *free*, Cat?"

He let me ponder for a moment, but before I could answer, he blew out a chuff of laughter. "You may have just started a pretty wild fire, girl. They're hunting for Eris, no doubt. And Hades has the Apple of Discord. Not sure that was the smartest move. Now he has all her secrets."

"Hoping you'd get a hold of the Apple for yourself?" I asked with a sideways smile.

"Won't lie, the idea had crossed my mind."

I shook my head. "Pretty dangerous thing to have floating around in the world."

"Dangerous is half the fun!" he sang.

"Wouldn't do you much good right now anyway."

Loki grinned playfully. "Oh really? Why is that?"

"Well, in techie terms, I wiped the hard drive before I handed it to Hades."

His eyes wide as saucers, he crossed his arms. "It's really empty?"

"No more than a pretty paperweight."

Something akin to disappointment flashed over his features. "All that information is gone?" he whined. "Do you know what could have become of it? What I—or someone else who was so inclined," he added quickly, "could have done with all those schemes?"

"Yup." Too well. All Eris's sins were still filed in my head. I desperately wanted a shower to get the grime of her magic off me—assuming that would help. I wondered if I could download it all somewhere else. That would have to come later, though. There was still business I had with Marius.

Loki stared at me, his expression unreadable. "I underestimated you, Cat. Which I must admit, is difficult to do."

"Bet you won't make that mistake twice," I said, half joking.

"No. No, I won't. And neither will anyone else."

I didn't like the sound of warning in his voice. "By that, of course, you mean everyone will be banging down my door to tell me how awesome and cool I am, right?"

Loki chuckled. "You're so cute."

"Speaking of people who dig me...who did that to your face?"

"Still not going to tell you, Cat."

"Dammit."

THIRTY-SIX

"Waiting"

After a while, the Sileni surrounded Malcolm and began spouting off all that was expected of him in his new position. Marius backed away and headed up the stairs, out of the Temple with a decidedly morose slump to his shoulders. Loki took off to take care of his own affairs, leaving me in a cave full of satyrs of various stripes. Figuring this might not be the place to linger—especially without Marius's braid in my hair to keep me from succumbing to Mal's charms—I mounted the stairs two at a time and shuffled back to the real world.

I looked left and right for some hint of Marius, perhaps a glimmer of that silver cloak. But I didn't see him. Dusk had descended, and a strip of purple was all that remained of daylight along the western horizon. The constellations glittered above while the lights of a city twinkled below. A gust of summer wind rattled through the dry grass, whispered through the trees farther up the slope.

"Quite an interesting evening, don't you think, Cat?"

I closed my eyes and drew a breath. As I let it out, I said her name. "Dahlia."

"Did you get what you wanted?" she asked.

"Did you?" I opened my eyes, and she stepped out of the gloaming, walking up the slope with the grace of an angel and the silence of a ghost.

She shrugged, a dainty yet elegant gesture. "As much as anyone else who came to bid on the satyr. Perhaps more. Perhaps less."

"You're so Fae sometimes," I said with a chuckle.

"I am what I am. No more. No less."

"So who sent you? For Marius, I mean?"

Another shrug. "No one, really. I heard he was on the auction block and figured you'd be here."

"Oh, so it's not about him," I said, incredulously. "You're pretending to be here for my benefit?"

"Is that so hard to believe?"

Though I don't think she realized she was doing it, Dahlia gave the slightest of pouts, her lower lip jutting out just so. Her eyes commanded my attention, and in staring at her, I remembered our time together. Nights out on the town. Mornings in her bed.

In her palms, something began to shine with a wan but pure white light.

"You know—" she chuckled as she took a step closer "—you're the one who left."

"You're the one who gambled with my soul," I simmered. "That's worse than leaving."

She looked away, chastened. "Right."

"Look," I said after a sigh. I was too tired to fight her, too exhausted to pretend she didn't infuriate me. "I know that sometimes our paths will cross because of our jobs, but, really, you screwed me over in ways I don't know that I'll ever forgive. You lost my soul to Eris, and she wasn't exactly gentle with it. You bound my powers when I didn't even know about them. You... Frankly, Dahlia, you broke my heart."

She stared into the white light, a rueful smile dimpling her cheek. "I know." Dahlia gazed up at me. "Has there been anyone else, Cat? Since me?"

I thought about Marius and the dance on the balcony. The kiss. The desire. And my fear.

I shrugged.

"I was afraid of that," she murmured.

Dahlia glided to me, her wraithlike steps silent even on the rocky ground. The light from her hands glowed like a tiny star, illuminating her mahogany skin and raven hair. My chest ached with how beautiful she was. Like a rich dessert, she was too much of a decadent thing.

"Hold out your hand," she urged, "and close your eyes."

I raised an eyebrow. "Do you think I trust you that much? I sure as hell don't think so."

"Please."

Something of the old Dahlia—*my* Dahlia—shone in that one word. Though it went against everything I knew and felt, I decided to give that ghost of my first love a chance. I closed my eyes—and quickly popped one open to look for a dagger. When I didn't see one, I closed that eye again.

"Okay, now what?" I asked.

"Hold out your hands."

I did. A moment later, something touched my skin. Warm and fluttering like a tiny bird or a baby rabbit. I opened my eyes to find that she'd laid the small star—the gift she'd offered Hades—in my palms.

I gasped. Before I could question her motives, the light flared from a star to a supernova. I slammed my eyes shut but still saw the bright nimbus of Dahlia's trinket. Reflexively, I reached out with my senses but saw nothing. No magic, no machinations. Just light. The filaments of this power streamed into me, into my chest, with a throbbing sensation. Without knowing the reason, I began to cry. Sobs without purpose, emotions without a cause... I fell to my knees under the overwhelming wave of that light.

Soon, that tide washed away, and the light ebbed to darkness. When I looked up at Dahlia, she smiled at me with sincerity. She kneeled before me and wiped the tears away. Then she leaned forward and placed a kiss on my cheek.

"It's yours again," she whispered. "I'm sorry to have kept it for so long."

I remembered that night, that fateful night when I had lain in her arms, flush with emotions. What had I said to her? *I love you. Heart and soul, I'm yours.*

I hadn't understood then, but those words had given Dahlia very real possession of my soul. She'd squandered it, gambled with it, lost it to Eris. But I'd never thought about the other part of that promise.

A human heart. Freely given.

I choked. "Mine?"

She nodded. "Enjoy."

A few soundless steps, a wink beneath the starlight, and Dahlia was gone.

I sat there, trying to quantify what the hell had just happened, when I heard the sound of music on the wind. Pipes.

No shit, I thought. *You're sitting near the Temple of Pan and they just had a ritual. You're going to hear pipes.*

But no. I knew that music came not from Mal or the Sileni, but from another satyr.

My satyr.

I followed the tune up the path, around the other side of the cave, and into the dense trees. The terrain moved down into a sort of valley. The sounds of pipes and a waterfall grew louder, spurring me forward.

After a few minutes, I came to a pool. Stars twinkled in every ripple of the water. Beneath the silvery sheen of the moon, Marius's cloak gleamed.

He knelt at the edge of the lagoon, his bare feet sinking into the mossy earth. Eyes closed, his lips traced gentle lines over the pan pipes, coaxing sweet music from the reeds. The tune was light and languid, like sunbeams through the window on a lazy Sunday morning. While he played, I took in this place—the place he'd told me about and described so lovingly.

The water flowed around a large boulder, its top carpeted with moss and lichen. Similar rocks surrounded the pool, as if someone had created a stage of it and these smaller stones were seats for the audience. Perhaps, one day long ago, Pan had held court here under the stars. Or hell, even Marius. The trees surrounding the lagoon had droopy branches with cascading leaves. The bark was thin and silvery, casting back hints of light. In the boughs, more than the wind sighed. I caught the twinkling eyes of spirits. Nymphs, perhaps, sitting and listening in awe of the music.

I caught sight of a long white caftan moving among the trunks of the trees across the pond. Stalking from tree to tree, her stare cold, was the Lady of Olympus. She stopped her movements and fixed me with those hard, sour eyes.

I moved up beside Marius and glared at Hera. I wasn't sure what she wanted of me—or him—but I'd gone through Hell to protect Marius. I'd give the queen a run for her money, too, if she wanted a fight.

But that didn't seem to be the case. She stared at us, eyes flickering back and forth between me and the satyr. At first, her expression offered nothing but malice. But soon, her features softened to confusion. Brow furrowed with consternation, she slunk behind a tree.

Only then did I notice Marius had stopped playing. He stood beside me, stare resting on the shifting waters.

"What do you think?" he asked.

"It's...breathtaking."

"I've missed this place. Didn't think I'd ever see it again. Or you," he added. Finally, he took his eyes off the water and looked at me. No Sileni. No deified brother. No gods or monsters bidding on his soul. Just me. Marius's attention swept down on me with heavy focus that made my knees quake and my body crave his touch.

"That makes two of us," I said dumbly.

We gazed into each other's eyes. *What's next?* his expression asked. There was so much to explain. There were so many words to stumble over and choose and worry about getting wrong. Words I didn't remember how to say with perfect trust and without fear.

"I..." The syllable trembled in my throat. "I'm sor—"

He didn't let me finish my apology. "You came to Hades looking for me, Catherine. You tried to barter with the Lord of the Dead. You never need to apologize to me again, do you understand?"

I flushed, my cheeks burning. I couldn't keep the smile off my face, though.

"You're practically glowing," he said, stroking my hair. "What has gotten into you?"

"Oh," I said flippantly. "Dahlia. She... We just... I mean, she stopped me to talk."

"Did she? And did she have anything of interest to say?"

"She gave me...what she had offered to Hades."

"Really?" Marius asked. "Well, it certainly suits you."

With the awkwardness of two nerds at a junior prom, we danced around the real conversation, keeping each other at an uncomfortably vast distance. I was supposed to say something here. I was supposed to tell him all those things that had me running right across the River Styx, right? But my throat went dry, and my brain wouldn't do that thing that makes words possible. I'd kept my cool in a room full of deities while holding the goddamn Apple of Discord, but standing next to Marius by this beautiful pond, I went dumb. Completely and utterly devoid of thought.

"Christ, you make me stupid," I breathed.

"What was that?"

Say it, a part of me prodded. Instead, I reached out and touched the silver robe. "Some threads you've got there."

"It's that or go starkers."

Heat flared in my cheeks. Just a thin wisp of fabric between me and his naked body. With all the excitement and craziness inside the Temple, it hadn't occurred to me to ogle him. Now I lamented that damn robe.

A bird called into the night, and Marius looked off to the sky. "Somewhere out there, Eris is screaming for mercy."

"Do you care?"

"Not a damn bit. I'm no saint, but that woman deserves a taste of Hell for all she's done."

I shifted from foot to foot and cleared my throat. "So, now that this is all over, what's going to happen?"

Marius drew in a breath. "Well, Malcolm is going to need some help adjusting, that's for sure. I figure he and I should go home and see Father. Explain to him what happened. Mal has a lot to learn after a lifetime of shirking the history of his heritage."

Disappointment and fear writhed in my stomach. "So you're staying here."

"Oh gods, no. I'll be going back to Vegas soon enough. Maybe a week or two with Mal before heading back to Sin City."

"Really?" I said, perhaps a little too excitedly. "I mean, um...really? Why Vegas? I thought this was your home."

The shadows obscured his face, but the smile there was plain to see. "Sometimes home is more than a place. Besides, all my stuff's there."

I smiled. "Good. You know, I was thinking. I know someone who's been out of the loop for a while and needs some help navigating the twisty landscape of deities and such."

"Oh really? Do tell."

"Flynn would never ask you outright, but he's on the radar now. In a big way. He's going to need a trained professional."

"A friendly native guide, perhaps?"

"Something like that."

Marius stroked his beard. "Hmm, well, the idea has some merits to it, I suppose. When I get back into town, I'll pay Flynn a visit. And you. Assuming you're available," he added.

"You know how to find me," I said, grinning like an idiot. This wouldn't be so hard. I could just tell him now. "Do you think— I mean, well..." And then my words locked up again. Stupid brain! "Maybe we could try that date thing again. Sometime. If you're interested."

"No gods or monsters?"

"No foul beasties. And no running away. Promise."

"I'd enjoy that," he whispered.

My heart swelled in my chest, hope turning into a blazing bonfire. Maybe we could do this after all. "I would, too."

Marius brought his pipes back to his lips and blew an airy glissando. "I don't know what the hell Mal was thinking, offering these to Hades for my stupid life."

I chewed my lip. "Yeah. Dumb idea. But hey, he missed you and wanted to do anything to get you back."

"Did he?"

I nodded. "Yeah."

"Well, now he's going to see plenty of me."

Frogs began to croak, their songs a counterpoint to the gurgling of the lagoon and the soft drone of the waterfall. Marius lifted his pipes to his mouth and started playing. This tune carried a complex depth. The high notes were cheerful and brimming with vitality, but the lower register sang with just a hint of mourning. Of loss. As he played, I sat down on a stone and enjoyed this private concert. Listening, I found the unconsummated tension, the longing in each phrase, resonated with me.

Say it, I urged myself. *Tell him now.*

The melody wound around me like a cat between my ankles, all purrs and adoration. And I thought of Linux at home, probably very cross with me by now. He'd always approved of Marius, regardless of my ideas on the matter. Maybe that was a sign. Maybe Karma was right, too. I'd never be happy with someone I had to protect from this odd little life of mine. I closed my eyes and tried to imagine what life with Marius would be like. Not one where we went on these sadistic missions for Eris, or where we ran for our lives. But going for coffee. Having a drink. Dinner at the little shawarma joint down the street from my apartment. Giggling as we passed Mrs. M's apartment at oh-god-thirty. Sharing passion and getting to know each other, bodies and minds.

What would *that* be like with Marius?

I could find out. I wanted to.

I drew in a long breath and practiced the words in my mind, those three syllables that seemed to catch in my throat and trigger my gag reflex. I could say it. Here in his sacred place. Now, after all we'd been through.

I opened my mouth. "I love you."

The music stopped.

I opened my eyes, nearly blinded by afternoon sun pouring into my apartment. Linux's mew was pitiful and full of disdain as he stepped around my ankles. It took me too many seconds to realize that Marius had sent me home with his own brand of magic. But where was he? Still with Mal, just as he'd said. And soon the two would go back to Glastonbury to be with Llyr.

But Marius said he'd be back.

Anticipation of that moment already had me on edge. As I padded into the kitchen to feed Linux and get him fresh water, I glanced at the calendar. A week or two seemed like eternity. Had he heard my confession before I'd faded away from Greece and back to Vegas? What did he think? If he didn't, could I say it again?

A week or two. They'd be a new kind of hell without him, just this empty ache in my heart at his absence.

But he'd be back. I trusted his word on that.

You do that when you love someone.

ACKNOWLEDGMENTS

Here we are again, my loves, and I'm thrilled. Seriously, you don't even know. I wrote the rough draft of this book before the *Unveiled* (Book 2) Kickstarter in 2014. Even then I was vibrating with excitement to share this story with you because I'm incredibly proud of it. Being able to finally get this book into your hands and the story into your brain? Epic. So, above all else, thank you, dear reader, for slaking this thirst of mine.

As always, tremendous thanks go to my editor, Danielle Poiesz, and my fantastic cover artist, Nathalia Suellen. Special thanks also to Zach Reddy and Emma Lysyk for their artwork for merchandise; to Beverly Bambury, my publicist; to Mandy Nelson, who voices Cat on the audiobooks; to Lejon Johnson, whose council helped these first three books not suck; and to my glorious Attack Fish. Your screams and tears are sustenance upon which I gladly feast.

I also have to thank my dear family for all their support and love. My daughter, my husband, Sean, and our cats have dealt with all manner of hell just by living with a writer.

Like its predecessor, *Uninvited* was brought to you by viewers like you. Thanks to Open Beta (www.openbetamusic.com) and Gotham City Comics in Mesa, AZ, for hosting Satyrthon, our small fundraiser concert and auction in September 2015. And eternal gratitude to the many backers of the *Uninvited* Kickstarter. Those kind souls are:

L. Laufeyson, Nacole Vickery, Nedra Wilson, Jim Wyman, Ethan and Kaitlyn Kincaid, Kristin D., T. Costa, Kitty Spaven, Tiffany Meuret, Delilah S. Dawson, Jonni Greenburg, Tex Thompson, Michael R. Underwood, Head Knacker MGL, Axex Dental, summervillain, Rene Sears, Philda Todzaniso, Cyrano Jones, Eric Lloyd, Beth Cato, Pim and Carin Klabers, Craig Coxon, Tracy Canfield, Michelle Welch, Sandra Roberts, John Idor, Lorena Dinger, Dr. DeAnna Woeller, Joe O'Toole, FrozenFoxy, Rylee Keys, Matthew Kinney, Brian McDonald, Eric May, Florian Schock, Tara Zuber, Krysi, Tibicina, Sam Slessor, Jessica Meade, Karen Lindsay, Melissa Tabon, Lord Fancypants, Bob Mungovan, Bob Jackson of the Spongeworks Clan, Gordon Tyus, Neliza Drew, Christopher "Titan" James, Ken Bowley, Emma Maree (@emaree), Max Kaehn, Sara Wilmber, Nathan Duby, Andrea Feeney, Cliff Winnig, Lisa McCurrach, Sarah Mack, Zen Dog, Stephanie Cranford, Justin Greenburg, Angie Kones, M.E. Gibbs, Janet Armentani, Veranica and James Stephan, Andrew Barton, Sally Novak Janin, Cat Faber, Kathleen O'Connell, Bry Hitchcock, Eleri & Scott Hamilton, Thom Slattery, Rachel M. Thompson, Knat, Rhys Edan McNamee, Yeti, Paulie, Elfling, Cindy Durand, Jenybeth Durand, Ashley Dryer, Ryan Dalton, Inger Burnicle, Stephen Makofske: Spawn of Awesome, The Bald Pirate, Mandy Nelson, Doty, Sarah Lynn, Amie Deichert, Alyssa Marie Bethancourt, Tracy Richardson, Sara Fleishman Nelson, Ivy Faulkner, Nicola Chick, Brady Barnett, Cathy Corman, Rachel Sharp, Jamie Rapose, Jaileigh McIntyre, Lorri Angus, Sara Rebennack, Stefanie Muniz, Vicki Riddick Nelson, Michelle R. Lyon, TS, Ambrosia Rose: Queen of the Color Pixies, Pam Greenway, Andrew Gilbert, Alison M Diem, Paul Krueger, Jason Boudon, Sabrina Poulsen, Heather Bragg, Cat Magic, Cheryl Doebler, Leigh Flynn, John Groseclose, Emma Lysyk & Guillermo Hernandez, Julia M., Heather Wilson, Isaac "Will It Work" Dansicker, David Gates, Mel, Rosanne Girton, Sheila, Tina Beychok, Gunnar Högberg, Sage Christofferson, Andreas Gustafsson, Allison Pang, MC, Cheryl Busfield, Stephanie B., Clare A. Bohn, Jennifer McCormick, Crowfae, Sam-ish, Caitlyn DeAmbra, Vicki Colbert, Krista Long & Chris Seggerman, Tim Stapleton, Melissa Lotspeich, Alma E Heinrichs, Christine Jackson, Kristin Gwinn, Angela Melton, Loralei Riney, Steven Cowles, Rachel

Caine, Melissa Crandall, the other Catherine Sharp, Erin Paxton, Gabi & Dave Burtless, Betty Campbell, Mrs. McIntyre, The Legion of Leaches, Jeff Carlson, Jane Hanmer, Zach Reddy, beckymmoe, Jeremy McCliment, anon, Joseph M Benzer, Ariel Byrne, Jarred Harris, Aa, Chris Hartwig, Elizabeth Davis, Brian Abernethy, Phil & Gabby, MOM, Melissa McCollum, Susana La Luz-Hawkins, @stevedave47, Judy Little, Wanda Baum, Jennie Goloboy, Gabrielle Davis, Lejon A Johnson, Brian McGuire, Jessie Le Fey, Govneh, Rissa, Andrew Terranova, Inge Atkinson, Jim Barrows.

Thank you all for your enthusiasm. Thank you all for believing in me.

Can't wait to show you what comes next.

With love and chai,
J.

www.ingramcontent.com/pod-product-compliance
Lightning Source LLC
Chambersburg PA
CBHW070650180626
46817CB00006B/2300